MC

Born in Bologna in 1962, Giampiero Rigosi is a philosophy graduate and a former bus driver. He is a critically acclaimed novelist, playwright and author of screenplays. *Night Bus* is his first crime novel.

NIGHT BUS

Giampiero Rigosi

Translated from the Italian
by Ann Goldstein

BITTER LEMON PRESS
LONDON

BITTER LEMON PRESS

First published in the United Kingdom in 2006 by
Bitter Lemon Press, 37 Arundel Gardens, London W11 2LW

www.bitterlemonpress.com

First published in Italian as *Notturno Bus* by
Giulio Einuadi editore s.p.a., Torino, 2000
(Part of the Einaudi Tascabili Stile Libero Noir series)

Bitter Lemon Press gratefully acknowledges the financial
assistance of the Arts Council of England

Published with the financial assistance of the
Italian Ministry of Foreign Affairs

A CIP record for this book is available from the British Library

ISBN 1-904738-11-7

Typeset by RefineCatch Limited, Broad Street, Bungay, Suffolk
Printed and bound by WS Bookwell, Finland

ARTS COUNCIL
ENGLAND

To Ishmael
and his future voyages

Bologna, navel of everything,
you drive me to a sigh and a burp.
Francesco Guccini, *Bologna*

. . . Flight, who knows . . .
whether it may not be the quintessence of life,
. . . so few of us can do without it . . .
Paolo Conte, *Flight English-style*

I wish to express my gratitude to all those who were close to me during the writing of this novel. Special thanks to Antonella, Simona, Deborah, and Carlo for their support and encouragement, to Pacho for his suggestions, to Guido for his valuable advice, and to Luigi, for the meticulous patience with which he read the text, helping me make it better.

Thursday, 1 April 1993, 7:30 P.M.–
Friday, 2 April 1993, 2:30 A.M.

Hearts do not grieve and can suffer
Hour by hour, even for an entire life,
Without any of us ever knowing,
With too much certainty, what is happening.
Camilo José Cela, *La Colmena*

In the parabolic mirror, he sees the silhouette advancing. He holds his breath. Then the man takes another step, and Francesco breathes again, relaxing his shoulders. For an instant, he was afraid it was the Bear. But though the stranger is tall and robust, he's at least four inches shorter, has grey hair and is wearing a herringbone jacket that the Bear wouldn't be caught dead in.

As the bus approaches the stop, the man makes his way among the other passengers until he reaches the driver's seat. When he leans towards him, Francesco notices an intense odour of aftershave.

"Excuse me," the man says, with a Roman accent. "Could you let me know when we reach the stop closest to the Teatro delle Celebrazioni?"

Francesco gives him an affirmative nod, while he presses the button that opens the pneumatic doors. People crowd on, permeating the bus with a smell of sweat, fried potatoes and smoke.

"You have to get out at Arco del Meloncello, at the end of Via Saragozza. I'll let you know when we get close."

"Thanks. Then I'll wait here," the other says. He takes a step back and settles himself by a window.

Francesco closes the door and glances in the left-hand mirror. He sees a scooter approaching, driven by an elegant-looking man in a brown overcoat that flies out behind him. He lets the man go by, then presses the accelerator and moves on again.

One of these days the Bear will present him with the bill, and, as always, he'll find himself without a penny in his pocket, inventing ridiculous excuses, looking out of the corner of his eye for a possible escape route.

He stops the bus at a pedestrian crossing. Among the people going by is a tall girl with a backpack, from which the head of a tiny infant sticks out. Passing in front of the bus, the newborn looks up, staring at him with an expression of astonishment.

Francesco leaves Strada Maggiore on the left and turns onto Via Castiglione. Opposite is the Palazzo della Mercanzia, with its tall gothic arcades and the white balcony that stands out against the dark brick.

The anxiety of this evening is a new sensation, which he can't explain. His life is a total disaster, obviously, but by now he should be used to it. How long has it been since he's had his head above water? And yet, one way or another, he has always got by.

His gaze detaches itself from the street and slides diagonally along the surface of the windscreen. The dark silhouettes of the passengers, slightly distorted by the convexity of the mirror, are reflected in the rect-angular frame. Cold neon light rains on their heads and shoulders, but the bodies are immersed in a livid obscurity, where forms commingle. That mass of fig-ures, swaying as they grip the support poles, has some-thing spectral about it.

The grey-haired man, holding on to a pole, lets his

eyes wander out the window. Sprawled on the seat beside him is an acne-faced kid who is picking his nose. Next to him, two women in their fifties chatter in loud voices.

"So, in the end she decided to dump him?"

"She told him to go to hell, I'm telling you. She packed her bags, threw them in the back of the Volkswagen and went off."

"Oh, so she took the Golf?"

"What do you think she did? Walk?"

From the compressed-air tank comes a continuous hiss that grows in intensity until, every four or five minutes, it erupts, in a kind of elephant bellow. It must be that the discharge valve isn't properly calibrated.

The bus passes Piazza Galvani, which is swarming with kids. At the bus stop, the first to get on is a stiff-legged old man, with a broad-brimmed hat and a cane. He hooks the cane over one arm and climbs up the steps, followed by a girl and boy entwined around each other, who get on without a pause in their kiss.

Francesco presses in sequence the three buttons that close the doors, lowers the turn-signal lever.

*

The man in the armchair has a thin, bony skull that looks like an insect's. His lips are rigidly set in a sad-looking line. On the television in front of him the images of a movie rush by. Four police cars, sirens blaring, are following a big blue car with a good suspension system, which one way or another always manages to avoid being stopped.

The thin man is examining his fingers, looking for a possible cut, or even just a small superficial scratch. He pays closest attention to the area around the nails. It

3

must be the twentieth time that he has completed this minute inspection, but still he's not satisfied. He rotates the hand an inch or so from his eyes, slowly, then lays it again on the arm of the chair and returns to the TV with his impenetrable expression.

Now the blue car seems done for. The police cars have increased in number and are pursuing the fugitives through an unpaved area that runs under a viaduct. A little farther ahead you can see there's a sudden drop. Meanwhile steep banks of earth rise up on both sides, keeping the car from making a U-turn. Now it's hemmed in and has to go straight towards the precipice.

The man with the face of an insect stares at the screen, thinks again of the job he's just done. He sees the informer again, in profile, while he's putting the key in the door of his car. He seems to feel again the pressure of the recoil in the palm of his hand. The informer pirouetted against the car and slid to the ground, his fingers searching for a hold; then he stiffened on the asphalt, dying, with his head stuck under the body of the car. To finish him off, he shot him in the chest. He sees again the two gashes opening in the man's shirt, the body jolting as if hit by electric shocks.

Now that there seems to be no way out, the pursued car suddenly accelerates and, with a sharp jerk of the wheel, swerves. It skids, slips neatly between two pylons and heads at top speed towards a truck trailer providentially abandoned on the edge of the cliff. The bed of the trailer creates a sort of trampoline. The girl next to the driver is screaming, covering her eyes with her hands.

Unfortunately it wasn't just a matter of getting rid of the man. He also had to retrieve an envelope. So, after murdering him, he had to search the corpse. And at that point he cursed himself for not having at least brought a pair of gloves. He shifted the edge of the jacket with the point of the silencer and stuck his hand under the blood-soaked material. At that moment there was a noisy rumbling from the dead man's intestines. It seems to him that he can still smell that sweetish stench and feel the warm wet material under his fingertips. After retrieving the envelope, he got away in a hurry, rubbing his sticky fingers together. Panic forced him to stop after barely twenty yards. The blood was already starting to coagulate. He wiped the blood off his fingers with his handkerchief, then threw it into the first trashcan he saw.

The blue car hits the trampoline at full speed and, a moment before the inclined platform starts to sink under its weight, takes off towards the opposite bank of the precipice. The car is thrust upward, but the one pursuing car that tries the same manoeuvre finds itself with a much lower launching pad and ends up at the bottom of the ravine. Amid a roar of revving engines, wailing sirens, squealing brakes and the clash of crumpling metal, the television screen shows the blue car landing with a series of bounces on the opposite side of the ravine, while on the near side the six surviving vehicles are crashing into one another to avoid going over the edge.

The man with the face of an insect twists his mouth in a grimace of disgust.

"How idiotic!"

Then he looks at the clock and presses a button on the remote. In the room silence falls, while the images continue to flicker on the screen. The man puts on his slippers and gets up. He goes to a low glass table on which a telephone sits.

He dials a number. One ring. Two. Three. Four.

The man can still see the television from there. His lips are set in the usual bitter, suffering line. He is so still that his face seems cut in stone. In his right eyelid a tear has formed.

"Hello, signora? It's Diolaiti. Is your husband at home?"

While he waits, the receiver leaning against his ear, he takes a handkerchief out of his pants pocket, delicately wipes away the tear.

*

Well, yes, all in all not bad, thinks Leila, barefoot before the mirror. She rotates her body, inclines her head. Her dark hair, cut like a helmet, cascades from one side, covering part of her face. Not bad, but time is passing. She examines her legs, below the tight miniskirt. They are slender, well-formed legs. Her feet, too, are shapely. But Leila is in the mood for inspection. She lifts up the miniskirt, and with the index finger and thumb of both hands pinches the flesh on the outer part of the left thigh. Some small indentations appear on the skin. She squeezes harder, to see if the cellulite holes increase in number and depth. The skin turns red at the centre, whitens along the edge of the pressure. The number of little indentations, however, remains the same. Leila lets the edge of her skirt fall. She takes a step forward, brings her face close to the mirror. No doubt about it: here, too, a few signs are starting to be visible. At the corners of her eyes, for instance, and around the mouth. Not really wrinkles. Rather, small superficial marks. But visible.

Time is passing, even if she doesn't show her thirty-three years.

She backs away again. There she is: slim, well

proportioned, sexy. That mini, then, is particularly flattering. It accentuates her shapely legs, with their narrow calves. Her legs are very good; her bosom, on the other hand, has always seemed to her too small, even if that's the reason it has remained high and firm. Five-five and 117 pounds, you can't complain. Especially since, until now, staying in shape hasn't taken much of an effort. Until now.

She feels like smiling. She looks at herself in the mirror again, examines the marks of time on the geography of her skin, starts to worry about the future. Thirty-three, the beginnings of cellulite in the upper part of the thighs, six million in cash hidden in the false bottom of a closet and another twenty-five in a bank account. Nothing solid on which to rely, apart from her ability to *fend for herself.* But security is not of this world, thinks Leila, trying to get rid of the sticky sensation that's caught her.

She bends over, puts on low, black-leather boots. She zips them up, then stands and with her palms smoothes the creases in the miniskirt, which is tight across her hips. She pinches the material of her body stocking, to adjust the neckline. She opens the closet, chooses a short, very soft black suede jacket. While she's putting it on she thinks that what she'd really like, once and for all, is a good stroke of luck.

*

The large, squarish man sitting at the head of the table pounds his fist down a couple of inches from his plate.

"You'll do what I say, and that's it! Understand?"

His wife looks at him, frightened. She knows his rages, and knows that nothing good can be expected.

Whereas the girl, it seems, couldn't care less about her father's shouting.

"You think you can tell everyone what to do," she says. "Why don't you try instead to understand that I have my own life, and . . ."

"Your own life . . ." the man interrupts, with a threatening look, but his daughter won't let him continue.

"Yes, Papa, my own life! And you'd better not interfere with it!"

"You be careful what you say! If I order you . . ."

"Do you hear yourself talking?" cries the girl. "*I order you!* If you want to know, I don't give a damn about your orders!"

His daughter's words have a surprising effect on the man. He jumps to his feet with an agility that is surprising in such a heavyset person, and in an instant has come around the table. The girl, seeing him lunging towards her, tries to get up, but the man stops her, grabbing her wrist.

"Who do you think you're talking to? One of those imbecile friends of yours?"

The girl struggles, but the man tightens his grip.

"Ow, Papa, you're hurting me!"

"I'm hurting you? You have no idea how much I can hurt you!"

The wife, still sitting in her place, throws her napkin on the table.

"For heaven's sake, Giuseppe! Enough! What kind of behaviour is this?"

The man turns his head, gives the woman an angry glance. The daughter takes advantage of this to free herself with a sudden tug, and, before he can manage to grab her again, is in the hallway. She runs to her room, the man follows but isn't in time. The door closes with a thud and the key turns rapidly in the lock.

"Elisabetta!" the man shouts, his nose an inch from the door. "There's no point locking yourself in. I can knock down this door if I feel like it!"

He stands there, panting, in the yellow glow of the ceiling light that reflects off his square, bald head, shiny with sweat. Rage builds up inside him like steam in a pressure cooker.

He raises one hand and slams the palm, hard, against the surface of the door.

"Get that clown out of your head! Either you stop going out with him or I'll throw you out of the house!"

"Go away!" the girl cries, from inside. "Leave me alone!"

His wife, behind him, says: "Do you think it's necessary to treat her like this?"

"You be quiet," he snarls at her, darkly. "It's your fault if our daughter is out of control."

"Things can't always go the way you want, Giuseppe."

"I told you to keep your mouth shut."

"Anyway, you'll get nowhere like this."

The man's shirtsleeves are rolled up to the elbows, revealing thick, muscular arms. His fingers fidget near his hips. He turns towards his wife and glares at her. She tries to meet his gaze, but there is something in his look that scares her. She and her daughter have always been afraid him. The woman tries to remember if she felt that fear even before she married him, when they went out together and he'd take her to the movies, to a dancehall, a restaurant.

At that moment, the telephone rings, at the far end of the hall. The woman, glad to have a reason to leave, turns on her heels and heads towards the front entrance.

The man stands staring at his wife's back as she walks away.

"Hello? Oh, it's you. Yes, my husband is home. I'll get him right now."

The woman reappears.

"It's for you. That colleague of yours. Diolaiti."

He snatches the phone out of her hand.

"Is that you, Diolaiti? Yes, go on. What's up?"

At the other end of the line, the thin man with the face of an insect puts the handkerchief back in his pocket.

"What do you mean, what's up? We agreed that you would call me at dinnertime, don't you remember?"

"Oh yes, right, I'm sorry. I had something else on my mind just then. So, how did the job go?"

Diolaiti raises one hand and examines it.

"Done," he answers, while he studies the outlines of his nails, one by one. "I've already seen the boss, and he confirmed the Bologna job. Shall I come by and pick you up tomorrow morning?"

"Tomorrow morning? Yes, fine."

Diolaiti frowns.

"Tell me, Garofano, is something wrong?"

The heavyset man looks in the mirror above the shelf, to inspect his balding head.

"No, nothing in particular. The usual family problems. You want to know something, Diolaiti? You did well, not to get married and bring children into the world. They're nothing but a big pain in the neck!"

Diolaiti is silent for a couple of seconds. He stares at the figures moving across the screen of the television, on the other side of the room.

"So, I'll come by around nine tomorrow morning. OK?"

"Yes, of course. See you tomorrow," says Garofano, then he hangs up the phone and smooths the lock of hair on his forehead with the palm of his hand.

Diolaiti puts down the receiver. He rubs one hand over his stomach. These damn burning sensations have come back to torture him.

He goes into the kitchenette, fills a glass under the tap, drops an effervescent tablet into the water. He goes back to the living room, sits down on the sofa and stares again at the TV. He balances the glass on an arm of the sofa. A tiny sliver of the tablet, which by now is almost completely dissolved, eddies in the water in a swirl of bubbles.

*

What was it the instructor was always saying during the training course?

"The driver's true eyes are the rear-view mirrors. Never forget that, kids. It's the mirrors that allow you to keep an eye on the situation."

He must have repeated it a million times. Francesco recalls his oblong face, with the high forehead and dirty-blond eyebrows, inclining downward, that gave him the look of a whipped puppy. His name was Marchetti and he had a habit of sucking on mints.

"I'm telling you this for your own good. You have to pay more attention to what's going on *behind* you than to what is *in front of* you. Keeping an eye on the street is nothing. The hard part is not to be caught by surprise by what's happening behind you! It doesn't take much to crush a cyclist who's caught between the curb and the side of the bus."

He rolled one of his mints around in his mouth and leaned forward to smack the student who was driving at that moment.

"Did you hear what I said? Check the rear-view

mirrors, damn it! Did you notice that scooter that's passing us?"

Francesco, in time, began to consider even more useful the inside rear-view mirror, the one that allows you to keep an eye on what is happening *inside* the bus. The eye in the back of your head, as many of his colleagues call it. It's the inside rear-view mirror that allows you to distinguish possible bores, old people with precarious balance, beautiful girls. And, above all, to intercept the pain in the ass. Cities are full of annoying people who get on the bus solely to find someone to torture with their confidences, complaints or misfortunes. And that someone is there, just within reach, all they have to do is settle in next to the driver and ignore the sign that forbids them to speak to him.

In big cities people end up feeling alone, and it's not easy to find someone to unburden themselves to. The psychiatrist's couch has a steep price, while a ticket for an hour's ride on a public bus is cheap and can be bought at any newsstand or tobacconist. For the most part, people don't *really* think they can improve their lives and, in fact, have no intention of making an effort to do so. They simply look for someone who will listen to them. A friend, a Mormon, a counterman in a deli, a bus driver. Understanding friends are extremely rare, Mormons have the downside of giving advice, and countermen are in a hurry to serve other customers. Bus drivers represent the best solution. That's why the inside rear-view mirror has a fundamental importance. It allows you to identify the pain in the ass before he goes into action and offers the possibility of beating him to the punch. Sometimes it's sufficient to appear to be in the middle of some manoeuvre or to grab the radio and pretend to be engaged in a conversation with the dispatcher. Francesco had taken the words of his instructor to heart, and looking behind him became one of his principal activities. Ever since troubles and creditors had begun to pursue him, this habit had been transformed into an obsession.

Francesco stops the bus at the signal at Porta Saragozza. The flower seller is carrying the plants inside the shop. The usual fifteen or twenty old ladies have gathered to say their prayers, sitting on chairs arranged on the broad pavement that separates the Porta from the boulevards, where at eight in the evening the traffic is beginning to thin out.

In Via Saragozza the traffic is moving pretty well, and soon they come up to Villa delle Rose. As Francesco approaches the portico, he turns to get the attention of the grey-haired man.

"Here we are, get off here. That place opposite is the Teatro delle Celebrazioni."

"Thank you," says the man.

In the side mirror Francesco sees the acne-faced kid get out, followed by the old man in the broad-brimmed hat and the grey-haired man. As soon as they've got down from the last step he closes the doors and starts off again.

Tomorrow he's on the night shift, but tonight his shift ends at one-fifteen. He could make a stop at the bar, have a quick beer and see what's happening. Maybe sit at a table, just for a couple of hands.

He cracks the window to get a little air.

He has more or less 300,000 lire remaining. Ultimately, what's the risk? He doesn't have far to go, with 300,000 to get to the end of the month and a few dozen creditors hassling him for money.

The dark hills run by on his left. The yellow of a flashing traffic light pulses in the night. Francesco takes his foot off the accelerator. The fresh air hits his face and he breathes in deeply. Well, yes, all things considered, why not? With spring arriving, who knows, maybe tonight the cards will go his way.

*

Andrea sticks the card in the slot in the telephone, then presses the numbers.

The voice of the Secretary answers.

"Who is it?"

"It's me," says Andrea. "I want the confirmation for tomorrow. Everything is set?"

"Of course. Exactly as you arranged it."

"I want to be sure, I don't want any surprises at the moment of the handover."

"Calm down, Fabbri. Everything will go as planned."

"That will be best. Otherwise you know what could happen."

"I've told you that you don't have to worry."

"Good, then I'll just say goodbye. Give my regards to the Minister."

Andrea hangs up, checks the time on his wristwatch. He takes a slow look around the place. He goes over to the bar and sits on a stool a little apart. After a few moments the bartender comes up to him.

"What can I get you?"

"A Coke," Andrea answers. "And put a slice of lemon in it."

*

The bus moves off, and the man in the herringbone jacket looks at the posters outside the theatre, on the other side of the street. Next to him an old man in a broad-brimmed hat walks slowly away, leaning on a

14

cane. He checks his watch. It's still early. The concert begins at nine-thirty, there's plenty of time for a stroll and a cigarette. He takes a pack of Marlboros out of his jacket pocket.

He walks slowly under the portico, towards the Arco del Meloncello. His knee is hurting again. Who knows, maybe the weather is about to change.

It must be at least six years since he was in Bologna. And that time too it was a brief stay. He turns to the right, up the steps. One flight, and he is above the arch, suspended over Via Porrettana. The cars pass beneath him. From here, following the portico, one can reach the sanctuary of San Luca. He went up there often, many years ago. But not on a pilgrimage. He smiles, blowing the smoke out of his nose. He went to have sex with a student, on the backseat of the car, hidden behind a stand of bushes, in a small space littered with used condoms, cigarette butts and Kleenex. It was '75. The car was a blue Opel, fourth-hand. The girl was called Sonia, and she was studying literature; she was one of the hothead radicals who were around in those days. She was twenty-one and came from Pescara. He was fifteen years older, working for the secret service, and had been transferred to Bologna precisely to keep an eye on people like her. Not being Bolognese was perhaps the only thing they had in common.

The quarrels, the shouting, the insults return to mind. After they had talked a while, the blood would go to Sonia's head and she would say that he was a servant of the state, a watchdog in the service of power, that between them there could be nothing, and it was better to cut off that absurd relationship. He listened, but usually he didn't get mad, he could even understand the reasons for Sonia's protests. But mainly he was fascinated by the colour her face got, by the Abruzzese accent that grew thicker, and by the odour of her skin when she was angry.

Now, thinking back, he can't believe there was a time when he was discussing politics with a girl who was a member of the radical left. One of the types the police would have shot.

He throws the cigarette stub on the ground, crushes it under his heel.

Good times, shit, yes. A student of the ultra-left being fucked by a cop from the secret service, on the backseat of a dilapidated car or in the toilet of a cinema.

He looks at his watch again. If this damn knee didn't hurt so much, he wouldn't mind climbing up to the top and seeing Bologna from on high. He puts his hands in his pockets. Maybe another time. In three-quarters of an hour he will be comfortably seated, listening to the notes conjured by the magic fingers of Michel Petrucciani.

Down at the corner there's a bar. He'll be able to order an espresso and smoke another cigarette, peacefully, as he waits for the concert to begin.

*

Leila opens the door of her Y10. She throws handbag and jacket on the right-hand seat, gets into the driver's seat and starts the car. At the intersection the signal is red. She takes advantage of it to shift her head to the side and glance at herself in the rear-view mirror. What she catches is the part of her face that goes from her dark bangs to the base of her nose. At the centre of the rectangle, two grey-green eyes, vaguely oriental in shape. The mascara is perfect.

She opens the handbag, grabs a Gauloise Blonde, puts it between her lips. She clicks the lighter. She inhales deeply, blows the smoke out towards the windscreen. She sticks her hand in the handbag to make sure once again that everything is there. The cloth for fingerprints, the folded-up nylon knapsack, the latex gloves. Behind her a horn beeps. She looks up, realizes the light has already changed. She goes into first and quickly releases the clutch.

At the end of Via Irnerio she turns right. While she goes along the tree-lined avenue, she lowers the window a couple of inches, to let out the smoke. Reaching Viale Gozzadini, she puts on the indicator and shifts left towards the centre strip. Red light. Then green. She turns into Via Castiglione and takes it past the Margherita gardens. The discotheque is at the top of the hill.

The tyres squeal on the gravel of the car park. Leila parks her car in a spot far from the entrance. Before getting out she opens her lipstick and, looking at herself in the rear-view mirror, runs it over her lips.

*

Bobby, with his foot on the brake pedal, revs the motor of his Harley. Opaque black helmet, leather motorcycle jacket, black leather trousers, gloves, boots. When the light changes, he goes rapidly into first, second and third, leaving all the other vehicles standing. Fourth, fifth, a tight slalom between two cars, and the street is his alone. The headlight of the motorcycle cuts the air like the prow of a ship. The chrome of the handlebars gleams, reflecting the lights of street lamps and cars. He's a little late for the appointment, but Andrea will wait.

Arriving in front of the bar, he rides up onto the pavement with a soft spring in the shocks. With his heel, he lowers the kickstand so the bike is leaning to one side. He dismounts, takes off his helmet, shakes his head. His hair falls over his shoulders.

As soon as he crosses the threshold he sees his friend sitting on a stool. In front of him is a glass, with a couple of drops of Coke in it and a soggy slice of lemon at the bottom. Bobby sits down next to him, puts his helmet on the bar, nods to the bartender.

"A Ceres!" he calls out. Then, turning to Andrea: "So, how's it going?"

"Everything's set. I've had the confirmation. We finish up tomorrow night."

"Finally!" says Bobby, taking a handful of nuts from a little bowl. "Everything as planned?"

Andrea lowers his eyes to his glass.

"You just have to do what we decided. No more, no less. Do you want to go over the moves?"

"Like school? Come on, Andrea, that's unnecessary. I'm not a halfwit."

The bartender puts down a bottle of Ceres and a glass next to Bobby's black helmet.

Andrea waits for the man to move off.

"Good. So from here on the ball is in your hands. We'll meet tomorrow at the Porto di Mare with the key."

"Don't worry," Bobby says, pouring the beer slowly into the tilted glass. "You'll see, it'll all go fine."

*

He laughs a lot, drinks a lot and is wearing expensive clothes. Above all, Leila has enjoyed the casual way he takes the wallet out of his pocket, leaving a generous tip whenever he pays for something. After a few minutes of talking about nothing in particular he introduced himself.

"Mauro Breventani," he told her, offering his hand.

When he took his elbow off the bar, he swayed a little.

"Pleasure," Leila answered. "I'm Patricia."

He turned on her a broad smile, gripping her hand as if he would never give it back to her. He suggested a dance. So she found herself on the dance floor, in front of this guy who was moving out of time and with every new tune came a little bit closer. They kissed as they were returning to the bar. Leila didn't like the taste of his mouth. But now that the game had begun, she might as well keep going. Basically Breventani was nice, and the fact that he was drunk would simplify things. When he proposed leaving the discotheque, Leila accepted willingly, happy to speed things along and be able to breathe a little fresh air.

Outside, Breventani takes her by the arm, guides her with shaky steps towards a grey Mercedes. As he opens the door for her, he staggers slightly, and his eyes are blurry.

Leila asks him, "Everything OK?"

"Mag-ni-fi-cent," he says thickly, syllable by syllable.

Then he gets into the driver's seat, slumps against the seatback.

"You have a nice big car," Leila says.

Now he hunches over the steering wheel, trying to insert the key into the ignition.

"The car?" he mumbles.

He stares at the dashboard and runs his hands over the steering wheel, as if he were caressing it.

"Yes. As long as they let me keep it."

From the way he concentrates on the gearshift, one

would say that putting it in reverse is quite a complicated operation.

"Excuse me," Leila asks. "Why 'as long as they let me keep it'? You think it's going to be stolen?"

Breventani rolls his chest around and extends his arm over the seatback. He backs up a few feet. Then he turns around and puts it in first, stripping the gears.

"Steal?" He shakes his head. "No. I don't think anyone will be in time to steal it. The bailiff will get there first."

The Mercedes takes off suddenly. A burst of gravel sprays the underbody.

*

The sign outside the bar is off and the gate almost completely lowered. The usual clients know that in the back rooms a couple of tables are ready.

Francesco stops fifteen feet from the entrance. And if the Bear should be inside? He weighs the possibility of turning back, but an instant later he is crouching down to go under the steel gate.

In the room on the right are seven people. Bobo, the bartender, is chatting with two customers. Four other men are sitting at one of the small, round tables. The light from a cone-shaped lamp falls over the table, illuminating the dark-green cloth. The hands of three players are motionless. The fourth is shuffling the cards.

Francesco feels his fingers tingling. A kind of cramp grips his stomach. He knows there is only one way to relieve that bite. Bonetti, one of the men chatting with Bobo, nods in his direction. The bartender looks at him with a dubious expression, then lifts his chin in greeting.

This business of the bailiff is bugging her. What's behind it? An overdue payment? A bad cheque? She asks him some questions, to try to get a clearer picture. Breventani's vague answers make her suspect that the car isn't even his.

"No, no," he explains, with a pasty mouth. "The Mercedes is mine, it's not that. It's that I'm about to drown in debt. Just a matter of days now."

So Breventani has decided to come clean. Leila listens to a complicated story of bad investments, unreliable partners, failed marriages, children to support, even a mother with Alzheimer's, staying in a nursing home at three million a month. In short, a catastrophe.

"I've got nothing. Not a single lira. Tonight I spent everything I had left. The last 10,000 lire went for a tip to the coat-check girl. Now I don't even have money for petrol. My bank credit has been blocked for weeks, my house has been seized, and my two ex-wives don't give a damn – vampires, they go on sucking my blood even though I'm already dead."

And he laughs, the fool.

"Why are you looking at me like that? Doesn't my story amuse you?"

His laughs become sobs, which shake him like a poisonous cough.

"I'm ruined," he laments. "Ruined. And there's no way to start over. Shit, if I had any balls I'd end it all."

Leila is paralysed, her back rigid as an iron bar. Breventani's sobs slowly diminish.

"Anyway, you know what I say? I don't give a damn! I'm not the first to fail! One way or another I'll get back to the surface. Is it possible that things can continue to go wrong? For example, tonight I met you."

Leila can't even manage a smile. She lights a cigarette, tries to think up a good reason to persuade him to stop and take her back to the disco. Breventani reaches a hand over her thigh. Her muscles stiffen.

"Listen," she says to him. "Maybe it would be better if I went home."

Breventani looks at her darkly.

"Home? Why?"

"I don't feel very well. I've got a headache."

"Oh no, no," he says. "Shit, it's my fault. I didn't mean to depress you."

He slows down, heads for the side of the road, puts the car in neutral.

"Seriously," he says. "I don't even know why I started telling you my troubles. That's enough, let's not think about it anymore. Do you feel like going to my house?"

Leila wouldn't even think of it. But she realizes it won't be easy to get rid of him. Especially since from there to the discotheque is quite a ways. She has no intention of walking. Breventani, meanwhile, has attached his lips to hers and is trying to stick his tongue between her teeth. Leila gives in to the kiss, nauseated by the smell of alcohol.

"Listen, Mauro," she says to him as soon as she manages to get free. "Don't be mad, but I really have a terrible migraine. It's better if we see each other some other time. Maybe when you're in better shape, too."

"Look here, I'm very well. Feel."

He grabs one hand and presses it against the bulge in his pants. It's not the hardest thing she's ever touched, but Breventani seems quite proud of it. Then, suddenly, his mood drops again. He stops smiling and relaxes his grip.

"It's obvious . . . I annoyed you with my whining."

"No, I swear. It's not that."

"Then why? Until ten minutes ago we seemed to be going full steam ahead!"

"Yes, but . . ."

"Forget it, I know the reason. I understand perfectly."

Leila stiffens.

"The stink of failure," Breventani states. "Nobody likes a failure. Not even you. Rather, especially you. You're so beautiful."

Breventani bows forward, as if deflated. Leila looks at him, undecided between pity and disgust. She hopes that at least he won't start crying again.

*

"Thirty thousand," says the guy with the blond beard.

The bald man in the brown shirt reflects a few seconds before sticking.

"Fifty." The big shot with the Rolex, his hair shiny with gel, raises it, throwing a creased bill into the middle of the table.

Francesco looks down at his cards. Three queens, an ace of spades and a seven of hearts. He has no desire to get out, with three of a kind, and even less to chicken out in front of that asshole. But is it better to raise it or see the fifty? He looks up at the guy with the Rolex, wonders what he's got in his hand.

"Hey, we're waiting for you," the other says, with an arrogant stare. "Do you intend to decide by morning?"

As his left thumb caresses the cards, Francesco feels his fingers tingle.

*

Leila presses the switch. A warm light illumines the fabric of the sofa, the television, the amber highlights of the dining table, the stainless steel of the kitchen. She closes the door behind her, leans her back against it. It's a relief to re-enter her lair and find the well-known smells. She turns the gas on under the kettle, then goes into the bathroom. The light over the mirror falls onto her face, which seems to her much older and wearier than a few hours ago. She turns on the tap, rubs the soap between her hands. She holds them for a long time under the water. Then she takes off her make-up, washes her face, brushes her teeth.

When she goes back to the living room, the clock says 2:25. She drops onto the couch, looks for the remote buried in the cushions. She pushes the button that turns on the TV, but immediately turns off the sound. Then she kicks off her shoes, folds her legs under her, sits watching the mute images jump around on the screen. She thinks again of Breventani, with his look of distress, his breath saturated with alcohol. In order to get rid of him she ended up masturbating him. A hand job is better than nothing, he must have thought. He made himself comfortable, leaned his neck on the seat back and let her do it, panting through half-closed lips.

The kettle whistles. Leila gets up and goes to the kitchen barefoot. She puts a lime tisane in a cup, pours the hot water over it. She rotates the bag slowly in the cup, watching, on the TV, two girls stripping as they dance on a deserted beach. One of the two, with curly hair, has an enormous bosom. When she takes off her T-shirt, her breasts burst out of her bra. The other, a thin blonde with a turned-up nose, bares her tiny pointed, widely spaced nipples. Leila drinks the infusion in small sips. Sooner or later she'll have to leave this city too. The longer you stay in the same place, the greater the risks become. The blonde whirls her hair in the air. The curly-headed one laughs, revealing a mouth with too many teeth. Getting ahead is hard for everyone. Who can say how much you might earn, appearing in a video like this?

In front of the discotheque, Breventani asked for her phone number. She recited some numbers at random, which he scribbled on the pack of Camels.

"One of these days I'll call you," he said to her. "As soon as I've settled a couple of things, I'll invite you to dinner in a nice restaurant."

Leila nodded assent and got out of the Mercedes, avoiding having to kiss him.

The fact is that the guy tonight isn't the first miss she's had lately. She has a feeling that a few years ago she would have managed to pick up something better. They all seemed to have a greater desire for fun and more money to spend.

Suddenly her eyelids feel heavy, and she has only a deep wish to go to bed. She gulps down the last mouthfuls of her tisane, while the images of a chewing-gum ad appear on the TV screen.

Friday, 2 April 1993, 8:45 A.M.– 3:45 P.M.

I do not understand how you can love the air of Italy so much,
in which so often one breathes the plague,
where the heat of the day is always unbearable,
the cool of the evening unhealthy,
and where the obscurity of the night
hides robberies and murders.

From a letter of René Descartes, 5 May 1631

Garofano, in front of the closet mirror, is straightening the knot of his tie. He puts on the jacket, makes sure that the bulge under his arm isn't too noticeable.

When he goes into the kitchen, his wife is putting the coffeepot on the stove.

"Did you get everything packed?" she asks him, filling the milk jug.

He yawns, sits down at the head of the table.

"I think so. Anyway, I won't be away long."

"Did you take your electric razor?"

"Yes."

"Socks?"

Garofano scratches one ear.

"Yes."

"A change of undershirt?"

"I've got that too. Where's Elisabetta?"

His wife looks at him.

"What kind of question is that? She left for school at seven-thirty, as usual."

"Did she say anything to you about last night?"

"What do you think she said to me? Nothing. But her eyes were swollen."

Garofano shrugs his shoulders.

"I don't care. The important thing is that she forgets about that jerk."

"She must have cried all night."

"Don't exaggerate. What do you know about it?"

"I heard her. When you weren't snoring too loudly."

"It almost seems like you're on her side. Our daughter had better get it into her head that she can't do whatever she feels like. And I can assure you that I'll make her understand, one way or another!"

He grabs a brioche from the box in front of him and tears off the cellophane. As he's biting into it, the doorbell rings. Garofano looks at his wife. Without speaking, the woman leaves the kitchen.

"It's Diolaiti," she calls to him from the hall. "Shall I tell him to come up?"

"No," he says. "I'm going down."

*

Leila opens the window and breathes in deeply. From the street rises the usual odour of smog. But it's a clear day. The sun strikes the façade of the house opposite, giving it an intense red colour. A group of university students pass under her window. Their cheerful voices put her in a good mood.

While she makes coffee, her gaze falls on the cup that she left on the edge of the sink last night. For a second she thinks of Breventani. But this morning she feels impervious to misery.

She drinks the hot coffee. Then she lights a cigarette and again looks out the window. She inhales, closes her eyes. She basks in the fresh air and the warmth of

the sun, which is reflected on her face from the façade
of the building opposite.

*

"Stop here," Garofano says.

Diolaiti steers the car close to the curb. He switches
off the engine, turns to his colleague and stares at him.

"I'll be quick, five minutes, don't worry," the other
reassures him before getting out.

Diolaiti watches him move off, then checks the tips
of his fingers yet again. Even in the light of day he sees
neither cuts, nor wounds, nor scratches. There
shouldn't be any risk of infection.

Garofano approaches the entrance of a building. He
looks at the names on the bells. He takes a penknife
from his jacket pocket, fiddles with the lock for a
couple of seconds.

While the lift ascends, Garofano brings his face close
to the mirror. Left cheek, right cheek, chin, then he
sticks out his tongue to examine the colour. Then he
inclines his head forward and with the palm of his
hand smoothes the comb-over against his head.

The man who half opens the door has bovine eyes
and is holding a stained rag in one hand. On his chin
is several days' growth of beard. He wears a baggy
faded shirt, cotton trousers and a pair of carpet slippers. His straw-coloured hair is tied behind his neck
in a ponytail. From inside comes a dirge that Garofano classifies as Arab or Indian. Music for fags, in any
case.

"Are you Bellini?"

The man studies him with diffidence through the
half-open door, wiping his hands on the rag.

"Yes, I am. And who are you?"

"I'm the father of Elisabetta Garofano. Does that name mean anything to you?"

The man with the ponytail tries to close the door, but Garofano places his hand in the middle of it and pushes with all his weight, sending the man backward.

"What do you want from me?" asks Bellini, recovering his balance.

There's a penetrating odour in the air, which Garofano can't identify. Then he sees paintings hanging on the walls, piles of canvases leaning against the walls and an unfinished painting on the easel in front of the window. He realizes that the stink comes from the painting materials. Paints, varnish, solvents, all that stuff. On a table is a heap of half-used tubes, dirty rags, cans overflowing with brushes, a couple of palettes smeared with paints. Smoke rises from half of a cigarette left lying in an ashtray. Garofano takes the butt between thumb and index finger, sniffs it, winks at Bellini.

"Bravo, painter! If you piss me off, I'll put this joint out in your eye."

On the wall, next to a dilapidated cabinet, Garofano notices a painting done in broad brushstrokes. It shows a female nude. The subject isn't rendered in a realistic manner, but something in the picture reminds him of his daughter. He imagines Betta taking off her clothes in front of this creep who, more or less, can't be more than four or five years younger than he is. A shit who teaches art history in a shitty high school and takes his students to bed. The thought of his daughter naked in the hands of that asshole makes his blood boil. He punches him, catapulting him to the floor.

"What are you doing?" Bellini says, dragging himself up on one side. "Are you crazy?"

Garofano bends over, grabs him by the lapel of his shirt and picks him up bodily. He knees him between the legs, and the man contracts, rolling his eyes in pain. Garofano lets go of the shirt and watches as he sinks to the floor like a punctured balloon. As he flails around, the painter kicks off one of his slippers. Garofano observes that pale foot, and its hairy back, with an expression of disgust. He takes a pack of cigars out of his pocket, puts one in his mouth. A dense cloud of smoke rises. "It makes me sick to think of my daughter being screwed by a shit like you."

Bellini groans, with his hands between his thighs. Garofano feels a blind rage mounting to his brain. He puts his hand inside his jacket, takes out the Smith & Wesson. He kneels down, presses the heavy stainless-steel barrel up under the painter's chin, forcing him to raise his head.

"Now, dickhead, let's have a little talk. If it was up to me, I would blow your brains out and good riddance. But I don't want to make you into a hero. And above all I don't want Betta to have any suspicions about her father. You see? You're lucky. You have within your reach a chance to stay alive. You've been fucking a girl young enough to be your daughter. What's done is done, and even if I were to cut off your dick and stick it up your ass, there would be no going back. But starting tomorrow, if you want that dick of yours to stay in its place, get lost. Rather, you don't just take off and that's it. Because I don't want Betta to stay attached to you. You have to disappoint her, be a worm, disgust her. It won't be hard for you. Just do now what you would have done in a couple of months anyway. Telephone her and tell her that it's all over between you, that all you wanted was to go to bed with her, that in the meantime you've been doing it with four or five other girls. Have I made myself clear?"

The man widens his cow-like eyes.

"I'll do whatever you say, I swear."

Garofano smiles, but at heart he is a little disappointed. He would have preferred the game to continue a little longer, so he could really let go. The thought that this piece of shit has laid hands on his Betta makes his head spin with nausea. Better not to think about it, because it wouldn't take much to pull the trigger. He gets up, puts the .45 away and waits for Bellini to stand up again. Then, with the full force of one arm, he punches him in the face.

"That," he explains, massaging his knuckles, "is because I've read that to repress your aggression is bad for your health. And so that later you won't have any suspicions that I was only joking."

The painter writhes on the floor, pressing both hands to his face. Rivulets of blood drip between his fingers. Garofano pulls the nude off the wall, smashes it against a corner of the credenza. Then he kicks a stack of paintings that are leaning against the wall. His foot plunges through canvases up to the ankle. He jumps back, cursing as he attempts to free his shoe.

*

Bobo looks up and immediately sniffs trouble in the air. The Bear has the face of one who is seeking some prey to tear to pieces. The bartender screws the top back on the bottle of Campari, goes to place it on the shelf. When he turns back he finds himself facing the Bear, big as a mountain.

"Hey there, Bear. How's it going?"

"Have you seen our young friend?"

31

"Who?"

"Listen, Bobo, watch I don't break your balls too. You know perfectly well who I'm talking about."

Black mood. And, indeed, the bartender knows that, in this situation, it's more prudent not to contradict him.

"You're looking for Franz?"

"Bravo. Have you seen him around here?"

"No, I don't think so. Unless he came in without my noticing."

The Bear looks at him as if he were about to strangle him. And for a moment Bobo is afraid that he really will. He imagines the hands reaching over the bar and grabbing him by the neck.

"And yesterday?"

"Yes, he came into the bar around one in the morning."

"I bet he lost again, right?"

Bobo, looking gloomy, extends his arms with a shrug.

"He was unlucky."

"He's an idiot! And I bet he played on credit!"

The bartender looks down, and the Bear bursts into a joyless laugh.

"There's nothing to do, Bobo. He's always been a jerk and a jerk he'll die. But don't think that I'm going to be made a fool of forever. Sooner or later I'll get my hands on him, and you'll see, I'll make him cough it up!"

*

"There he is," Diolaiti says.

The man in the herringbone jacket comes out of the sliding door of bullet-proof glass. In his hands he

32

carries two small black suitcases, like overnight bags. Reaching a blue Alfa 90, he sticks one under his left arm and takes the car keys out of his pocket.

"Now pay attention," Garofano says. "Matera is an old fox. Even if he isn't suspicious, he watches his back out of habit."

Diolaiti nods, then starts the engine and puts the car in gear. Before setting off in the wake of the Alfa 90, he lets five or six cars go by.

"Let's hope he doesn't notice we're following him."

"It seems to me that the guy scares you a little."

"What the fuck does being scared have to do with it? You may be a champion at shooting morons in the back when they don't expect it, but I can tell you, that man is a horse of a different colour. I know him. He's the one who taught me the job."

*

The alarm clock on the dresser says 3:28. Francesco puts on one slipper, then spends at least a minute finding the second.

He unscrews the top of the coffeepot, empties the filter into the sink, runs the water to refill the pot. Even last night, after losing everything he had, he kept playing, on his word. He scratches the inside of one ear. How long has it been since he won anything? He massages his chin. He can't remember the last time he managed to come out even. Better to forget about it. What's the point of getting all worked up about tomorrow's good intentions? Just calculate how much it would take to pay all the debts he's accumulated. A year's salary? Two? He shakes his head. Two years wouldn't be enough even if by a miracle he stopped doing stupid things. You can't use a pay packet just

33

to liquidate debts. In the meantime you have to eat, buy coffee, beer, cigarettes, shampoo, detergent, pay the rent, the bills, the garbage tax . . . what else?

So, now he really could cry.

There's always his *reserve*. A few tens of thousands of lire, which he has the habit of keeping in an old wallet. He gets up and shuffles in his slippers to the bedroom. He opens the drawer. Seventy-four thousand lire, plus a little change. He throws the wallet back in the drawer and returns to the kitchen.

The coffeepot has splattered coffee all over the cooker.

Friday, 2 April 1993, 6 P.M.–12 A.M.

The future encounters of beautiful evil lovers
will be clashes
will be hunts with dogs and wild boars
will be runs bites and troubles for a thousand years
Fabrizio De André, *Anime Salve*

Matera left the Alfa 90 in a covered car park. Then he went to the hotel and waited for a couple of hours.

When he comes out again, he has only one of the suitcases.

Diolaiti and Garofano, in the grey Audi, follow at a distance. Via Saragozza, Viale Pepoli, Viale Vicini, Via Saffi, Via Emilia, Via del Triumvirato. When the blue Alfa turns onto the road to the airport, they look at one another.

"What the fuck is he doing?" Garofano says. "He's not going to take a plane and leave us sitting here like a couple of imbeciles?"

Diolaiti shrugs his shoulders without answering.

They follow Matera's car into the parking garage. Garofano feels his legs tingling with the tension. And if Matera realized that they were tailing him? Diolaiti turns off the engine. Through the windscreen the two men observe Matera as, suitcase in hand, he crosses the plaza to the terminal.

"It's better if you go," Garofano says. "If he sees me, he'll certainly recognize me."

Matera passes the big round columns and the people waiting in the lobby. He heads decisively towards the row of benches opposite the luggage lockers. All the seats are free. He sits down in the last one on the right, places the suitcase beside him and lights a cigarette. The chairs are of red-painted metal. The seats and backs are padded in a washable red fabric. Matera slides his fingers under the seat, until he meets a small hard thing, stuck to the metal with a strip of tape. He detaches it by scratching at the tape with a fingernail. Then he withdraws his hand, holding in his fist the tiny object that he has retrieved. He taps the cigarette, looks around, then down. It's a key. On the rectangular grip is stamped in relief the number 37.

*

Bobby, with his helmet hanging over one arm by the strap and his shoulder resting against one of the imposing columns of the lobby, is leafing through a copy of *Diabolik*. He tries to follow the story, but every ten or fifteen seconds he gives a rapid glance at the luggage lockers. So, alternating reading the comic with surveillance, he has to keep looking back at the plot. On page 27 a curly-haired girl appears, in a checked miniskirt and tennis shoes, and he can't remember that it's actually Eva Kant, who in the meantime has taken the place of the daughter of a rich jeweller. When, however, the girl, taking care not to be surprised by her father, starts going through the papers in his desk, Bobby realizes that he has lost the thread. He leafs back through the magazine and finally reconstructs the sequence of events. He nods with satisfaction, and when he looks up again from the comic he sees a tall man with grey hair and a herring-bone jacket who is doing something in front of the lockers. He shifts his head a little to the side to see which one he's opening. When he realizes that it's number 37, he throws the comic book into his helmet, thrusts his hands deeper into his jacket pockets and shifts a couple of steps, so that he can follow the man's moves.

*

Number 37 is in the next-to-last row on the bottom, where the larger lockers are. Matera closes the door and leaves, holding the key between thumb and forefinger.

Near the bank of seats where he sat before is a wall with three payphones. Farther on there is a waste basket: a tall rectangular one, painted red. Matera lets the key fall in, then takes out the pack of Marlboros and lights a cigarette. He inhales, pushes the smoke down into his lungs and walks towards the exit. On the way he notices a priest with a pockmarked face walking beside a tall, beautiful red-haired woman. The two proceed at a quick pace, talking animatedly in French. Matera exhales the smoke and, when he passes them, sniffs the air, trying to smell the woman's perfume. He manages to catch a dense, resinous scent, which reminds him vaguely of bitter figs. He slows down, tempted to take a look at the woman's ass, then decides to continue on without turning, as the Secretary advised.

*

Andrea opens the top drawer of the wardrobe. He chooses a tie with a loud pattern in shades of blue and yellow. He holds it against the shirtfront and turns to the mirror. Before him is the image of a handsome, athletic man of twenty-eight, with thick dark hair and a good tan. Andrea smiles with satisfaction. It doesn't take much to see that it's the face of a man who's going to go far in life.

The tie goes perfectly with the shirt. The fellow in the mirror agrees, and Andrea gives a conspiratorial wink. Then he smiles again.

*

Diolaiti, pretending to make a phone call, observes Matera's movements. Then he sees a man with a motorcycle helmet dangling from one arm approach the waste basket and give a sidelong glance inside, trying not to be conspicuous. He looks around, fishes something out of the can with one hand and heads quickly towards the exit.

Garofano, with his rear-end resting against the hood of the Audi, is talking on his mobile phone. Seeing his colleague approach, he makes a questioning motion with his chin.

"We have to follow the guy on the bike." Diolaiti comes straight to the point.

Garofano cranes his neck, looking in the direction indicated by his colleague.

"Listen, Giovanna, I'm busy now. I'll call you as soon as I have some time."

Garofano closes the phone and gets in the car as Diolaiti starts the engine.

"My daughter's going to drive me mad!" he says, sticking the phone in his pocket. "My wife told me that when Betta came home from school she locked herself in her room and hasn't said a word."

*

The big motorcycles standing on the pavement in front of the Palazzo dello Sport lean on their kickstands. Many of the tanks have pictures painted on them – dragons, horses, skulls, naked girls, tigers. The group of bikers who hang out in the neighbourhood welcome Bobby's arrival with shouts of greeting.

"Where the fuck have you been, brother?"

"Let's have a drink, Bobby! You're buying!"

"Hey, Bobby, got any plans for the evening?"

"Nothing particular. Why?"

"We had an idea of taking a ride to the coast. What do you say?"

"The coast?"

"It's Manser's idea. Come on, Manser, explain it to Bobby."

A thickset man, wearing Ray Bans and a patchwork jacket, gets off a blue-and-black Ducati.

"My cousin, with a couple of friends, has just taken over a bar near Riccione. Tonight's the opening. So I'm thinking we ought to go have a drink."

Bobby lowers his kickstand with the heel of his boot.

"Sure, why not? But first I have to do a couple of errands."

Manser shrugs, extending his heavy arms.

"No problemo. Meet you here around eleven, and when everyone shows, we'll take off."

"OK, then it's set!" Bobby says. "Who said something about drinks?"

"Me," answers a thin, hunched individual, with a

goatee. "But, if you recall correctly, I said you were buying."

*

Six old men are sitting at one of the tables under the portico. Four are playing cards. They slap the cards down hard on the tabletop, exchanging advice and opinions in loud voices. The other two follow the game and every so often venture a comment.

Francesco goes into the bar. The Rabbit and Gandini, elbows resting on the bar, are discussing off-road vehicles, while Bobo is lining up the liquor bottles on the shelf. In the back room a kid is stuck to the controls of a videogame.

Francesco says hello. The Rabbit and Gandini are silent. Bobo, with a bottle of vermouth in his hand, looks at him as if he's seeing a ghost.

"Hey, why are you looking at me like that? Have I grown horns?"

Gandini shakes his head and tosses back a swallow of Fernet.

The Rabbit pinches the lobe of one ear.

"Barely an hour ago the Bear was here," he says. "He was looking for you."

"The Bear?"

"The same. And, to tell you the truth, he seemed kind of mad."

Bobo waves the bottle of vermouth in the air.

"You think? I'd say he was furious. He practically started fighting with me too."

"Just a minute, just a minute. What did he want? If it's about money . . ."

"What do you think it's about?" the Rabbit interrupts him.

40

"When he found out that you lost your shirt again last night, he went ballistic."

"All right, so what the fuck should I do? Start handing over my salary?"

"Franz, you know yourself how it works. When you're already drowning, then you're dead before you've started."

"Son of a bitch, Rabbit! What would you do, in my place?"

Rabbit shrugs.

"I'd try to keep on friendly terms with the Bear. Because if he gets seriously steamed, he's nasty. You know that Battise and the Tailor have him collecting on their account too?"

Francesco runs a hand through his hair.

"Yes, worse luck. Because I don't owe all that much to the Bear, but I've lost a lot of dough to those two vultures!"

"There's more. The Bear has begun to pick up all your debts."

"What?"

"I saw him with my own eyes, Franz. When he runs into someone you owe money to, he collars him and makes a proposal. He offers to pay half the debt, on the spot and in cash. If the person agrees, the Bear takes out the money and marks in a notebook the name of the creditor, the sum you owe him, the night you lost it and the possible witnesses. He says he'll manage to get it out of you, one way or another."

"But that's nuts! Why's he doing it?"

"You're asking me? He's putting together an enormous sum. Soon he'll be your only creditor."

"Holy shit, I'm in a real mess."

"Yes. But couldn't you give him something now and the rest a little at a time?"

Francesco shakes his head.

"I don't have a cent."

"Then, Franz, it seems to me that you're in deep shit."

*

"Where did those clowns come from?" Garofano asks.

Diolaiti runs his hand over his chin, looking at the group of bikers from behind the windscreen.

"I haven't the faintest idea."

"You want to know something? In my opinion, they don't have a damn thing to do with it. You're sure that hippie took Matera's key out of the waste basket?"

"I already told you, Garofano. I couldn't see that well, but it certainly looked like a planned operation. Matera put the suitcase in a luggage locker in the baggage-storage area, then he threw something in the bin. In less than thirty seconds this jerk shows up and starts going through the rubbish. It can't be by chance."

"Maybe he's one of those people who like going through garbage. Maybe he took out a cigarette butt."

"Let's not talk crap. Does he seem the type to root around in a rubbish bin for a butt? With a motorcycle like that?"

Garofano stretches his knees forward and settles his back into the seat.

"Well, let's hope you're right. I wouldn't like to waste time with the wrong man."

*

Francesco doesn't feel like going home and eating alone. He gets back in his old Peugeot, turns right onto Via Marco Emilio Lepido and heads for the entrance to the ring road. In Corticella there's a trattoria where his credit's still good. On the avenue behind the supermarket, he sees some Slav prostitutes. After about half a mile he turns onto the ramp. Rays of red light from the sun, low on the horizon of streets, junctions and elevated highways, are reflected opaquely on the galvanized metal of the guardrails and flash suddenly on the bodies or windscreens of the cars. Francesco, hypnotized by the sight, drives lost in the dark buzz of his thoughts.

He takes exit 6 onto Via Corticella, then left to Via delle Fonti. He parks right in front of the restaurant.

When the waiter sees him, he goes to meet him with a friendly smile.

"Franz! How's it going? It's a while since we've seen you here."

Francesco makes an effort to smile. He heads for the inside room and sits at a table in a corner. The waiter leans forward and rests his hands on the edge of the table.

"If I may suggest, tonight we have black linguine made with squid ink that is truly spectacular."

"OK, I'll try it. And bring me a half bottle of white wine."

In a few moments the waiter is back with a cloudy carafe in his hand.

"Are you off or did you work this morning?"

"I haven't started yet," Francesco answers, filling the glass. "I'm on the night shift."

*

Andrea wipes his lips with the napkin. The dessert, ricotta with strawberry mousse, was delicious. He chose one of the best restaurants in the city and he's

43

not sorry. He nods at the waiter, who hurries to his table.

"I'd like coffee, please. And the bill. Oh, and bring me a whisky."

"What kind would you like?"

"Do you have Lagavulin?"

"Of course."

"Then a Lagavulin, neat."

He glances at the clock. The waiter is back in a flash, with a tray balanced on his arm. He places before him a steaming cup, a small, potbellied sugar bowl, a glass of whisky and a folded paper on a silver plate.

The coffee is excellent; the total 86,500. Andrea swirls his cup, sips the dense, frothy liquid, wipes his mouth with the napkin, then goes on to the Lagavulin. He puts the glass back on the table, takes his wallet out of his pocket. He leaves a 100,000-lire bill. Now he is on the home stretch, and, if everything goes as it should, this dinner is just a tiny taste of the luxuries that he will enjoy when the deal is done.

*

To follow the acrobatics of the Harley, without losing it or getting too close, is not an easy undertaking. Diolaiti's driving is more and more nervous. The car's progress is jerky, as he accelerates rapidly and brakes abruptly.

Garofano lowers the window a few inches.

"Diolaiti, if anyone tells you you're a good driver, don't believe him."

"You think it's easy to stay behind that idiot? If you want to know the truth, I'm fed up. At the first chance, I'm handing you the wheel."

"I'm happy to switch. By the way, I can't wait to eat.

I'm dying of hunger, and that son of a bitch keeps going around and around on that fucking bike. If I'd known it was going to be like this, I would have brought something."

"And now where's he gone?"

"He turned down there. Past the sign for the Chinese restaurant."

*

Leila still doesn't have a definite plan for the evening. She went to a pizzeria, ordered a *romana* and a beer. She had coffee and went out onto Via Augusto Righi and headed towards Via Indipendenza. Under the portico across the street a guy with red hair and an olive-green tailcoat picks out popular tunes on an electronic keyboard. Two dogs are lying at his feet, watching the passers-by with looks of annoyance.

Leila crosses Via Rizzoli and as she comes out into Piazza Maggiore a gust of fresh air hits her face. She fills her lungs and looks up at the sky. It's a clear evening. The white light of a star manages to pierce the violet halo suspended over the city. The spotlights trained on the Palazzo Comunale illuminate the façade with a delicate orange light that creates a beautiful play of shadows.

The anchovies and capers on the pizza have made her thirsty. She goes into one of the bars on the piazza and orders a beer. She drinks it standing in the doorway of the bar, watching the people passing through the centre of the piazza. Several people sit talking on the steps of the basilica. Leila observes a group of young people singing while one of them plays a guitar. Leila takes a swallow of beer. It seems to her a century has passed since the last time she sang along with anyone.

Suddenly, in the liquid night, the memories float up, unbidden. They splash for a few moments on the surface, then flee again to the depths. A bittersweet nostalgia is stirred up inside her.

She recalls her first years of high school, when she studied like a madwoman, seeking the approval of teachers and parents. Then came the startling discovery that there was another way to live. Many other ways. And the nights at the *osteria*, Marilena, Giovanni, Gianfranco, the first joints, sex, sleepless nights. The deathlike sleepiness of waking up, mornings when she didn't go to school and hid out in a bar or the park, talking to a friend. The discussions with the teachers, troubled by her new behaviour, and the exhausting quarrels with her father, who at first was angry and then more and more bitter and disappointed. And after high school, university. Alessandro, the action committees, saving humanity. The interminable discussions on subjects that she can no longer remember.

She swirls the beer around in the glass and her lips stretch into a smile. That was the period of grand ideals. Alessandro took her to meetings, explained to her how they would change the world. She postponed her exams for months, while her father became a peevish stranger who doled out money in tiny amounts. Meanwhile, Alessandro, more practical, got a law degree, joined a party and began to make a career in the moderate wing of the left. When he started buying ties that matched his jackets, she had said the hell with it and taken up with someone else. Federico was a wanderer in the spirit of the Beat generation; he was thin, with a tuft of curly hair in the middle of his narrow, sunken chest, and he played the guitar very badly. His only ideal was to be stoned out of his mind. As quickly as possible, and to the point of not knowing where in the world he would wake up in the morning. With him she had travelled a lot. Algeria, Seville, Lisbon, Amsterdam, Stockholm. Then farther and farther: Mexico, Guatemala, Costa Rica, Colombia, Venezuela, Brazil. An endurance test. Under big cotton shirts they were reduced to skin and bone, their armpits stank, their hair, in dreadlocks, was covered by a layer of dirt impervious to water. They never got to Argentina. One day, in agony from the dysentery that had been tormenting him for weeks, Federico had telephoned his grandparents. The old people, taking pity, had sent them money and return tickets. Leila recalls that interminable flight, the landing at Milan, the train to Bologna. The longest journey of her life. Nausea when she arrived.

Then a period of rest at her parents' house, a kind of convalescence. Her father didn't speak, her mother worried. She would have liked to know a lot of things. How Leila felt, where she had been, how she had grown so thin. Leila was too confused to want to answer those questions. After a few weeks, Federico telephoned to tell her that he had got money for another trip, and off they went again. This time to the East. India, Nepal, Pakistan, Thailand.

Suddenly, one morning in a godforsaken village on the banks of the Mae Nam Ping, while she was washing her face in an aluminium basin, she had the sensation of being very far from home, from herself, from everything. For an instant, she had seen her own face reflected in the water, disfigured by the ripples on the surface. Then she had stopped, leaned over to see better. When she had met her own eyes, staring back at her with a savage, frightened gaze, she had jumped, startled by that unknown person observing her as if she had surfaced from the bottom of a lake.

In the last image she has of Federico, he's squatting on his heels, keeping her company as she waits for the bus to Bangkok. Who knows where he would have dragged her if she had stayed? And who knows where he had ended up?

As soon as she was back in Italy, she had got herself into the clutches of that son of a bitch Paolo. She had met him in a discotheque in Florence and in less than two weeks had moved into his apartment in Genoa. From then on, she had let herself get mixed up in his whirl of smuggling, nightclubs, women, coke, gambling, always on the edge between wealth and ruin. After a few months of that life, she couldn't even breathe. She remembers with a sense of anguish moving from one mess to the next, the attempts to change, to run away, to get herself back on track, only to return, one way or another, to him, with his gold watches, designer clothes, cars with illegal registrations, his air of a farm boy who's made it big. He did know how the world works. He knew the price of everything. How much it costs to corrupt a customs officer, fuck a thirteen-year-old girl, buy a stolen Jaguar. Of all the lovers she's had, he was the biggest villain, the worst shit, the most useful. The only one who taught her some good tricks. From then on she's lived alone. Never more than a couple of years in the same city. Turin, Rome, Florence, Milan, Bologna, one place the same as the others. And soon she'll have to get away from here.

Paolo has looked for her only once since she left him. Maybe to show that she couldn't escape. One day, in a hotel in Verona, she had gone to her room, closed the door behind her. When she turned on the light, she found him there, sitting in an armchair. He looked at her with a smile, a cigarette between his fingers.

Leila had imagined him sneaking into the room, carefully preparing the scene, inspired by some American B movie. The only kind of film he had ever managed to sit through from beginning to end. He had spoken in a low voice, in a regretful voice. She was astonished when she realized that he wasn't trying to persuade her to go back to him.

"I just wanted to see you. And wish you good luck, that's all."

She had remained silent, without managing to smile at him, while he, as if following a script, had continued: "I also wanted to tell you that with you I was happy and that we can part as friends. If you ever need anything, you can count on me. But you could have left whenever you felt like it. There was no need to disappear like that."

Leila finishes her beer and goes back into the bar. As she sets the glass on the counter, she decides that the first stop of the night will be the Porto di Mare. A lot of people go there. Who knows? Maybe tonight she'll find someone to pick up. But she doesn't feel like making predictions. If it happens, it happens. And the hell with her worries.

*

"I wonder what the fuck that idiot is doing," Garofano protests, now at the wheel. "Son of a bitch, shouldn't he be making a swap? It seems to me he's out taking care of his own business!"

Diolaiti doesn't answer. Bobby turns onto Via San Vitale and accelerates hard, speeding his Harley along the narrow street, which is flanked by low porticos. The grey Audi follows the motorcycle, a hundred yards back.

"Do you think he realized we're on his tail?" Garofano asks.

"How should I know?"

"Maybe we'd be better off stopping him and making him tell us what his role is in this thing."

"I don't think he has what we're looking for."

"*I don't think, I don't think.* Meanwhile we're following him like two retards, and all we know is he stuck his hand in a waste bin."

The Harley bends left, passes the towers and continues onto Via Castiglione. Then it turns right into Piazza del Francia and stops beside a newsstand.

The Audi reaches the piazza while Bobby is putting on his lock.

"And now what?" Garofano asks.

"Go straight ahead. Let's circle around the piazza and get him from behind."

Garofano accelerates. The traffic light is red, but he goes through anyway, keeping to the right, then turns right again in Piazza Minghetti. When they enter Piazza Francia, they see Bobby crossing Via Castiglione on foot.

"Find a place to leave the car," Diolaiti says, getting out quickly. "I'll follow him."

*

The drinks are good, the music isn't bad, but Andrea doesn't feel at ease. He would prefer to be in a quieter place, maybe. Or would simply like the game to be over.

Bobby chose the place. The Porto di Mare opened a little over a year ago and immediately became one of the most popular bars in the city. It's in Via de' Pepoli, right in the centre of Bologna, in an old palazzo, where it takes up three floors. It's divided into different venues, and there's something for all tastes. Pub, concert space, discotheque, smaller, more private rooms with couches and low lights, piano bar, restaurant. There's no cover. From nine at night till three in the morning, thousands of people go there. Friday evening there's barely room to move.

Andrea has been there for about twenty minutes and is already tired of the crush that makes the air almost unbreathable. He is once again asking himself if he was right to trust Bobby. It's true that at one time they were inseparable and that Bobby has always been famous for his cool. But Andrea has the feeling that he's not taking this thing seriously.

He has just ordered another *mojito* when finally he sees him. Bobby stops a little beyond the entrance. He looks around, trying to pick out Andrea in the crowd. Andrea stands motionless, with the icy glass in his hand. The arrangement was for the first room, near the bar. Sooner or later he'll see him. There, now he's turned his eyes in his direction. And has nodded his head slightly, even though, out of caution, Andrea had warned him to avoid any gesture of greeting. Andrea lowers his gaze to his drink. He concentrates on the green of the mint. Out of the corner of his eye he sees Bobby elbowing his way through the crowd. He breathes in deeply, then exhales through his mouth and drains the *mojito* in one gulp. He gets off the stool and heads for the rest rooms.

*

When Diolaiti sees the crowd thronging the entrance to the club, he slows down, with an expression of disgust. Just the sort of place that guy would drag them to.

And if in the end Garofano was right? If he had made a mistake? He tightens his jaw. Pointless to have second thoughts now.

He manages to slip in among the dozens of kids who, going in and out, block the entrance. The music assails him, it's deafening, he has to make an effort not to bring his hands to his ears. He stands on tiptoe, trying to locate the biker in the leather jacket. But it's not easy. In the first room alone he can see at least a dozen jackets like the one his man is wearing. He struggles to advance, pushed and shoved from all directions. With his left arm he tries to protect his chest, at the height of the shoulder holster. The smoke burns his eyes. In his right eyelid he feels a tear welling, which soon slides down his cheek. He gives up trying to get his handkerchief out of his pocket and wipes it off with the back of his hand.

When he discovers that there's a flight of stairs leading up, he feels his rage grow. To find that jerk will be some job. Provided there are no other exits, because if so, he might have already shaken them. But to give up is not his style. So he goes back to pushing and shoving, and continues his inspection, venting his nerves with his elbows. Suddenly someone grabs his shoulder. He turns and finds himself a few inches from the broad, square face of Garofano, who is shouting something at him.

"What did you say?" he yells, with his hand cupped behind his ear.

"Did you see him come in here?"

"Yes. But I've lost sight of him."

"It's a real mess . . ."

"What?"

"I said it's a real mess to find him!"

Diolaiti makes a sign of agreement, then moves on

again, searching with his gaze among the dozens of moving bodies. For an instant he seems to see the biker pass behind a group of girls who are laughing at something said by a man balding at the temples but with yellow hair tied back in a ponytail. Diolaiti nods at Garofano and heads with an effort in that direction. But the biker has already disappeared.

He looks around in exasperation. The man with the ponytail is gesticulating and the girls are waiting for the next remark. Diolaiti brings a hand to his stomach. He feels a burning sensation. And his eye is dripping again.

Garofano grabs his arm.

"Listen, if I don't eat something I'm going to faint!" he shouts, his mouth stuck to Diolaiti's ear. "I'm going to make a run to the bar and get a couple of sandwiches."

Diolaiti makes a sign of agreement.

"Shall I get one for you?"

He shakes his head. The mere thought of chewing brings a foamy acid to his throat.

"OK. I'll be back. Keep looking around."

The man with the ponytail has finished his story and a new burst of laughter rises from the group of girls. Diolaiti looks at them with hatred. One is sort of attractive, with red hair and big boobs, covering her mouth with the palm of her hand as she laughs.

A little farther on, he notices the door of the men's room. Maybe the biker went to the toilet. His head is bursting and he allows himself to be tempted by the idea of getting out of that unbearable confusion.

*

Andrea is standing in front of the toilet, in the last stall

53

in the row. On the tiles next to the button you push to flush someone has written:

SOUTHERNERS GO HOME

He hears the sound of water running and the voices of two kids talking about a certain Stefania.

"So did she put out?"

"Did she ever! Believe it or not, if I hadn't stopped her, we'd still be fucking!"

The two laugh, start the dryers for their hands. Their voices reach him in a jumble, overpowered by the noise of the fans. When the machines go off, Andrea catches a last shred of the conversation.

". . . satisfy my curiosity on one thing. Did your father fork over any money?"

"Are you nuts? The old man's wallet is sewed up tight. If I want to buy it, the only thing is . . ."

The din of the crowd and the music cover the rest of the conversation. The sound fades and then, as soon as the door closes behind them, disappears.

As he stands there, the stink of pee becomes irritating. Andrea puts his hands in his pockets and bites the inside of one cheek. From another stall comes the roar of a flush. Then a door slams and steps cross the floor. Again he hears, for a few instants, the noise and music at high volume. While he waits, he turns towards the closed door and reads the writing scribbled on the back of the light-brown laminated surface.

FOREIGNERS OUT OF ITALY
WE LIKE PUSSY
I'M VOMITING, I'M SICK AS A DOG
CHRIST HAVE PITY
SYLVIA I LOVE YOU

INTER FANS ARE FAGS

MY NAME IS NICOLETTA, I HAVE BLUE EYES, I'M BLONDE, SLENDER AND I LIKE TO GIVE BLOWJOBS. MY NUMBER IS 217638

FASCISTS EAT SHIT

A broad black ink mark has almost obliterated this last saying, replacing it with:

DEATH TO COMMUNISTS

A current of air from somewhere hits his calves. There must be an open window. Again the door opens and closes. Music at top volume, buzz of voices, silence. Andrea can't figure out which direction the steps are going. He bows his head and concentrates. He hears a lock slide.

From the next stall comes a whisper.

"Andrea, are you there?"

It's Bobby.

"Yes. Everything OK?"

"Smooth as can be. I'll hand it over the top."

Andrea gazes upward and along the top of the dividing wall. He reaches his hand up and runs it along the edge. His fingers encounter the metal of the key.

"Did you get it?" asks Bobby from the other side.

"Yes."

Andrea opens his wallet and slips the key into the change compartment.

"Who's leaving first?"

"I am. You wait a minute."

"OK. Good luck."

Bobby hears the door of the stall next to him open and the sound of footsteps growing distant. He unzips his pants and pees.

The instant he puts his hand on the knob, Diolaiti feels the door being pulled from the inside. He lets the kid who appears on the threshold go by.

Once he is in the men's room, he has an immediate sense of relief. Finally he can breathe. On the left, the mirrors and sinks. On the back wall, a half-open window. On the right, four stalls. The one at the end is closed. Diolaiti loosens the knot of his tie and approaches the row of sinks. The taps don't have handles. He leans over. Pedals on the floor control the water. He steps on one, then presses the button for soap. He washes his hands, rinses his face. When he looks up into the mirror, he sees the motorcyclist passing behind him.

*

As soon as she turns onto Via de' Pepoli, she notices the crowd outside the club. A continuous crush of people, some of whom stand chatting in small groups in front of the entrance or along the street.

Leila approaches slowly, undecided whether to join the mob. Maybe it would be better to spend the evening somewhere else, somewhere more peaceful. But now that she's here, she might as well go in.

*

At the door of the men's room, a man with the face of an ant moves aside to let him pass. Andrea smiles, thanking him. He's in the mood to be polite, now that he has the key. As soon as he comes out, he is assaulted by the noise and the heat of massed bodies. But the atmosphere no longer seems so irritating. In fact, he has half a desire to order another *mojito*. Two girls in very short skirts go by. One is wearing boots up to her knees and has stupendous thighs. The other looks at him and smiles. On her cheeks intriguing dimples form. Well, yes, why not have another drink? The place is full of beautiful girls and he still has three hours before he has to play his part. After all, everything is going according to plan. It's worth the trouble to celebrate.

While the bartender prepares his cocktail, he looks around with his elbows on the bar. Then, glass in hand, he moves to the discotheque.

A tall, thin, very young red-head goes by; her ass is a little flat but she has boobs you could applaud. She's wearing skin-tight jeans and a red and white striped T-shirt, against which the nipples push out. But there's one detail that excites him more than anything else: the girl is wearing braces on her teeth.

Andrea looks again at his watch. Calculating that he needs an hour for the exchange, how much time does he have available? His veins are fizzy with excitement. To pick up someone he's never seen before and fuck her in less than two hours. It's a good bet.

He's on the point of throwing himself into it when a baldish guy with a blond ponytail approaches the red-head and embraces her from behind, guiding her to the rhythm of the music. Laughing, the girl lets him kiss her on the neck. The man entwines his forearms around her waist. A wave of annoyance washes over him.

He continues to explore the room, with slow panoramic glances, until he picks out another prey. A dark girl, her hair like a helmet, sheathed in a miniskirt and low-cut black body stocking, which is stamped across her chest like a second skin. She's not as young as the redhead, and her tits are a little small. But she is not to be sneezed at; why look for flaws?

The girl stops at the edge of the dance floor. A glass in her hand, she sways slightly to the rhythm of the music as she observes the others dancing.

*

Garofano reads the list of sandwiches distrustfully, while the waiter, a kid in a checked waistcoat, his forehead covered with pimples, waits, tapping a ballpoint pen on a spiral notebook. Prosciutto-lettuce mayonnaise. Ham-mozzarella-mushroom sauce. Tuna-tomato-olive paste. Ham-fontina-mixed greens. Bacon-tartar sauce-Tabasco. Aubergine-mushroom-pepper. Why the fuck don't they ever use more than three ingredients?

"Excuse me, could you make a couple of those and put in what I tell you?"

The waiter looks at him askance.

"Why? Don't you like our sandwiches?"

Garofano stares at him severely.

"No. I don't like them. Personally, I prefer sandwiches with more filling and without those cheap sauces you slather on."

The waiter grimaces and shrugs his shoulders, turning his gaze in another direction. He doesn't seem in the least impressed by Garofano's attitude.

"OK. What do you want?"

"On one you put butter, capers, artichokes, olives, tuna, anchovies, lettuce, hardboiled egg, tomato. How are the peppers cooked?"

The kid scratches the pimples on his forehead with the pen point.

"The peppers? Grilled, I think."

"They're bound to be frozen. But all right, peppers. Have you got everything?"

The waiter makes a sign that he has, while he adds peppers to the list.

"Good. On the other you'll put bacon, mushrooms, black olives, marinated aubergine, artichokes, a few drops of Tabasco and cheese. But here we've got to have a little discussion. Is fontina all you've got?"

"I don't know. I'll have to ask."

"Good boy. See what they tell you in the kitchen, because I don't like fontina. I would prefer something a little stronger. But I'm not particular. Pecorino, scamorza, taleggio, caciocavallo, whatever you find. See, I like cheese a lot, but when they talk of fontina in a place like this, I hear processed cheese. And that's not cheese. It's rubber. I don't know if you understand me."

"Yes, more or less."

"Well, I'm going to explain more clearly. If you bring me a sandwich with processed cheese in it, I will stick it up your ass, with the napkin and all the trimmings."

Now the boy looks a little more worried. He finishes writing the order on his pad and slips away without another word.

When he reappears with the sandwiches, Garofano orders a couple of cans of beer. At that moment Diolaiti appears.

"What are you doing? Didn't you see him go by?"

"Who?"

"Let's go, he's going to get away from us," Diolaiti shouts, making his way into the crowd.

"Just a second, I'm getting the sandwiches."

He hurries towards the waiter, tears the two sandwiches out of his hands and puts them in the pockets of his jacket, one on each side. Then he grabs the beers and rushes after Diolaiti, who by now has reached the door.

Leila sets the empty glass on the bar and nods to the bartender.

"Another gin and tonic, please," she says to him as soon as he is in earshot.

She is putting a hand in her handbag when a man in a jacket and tie appears at her side, with a smile as if he'd conquered the world.

"If I may," he says, sliding a fifty across the bar. "Let me get this for you."

Leila smiles and shrugs. Then she sticks a Gauloise between her lips. He makes no move to light the cigarette. Probably he doesn't smoke.

"Consider it as homage to your fascination," Andrea says and puts the change in his pocket without looking at it.

Leila lights a match, inhales.

As long as he doesn't turn out to be another disaster.

*

This group isn't bad. Matera looks at the clock. Still two hours to go, and the Secretary warned him to pay close attention to the schedule. First delivery at six o'clock sharp. Retrieval and second delivery not before one. He would like to know what nitwit thought up such an absurd plan.

He nods to the waiter.

"Another beer please."

"Amber?"

Yes, a small amber. Thank you."

Luckily he had been told about this bar, where he could pass the time listening to some good music. It's not the kind of jazz he likes best, he prefers the old standards, but it's better than wandering around like an imbecile, waiting till it's time to finish the job.

*

It's done, she's let herself be hooked. The guy, all in all, seems like a good prospect. Maybe too full of himself, but it's not as if she has to marry him. He's wearing designer clothes and has a nice fat wallet: that's the important thing. And physically he's not bad at all. Certainly he doesn't waste time. He moved in a hurry from compliments to allusions and point blank invites her to his house. Leila accepts the proposal stylishly, letting him imagine that in his case she'll make an exception to the rule, but that it's not her habit to go to bed with the first guy who comes along. He seems satisfied. He must think he's made an impression. There is nothing more satisfying to men than to believe they possess a unique attraction. On the other hand, it's sufficient to let them believe it. It's what they expect.

As soon as they leave the bar, Andrea takes her by the arm.

"I'm parked just a step away," he tells her, guiding her towards Via Castiglione.

As they turn onto Via Farini, Andrea looks at his watch and quickens the pace. He is already beginning to regret the enterprise he's embarked on. It would be much better to get the exchange over with and allow himself all the fucking he wants afterward, when he's got all the time in the world. What sense is there in having a quickie, with the risk of arriving late at the most important appointment of his life?

"Where did you leave the car?" she asks.

Andrea shakes himself out of his thoughts, tells her

he parked in Via de' Poeti. In Piazza Cavour a tramp approaches them. In one hand he has three plastic shopping bags full of rags, in the other a carton of wine.

"Won't you give me a thousand lire?"

The stink of rancid sweat is noticeable three feet away. Andrea holds Leila's arm tighter, pulls her along without even turning.

"Hey, mister," the tramp calls after him. "I asked you something. You could at least answer me!"

"Wait," Leila says.

"What are you doing?"

She opens her handbag.

"I'm going to give that man a thousand lire. What's the harm?"

The tramp shuffles towards them.

"You changed your mind?" he asks, with a smile that reveals a mouth full of decayed teeth.

"Yes," Leila answers, looking in her wallet. "Just a second."

Andrea, impatient, digs in his jacket pocket.

"Forget it. I'll take care of it."

His fingers fall on a 10,000-lire note. He sticks it in the man's hands and drags Leila away as she's closing her handbag.

The car is a metallic-blue BMW. Andrea has parked so close to the wall that not even a contortionist could get to the passenger side. With four frenetic man-oeuvres he frees the car from its slot. Then he gets out and runs to open the door for her. So he can get a quick glimpse of her legs as she gets in and the mini-skirt hikes up her thighs.

Via de' Poeti is very narrow. Andrea drives slowly to Via Castiglione. He turns right, goes past the tower, and at the intersection takes the boulevards in the direction of Porta San Mamolo.

The BMW starts off smoothly, avoiding the cars that go more slowly or that are slowing down to stop. Through the window, Leila glances at the prostitutes on the pavements. Then she looks at Andrea's profile as he concentrates on driving. She has the impression that something in his attitude has changed. Ever since she agreed to go to his house, he has begun to act as if he had lost interest. Usually they keep up their attention at least until they've fucked. Leila decides she doesn't give a damn. She relaxes on the seat, enjoying the comfort of the anatomically correct seatback.

Andrea glances at the clock on the dashboard. Eleven-ten. No, this is no good. If he wants to succeed, he has to calm down. The important thing is to stay in control. Didn't he want to take a girl to bed? Well, here's one who in just a short time is going to spread her legs.

"We haven't even introduced ourselves," Leila says.

"What do you mean? Oh yes, it's true. My name is Andrea. And you?"

"Angela."

"That's a pretty name, Angela. Do you feel like some music?"

"Yes, that would be nice."

Andrea opens a compartment on the dashboard. In the dark emerge the little green lights of a hi-fi. He presses a couple of buttons. A synthesizer background, followed by the notes of a piano. Then a voice. Elton John. "Sorry Seems to Be the Hardest Word".

Leila runs a hand through her hair and moves a lock behind her ear. She rests her neck on the headrest and lets the glow of the street lamps and headlights slide over the convex surface of her eyes. She feels good. In excellent shape, relaxed, ready for action. In the air is a slight scent of woodland pine.

The audience applauds. The saxophonist brings the microphone to his mouth, thanks everyone and explains that the piece that just ended was called "Lítost". The bass player composed it, while the next one he wrote himself, dedicating it to Che Guevara. The title of the piece is "Aplomado". A term that refers to the final phase of the bullfight, when the bull is beaten.

Matera smiles and shakes his head. He has never understood why, but almost all artists are on the other side. However you look at it, in the end you discover that the majority of musicians are deadbeats, addicts, practically anarchists. There's little to do about it, it seems that they can't stand rules. They are allergic to laws, and usually also to the State. Even those who manage to survive, thanks to the government. They're made like that. They like to bite the hand that feeds them.

He looks at his watch. These kids may be reds, but they're good. The time has flown by. He turns, looks for the waiter, raises an arm to attract his attention. He sees him and heads over, slaloming among the tables.

"Sir?"

"May I have the bill?"

"Right away."

Meanwhile the next piece begins. The musician pumps into his tenor an obsessive phrase, which soon flows into an enthralling solo, full of energy.

*

"You know something?" Garofano says with his mouth full. "I've had enough."

On the autostrada he glances at his colleague sitting beside him. He holds the sandwich with two hands in front of his face. He bites off an enormous chunk, even before he's swallowed the one he's chewing, then tears off the top of the beer can that he holds between his thighs and washes down the mouthful with a swallow of beer.

"Are you listening to me? We can't go on following that imbecile forever!"

"And what would you suggest we do? Let's hear it."

Garofano bites into his sandwich again, stares at the group of motorcyclists in front of them.

"I'd like to pass them," he says, spitting out bits of bread. "And while we're passing them, take target practice."

He raises his right hand and points the index finger at the rear lights of the motorcycles.

"Bam, bam, bam. Don't you think that would be a lot of fun?"

Diolaiti looks at him again. Garofano turns towards him and smiles, with bits of food stuck in his teeth.

*

It looks like a furnished apartment. Not many clothes around and almost no knick-knacks. A pied-à-terre where he goes for sex? Maybe. But, come to think of it, Andrea has a strange accent. A clean and impersonal pronunciation, with a slight cadence of the south. Maybe he's someone who travels for his job and is often in Bologna. Who knows, maybe he's rented the place just in case he needs it? If so, he must have a lot of money, with prices what they are.

Andrea throws the keys on a desk.

"Well, here we are," he says, with a rather forced

smile. "What would you say to a couple of lines, just to loosen up a little?"

Well, well, the big shot has snow. Why not? It can't hurt. But she doesn't want to give him the impression that she's someone who sucks up coke like a vacuum cleaner.

"Why not?" she answers.

"You'll see. It'll help things get started. I'll have it ready in a second. In the meantime relax, make yourself at home."

As if to say: if you want to start getting undressed, go ahead.

Leila takes off her jacket and throws it over an arm of a sofa. He loosens his tie, opens a drawer of the desk, takes out a cellophane envelope. He tears a corner off the envelope and the coke spills out on the desk.

"Damn," he says.

He takes his wallet out of his pocket, pulls out a 50,000-lire note. With the edge of the bill he rakes up the coke. He leaves a little pile on one side, which he separates into four parallel lines. Then he rolls up the banknote to make a straw, sticks it in his right nostril. He leans over the desk and sniffs it up in a single draw. He repeats the operation with the other nostril, then offers the rolled-up note to Leila, who does the two remaining lines.

Andrea picks up the rest of the dust with his fingertip, rubs it on his gum. Then he goes over to her and kisses her. While their tongues entangle, he caresses her cheek, moves his fingers down her neck until his palm is cupping her breast. With the other hand he raises her miniskirt, sticks his fingers inside her knickers.

He draws her towards the bed. He kisses her neck,

touches her thighs, tries to figure out how to take off her body stocking. He gets up and sits Leila opposite him. He kneels down in front of her. He picks up her right foot. He unzips her boot and takes it off. He kisses her ankle. Then he takes off the other. He caresses her calves, her thighs, pulls down the zipper of her skirt. Leila lifts her bottom, arches her back while Andrea takes off the skirt. He stops a moment to admire her legs, then dives into her groin, while with his nails he fumbles with the hooks of the body stocking. He grasps the two edges of the garment, stands up, and pulls it off from above.

Leila looks up. Through her hair, which has fallen over her face, she sees him standing in front of her, with his groin at the level of her eyes. He drops the body stocking on the floor and with one hand caresses her neck. OK, Leila thinks. Message received. She slowly unzips his trousers. She sticks two fingers inside, as if she were handling something extremely fragile. She touches the swelling in his underpants, then, delicately, frees the penis from the elastic. He looks down at her, breathing deeply through his mouth. Leila pulls down his pants. She bends over to lick one knee, slides her tongue along the thigh. When she comes to the scrotum she slows down. She goes from the bottom to the top, slowly. Then she begins to lick the base of the penis, while with her hands she caresses the buttocks and sticks two fingers in the crack. Only then does she take it in her mouth, slowly, between tight lips.

Andrea, in a hoarse voice that he himself barely recognizes, says to her, "If you go on like that I'll come in five seconds."

Leila withdraws. She caresses the scrotum with the tip of her finger.

"What would you prefer?" she asks.

He lifts her chin with one hand. He clears his voice. "I want to fuck you."

"Good," says Leila. "I'd like that too."

He pushes her backwards, while he tries to free his ankles from the knot of shoes and socks. He kneels in front of her and kisses the insides of her thighs. He has to hurry if he doesn't want to be late. In the worst case, he can always leave her here, to sleep, and return after making the exchange. His tongue goes to the clitoris, then moves up to lick her stomach and breasts.

Leila tears off the edge of the packet that she's kept within reach.

Andrea sucks her nipples, with the corner of his eye finds a way to look at his wrist watch. It's already 11:45. Too bad, he thinks, with a whore like this it would be worth taking your time.

He lies on top of her and tries to penetrate her. Leila, rapid and precise, sheathes his prick in the condom and guides it inside.

Andrea is in a big hurry. In little more than an hour, he will have concluded the operation, and he wants to have time to make sure that everything is in order, before delivering the document.

After four or five heaves he grabs Leila's back, while from his throat a suffocated groan escapes.

Saturday, 3 April 1993, 12:30 A.M.– 7 A.M.

You say "Anyway's the only way", be careful not to gamble
On a guy with a suitcase and a ticket getting out of here
It's a tired bus station and an old pair of shoes
This ain't nothing but an invitation to the blues
                                    Tom Waits, *Invitation to the Blues*

He's tired even before he starts. He can barely stand this job anymore. In fact, maybe he started playing cards precisely in the hope of scraping together enough money to escape. Go and live in some tropical place, open a bar on the beach.

What nonsense! Francesco wonders how, at the age of thirty, a person can go on believing in such fantasies. The only thing he's getting out of cards is a faster trip to the bottom. Stick his life in the toilet and flush. Or end up with someone like the Bear.

He recalls a scene he witnessed one afternoon last summer, when he was having a spumante at the bar. A guy in a Ford Escort started getting huffy because of a parking place. He wanted to know who owned the car that was parked sideways, taking up three places. The car, unfortunately for him, belonged to the Bear, who was observing things from a table a few feet away. The man with the Ford was shouting, gesticulating, nodding in their direction. At first, the Bear pretended not to be paying attention. He turned to the others at the bar and said, "Sooner or later that pain in the ass is going to get tired of making a fuss."

But the pain in the ass didn't get tired. Rather, he began to pound on the horn. The Bear stayed quiet. He just crossed his arms and leaned back in his chair so that it balanced on its back legs.

Bianchini, who was sitting at the table with him, asked, "Hey, Bear, why don't you move your Volvo, so that idiot will shut up?"

"Because I don't feel like it."

Bianchini had guessed that it was better not to insist. But the guy had stopped the Ford in the middle of the street and was coming towards them quickly.

Reaching the bar, he shouted, "Does anyone know who the fuck that Volvo belongs to?"

The Bear stood up.

"It's mine, and I park it however the fuck I feel like. Turn around and go find another place."

"If you don't move that piece of shit immediately, I'm warning you I'll kick it."

The Bear laughed in his face.

"Try it, and I'll kick you in the teeth. Let's see who can do more damage."

The Bear stood in front of him, six-five and nearly 300 pounds, but the guy with the Ford Escort must have blown a gasket, because he looked around like a lunatic, grabbed a glass off the table and threw it in the Bear's face. The glass, along with the Martini that was in it, and the little ice cubes, the olive, and the tooth-pick. Then he rushed him. But before he could even touch him the Bear had thrown a punch at the level of his ear and, without letting him fall, had seized his wrist and twisted his arm behind his back. He had picked him up, carried him to the Ford and thrown him in through the open door. Then he leaned over

70

and grabbed onto the car's body. Francesco remembered with a shudder the muscles straining in the Bear's neck, as he hoisted the Ford and pushed it over on its side. Francesco saw again the dark belly of the car, with its skeleton of pipes, axles and shock absorbers, and the back wheel spinning in the air.

And now, one after the other, he remembered all the stories he'd heard about the Bear. Of the time he had laid out two tough, hulking car mechanics on Via Bencivenni. Of the time he had argued with a kick-boxing teacher, a nervous kid with hair like a helmet, who had started to hop around in front of him until the Bear ended the match by landing a punch that lifted him two feet off the ground. Or of the fight outside the stadium when, by himself, he had taken out seven Fiorentina fans who attacked him with crowbars and chains.

Francesco parks his Peugeot, slowly crosses the dark, deserted piazza. He heads for the dispatcher's glass booth, illuminated by the bluish reflection of the television. He goes in, mumbles a greeting, the dispatcher gives him the information about the bus he is to drive tonight. Vehicle 5017, Section A, Row 16. Route 61. The shift begins at 00:39 and ends at 6:25.

He goes to the bathroom. While he aims the jet at the urinal, he broods again on the meagre possibilities for getting out of his troubles. He shakes off, zips up his pants. Passing the mirror, he looks at himself.

He leans over the stainless-steel drinking fountain, pushes the button that starts the vertical stream, takes a swallow of icy water. He wipes his mouth with the back of his hand, then walks along the empty corridors of the depot. He casts a glance at the naked girls who smile, in the shadows, from the calendars hanging on the wall.

He goes through the double doors and out into the parking lot. A gust of cool air hits him in the face, with an odour of gas and burned rubber.

He heads for Section A. Bus number 5017 is the first in row 16. He climbs the two steps to the back door as if it were a gallows. He sits down in the driver's seat. He turns on the lights, starts the engine, adjusts the seatback. Then he gets up to put the route number on the outside panels.

From his stomach rises a silent burp that tastes of parsley. One after another he presses the three buttons for the pneumatic doors. He engages the gearshift to go into automatic. He releases the handbrake and presses the accelerator. The bus starts off, bouncing on the uneven asphalt of the parking lot. The compressed-air shock absorbers aren't yet fully charged.

*

The sliding doors open and Matera enters the airport. He has the impression that he is not in the same place he was that afternoon. A black cleaning woman in a blue shirt is pushing a cart holding brooms, buckets and cleaning supplies. Matera heads for the luggage lockers.

He skirts the columns, sits down on the last seat in the row, just as he did a few hours ago. He looks around, distracted, wondering if anyone is watching him. He reaches a hand under the seat, running his fingers securely along the edge. But at the point where, this afternoon, he found the key, there is now nothing. He leans to the side, runs his hand forward and back along the smooth surface.

He looks around again. No one seems to be paying

attention. He takes the pack of Marlboros out of his pocket, sticks one between his lips. He takes out his lighter. He lets go of it on purpose, so that it drops on the floor of red-veined marble. He goes down on one knee and bends over to look under the seat. Nothing. He retrieves the lighter, lights his cigarette. He feels a knot at the opposite edge of the seat. He detaches it and rolls it between his fingers. It's a piece of chewing gum that someone has stuck there.

*

There is something both sad and comical about the cock of a man who has just had an orgasm. Andrea's is no exception: sticky, soft and a little wrinkled. Lying against his right thigh, with a drop of liquid trickling slowly. Fifteen minutes ago he was rearing proudly, now he's like a dead snail. The clearing of hairs around his navel rises and falls with deep, regular movements. A sign that he is asleep. Leila looks at him almost tenderly. Certain that the amount of Valium she put in the vodka would have knocked out even an ox.

She goes into the bathroom to wash. She gets dressed. It's time to go to work.

She goes to the bed, to the side opposite where Andrea is sleeping. She dumps out the contents of her handbag. On the sheet fall the package of Gauloises, the lipstick, the house keys, car keys, a nail file, the small square box of blusher, the lighter. Leila takes the cloth, the latex gloves and the nylon backpack, which is folded into a thin package. She puts on the gloves. With the rag, she begins meticulously wiping all the surfaces that, as far as she can recall, she touched.

Andrea's jacket is thrown over the back of an

73

armchair. Leila searches the inside pocket, takes out the wallet. It's Gucci, dark brown leather, very soft. It's full of bills, mostly big ones. She throws it on the bed, with the handbag and the rest of her stuff. Systematically she examines the apartment. She puts in her backpack everything of value that she finds.

In the drawer of the night table she finds a revolver. A nickel-plated Colt Detective Special, with ivory stock. A real jewel. She glances with curiosity at the man who is sleeping there, lying on his side. Quite a guy, this yuppie, keeping a revolver in his bedside drawer. She extends her arm, closes her left eye and takes aim. She points the barrel of the gun at Andrea's forehead.

"Bang, bang," she whispers.

Then she blows on the end of the barrel, smiles. She flicks the clasp that unlocks the cylinder. All six bullets are there. She closes it, weighs the .38 in her hands. You could get a lot of money for that. She throws it into the backpack.

The mound of coke and the cellophane envelope are still on the desk. Leila opens the drawers, one after the other. A passport, a penknife, a gold tie clip, a Parker ballpoint, a telephone card, a white envelope, a couple of pencils, a travel alarm clock, some change. She puts the tie clip and the pen in the backpack. Using the edge of the passport, she slides the pile of cocaine to the edge of the desk, then, carefully, into the open envelope, which she seals, folds in quarters and sticks in her jacket pocket.

She goes to the closet, carefully examines the clothes. After the closet, it's the chest of drawers. Then the bathroom cabinets have their turn.

When she's finished her inspection, Leila takes off the gloves. In one of them she puts the condom that Andrea placed on the night table, sticks that inside the second, knots it at the wrist and puts it in her handbag. She'll throw it away later in a trashcan. Eliminating traces is important, even though many of the people she robs, because they don't want the circumstances to be known, don't report it, accepting the theft as the price for a night of sex. You can never be too prudent. She opens the window to dissipate the scent of her perfume that hovers in the air. When she leaves that apartment, it will be as if she had never been there.

She picks up the things scattered on the sheet and puts them in her handbag, together with Andrea's wallet. She zips up the backpack and throws it over her shoulder. Before leaving, she stops in front of a mirror. She redoes her lipstick, straightens her bangs. The evening didn't go badly, after all. She screws the top on the lipstick and lets it fall into her handbag.

Andrea is sleeping like a child, naked and curled up on one side. Leila plants a kiss on her fingertips and, from the doorway, blows it in his direction.

*

Sacchetti, heading home, feels both melancholy and cheerful. The sounds that echo amid the gym's yellowed walls and high ceiling are still in his ears. The kicks that hit the leather sphere like gunshots, the high squeak of rubber soles on linoleum, the cries of the boys, the thud of the ball as it rebounds off the floor. The wood of the bench under him, the faint odour rising from Pisani's T-shirt and the drop of sweat that sparkles on the tip of his aquiline nose as he comes over and says: "If we don't improve our dribbling, Sunday the kids from Calderara will kick our asses big time."

Sacchetti turns onto Via Mazzini and feels again the

warm fog of the locker room, cut by sudden cold drafts and saturated with the scent of shampoo, socks and sponge towels. The boys' chatter and their noisy laughter amid the roar of the showers. The long, pale bodies that emerge, steamy, from the halo of humidity, skin shiny with water under the white neon lights.

Perhaps Sacchetti ordered a couple of grappas too many, after the *panna cotta* and the decaf. When he goes to the pizzeria with the boys after practice, he always ends up drinking too much. He starts telling dirty jokes, laughs at the same old punchlines. They tease the stupid one, comment on the length of Calcaterra's dick, discuss the soccer teams, agonize over girls. They say *cunts*. And Sacchetti goes along, he too says cunts. They are young and want to have fun. He remembers when he was their age and played on a team in the outskirts. Eventually they pay the bill, get up. The boys stand talking in front of the pizzeria or organize a stop at some discothèque. Sacchetti says goodbye and see you Sunday morning, yes, until Sunday, good night, good night, then he gets in his Lancia Delta and goes home. And almost always, on the way, this indefinable mood comes upon him. A mixture of nostalgia and gratitude that makes him smile and, at times, pushes him to the brink of tears.

He thinks back to the boys' conversation. Soccer, motorcycles, cars, a film that made them laugh, cunts. Sooner or later, they always end up talking about sex. Fucks scored, imagined, reported or missed by a hair. The boastful ones describe them down to the smallest detail, the more introverted refuse to talk, hiding behind smiles that admit success and excite the curiosity of the others.

"Tell the truth, Boxer, you did it!"

"No point in pushing him, Gerry. Boxer doesn't

want to say, but everybody knows he's fucking Federica. Even Piero saw them, the other night, in the car park of the Ospedale Maggiore, and he swore she was giving him a blowjob."

"A blowjob? Come on, Boxer, at least tell us how she sucks!"

Sacchetti is amused and laughs along with them. But as he is heading home with those grappas in his stomach, he finds himself alone with his melancholy.

He stops at a signal, emits a burp that tastes of sausage. He thinks of how the desire to laugh and be together will vanish as soon as they've embarked on their own roads and find themselves having to think about the job, the apartment, the wife, the children, money, ageing parents. And at this point a bitter sadness rises in his throat at the thought that they, at least, still have some years ahead.

Many of the prostitutes who walk the streets are beautiful. They weren't so good-looking fifteen years ago. Sacchetti and his friends used to cruise the boulevards and, if things went well, they'd meet seven or eight whores, most of them at least forty, ill-tempered and gone to seed. There was even one who was a cripple, and they amused themselves by teasing her. They would ask the price and argue about it, until she lost patience and sent them packing, waving her stick and yelling insults like a sailor. One of the few passable ones was a Calabrian girl who usually worked at Porta Lame. In any case, no comparison with these Slavs and mulattos, whose bodies make your head spin.

Sacchetti slows down, to get a better view of the half-naked girls along the edge of the street. From Porta Santo Stefano on, they are almost all coloured. There's one with long, powerful legs, like a wrestler. Another, her black hair pulled straight back, has an enormous ass, which seems pasted onto her, round and high, as if not subject to the force of gravity. Sacchetti imagines squeezing those buttocks with his entire hands while inserting himself between the muscular legs of the wrestler. From the fusion of the two whores, he creates a mastodon Negro, who picks him up like a baby and plunges his face into her tits. Black, soft, enormous tits. Hot as the air in the locker rooms during the showers. Sinking his face into that immense breast, he seems to have in his nostrils the scent of the nipples, as big as cooking pots, which smell of African spices, cloves, cinnamon and pepper. Then the image dissolves, swept away by the sight of a black girl with the narrow hips of a child and a curly head, who shows him her tongue as he goes by. She must be about sixteen. Her legs, as slender as flagpoles, are sheathed in a pair of white net stockings. Saccchetti touches the bulge in his pants and gently massages his prick, which responds immediately to the pressure of his fingers. He slows down further, holding the wheel with his left hand alone, while with the right he presses harder on the bulge. He passes Porta San Mamolo with his prick swelling in his underpants, but on this stretch there are only a couple of fat whores, who are sitting on a wall talking. Sacchetti turns his gaze to the right and the left. Where did those good-looking ones go? On the other side of the boulevards, he glimpses a very thin black girl who seems to him practically naked. Sacchetti turns his head around, trying to get a better view. As he went by, he made out in the darkness a flash of white stuff against skin as black as night.

He accelerates and goes into fifth. Reaching Porta Saragozza he slams on the brakes, goes into second and makes a U-turn. He goes back along Viale Aldini, searching the edge of the street. Where was that marvel? His penis is getting a little soft, he wonders if someone has already taken her. Then suddenly he sees her. The breasts visible above the embroidered bosom of the white body stocking, nipples appearing along the edge, and those long, long, black thighs, which gleam in the glow of dimmed headlights. Sacchetti hits the brake pedal and swerves to the right, towards the pavement. He leans across the passenger seat to lower the window. As the young prostitute approaches, he hears a sound of brakes behind him and sees the headlights of a bus getting bigger and bigger in the rear-view mirror.

Sacchetti ducks his head, preparing for the impact.

*

The leather-jacketed bikers are gulping enormous pitchers of beer, slapping each other on the back and making a terrific racket, which can be heard in the Audi, parked 150 feet away on the other side of the street. Every so often someone goes inside for a refill. But for the most part they stay outside, standing around the motorcycles in front of the entrance. Bobby has been inside almost ten minutes.

"Do you think we should go in and see what's happening?" Diolaiti asks.

"In my view we should just go home. When you make a mistake, you have to have the courage to admit it."

Diolaiti keeps his gaze on the wooden door of the bar. The neon sign keeps changing colours.

Garofano snorts.

"You want to know something? This is the first time I've ever tailed a bunch of retards. Shit. If it was up to me, I'd throw them all in jail. And shave their heads."

Diolaiti compresses his lips. He doesn't want to

discuss it. He too is sick of this absurd chase, but he doesn't like to admit a mistake or to let go. He pictures the scene again. He sees the biker, with the helmet hanging over his arm, stick his hand in the waste basket and pull something out. He doesn't keep searching, he goes off without hesitating. And this can mean only one thing: that he too saw Matera throw the key to the locker in there. The more he thinks about it, the more certain he is that, absurd though it might seem, the two had some agreement.

"A bar, get it? They've led us to a hell of a bar!"

Diolaiti takes out his handkerchief and wipes it across his right eye. But Garofano has no intention of keeping quiet.

"And while they guzzle beer, we sit here mouldering like a couple of halfwits. A lovely evening."

Diolaiti puts the handkerchief back in his pocket.

"And if we were to make a phone call to the chief?"

Diolaiti turns his bony face towards Garofano.

"At one in the morning? And tell him what?"

Garofano shakes his head.

"We explain to him how things stand and get his opinion. Do you have a better idea? When are you going to admit it? That big jerk has nothing to do with it, and we've made a stupid mistake. Never mind. We won't be the first or the last who . . ."

"Look," Diolaiti interrupts him. "He's leaving!"

*

"Hey, boss, I'm talking to you, can't you hear me?"

"What did you say?"

"I'm asking you if I was right or not. Wasn't I right to get rid of that whore? Talk to me. What would you have done in my place?"

"Well, you know, it depends. It's not that . . ."

"Sixteen years! No, but do you realize? If I think about it, I could weep. Sixteen years down the toilet. It's easy to say I can't take it anymore. And then what? What should I say?"

At the intersection the signal is green. Francesco turns onto Viale Pepoli and gnashes his teeth. Hold on, he says to himself. This too will pass. Sooner or later this pain in the neck will have to get off. The drunk regurgitates. He burps, emitting an odour of vermouth and salami, and continues his monologue.

"It's always like that, let me tell you. Always like that. Soon or later they screw you. I should have kicked her out, that whore, rather than stay and listen to her. You know what the Chinese say? When you come home, beat your wife, she'll know why. They know what they're talking about and then some! You want to go? What does it take? There's the door! That's what I should have done. Kick her out and good riddance."

The guy sniffs and starts chewing over something. Francesco has the impression that the engine is making a strange noise. A ringing sound. Maybe it's the bearings.

"But no. Darling this, darling that. Like a poor fool. Come, love, tell me what's bothering you. Talk to me, dear, try to explain. Always nice, always available. I swear, boss, I tried to understand what the hell was going on in that sick head. I was busy trying to make things better. And she, with that voice like a goose, retorted, *I've told you a thousand times what's wrong, but you won't listen to me.* According to her I didn't listen to her, you see? But I wasn't doing anything else! I listened to her until the complaints were coming out of my ears."

The bus passes a group of black prostitutes, waiting for clients along the edge of the street. The drunk turns his head to look at them.

"Whatever," he says. "Not bad, eh, boss? Look at those legs."

Francesco glances in the direction indicated by the drunk. When he looks back at the street, he realizes that the car in front of him has jammed on its brakes. He presses the brake pedal to the floor and manages to stop the bus a few inches from the bumper of the light-brown Lancia Delta, which has stopped beside a tall, thin young whore who is wearing nothing but a minuscule white lace body stocking.

Out of the corner of his eye, Francesco sees the drunk swaying. Then he hears him protest.

"Hey, boss! Pay attention. Shit, we were almost up his ass!"

The prostitute, illuminated by the headlights of the bus, is leaning towards the window of the Lancia. The black skin of her legs sparkles in the band of light.

*

Usually she doesn't mind walking, but now she's tired and doesn't feel much like going all that distance on foot, lugging the backpack with her booty. With a little luck, she might still find a taxi in Piazza Azzarita. She walks along Via Calori. She hasn't gone even a hundred yards when she passes one that's free.

Leila rushes into the street waving an arm.

"Taxi!" she shouts. "Taxi!"

She is about to give up when she sees the red tail-lights brighten. The car slows, stops. She starts running again.

She opens the door and gets in. Without turning

around, the driver mumbles a very irritated hello and asks where she's going.

"Via del Borgo San Pietro," Leila answers. She takes off the backpack and lays it on the seat. "Number 16."

The driver starts the meter.

After a few moments, Leila asks if she can smoke.

The man looks at her in the rear-view mirror.

"Why not? Go ahead."

Leila opens her handbag, looks for the Gauloises. She lights one and inhales with pleasure, as she relaxes against the seat. She is a little tired, but the evening is over. Soon, finally, she will be able to go to bed. And tomorrow she doesn't have to wake up until noon.

The handbag is open on her knees. Between the compact with the blusher and the red cigarette pack, Leila glimpses Andrea's wallet. She opens it. She runs her fingers over the bills. With the cigarette between her lips she takes out the license. Surname Fabbri. Name Andrea. Born 19/1/65, in Bologna. Residence: Rome. Via Monserrato 108. Licence issued by the Prefecture of Bologna, 24 July, 1983.

She puts back the document and opens the clasp of the change compartment. A small key slides into her hand. On one side is stamped in relief the number 37. She has the feeling that she's had a key like that in her hands before. But of course! It's one of those from the baggage lockers at the airport.

Leila takes a drag on her cigarette. What if she were to have a look? Probably all he left in that locker is a suitcase full of underwear, shirts, designer ties, socks and aftershave. But you never know. There could be something valuable. She glances at her watch. One-thirty.

"Excuse me," she says to the taxi driver. "I've changed my mind. I have to make a stop at the airport."

The man shrugs his shoulders. He pulls up and turns around. Leila puts the cigarette out in the ashtray.

Meanwhile, the taxi driver keeps glancing at her in the rear-view mirror. She's not bad at all, this whore he's picked up. Even if her thinking is a little confused. First she sends him to an address, then she says she has to make a stop at the airport. What does he care! As long as she pays, he is willing to drive her around all night. In fact, to tell the truth, he'd halfway like to start a conversation. The whore doesn't seem in the mood to talk, but nothing ventured, nothing gained. Why not try? A girl who goes around at this hour, dressed like that, has to be a girl who gives it away easily.

"You're cute, you know that?"

Leila looks up. In the rear-view mirror she meets the gaze of the taxi driver.

"Thank you," she answers in a glacial tone.

As a reaction it's not much, but the man has no intention of being defeated.

"Well, I'm sure I'm not the first to say it. There've been plenty of others before me."

Leila remains silent, but he continues to stare at her in the mirror.

"So tell me, where did you spend the evening?"

She almost laughs. Here's the Latin male in action. Indolent, lazy, but he has to try. It's almost a moral obligation. Leila looks out the window. The taxi is heading along Via Emilia, in ten minutes they'll be at the airport. Why not amuse herself a little?

"You want to know what I did? I got picked up by someone I didn't know and went to bed with him."

The taxi driver practically has a stroke.

"Ah, that sounds good. So you're in favour of free love," he says.

84

"Well, not exactly," Leila answers. "But if you want to put it like that."

The taxi turns right on Via del Triumvirato and the man sees the available time diminishing. He has to try to bring things to a conclusion in a hurry. In any case, there's no point in dragging it out.

"Listen, what do you say we have a little fun together, you and I? Just to end the evening on a nice note."

Leila shakes her head.

"No. I don't think I feel like it."

"Why not?"

"I'm afraid you're not my type."

"Come on. You're not going to get difficult now, are you?"

Leila doesn't like the turn the conversation is taking.

"Why, do you think I should go to bed with anyone who asks?"

The taxi driver is silent for a moment, a little disconcerted. What game is this little whore playing? She can't be making fun of him?

"I'm not saying that. But you can be sure that I know what to do. You wouldn't be sorry."

"I'm certain of that. But I don't feel like it."

The taxi driver feels a blind rage clouding his brain. Who does she think she is, this little piece of ass? Suddenly he has a deep desire to hit her.

"I don't see any reason for you to be so fussy. If you do one, you can do two. How much for a blow-job? A hundred? Hundred and fifty? I've got the money!"

In silence Leila observes the man's eyes, framed in the rectangle of the rear-view mirror. In addition to being a Latin male, this guy is a real shit.

"You've stopped talking? Come on, tell me how much you want to suck my dick."

The airport is very close now. Leila sees the lights, on the left, closer and closer. She'd better cut this off.

"Listen to me, you fat pig. I don't know if there's a woman who has the stomach to go to bed with you, but I would rather sew up my lips than suck your dick. Got it?"

It's only a couple of hundred yards to the intersection with the road to the airport. The taxi driver is furious. He has no intention of wasting an opportunity like this. The whore's getting particular? He knows how to soften her up.

Leila says nothing. The man's gaze is on the road now. Did she go a little too far? But no, this bastard deserved it.

Fifty yards from the airport entrance. Twenty. Ten.

The car doesn't slow down. Leila leans forward.

"What are you doing? This is the turn!"

The taxi driver doesn't answer. He accelerates to the floor and goes straight on.

"What's got into you? I told you to take me to the airport!"

The taxi driver doesn't open his mouth. The only sounds are the revving engine and the voice of the dispatcher croaking from the small radio speaker.

Leila looks around quickly. The road they're on is barely illuminated. To the left, the airport enclosure, to the right a vast plain sunk in obscurity, beyond which shine the lights of the ring road. The taxi takes a couple of curves at high speed, tyres squealing on the asphalt, and dives between two dark embankments that rise along the edge of the road.

Leila pushes her back against the seat. The eyes of the taxi driver, in the rear-view mirror, are staring at her without expression.

*

With the last drag he burns the filter. Matera throws the butt on the floor and crushes it with his shoe. It could be worse. For example, he could be outside, in the rain. Then it would be a real problem, because of the metal in his knee. He stretches one hand out to palpate the right kneecap. The damn joint continues to hurt. But even the doctor told him there was little to be done.

"I'm sorry, Mr Matera, but you have to resign yourself. With a metal support in place of the joint, you can't pretend you're able to turn somersaults. If the pain becomes very bothersome, take one of these capsules."

Matera takes the blue-and-white box out of his pocket. He opens it, unfolds the instructions.

Side effects: diarrhoea, burning, stomach pain, nausea, haemorrhoids, headache, dizziness, sleepiness, phenomena of sensitization, cutaneous irruptions and allergic reactions of various types, blood in the stool (probably linked to gastrointestinal ulcers and haemorrhoids). Taking this product could result in serious reactions of hypersensitivity, such as Stevens-Johnson syndrome, Lyell syndrome, or anaphylactic reactions.

Better to put up with the pain. He puts the box back in his pocket, takes out the pack of Marlboros. There are only two left.

He inhales the first puff deeply. Locker number 37 is locked, but the key isn't where it should be. Perhaps it would be better to give the Secretary a call. But if he knew that there had been a hitch, he certainly would have let him know. He decides that, all in all, it's better to wait. Sooner or later someone will show up.

He feels his belt pinching his waist. He pulls in his

stomach and loosens the belt one hole. He pats his stomach with the palm of his hand, as if it were an old dog that he had grown attached to. Maybe it's time to go on a diet. Between the bad knee and the bulging belly, his agility has gone to hell. He takes another drag on the cigarette and smiles to himself. It's a matter not of pounds but of age.

In any case, he can't complain, he can still operate with a certain amount of dignity. And this job is proof that they trust him the way they used to. It's obvious that at fifty-four, and with the sort of life he's lived, he can't claim to be in perfect shape.

Certainly a lot of water has gone under the bridge since his early assignments. Ex-cop, ex-political-intelligence agent, ex-civilian-intelligence agent, ex-bodyguard for a member of parliament, who then hired him as a special agent. And here he is, in the middle of one of his special assignments, posted on a bench in an airport, smoking one cigarette after another, with the task of retrieving a very private document from a luggage locker. Too bad that no one delivered the key.

And yet the Secretary had said precisely that.

"Under the last seat you will find the key. In the same position as the first time. These are the instructions. But I warn you, Matera, pay attention to the schedule. The first delivery is at exactly six. The retrieval of the document and the delivery of the second suitcase not before one."

It didn't seem that difficult. But the key is not where it should be.

Matera takes another drag, taps off the ash with the nail of his little finger. He lowers his gaze to the black suitcase that he holds between his legs. The one sure thing is that it won't get stolen. With the fingers of his right hand he touches the butt of his Beretta 92 SB. As long as he has the .9 calibre within reach it won't be so easy to rob him.

The next-to-last cigarette is finished.

He lets the butt fall among the others. He counts them. Five yellow filters, scattered on that floor that seems striped with blood.

*

The taxi is going along this goddamn pitch-dark road. Not a living soul around.

The driver isn't speaking.

Leila half closes her handbag. She touches with her fingertips the canister of teargas that, for safety, she always carries with her. Then she thinks again. If she sprays this stuff in his eyes there could be an accident. But maybe there's another way. She reaches her hand towards the backpack. She slowly undoes the zipper. She digs around inside. She finds the butt of Andrea's revolver. She grabs it. In the mirror, she catches the gaze of the taxi driver. He too now seems worried by the silence.

Leila leans forward, against the front seat. She brings the revolver to the man's face, in such a way that he can see clearly what's going on. With her thumb she cocks the hammer. Then she presses the barrel against his fat cheek.

The car slows down.

"What's got into you?" the taxi driver asks, in alarm.

"I'll plant a bullet in your shit brain if you don't stop in five seconds."

"You're crazy! Put away the gun!"

"One, two . . ."

The taxi driver brakes hard, pulls up on the right.

"All right, all right. No need to get agitated."

"I'm not agitated. Now turn around and take me to the airport."

The taxi driver puts the car in first, makes a U-turn. He takes the road in the opposite direction. Leila keeps the barrel pressed against his neck, which is shiny with sweat.

"Couldn't you put that away now? Shit, it bothers me to have that thing pointed at me."

"I don't give a damn."

"OK, what's the point of getting mad like that? I was only joking."

"It's better if you keep your mouth shut. I have a strong desire to pulverize that piece of shit you have between your legs."

The taxi driver doesn't say another word. Leila wonders how it would have ended if she hadn't had a weapon in reach. Maybe she really should shoot this pig.

As soon as they turn onto the airport road, she puts the Detective Special into her handbag. The taxi driver stops in front of the terminal. Leila grabs her handbag and the backpack, opens the door.

The man turns.

"The meter says 37,500," he says.

"You must be kidding. You really have got a nerve! You really think I should pay you, for that nice little ride you took me on?"

"All right, forget the last part. But there's still the trip from downtown!"

"Fuck you," Leila says, slamming the door.

The taxi driver yells an insult at her from behind the closed window and takes off with a rapid acceleration, while the tyres screech on the smooth asphalt of the roadway.

*

Before starting off again, they got a supply of beer. Right after passing the tollbooth on the autostrada, Bobby bends over and sticks his hand in one of his side pockets. Gripping the handlebar with his right hand, the beer can with his left, he tears off the top with his teeth, spits it out to the side and takes a couple of swallows. Then he settles the can between his thighs. He can't take another drop unless he stops to pee. His bladder is so full that the vibrations from the engine are going to make him burst. He sees the signs for a rest area. He puts on the turn signal and down-shifts. Most of the others are ahead of him. The two or three who are following go straight on without stopping. As soon as he's relieved himself, he'll catch up easily.

The headlight of the Harley illumines the ramp and pans across the big dark outlines of the trucks that sit motionless in the parking area.

Bobby stops the bike behind a trailer truck. He turns off the engine, pushes down the kickstand. He takes off his helmet and hangs it on the handlebars. He walks over to the edge of the paved area. He places the beer can on the ground and pees into the darkness, sighing with relief. Then he shakes off, pulls up his zipper, bends over to pick up his Heineken. He tosses down a long swallow and turns to go back to his bike.

The punch lands in the pit of his stomach. Bobby folds forward suddenly, his breath cut off. The beer can jumps out of his hand, rebounds against Garofano's chest and rolls away foaming.

Bobby teeters backward, breathless.

"Son of a bitch," Garofano protests, sweeping away

the foam with the back of his hand. "Look what this shit's done to me. Him and his shitty beer!"

"It's not a big deal," Diolaiti minimizes it. "It's only a couple of squirts."

"Like hell," Garofano insists. He takes his handkerchief out of his pocket and dries the spots. "I'd like to see you, shit. I just bought this jacket a week ago. And paid almost 200,000, I don't know if I make myself clear."

"Big deal!"

"What's that, now 200,000 for a jacket's nothing?"

"If you're so fond of it, you shouldn't wear it on a job like this. And anyway, you'll see, when it dries you'll hardly notice a thing."

Garofano strokes the material of the jacket.

"You say the beer stains will disappear?"

"Of course they'll disappear. With a little water, maybe."

Bobby, curled up on the ground, gasps, pressing his hands to his stomach. Garofano moves forward and kicks him in the side, as if he were a sack of rags to be rolled as far away as possible. Bobby groans and starts writhing again and coughing.

"What a dickhead!" Garofano grumbles. "He spills a can of beer on me and then he complains."

A man's head emerges from the front window of the trailer truck. "Hey, what's going on? What the fuck are you doing behind my truck?"

Garofano takes out the .45, points it at the man's emerging outline.

"You want a bullet in your brain?" he snarls. "Mind your own business and go back to sleep."

The truck driver pulls his head in and closes the window in a hurry.

Diolaiti stares at Garofano.

"Is it necessary to make all this noise? Don't you know that most trucks have a radio?"

"OK, it's over now," Garofano cuts him off, putting the Smith & Wesson back in its holster. "Come on, let's pick up this piece of shit."

They grab Bobby by the armpits and drag him bodily to the Audi, parked twenty yards farther back.

"Who are you?" he asks, in a faint voice. "What do you want from me?"

The two men don't answer. They lay him on the ground, behind the car.

Diolaiti rubs the palms of his hands together, to clean them off, while Garofano puts a cigar in his mouth.

Through half-closed eyes, Bobby sees a flame leap up. The reddish light illumines Garofano's face, as he inhales deeply to get the cigar going.

"So," Garofano says, putting the lighter back in his pocket. "Here we are. Now you have two alternatives. Either you tell us immediately what you know or we torture you until you tell us. I've already wasted too much time, and I have no desire to waste any more. Therefore, just so you don't think we're bluffing, I'll explain to you our methods."

He gives him another kick. The point of his shoe stabs Bobby in the liver, and he writhes without being able to let out a cry. Garofano takes a couple of deep drags on his cigar and smiles with satisfaction. The tip of the cigar, revived, glows behind the cloud of grey smoke that vanishes in the air. He bends over Bobby. With his left hand he covers his mouth, while between the thumb and index finger of the right he holds the cigar. Without saying a word, he rests the burning tip against one of Bobby's cheeks. Bobby's eyes go wide and he thrashes around, his neck pressed against the asphalt. The cry that he lets out, muffled by Garofano's palm, is little more than a whimper. An acrid odour of burned flesh spreads in the air.

"There we go," Garofano says. He smiles at Bobby's terrified gaze, the eyes wide open and staring. Then he looks at Diolaiti.

"What do you say? Think he's got the idea?"

Diolaiti nods his insect head.

"Yes, maybe."

"Good," Garofano says, putting the cigar in his mouth. "So, you little shit, now listen to me. At this point you are pretty certain that, between me and my colleague, I am the bad guy. And yet you're wrong. I'm just a little angry because you got my jacket dirty. But what I did is nothing compared to what he'll do if he gets his hands on you."

"OK, OK," Bobby says, gasping. "I'll tell you whatever you want. But don't hurt me, please!"

Garofano gets up, revolves the cigar between his teeth and takes off his belt.

"Good. That means you're not as stupid as I thought. Now that I've made the introductions, I'll leave him to you."

Bobby sees the one with the angular face bend over him.

"First of all I'd like to know your name."

Bobby swallows. In the man's eye a tear glistens, and his lips are curved in a strange line, which gives him an expression halfway between ruthless and suffering.

"My name is Bobby."

"Bobby?" the big one sneers, blowing out a cloud of smoke. "What are you, a puppy?"

"All right, Bobby," Diolaiti continues, bringing his face closer. "You can begin by telling us where you put the key to the baggage locker."

As Sacchetti goes up in the lift, he thinks again of the black girl who leaned into his window as if it were nothing, not giving a damn about the bus that was about to ram him. She had gorgeous legs. But her cheeks were pitted by smallpox. Maybe that was partly why his desire evaporated and he let the whole thing go.

The doors of the lift slide open and Sacchetti heads for his apartment. He puts the key in the lock very cautiously. Then he closes the door slowly and tiptoes along the hall.

When he gets into bed and under the covers, his wife turns.

"Mmm. What time is it, Walter?"

"It's late. I stayed to chat with the boys."

He stretches his neck forward to kiss her. In the darkness, however, he can't find her mouth and places his lips between her nose and her cheekbone.

"I was sleeping," his wife says, turning onto her other side. "Good night, Walter."

"Good night, Luisa," and lying on his back he thinks of the black girl's legs and the amazing tits that were practically falling out of the body stocking.

*

The Marlboro package is crushed in Matera's large palm. Still no one has shown up. The problem isn't waiting. If it's that, he can stay here until tomorrow morning. By now, however, he is fairly certain that something must have gone wrong.

And at this point what would he be waiting for, exactly? For someone to deliver the document by hand? That was not the arrangement. He was not supposed to meet the person who is handling the exchange, or speak to anyone. The Secretary repeated this at least ten times.

Matera opens his hand, stares at the crumpled pack. The trouble is that he's finished the cigarettes. Usually he has an extra pack with him, but he wasn't expecting to have to stay so long. He had only to look for the key under the seat, open the locker, retrieve the document and deposit the second suitcase inside. Easy as drinking a glass of water. If the key had been in its place.

Maybe the person who was supposed to leave it was delayed for some reason and now is only waiting for him to step away to come over and stick it under the seat.

To clear off for ten minutes might be a good idea. He will take advantage of this to buy some cigarettes.

*

As she crosses the airport lobby, Leila realizes that her outfit is certainly not ideal for being inconspicuous. It's enough to look at the expression that appears on the face of every man she sees. Luckily there aren't many.

The corridor is deserted. Leila turns into the area where the luggage lockers are. She goes up to the lockers. Number 37 is in the next-to-last row on the bottom. She bends over, inserts the key in the lock. When she feels it turn, she can't contain a smile.

Inside is an overnight bag. She pulls it out and closes the door, leaving the key in the lock. Then she goes off with the bag in hand.

On one side of the lobby, a night guard is staring at

her. Leila smiles at him. The man in uniform responds by lowering his head in a nod of greeting.

*

Usually he is very careful. Before going to sleep he hooks the chain and leaves the key in the lock. Then he places a chair under the door handle. And finally he puts his Detective Special on the night table, within reach. But things didn't go right tonight. When Leila went out, she closed the door only with the latch, leaving him there like a cretin, naked and stuffed with Valium. Thus, when the two men enter his apartment, Andrea continues to sleep without a thought. He doesn't move even when one of the men, holding the barrel of the gun to his eye, tries to lift the eyelid with the point of the silencer.

Garofano stares at the opaque, motionless pupil.

"What the fuck's up with him? Isn't he awake?"

"He seems drugged," Diolaiti answers. "Try shaking him a little."

"He's in a deep sleep, poor fellow. Shall we give him a little refreshment?"

"Yes, let's try putting his head under the tap."

As they drag him off the bed, Andrea half opens his eyes.

"Who are you?" he asks, his mouth pasty.

"Did you hear that?" Garofano says. "He's asking who we are."

"Tell him."

"We're Donald and Mickey, champ. Satisfied?"

Through the fog of sleep, Andrea begins to realize what's happening. He tries to get free.

"Hold him, he's wriggling."

"He doesn't seem to like cartoons."

"Let me go. What do you want?"

"Try to guess, pretty boy. You think we're here for the Easter blessing?"

"Forget the shower, he's awake now. Help me get him on that chair."

Andrea realizes that he has nothing on. He tries to order his thoughts, but his brain is too groggy, he can't remember what the hell has happened.

The two men are tying him to the back of the chair. He is suffocating with anguish. They must be employed by the Minister and have been sent to retrieve the document. Calm down, he has to make an effort to think. But it's not easy when you're naked, and in front of two thugs who are tying your hands and feet to a chair.

"Now listen carefully, handsome. Your buddy gave you up. He told us everything in complete detail. So it's useless for you to try to deceive us. If you answer truthfully, you'll see, we'll be out of here in no time."

As soon as he stops speaking, he gives him a violent punch in the pit of the stomach.

"That," Garofano says to him as he watches him writhe, "was because talk by itself counts for little. Have you taken in the situation?"

Andrea nods, shaking his head.

"Bravo. Now pay attention, because the important questions are coming. Where did you hide the document?"

"Wha . . . what document?" Andrea gasps, struggling for breath.

"Aha, comrade. You see? We've met a tough guy. You think we should give up?"

Diolaiti smiles, wiping his eye with a corner of his handkerchief.

*

Matera pockets the change and the two packs of Marl-boros, then lights a cigarette and takes the escalator to the lower level. As soon as he gets off, a man with a pea-green tie and fanlike ears approaches him to ask for information. The man seems drunk, he speaks in drawling American English. Matera isn't that confident with languages and manages to catch only a few words. He looks at the man waving his arms and smiles at him, searching for a way to get rid of him. At that moment, a dark-haired girl passes behind the American; she's wearing a very short miniskirt, and her legs aren't bad. Continuing to nod, Matera eyes the brunette with the quick, elastic stride. He notices that she is carrying a soft backpack, a handbag and a small rectangular suit-case, an overnight bag, very similar to the one he has in his hand. He lowers his gaze to his and then looks at the other again. They seem identical.

He throws the cigarette to the floor and, dumping the American, hurries towards the baggage lockers.

He reaches the lockers out of breath. Number 37 is half closed, with the key in the lock. He opens it.

He retraces his steps, trying to run, but the pain in his knee forces him to slow down. Limping, he emerges onto the plaza outside the exit doors, just in time to see the girl get into a taxi. He descends the ramp on the left as quickly as he can, while the taxi is already heading down the one on the right. He reaches his Alfa 90 and throws the suitcase on the pas-senger seat. When he bends his leg to get in, a sharp pain in the joint tears a curse out of him. He puts his foot to the floor quickly and the car leaps towards the exit of the parking lot with the engine racing.

He speeds along Via del Triumvirato in pursuit of the taxi. Where did that girl in the miniskirt come from? Is she involved in the exchange? Why the hell did she pick up the suitcase only now? Too many questions, and not a shred of information on which to base conclusions. Doubt assails him: has he done something stupid, throwing himself into this pursuit?

The taxi is stopped at the intersection with Via Emilia. Matera slows down. He's on the taxi's tail. His breathing has returned almost to normal. The signal changes to green, the taxi turns left.

Good, from now on, avoid manoeuvres that might draw attention and don't get too close. He allows himself a smile, satisfied with at least having under control the two suitcases that they entrusted to him for the exchange. He glances at the one on the seat beside him. He reaches out his right hand to caress it.

*

Luckily this taxi driver seems normal. Leila looks at the overnight bag beside her, on the back seat. Why not take a look? She has all the time she wants. She settles the suitcase on her legs and presses the buttons that open it. She feels them yield under her thumbs, while the two locks click. Leila slowly raises the lid. Even in the faint light that filters through the window it's not hard to make out the contents. Her eyes suddenly widen.

"Shit," she whispers, staring at the little suitcase jiggling on her knees.

*

A perfect night. First the ravings of that drunk and now these four shits. Their outfits are classic. Bomber jackets, black steel-toed boots, red and blue scarves. Four shaved heads that glisten in the neon lights of the bus. They shout soccer chants, beating in time on the seats, pushing and shoving one another, exchanging stupid jokes.

"H-e-e-e-re we go-oo-oo, Bologna! H-e-e-e-re we go-oo-oo!"

They got on in Piazza Mickiewicz and the other passengers who were on board vanished after a couple of stops. Now it's just the four of them. And they are making a team-size uproar.

"So Sunday the game is away?"

"You said it. And you know what we're gonna do to those fags in Pisa?"

"Shit, we'll kick their ass!"

A fat kid, with a sweaty red face, raises one leg in imitation of a karate move and lets out a long, resounding fart. The laughter echoes through the whole bus. The tallest kid hangs from the support bars and swings back and forth, kicking the air with his bovver boots.

"I'll slaughter those faggots from Pisaaaa!"

Another takes out a spray can, shakes it, points it at the back of a seat.

Francesco keeps on eye on the situation in the parabolic mirror and goes straight on, driving in silence. For all he cares, they can paint the whole bus. As long as they leave him in peace.

Some moments earlier, when the skinheads were standing, joking and slapping each other around, he had the temptation to brake hard and send all four of them flying through the air. Then he thought it was better to leave them alone. He wouldn't be the first driver to spend forty days in hospital recovering, thanks to thugs like them. And he certainly has no wish to start playing the hero. He has enough troubles of his own.

She had the taxi stop in a very narrow street down-town. It pulled up on the right and Matera, following in his Alfa 90, passed by.

In the rear-view mirror, he sees her get out with the backpack over her shoulder, the handbag in one hand, the suitcase in the other. He stops his car in front of a "no parking" area. He gets out, goes back along the street on foot. His knee is still bothering him.

The girl is in front of a doorway. She's put the suit-case down.

Matera stays hidden behind a column and watches her digging through her handbag.

*

She gave the taxi driver a huge tip, and he stared at her in shock, afraid that she had made a mistake. Leila smiled at him, wishing him good night. The driver thanked her, put the car in gear and took off in a hurry.

In front of the door, Leila puts down the overnight bag. Ever since she saw the contents, she has been unable to master her agitation. What the hell sort of business has she stumbled into? As she hunts in her handbag for her keys, she tries to order her thoughts. Probably she intercepted a courier. Maybe Andrea had a job delivering or picking up the money.

She has to be careful now what she does, since this business could turn out to be dangerous. The suitcase is full of hundred-dollar bills. How many can there be in each bundle? She has to try to keep her nerves under control. The keys. Where did she put the keys? If she is cautious, nothing will happen to her. Andrea doesn't know her real name. He doesn't know anything about her. She didn't leave any traces at his house. Everything is in place. Of course, she'll have to drop out of circulation. But at the moment the most important thing is to stay cool. She has to try to calm down. Where did those damn keys go? Stay calm, Leila, she repeats, you have to stay calm. But her heart continues to race. And the house keys don't show up.

*

"I don't know anything besides what I've already told you! How many times do I have to repeat it?"

"Does the kid move you, Diolaiti?"

"Me? Not even a little."

"Hear that? My colleague isn't moved. I'm afraid you're in trouble. You should have seen how he skinned your friend. Revolting."

Andrea lets his head fall forward, shakes it slowly, sighing. His face is swollen, and blood is dripping from a cut on his lower lip.

"Please. If I knew anything else, I would have told you. It must have been that whore who robbed me. And if she wasn't working for you, it means there's someone else who's trying to get the document."

"Yes. Or else you've invented the whole story."

"I swear it's the truth!"

"Calm down. We're going to have a little chat, just to make sure. I don't remember, what did you say the whore's name was?"

"Angela."

"Oh yes, Angela. That's a very nice name."

"Yes, that's what I told her."

"You see? You're a romantic. Just like me. And then,

103

between us, even if a woman has a name like shit, it doesn't cost anything to say the opposite. Right?"

Andrea stares, exhausted, at Garofano without responding, his gaze moving from his feet to his head.

"OK, it doesn't matter. So you want me to believe that you went chasing a piece of ass on the very night you had a deal like this at stake?"

"It happened by chance. I was on top of the world – everything was going smoothly. There she was, in front of me, I liked her. I thought it was an opportunity not to be missed."

"As you see, things don't always go right. So let's recapitulate. You want to get laid. You manage to pick up a girl who's willing. You take her home and in less than no time you fuck her. It must have seemed like a fairy tale. How did it go in bed? Was she good?"

"Too good."

"So you can't complain. Let's go on. She lets you take off her knickers and you fuck quickly. Opportunity only knocks once. Except that the whore, after the fuck, offers you a drink. What did she offer you?"

"A vodka."

"Oh, yes, vodka. Excuse me, but didn't you say whisky earlier?"

"No. I'm sure. We had a vodka."

"Diolaiti, doesn't it seem to you that he mentioned whisky?"

Diolaiti shrugs without answering.

"It's all the same, it's not important. Maybe I'm mistaken. Anyway, you toast each other, and meanwhile the two of you keep busy. But amid the touching, you begin to feel sleepy. Who knows? Maybe it was all that grand fucking."

"No, I'm certain that bitch put something in my drink."

"And while you went off to dreamland, she took advantage of it to rob you blind."

"Exactly."

"You see? We've gotten this far. Too bad we can't find the slightest trace of the whore you're talking about."

"Well, it shows she was a professional."

Garofano snorts, crossing his arms.

"Listen, Diolaiti, I'm sick and tired of listening to this idiot. We're just wasting time. It's obvious that in this case a little slapping around isn't enough."

"For once I agree with you," Diolaiti says, wiping his right eye.

He puts the handkerchief back in his pocket and turns towards Andrea, who stares at them in terror.

"Here's what we do. You stuff his mouth and leave the work to me for a while. You'll see, when we take off the gag he'll feel much more like talking. I'm going to the kitchen to look for something."

Before Andrea can take a breath, Garofano sticks a rag in his mouth and winds a roll of tape around his head. Andrea groans and tries to kick, but Garofano grabs one ear and jerks it upward, almost tearing it off.

"Hold still. I told you to hold still, you shit! Now you're going to find out that with my friend here it's another story."

Diolaiti comes back wearing a yellow apron with a bib, and he knots the ties behind his back.

"There. This way I don't get my shirt dirty."

He sticks a hand in his pocket and takes out a razor. He opens it. Andrea's eyes seem to pop out of their sockets. Garofano, holding him by the hair, tugs on it. Diolaiti brings the razor close to Andrea's neck, as he cries out from under the gag.

"We've been nice up to now," Diolaiti says, almost in

a whisper. "And maybe you've decided we're kind-hearted. But that's not the case."

The blade runs slowly along his chest, cutting into the skin. The blood drips down his bare torso. The razor comes close to a nipple. It slices through it. A kind of grunt emerges from Andrea's throat. The veins in his neck are swollen, his face is red and sweating.

Diolaiti now inclines the blade, holding it flat in relation to the skin, as if he were going to shave, then moves it slowly along the stomach. Garofano, behind Andrea, follows as if hypnotized the movement of the razor as it cuts off the hair of the pubis, approaches the penis, then stops. Diolaiti looks up and stares into Andrea's eyes, with a smile that seems a grimace of pain.

"So, what shall I do? Cut?"

Andrea writhes, trying to get free, Garofano tugs on his hair. Although he knows the ritual well, an icy shudder descends along his spinal column. He wouldn't like to be in this kid's place, with that mad-man Diolaiti standing there, his damn razor resting on your prick. He hopes for his sake that it's over quickly. Since he's done for anyway.

*

She can't have been so stupid as to have left her keys at Andrea's house. On the other hand, if they aren't there, she must have lost them. When did she open her handbag? In the pizzeria, after ordering the beer at the bar on Piazza Maggiore, at Porto di Mare, in the two taxis that she took, and a thousand other times to light a cigarette or freshen her make-up. Of all these hypotheses, the one that frightens her most is that she left them in Andrea's apartment. She remembers dumping the contents of the handbag on the bed, to look for the things she needed.

What did she do afterward? She inspected the apartment. And when she finished, she put everything back in place. Everything? But surely she was careful, as always. She can't have made a mistake like that! And if Andrea, moving in his sleep, knocked the keys onto the floor? Or covered them with a corner of the sheet? Drops of cold sweat drip from her armpits. She can't risk having Andrea find her keys. Not after she's stolen a suitcase full of dollars.

Walking fast, she heads for Via delle Moline. She opens the door of the Y10, throws the suitcase inside, and the backpack, and gets in the driver's seat.

*

And now what in the world is this idiot girl doing? Matera feels more and more confused. She is about to enter a building, thinks again, jumps into a car and takes off at full speed. In order not to lose her, he is forced to run for the Alfa.

The Y10 goes around a ring road, at the centre of which is a circular flowerbed with a fountain. To stay behind her, Matera risks colliding with a couple on a Vespa, who curse at him. This business is starting to annoy him.

His questions increase when he sees her stop, jump out of the car, stick the overnight bag in the boot.

Matera looks around. He suspects that all these actions with neither rhyme nor reason are intended to throw him off. Yes, but throw him off what? If they wanted to rob him, they could have gone off with the suitcase and good riddance. Why wait until the middle of the night?

The girl closes the boot and runs towards the entrance of a building, taking only the handbag. It's madness to leave the car unguarded, with three-quarters of a million dollars in cash. So presumably she'll return shortly. OK, be that as it may, between her and the money, for the moment Matera decides it's more important to keep an eye on the money. He will stick to that fucking suitcase even if he has to stay awake all night!

He finds a comfortable position on the seat, takes a tape from the glove compartment. He inserts it in the tape deck. "Take the A Train". Ah, what style the Duke had! Timeless. He manages to relax you even in a mess like this.

Matera taps his finger on the steering wheel in time with the beat.

He puts a cigarette in his mouth, lights it and lowers the window a little. The smoke is sucked out through the crack.

*

Better to keep the teargas in reach, in case Andrea should wake up. Leila takes it out of the handbag, sticks it in a pocket of her jacket. Then she takes out a pair of latex gloves and puts them on.

She gets in the lift, presses the button for the fifth floor. She forces herself to inhale deeply and exhale slowly. Andrea shouldn't be awake yet, but you never know. The important thing is to go in without making any noise, find the keys, disappear. With a little luck, she'll manage it in a moment.

From the handbag she takes a small pencil flashlight and a flexible metal strip.

The lift stops with a soft thud, the doors open, sliding along the metal runners.

Leila takes one more deep breath.

*

Diolaiti and Garofano are standing in front of the body tied to the chair. The head is inclined backward. The neck, at the Adam's apple, makes an almost ninety-degree angle.

Garofano looks at Andrea, at Diolaiti, then again at Andrea. He takes a step forward and touches his neck. He turns towards his colleague, glares at him. A tear is sliding along his cheek. He really does look like a god-damn crocodile, weeping after ripping its prey to pieces.

"It's a bad habit, goddamn it! You've killed this one too! Tell me what the fuck we do now?"

"Be quiet, Garofano. Let me think."

He's still holding the razor in his right hand. A drop of blood gathers at the end of the blade, pools, drips on the floor.

"Yes, sure, think, fathead. You should have gone a little lighter!"

"Maybe he had heart trouble."

"You must be kidding, heart trouble! I nearly had a stroke, and I was only watching!"

Diolaiti opens his mouth to respond, but at that moment the sound of the lift stopping on the landing can be heard. The two men look at each other without speaking. Faint metallic noises come from the front door lock. Garofano scowls and sticks out his chin with a questioning gesture. Diolaiti brings his index finger to his lips, springs towards the switch, turns out the lights. Then he touches the sleeve of Garofano's jacket.

"Let's go in the other room," he whispers.

"Who could it be?"

"How should I know? Let's hide and see."

*

The lock gives. Leila puts the metal strip back in her handbag and delicately pushes the door, which opens into the dark apartment. She proceeds slowly, careful not to make a sound. She closes the door behind her, gently lowering the handle. Then she stands motionless for a few seconds, trying to make out Andrea's breathing, but in the darkness there is nothing but a profound, total silence. She takes the flashlight out of her pocket and turns it on, keeping it pointed at the floor. A small luminous circle appears between the tips of her boots. Slowly she raises the flashlight. The circle of light advances along the floor. It encounters something shiny and keeps going by. Then she stops. She backs up. The light falls on a thin tongue of dark liquid. Its luminous circle quickly follows the zigzagging trail, until it intercepts the legs of a chair, a pair of bare feet, and then up, and up, to discover the naked, martyred body of a man. And at the top of that body the face of Andrea, bent back, staring wide-eyed at the darkness of the ceiling. Leila is paralysed by horror, by a cry that struggles to explode from her chest. Before she can scream, someone grabs her from behind, fingers are digging into her cheeks, the palm of a hand covers her mouth.

*

The bus bounces as it rolls over the paving stones of Via delle Lame. Francesco lets himself be rocked by that hypnotic motion, swaying on the seat like a pioneer riding in a covered wagon over the prairie of an old Western.

Besides him, there are only two passengers on the bus. One is a man about forty, with a pockmarked face, a ponytail and a shapeless corduroy jacket. The second is a transvestite, no longer young, his face covered by a crust of make-up and on his head a red-orange wig.

The pockmarked man was waiting at the end of the line. He sat down and went to sleep after a few minutes, his neck resting against a window. The transvestite, on the other hand, got on near the fairgrounds. Francesco had just turned onto Via Donato Creti when he saw a dark shadow appear from behind a tree, waving to catch his attention. He braked and opened the doors. The transvestite ran after the bus. She climbed up the steps of the front entrance, a bit unsteady on her spike heels. She thanked him with a furry tongue and staggered away, holding onto the support poles.

A couple of times as the bus headed towards the station, Francesco met her eyes, which were studying him in the parabolic mirror. He averted his gaze quickly, afraid that she would start a conversation. Then he simply forgot about her presence. He put on his mental automatic pilot and continued to drive, brooding over his bad mood.

But suddenly, as he's turning into Via Riva di Reno, a voice beside him makes him jump.

"Excuse me, does this bus go to Via della Barca?"

He turns and finds himself facing scarlet-painted lips, a pair of quivering tits and two dry, gnarled legs inside net stockings that stick out from under an emerald-green miniskirt. The transvestite is smiling at him, gripping the pole, swaying on her high heels.

"Yes, of course it goes there," Francesco answers.

The other curves her lips even more. At the corners of her mouth, the lipstick is smeared.

"Oh, good. I was afraid I had the wrong bus."

The smile makes a network of wrinkles appear, even under the layer of make-up that ices her cheeks.

"Can I ask you a question?" she says.

Francesco shrugs.

"Have you been doing this job for a long time?"

Francesco takes a deep breath, glances in the mirror in the hope of finding help. But the man with the ponytail seems to be in a deep sleep, his neck bumping against the window glass.

"Six years, more or less. Why?"

"Do you like it?"

Francesco looks at the transvestite in annoyance, but she continues to turn on him that disarming smile, as she waits for an answer.

"It's a job like any other job."

As soon as he's said it, Francesco is sorry. In a situation like this it's better to keep to monosyllables.

And, indeed, the transvestite starts up again.

"Oh yes, you're absolutely right. Unless it's something you really like. You know, I mean something that you would do even for nothing, out of passion. In that case it's not so bad, don't you think?"

"Maybe."

There, better already. Don't totally give her free rein, wait for her to get tired of her own voice. But the transvestite seems to have no intention of letting up.

"Still, all in all, there must be some satisfactions in a job like yours. For example, isn't it interesting to deal with so many different people every day?"

"Depends."

OK, Franz, continue in this mode. Vague and irritated. He can't bear it much longer.

"Why does it depend? Don't you like people?"

"People? No. That's not what I said."

"Obviously, some people are sympathetic from the start, and some you can't get on the same wavelength with. But, to tell you the truth, I like human contact in general. Even if a lot of people are mean, most of the time it's the fault of the life they lead. All day running here and there, always worried about getting ripped off. And in the end they get all worked up, it's natural. But basically everybody has a deep need for love. Don't you think?"

Francesco is a little disoriented.

"If you say so."

"My name is Susanna, by the way. Susy to my friends. What's yours?"

"Francesco."

"Francesco? I like that. And let me tell you something confidential. I like you too."

Here we go, Francesco thinks, now comes the worst. As if that were not enough, he hears the bell. He glances in the mirror and sees the guy with the ponytail standing in front of the exit doors.

Susy returns to the charge without wasting any time.

"I'm serious. Hasn't anyone ever told you you have a lovely profile?"

What do you say in a situation like this? Francesco decides that the only thing is to say nothing.

"But of course, how stupid! You must have heard it a thousand times."

A few moments of silence: Francesco begins to hope that he's done it. But Susy starts again.

"Listen, excuse my asking you so shamelessly. Wouldn't you like to have a blowjob?"

Francesco can't believe his ears. He tries to keep his eyes on the road.

"Uh, no . . . I don't think . . . I would say no."

"See, I'll do it for you free."

"Thanks, but I don't feel like it. Really."

"You don't know what you're missing. My blowjobs, compared with the ones done by a woman, are in another class. You know, it's a matter of intuition, of experience and sensitivity. But I've got another little secret too. Wait, I'll show you."

Out of the corner of his eye Francesco sees the transvestite working two fingers in her mouth. He doesn't have the courage to watch what's happening. Susy's holding something out to him. A wave of disgust overwhelms him when he realizes it's a set of dentures. He stares at the transvestite, who smiles again, with her toothless gums.

"See?" she says radiantly. "No teeth. I have a mouth as smooth as a bar of soap. Tell the truth, I'll bet you've never had a blowjob with no teeth!"

Francesco is speechless. And at that moment he realizes that he is about to run a red light. He brakes hard, the transvestite loses her balance, grabbing the support pole in order not to fall. The dentures fly out of her hand and roll into the dark space between Francesco's feet.

"Oh damn!" she mumbles. "I lost my dentures. Did you see where they went?"

"They must be under there," Francesco answers, while nausea squeezes the pit of his stomach.

"Would you be so kind and get them for me, please?"

Francesco knows perfectly well what any of his colleagues, at a moment like this, would do. They would

114

pull the handbrake and kick this faggot off the bus. But when he turns to give a threatening look, Susy is smiling at him again. Suddenly, every violent intention evaporates. Francesco feels overcome by exhaustion, by compassion, by a resigned melancholy that reduces every other feeling to nothing. So he leans over and reaches his hand under the pedals, groping for the dentures. He picks them up, holding them with the tips of his fingers, and hands them to the transvestite. Susy thanks him, puts them back in her mouth without even bothering to clean them off.

Behind them, a car honks. The light has changed. Francesco takes his foot off the brake pedal, drives on. He swallows the wave of nausea.

Sooner or later, he thinks, even this shit night will end.

*

While Garofano checks her, covering her mouth with the palm of one hand, Diolaiti turns on the light and plants himself in front of her. Leila stares terrified at the man, with his bony, angular head, who slowly takes a handkerchief from his pocket and gently wipes his eye. She can hardly breathe, suffocated by fear and by the hand over her mouth. She doesn't move, not even struggling to get free. The little air that filters into her throat has a bitter, metallic odour. The man in front of her puts the handkerchief back in his pocket. Then he takes out a razor and waves it in front of her eyes as if it were a visiting card.

"Don't get hysterical, just listen to me. If you promise not to make a fuss, we'll let you breathe. That way we can have a few words in peace."

Leila widens her eyes in agreement. Diolaiti glances

at Garofano, who relaxes his grip. For a moment Leila is afraid she's going to fall. Her knees seem unable to support her weight any longer.

"Well, well," Diolaiti says, examining her from head to toe, with his lips frozen in a scowl. "What do you know? Maybe the stories that imbecile told us weren't all made up."

"You think this is the whore he was talking about?" asks Garofano.

Leila tries desperately to make her brain work.

"Let's say it seems possible," Diolaiti answers. "Although I'd like to know why she came back."

He closes the razor, puts it in his pocket, grabs the handbag out of her hands.

"To start with, let's have a look in here."

As soon as he undoes the clasp, the ivory stock of the Detective Special comes into view.

"How about that, look what the lady is carrying."

He picks up the .38, showing it to Garofano. Leila's skin breaks out in goosebumps while Diolaiti begins to rummage in her handbag with the barrel of the revolver.

"Let's see. Lipstick, powder. And how about this, look here," he says, pulling out the package of condoms. "Can you use these?"

Leila hears the man behind her sneer.

"You never know. If there's time."

"Did you hear that?" Diolaiti says, putting the condoms and the gun back in the handbag. "You might say that my friend likes you. Anyway, let's get back to us. You can begin by telling us who you're working for."

Paralysis. Who are these men? How many people are involved in this business? And, above all, what should she say? She decides that, for the moment, the best

116

thing is to keep her mouth shut. It seems advisable to wait and try to get a better understanding. But, after a couple of seconds, Diolaiti gives her a slap that makes her head spin. Then he grabs her chin, forces her to stare into his eyes. On the edge of his eyelid a tear hovers.

"This time it was a slap, next it will be the razor. We don't have time to waste and you don't want to ruin that pretty face. OK, who gave you the job?"

Leila realizes that to insist that she's not involved, or to confess that she stumbled on it by chance, might be more dangerous than to admit that she knows something. She has to improvise.

"Listen, I'm a professional. When I'm paid for a job I don't ask questions. The person who hired me didn't introduce himself. He explained what he wanted and that's it."

"Ah, you see, it's not so hard, is it? Now tell me the rest. You were told to pick up this jerk and find out where he was keeping the material."

"Exactly. They told me to pick up this jerk and find out where he was keeping the material."

"And you, being a smart girl, found out. Don't tell me you didn't."

Her brain is moving at maximum velocity. But she doesn't know enough to start inventing a credible story. To orient herself, she has to get this man with the insect face to talk some more. What is he looking for? The suitcase doesn't seem to interest him. He mentioned material. But what type of material? Unfortunately he doesn't seem to have much patience. His eyes bore into her, as if he can't decide whether to cut her throat or start crying.

"I did what they asked me to do. I came here, I gave him a sleeping pill."

117

"Hear that, Garofano? The story of the sleeping pill was true too."

"It's all hard to believe. Sounds like a pile of crap invented on the spot."

"Go on. What did you do afterwards? Did you take care of it yourself or did you turn things over to someone else?"

With every answer Leila feels she is at a fatal crossroads, as in a quiz in which her life is at stake. As long as they are convinced that she can reveal something, her life has value. But the bluff certainly can't go on indefinitely.

"No, no one else."

"Perfect! Then you know what we're looking for. Where did you hide it?"

"How can I be sure that if I tell you, you'll let me go?"

Suddenly, the one behind her grabs her hair, yanks her head backward.

"Hey, you little whore, do you think you can dictate conditions?"

"Take it easy, there's no need to get ugly. I'm sure that this young lady will be so kind as to give us what we're looking for without forcing us to hurt her. Am I right?"

"Yes," Leila answers.

Garofano lets go of her hair.

"So?"

"The problem is that I've already delivered it."

Diolaiti's eyelids narrow. Leila feels a shiver go down her back.

"When I left, the person who hired me was waiting."

"Oh, is that so?" Diolaiti says in a distrustful tone.

"You want to know what I think?" Garofano interrupts. "I think this whore is feeding us a lot of crap."

Diolaiti stares Leila in the eyes.

"And where might we find this person?"

Another crossroads, and no time to reflect. Everything on the black, unequal, *les jeux sont faits*.

"He came back with me and he's waiting outside, in the car."

Diolaiti's eyelids narrow even further, X-rays seeking to dig inside her. A tear slides from his right eye.

"Aha!" he says, stopping the course of the tear with the tip of his index finger. "And are you going to tell us why you came back?"

"Because I had to retrieve one other thing."

"Which was?"

Leila decides that the moment has arrived to play the only card she has in her hand.

"It seems that a key was missing."

Diolaiti glances at Garofano, who murmurs, "Shit. The locker."

Diolaiti nods, again fixes her with his pupils.

"Let me tell you one thing. Our friend here swore that that key you mention must have been stolen by you, along with his wallet."

Leila shrugs.

"I don't know what to tell you. I don't have it. Why else would I come back?"

"And the person who hired you is downstairs waiting for you now."

"Exactly."

"Man or woman?"

"Man. Around forty. With a moustache, not very tall, grizzled."

Leila tries to sustain Diolaiti's stare.

Garofano asks: "Now what do we do?"

"Let's go see if this man really is there."

"And her?"

Leila feels she's on the edge of a precipice, while the man looks at her, evaluating the possibilities.

"For the moment we'd better take her along."

Diolaiti steps aside, pointing to the door.

"Please. Lead the way."

When Diolaiti moves, Leila sees Andrea's corpse on the chair, spattered with blood and wounds. She looks away quickly. Only now does she see the face of the man who was behind her. A big man, with broad shoulders and a comb-over pasted to his forehead. As she walks in front of him, he takes advantage of the moment to pat her on the behind.

Diolaiti places a hand on her back and pushes her forward, away from Garofano. As he directs her towards the door, Leila thinks that she may have complicated things. When they get downstairs, she won't have many excuses left.

She reaches the threshold. Behind her are the two men. Beyond the door, the dark landing. Diolaiti raises a hand and clicks the switch. The lift is open in front of them. Now or never. Leila hurls herself into the lift. She presses a button at random with her left hand, puts the right in her pocket. She pulls out the teargas canister as the doors slide closed. She turns. Diolaiti is a couple of feet away, reaching towards her. She points the spray in his face. The jet whistles through the air. Diolaiti lets out a hoarse cry, while his features crumple. He throws himself forward anyway, blindly, in an attempt to stop the lift. Leila hits him hard in the chest, pushing him backward. Through the closing doors, she sees Garofano pointing an enormous gun at her. The barrel jerks aside each time Diolaiti, staggering, enters its trajectory. The weapon fires one, two, three times with a noise that sounds like a bottle of spumante being uncorked. Leila hears the thud of the bullets as they hit the wall behind her. The doors close. A big hole opens in the left panel. With a shudder the lift starts its descent. Leila can clearly make out the voices of the two men.

"Did you hit her?"

"I don't know. I don't think so. You were in the way and I couldn't aim."

"Where did she go? Up or down?"

"She's going down."

"Hurry up! I can't even keep my eyes open. Try to stop her before she gets away!"

The sound of steps thundering down the stairs. The thumps are louder and louder and then, after passing her, diminish in intensity, descending to the lower floors. Leila pushes the stop button. Then the button for the top floor. The lift stops with a jolt, starts up in the opposite direction.

This will gain her a little time. But what will she do once she gets to the top? She has to think in a hurry. The alarm. She could sound the alarm. Her finger hesitates on the red button. And if some resident should call the police? Probably that would make the two men flee, but only to throw her into the arms of the police. She has no wish to explain what she's doing there, with a body tied to a chair and a suitcase full of money in the boot of her car. She realizes that she still has the teargas canister in her hand. She puts it back in her pocket. She tries to figure out if the footsteps she hears echoing on the stairs now are going up in her direction. She imagines the big heavyset man struggling up the stairs with that enormous gun in his hand. If only this lift would move faster! Her legs are tingling with tension. She feels trapped, with no way out.

Finally the lift stops. The doors part with exasperating slowness. Leila slips out through the opening, finds herself on a broad landing. To the left, the stairs coming up from the floor below. On three sides, the entrances to the apartments. In the right corner, a small stairway leading up. It might be a dead end, or it might turn out to be an escape route. The footsteps are getting louder. She needs time. Time.

She can send the lift down, to make him think that she's still inside. She reaches a hand in and pushes the button for the ground floor, but nothing happens. Leila hears the man getting closer. She sticks a foot inside, tries to press down on the floor. The lift sinks a fraction of an inch. Some lifts have a safety device that disengages the action of the buttons when the lift's empty. So it's one of those.

*

Sacchetti tries another approach. Prudently. His wife, taking cover behind the usual excuses, has already demonstrated a certain impatience. I'm tired, it was a hard day, the child doesn't feel well, he may still be awake and hear us. Sacchetti's hand advances under the sheet. It travels those few inches with an unnerving slowness. Finally it establishes contact with the material of the nightgown. Once this objective is conquered, he moves with the delicacy of a bomb-disposal expert. Is it possible to kindle in her some physical desire? At times, in similar situations, he has succeeded in obtaining something. But he has never figured out if his success was really due to his techniques of seduction.

His wife's reaction is ambiguous. She doesn't retreat at the touch of his fingers, but she doesn't move, doesn't respond to his caress, which becomes more and more explicit. Now he has reached her pelvis. His hand lies on the nightgown, below what he recognizes as the edge of her knickers. At this point Sacchetti stops, indecisive. Immobility, in the end, could mean anything. Even that the woman is asleep. He concentrates on the rhythm of her breath. It's neither slow nor deep. He deduces from this that his wife isn't sleeping. Maybe the game is still on. His fingers slide. The skin is soft to the touch of his fingertips.

Sacchetti moves closer until he makes contact between his own belly and her back. Emboldened by his wife's unexpected yielding, he registers with disappointment some noise coming from the landing outside. He also realizes, among other things, that a few minutes earlier he heard the sound of voices and footsteps on the stairs, suspicious only by the fact of their existence, in a building where usually, at three in the morning, the residents are sleeping. Or in any case are quietly in their beds, not bothering anyone.

Sacchetti has decided to ignore the noise. It must be some kids coming in late, maybe they've smoked a joint. Maybe the Frattinis' son, with the long hair and studs in his ears. Unfortunately his wife is also aware of the noise and, unlike him, does not seem inclined to pretend it's nothing.

"Did you hear that, Walter?"

Sacchetti's caress is interrupted.

"No. What?"

"Come on! That noise on the stairs. I've been trying to figure out for a while now who is going up and down at this hour."

"It must be the Frattinis' son, who else could it be?"

"The Frattinis' son is in the hospital with a broken leg. He fell off his motorbike the other day, they admitted him at Rizzoli."

"All right, what do you want me to tell you? It must be someone else."

"Walter, I think you should take a look."

The idea doesn't thrill him. But he is well aware that when his wife gets something in her head, there's nothing to do about it. So he shrugs his shoulders and unwillingly pushes his legs out from under the covers.

As he walks with uncertain steps along the hallway, Sacchetti tries to foresee if, once he's back in bed, it will be possible to re-establish the favourable situation of a few minutes ago, or if for yet another night he will have to surrender to abstinence. With the tip of his index finger he pushes aside the plate that covers the peephole.

"Walter, do you see anything?"

"The light on the stairs is on."

"Can you see anyone?"

"No."

"But there's still that noise. Don't you hear it?"

Sacchetti snorts. The whole thing is of less and less interest to him, and just as he is about to say OK, Luisa, whoever it is, that's who it is, let's go back to bed and try to sleep, he sees a man he doesn't know, large and partly bald, who is certainly not a resident of the building. But the thing that makes him jerk his head back suddenly, as if he has had an electric shock, is that this man is holding in his hand a gun a foot and a half long.

"What is it? What did you see, Walter? For the love of God, don't frighten me."

Sacchetti puts his index finger on his nose, pushes his wife towards the dark, reassuring depths of the hallway.

"Sh-h-h! Be quiet and get out of the way. Get out of the way, please, there's a man with a gun."

"What do you mean? A man with a gun? Who is it?"

"I've never seen him before. It must be a cop. Or a criminal. I don't know and don't care."

"Are you mad? There's an armed man running

around the building, and you say you don't care? Walter, I think you'd better call the police."

Sacchetti doesn't like to get involved in things that have nothing to do with him. But it's also true that this business is not to his liking. And it costs nothing to make a phone call. So, with all the caution in the world, he picks up the receiver and dials 113. As he waits for someone to answer at the other end, he wonders if this unforeseen event might not end by serving his needs, pushing his wife to seek safety and comfort in his arms later, once the problem has been entrusted to the forces of order. The hardest part will be to persuade her to go back to bed.

*

When Garofano emerges onto the top landing, the lift has already left. Panting, he points his gun at the metal doors. Too late. He lowers the Smith & Wesson, rests one hand against the wall to catch his breath. He stares at the red light on the call button with rage. That bitch had time to go back down. He hopes at least that Diolaiti had the good sense to go to the lobby, to block the exit.

He wipes the sleeve of his jacket across his forehead to dry the sweat, looks around. On the landing are the closed doors of the apartments, and one small stairway leading up. Garofano takes the stairs three at a time. At the top of the staircase is a metal door. He grabs the handle, shakes it. It's locked. He goes down the stairway and rushes off in pursuit of the lift.

On the ground floor he finds Diolaiti standing in the middle of the lobby, wiping his eyes with his handkerchief.

"Don't tell me she's gone up again!" he says, gasping for breath.

"No," Diolaiti answers. "It sounds like the lift is about to arrive. You didn't stop her?"

"I missed her by a hair. When I got to the top floor, she had already started down."

"OK, now we'll nail her," Diolaiti says, pointing his SIG-Sauer at the sliding doors.

The indicator above the call button turns from red to green. The lift stops. Garofano also raises his .45, holding it with both hands. Index finger tense on the trigger. He rests the butt against the palm of his left hand, aims at the centre of the opening that is widening between the doors.

The lift is empty.

The two men's guns remain pointed at the bare metal wall. Garofano, still breathing hard, is the first to lower his. In the middle of the lift are two black leather boots, unzipped. The metal zippers sparkle in the white light.

*

Leila had had just enough time to lock the metal door from the inside when she felt it shaken hard from the other side. She is petrified, holding her breath, with her eyes fixed on the door handle. When she hears the footsteps move away, she exhales and finally breathes again.

She makes a quick circuit of the building's roof terrace. A concrete parapet surrounds it, and she finds only one possible way out: a rusty scaffolding put up on one side of the building, probably for some kind of renovation work. She leans over and looks down. The poles vanish into the darkness. The thought of getting down that way doesn't excite her, but she has no other choice. Either she tries it or she stays on the terrace, hoping that the two men don't decide to come back up and look for her.

She sits on the parapet, swings her legs over, reaches her hands forward. She grabs a pole. The scaffolding sways, but seems to hold. Leila abandons the terrace, grabbing onto the support bars with all her strength. The wind hits her face and whistles through the metal structure, blowing her hair in front of her eyes.

*

The two men look at one another. The barrels of their guns are pointing at the floor.

"That bitch has made fools of us. She's still up there somewhere."

"Yes, but where? You came down by the stairs, and she didn't come through there. Do you think she asked someone for help?"

"On the top floor I saw a staircase going up to a door. I checked, but it was locked. And since the lift had already left, I didn't waste time forcing it. I bet she's hiding up there."

"Then let's get her. But it's better to go up separately, one of us takes the stairs and the other the lift. I wouldn't want her to give us the slip again."

"I agree. But this time you take the stairs."

*

Matera wonders what in the world the girl is doing. She must be a little screwy to have left the suitcase in the boot of her car all this time. He goes over what the

Secretary told him, Tuesday morning, a little before he left the office.

"I warn you, Matera. The affair is very delicate. The Minister wants to avoid any type of complication."

Any type of complication. The fact is, there have been nothing but complications!

The Ellington cassette is over. Matera rummages in the glove compartment, pulls out another. Miles Davis. Side A: *Round About Midnight.* Side B: *Kind of Blue.* He takes it out of the case and holds it up to the windscreen, to observe it against the light of a street lamp. The spool is almost at the beginning of side B. He puts it in the tape deck, adjusts the volume.

Thinking again of the Secretary, he recalls the tortuous circumlocutions, as the Secretary explained what they wanted of him. First, the Secretary had taken almost an hour to repeat the precise instructions, step by step, meticulous and tedious as a catechism teacher. And only at the end had he conceded any explanations. The Secretary, like the Minister, is profoundly Catholic, and a deep moral sense requires them, if he, Matera, is going to risk his life, to provide him with at least a vague idea of their motive.

"Have you got the situation in focus?" the Secretary had asked, resting his elbows on the desk and joining his hands in front of his face, the fingers on a level with his nose.

Matera had propped himself up on his arms, had shifted his weight from the right buttock to the left.

"Yes, I would say so."

"Then let's go over it. What are your moves?"

"Friday, after closing hours, I am to go to the bank. The director will have prepared two briefcases with the money. I take them and deliver the first."

"When, where and how?"

"At six in the evening, at the airport. I go to the row of seats opposite the luggage lockers. Under the last seat on the right, I will find the key of the locker where I'm to put the suitcase."

"Very good, Matera. Very good. And then?"

"I throw the key in the first trashcan and leave without looking around. I wait until one in the morning, then I return to the airport, I sit in the same seat and look for the key under the seat again."

"Exactly. Same procedure as the first delivery. Go on."

"Inside the locker, this time, I should find the document that I'm supposed to retrieve. I take it and leave the second suitcase."

"Don't use the conditional, Matera. In that locker you *will* find the document. And now a couple of recommendations. First of all, I repeat, stick scrupulously to these instructions. You mustn't intervene. For no reason, listen to me carefully, Matera, *for no reason* should you interfere with the retrieval of the two suitcases. Is that clear? Your job is purely to carry out the exchange and do it so that everything can proceed in the best possible way. But if, and I say *if*, in the course of the operation difficulties should arise, you are authorized to make the decisions that you think most opportune. Remember that the retrieval of the document has absolute priority over everything and act accordingly. Am I clear?"

"Very clear."

"If you consider it advisable in the circumstances, call me. I will take care of helping you resolve any possible problem. Unless you're forced to, don't take initiatives that could compromise the successful outcome of the exchange. In this whole matter there have already been too many hitches. What the Minister and I are most afraid of is that the persons who at present are in possession of the document may lose control and allow the situation to get out of hand. Unfortunately, as far as we understand, other persons have gained knowledge of the negotiations in the meantime, and there may well be some kind of interference."

The Secretary had had a little outburst of coughing.

"You see, Matera, the fact is that we are not the only ones interested in that document. The Minister, obviously, wants to retrieve it for reasons of personal caution. But there are others who, if they should come into possession of it, would gain the opportunity to place a fair amount of pressure on him. To the point of being able to control, so to speak, some of his political decisions. You understand me."

Matera had nodded, but what he understood was that the Minister had found a skeleton in the closet and was in a hurry to do spring-cleaning. The sooner the evidence that could damage him disappeared, the sooner he would have a peaceful night's sleep. But who were these other persons the Secretary was referring to? And in what way did they enter the situation? Matera had tried to ask, and the Secretary, from behind his rosewood desk, had exhaled deeply before answering.

"You know how much trust we have in you, Matera. I will tell you what I can tell you, but don't ask me for more. It's in the interests of everyone that this ugly business be resolved as quickly as possible, and as quickly as possible forgotten. The fact is that the Minister, in the past, was forced to deal with individuals whose honesty, let's say, was not unexceptionable. Compromises that, as it happens, he had to accept; I don't have to explain to you how these things go. Unfortunately, in the case in question some documents exist that can prove the involvement of the Minister with these individuals. One of these documents is in the possession of a person who thought he could profit from it."

"Blackmail."

The Secretary had contracted his features, as if the word had released a nauseating stink in the deodorized air of his office.

"We could put it like that. But the most serious problem is that it is happening at a particularly delicate moment. I don't have to enlighten you on the current political situation of our country. Unfortunately, some significant changes have occurred in the balance of power that allowed representatives of the parties in the government to exercise their mandate effectively. Today, no one can feel safe from accusation or defamation. If that document, God forbid, should end up in the hands of certain political adversaries, or certain magistrates without scruples, whose work, as you well know, is constantly exploited by the opposition, if this should happen, Matera, the Minister would find himself in serious embarrassment. They wouldn't hesitate to use that document to compromise his reputation. This would provoke further damage to the political faction that he is part of, which lately has been undergoing a series of especially fierce attacks to the point of persecution, I would dare say. In short, you surely realize how important it is for these papers to disappear once and for all."

The Secretary's way of speaking always gives him a headache. He is a man of action. Those tangled sentences, which oblige him to concentrate as in the days when he had to study codes for the admission exams, always leave him with the sensation of not having grasped the heart of the problem.

"Tell me at least who I should watch out for."

The Secretary had emitted another long sigh.

"I can't say precisely. But, if I were to put faith in some confidential information that I have managed to obtain, some agents of the intelligence services are also concerned with this matter."

Matera had compressed his lips, letting out a faint whistle. Internal struggles. The affair became more complicated. It wouldn't take much to get one's fingers crushed in the gears. The Secretary, as usual, immediately tried to throw water on the fire.

"My sources of information weren't able to define more precisely the terms of this interest. On my own account, I wouldn't give excessive weight to these rumours. In any case, Matera, I want it to be plain that what I am revealing . . ."

"Yes, I know," he had interrupted. "What you're telling me is strictly confidential. I wasn't born yesterday. But it's important to be clear. If the men from the secret service try to eliminate me, how do I respond?"

"I've told you. In that case, consider yourself authorized to intervene."

"Agreed. But if someone gets killed?"

Matera knows perfectly well that the Secretary, with his sacristan's prudence and his circumlocutions, is allergic to that type of language, but sometimes it amuses him to embarrass him. In the end he's the one running the risk, and he thinks he has the right to some small revenge.

The Secretary had changed position. As if seized by a sudden attack of haemorrhoids. He had brought his closed fist up to his mouth, cleared his throat.

"Should it turn out to be necessary, Matera, have recourse to any arrangement you consider appropriate. I am sure there is no need to add anything. You understand the priorities. Act accordingly and don't worry if the situation requires an intervention that is, let's say, particularly drastic. You can count on the usual cover."

Matera had nodded in silence. If the cousins in the intelligence services should put a spoke in the wheel, he was authorized to use strong-arm tactics. Just as well. It would be more complicated to have to worry about being neighbourly.

But at the moment Rome is far away and he's the one in the fix. To begin with, he'd like to know what team the girl in the miniskirt is playing for, and why the hell she's wandering around with a briefcase full of money. But most of all he'd like to know where she's got to. Matera glances at the clock on the dashboard. Has the moment arrived to intervene? It's obvious that something hasn't gone right, and he can't go on sitting there twiddling his thumbs. He doesn't like leaving the suitcase in the boot of that car, with the risk of having the whole thing fall through. Of course, it's a dangerous decision, but it seems to him the only logical thing to do. Three-quarters of a million dollars is a good sum and he has no intention of letting it get stolen right from under his nose. He opens the glove compartment, takes out a leather case. He unzips it and feels around inside, looking for his skeleton key. The stereo is playing the first notes of "All Blues". The fingers of Bill Evans flutter over the keyboard, suddenly pursued by Coltrane's sax, as he sighs out his riff. As Matera gets out of the car, Miles starts his solo and, in spite of the fact that he knows the passage by heart, for a few seconds he stops to savour the cold sound of that trumpet. Then he hurries over to the Y10. He goes around it, inserts the skeleton key in the lock of the boot. He raises the lid, takes out the suitcase, closes it. He returns quickly to the Alfa. Just as he is about to open the door, he hears, distant but clear, the blare of sirens.

*

Leila moves from one support to the next, her ears alert. She is terrified of hearing any sounds from the roof terrace. It would not be amusing, now, to see the faces of the two men sticking over the edge of the parapet, looking down and trying to make her out. She extends her feet slowly, testing the solidity of the support below before letting go her grip. But when from above she hears the metallic crash of the door as, following a couple of gunshots, it gives way, she abandons all caution. She tries to quicken her descent, because it won't take long for them to figure out where she's fled.

She leans to one side, extending one foot towards the iron crossbar below her. Tension and exhaustion make her lose her footing and suddenly she finds herself kicking in the darkness, gripping a rusty bar. She tenses her muscles, locking her fingers as hard as she can. With an effort she raises one foot and manages to find a support. She places the sole on the horizontal bar. She lowers herself cautiously, in an attempt to recover her balance. Her heart is pounding in her ears, but, just the same, she can hear the words of the two men above her clearly.

"Did you hear that?"

"Of course I heard it. It came from over there."

"Then let's go. Move."

Leila is worn out. She can find nothing better to do than stay there, huddled on her pole, waiting for the tread of those feet to arrive at the parapet.

*

Matera opens the door, throws the suitcase in, settles himself quickly in the driver's seat. He wonders if it might have been stupid to go and get it. But the siren is getting closer and there seems no point in wasting time on regrets.

He is about to start the car, when he sees the outer door of the building open. He stops, with his fingers on the key, to see what disasters that girl is going to cause now. But it's not her he sees; rather, it's two men, who hurry out of the entrance. Matera follows them with his eyes as they run towards a grey Audi parked nearby. As they pass under the streetlight, he recognizes one. Men from the intelligence services, as he feared, have entered the scene. That must be the reason that the exchange went wrong.

Matera knows who they are. The bigger one is an old acquaintance of his. Giuseppe Garofano, class of '48, has worked in civilian intelligence since the early eighties. At the beginning they assigned him to Matera to act as his godfather. He's put on a few pounds since then and has less hair. Matera taught him a lot of things, when he was just a boy with a formidable appetite and a desire to be free with his fists. The second must be Diolaiti. He knows him only by reputation, but he's heard that he and Garofano have been working as a team for a while, and that he is feared like a poisonous snake. Someone told him that one of Diolaiti's eyes tears continually. That's how, in the business, he came to have the nickname of the Crocodile. First he rips his prey to pieces, then he weeps.

Matera certainly isn't happy to find those two in the way, but at least the Secretary has authorized him to do whatever's necessary. It would be annoying to have to do business with someone like Diolaiti and at the same time worry about being on good behaviour.

The grey Audi moves off rapidly. He waits to let it turn, and then he too hastily starts the engine.

As he turns onto the boulevards he repeats to himself the licence plate number of the Audi. The Y10's he has already transcribed onto his notepad.

*

Leila is running, barefoot, over the cracked asphalt of a dark, narrow alley. The air burns her lungs, she feels as though her head is going to burst from one moment to the next. The sirens have stopped.

She has to get out of this neighbourhood. The police, once they've found Andrea's body, might send other squads to the area.

She emerges into Piazza di Porta San Felice, amid rows of parked cars. On her right, at the intersection with the boulevards, a tall portico, under which the illuminated windows of a lamp shop give off a glow. Beyond the intersection, the headlights of the cars driving along the boulevards and the tall dark outline of the Porta. On her left, the dimly lit porticoes of Via San Felice. Which way should she go? Heading towards the centre could be risky. That area is easier to circumscribe and control. Maybe it's safer to walk on the boulevards. But she doesn't want to get stuck in yet another mess. Along that stretch there are white prostitutes, Austrians and Slavs, and with the clothes she's wearing she could easily be taken for one of them. While she is trying to decide, she sees a bus turning off of Via Riva di Reno.

*

"I'm sure she hid down there."

"What do you want to do? We can't stay here waiting for the police to arrive."

"And if they arrest her? You think she'll talk?"

"How should I know?"

"She'll talk about us too."

"What's wrong, you shitting in your pants? She doesn't even know who we are. If she talks about us, it doesn't change much. They'll rough her up, and they won't believe her. And even if they listen to her, they'll come to a dead end, as usual. In the worst case, we'll ask the chief to cover us."

*

The first thing he noticed was her legs. Hard not to, with that miniskirt. Then the girl went and sat on one of the side seats and Francesco noticed that she wasn't wearing any shoes. Of course, he thought, all he needed was a dopehead, to make a perfect end to the night. Let's hope that at least she doesn't throw up on the bus.

Yet she doesn't look like an addict. Francesco has continued to examine her in the parabolic mirror, and in the end he is almost certain. Even though there is certainly something that's not quite right, judging from her expression and from the fact that she's going around barefoot.

She doesn't even have a handbag. And Francesco wonders if she's been robbed, or even raped. Also, a woman who goes around alone at this time of night, in a miniskirt and body stocking, even if she's not an addict or a prostitute, must be a person who loves danger.

Francesco lets it go; in any case it's none of his business. Still, this doesn't prevent him from continuing to cast brief but intense looks at the girl's legs. Her legs and the rest of her. Because, addict or not, she's very attractive, you can't argue with that.

*

Leila tries to breathe deeply and analyse the situation.

So.

She meets this guy, who picks her up and takes her home. She fucks him, he falls asleep, she cleans out the apartment. Up to here, business as usual. Then the stroke of luck. In the wallet that she has just stolen is the key to a luggage locker at the airport. And in that locker she finds a suitcase full of dollars.

From that moment, however, things begin to go wrong. First, she realizes she's lost her house keys. She hurries to Andrea's, hoping to retrieve them. Instead she finds his body and is attacked by these two killers who stop her, threaten her and ask her to give them something. Only she hasn't the slightest idea what they want, and it's a miracle that she's managed to stay alive.

Calm down, she has to try to reason. Where did her handbag end up? Would they have taken it or left it at Andrea's house? She clutches her head in her hands. In any case, she is in trouble. In the handbag were the keys to her car. And in the boot is the suitcase with the money. A real mess. Plus the car is parked outside the building where they killed Andrea. She won't even mention going back there to force the lock and get the suitcase. And, anyway, what could she force the lock with? She has nothing, not even a nail file. No, she has one thing. In her jacket pocket she has the teargas spray. And her house keys? If she left them in the apartment, she's done for. If she lost them somewhere else, there shouldn't be any signs that link them to her.

Calm. She has to analyse the situation calmly. If the cops find her keys or her handbag, how much time will pass before they link her to the Y10 and decide to search it?

Her forehead is burning. She has a tremendous desire for a cigarette. But even the pack of Gauloises is in her handbag. She needs a little time. And money. And a place to spend the night. Tomorrow, with a little luck, she could try to retrieve the suitcase from the boot. If the police haven't already discovered the Y10.

Calm, Leila, stay calm. Getting worked up isn't helping anything. The important thing is for the brain to work. If you don't keep cool, you risk total disaster.

So, let's recapitulate.

*

"Look how that bitch screwed us. It pisses me off just thinking about it."

"What's done is done," says Diolaiti, drying his eye with the handkerchief. "Let me have a look inside the handbag."

"Yes, you're right, it's better not to get all worked up about it. But I swear, if I ever get my hands on that little whore, I'm going to have some fun. How are your eyes?"

"Bad. Hey, look what's in here. The wallet, with her identity card and licence. Do you think they're really hers?"

"I wouldn't swear to it. If she's a professional, she surely must have false documents. But we might as well stop at that address, what can we lose?"

Diolaiti thinks about it, tapping the identity card against his lower lip. His right eye is burning. It's tearing so much that he has to press the handkerchief against it. He would like to know who she's working for. He looks again at the photograph on the ID card. She's attractive, even if he isn't interested.

"So, Diolaiti, what do we do? Shall we go and have a look?"

"Why not? It says here that she lives in Via del Borgo di San Pietro."

"That's Arabic to me. Try to find it on the map."

Diolaiti runs his finger over the page, his eyes burning with the effort. A tear falls between Via Belfiore and Via Bella Costa.

"Borghese, Borghetto, Borghi Mamo. Here it is. Borgo di San Pietro. Map 14. B3."

"Let's go," Garofano says, putting the car in gear.

*

What can she do? For the moment she can't think up a strategy that's worth anything. She needs to lie down somewhere and close her eyes for at least a couple of hours. She can't continue to go back and forth on this bus forever.

The accumulated exhaustion and tension cause an almost hypnotic torpor. Her gaze continues to move over the objects and writings in front of her. She has stared so long at that part of the bus that she goes on seeing it even when she closes her eyes. A luminescent halo against the dark red background of her lowered eyelids.

The four plastic seats on whose backs someone has spray-painted a black swastika and a slogan.

BOLOGNA IS THE TRUE FAITH
WHOEVER DOESN'T BELIEVE IN IT MUST DIE
RED BLUE SKINS BOLOGNA

The dull-metal support poles. The hotel ad hanging high up, above the window: a rectangle of plastic-coated paper displaying a photo of a dream beach. Blue sky, white sand, palm trees and stupendous blue sea.

WHAT ARE YOU WAITING FOR?
THE CARIBBEAN IS WAITING FOR YOU

SEAGULL TRAVEL AGENCY

In the middle of the window, a red band with two sentences printed in white letters.

EMERGENCY EXIT
IN CASE OF NECESSITY BREAK GLASS

She can't think anymore. Her brain is empty, and suddenly it's as if the whole thing had to do with someone else.

The only thing she would really like, right now, is to smoke a cigarette.

*

The corridor is backlit and at the end the shape of a man is silhouetted. He can't make out his face. He tries to call him but no voice comes out of his throat. He feels sick, his head is spinning, as if he couldn't get enough oxygen. The man stands there, immobilized, while he is barely able to breathe, to utter even a syllable. He moves along the corridor, which now seems to him very long. The man is farther and farther away, he will never reach him. Then, at a certain point, the figure moves and disappears. Perhaps the stranger went into a room.

He looks around, to right and left. The corridor is lined with doors. He tries one door handle, then another, and another, but all the doors are locked, and the sense of anguish increases until he is suffocating. Suddenly, a door yields and opens. He is on a country lane bathed in a pale light, and far away, at the end of the lane, he sees the same man. He waves to get his attention, but the man ignores him. Then he runs towards him. When he finally reaches him, out of breath by now, he sees that his back is turned. Panting, he places a hand on his shoulder. The other man stops, turns. He has no face. Above the collar of his shirt he has only a kind of cavity, a mass of open, bleeding flesh. He knows that he should feel horror at that sight, and yet he is curious. It would be natural to cry out, be frightened, run away, and instead he moves closer, to get a better look. From the bottom of that cavity a weak sound emerges. Maybe the man is trying to tell him something. Maybe he needs help. By now he is a few inches from that shapeless mass. The sound grows louder. It's a kind of suffocated cry coming from inside. He observes with amazement his own hand rise up, approach the cavity the man has for a face. His fingers sink into the flesh, slowly. The other doesn't retreat, he waits without moving for him to do what he has to do. The hand descends gradually into the face, which now seems a flower with wet fleshy petals, not without an obscene beauty. The cry coming from inside increases in intensity. First it resembles a wail, then a siren, finally a tuneless concert of bells. His fingers go hesitantly into the soft heart of the flower, until they touch something hard and angular and icy. Suddenly, this mysterious object which he has grazed with his fingertips fills him with horror. He wants to pull his hand out, but the flower has closed over his wrist, blocking it. He pulls hard, but can't free his arm. Meanwhile the sound gets louder, higher, deafening, unbearable.

Commissioner Roccaforte wakes with a start, his breath in his throat, at the fourth ring of the telephone. In the dark, he tries to stretch out his hand to pick up the receiver, but his right arm, folded under his body, doesn't respond. It's as stiff and unfeeling as a piece of wood. The phone rings again, the Commissioner gropes, managing to reach the instrument with his left hand.

"Yes, hello," he says, holding the receiver between his jaw and his shoulder and massaging the painful arm with his free hand.

"Excuse me for disturbing you, sir, but there's a big mess."

"Is that you, Loiacono? What time is it?"

"Who do you think it is, sir? It's me. I know it's early, but I've got to disturb you. Someone's been killed – butchered! It's better if you come and have a look."

"All right, wait. Give me the address."

The flesh of his arm feels like pins and needles. Loiacono, at the other end of the line, reads out: "Via Battistelli, sir. Wait. Via Battistelli, number 8. You know the gardens behind the Palazzo dello Sport? The apartment is just opposite, on the fifth floor."

"OK, I've got it, 8, Via Battistelli. I'll be there immediately."

The lamp illumines the top of the night table. The telephone, the ashtray, the pack of Nazionali, the alarm clock. The hands show twenty to six. Commissioner Roccaforte scratches his neck, with the last repugnant images of the dream still floating in his head. A shiver runs down his back. He grabs the pack, lights a cigarette. He opens and closes his fist, to get

143

the circulation going. A homicide. Loiacono said someone was killed. Via Battistelli, number 8. His hands are tingling, his fingers feel as swollen and stiff as sausages. What a disgusting dream. He kicks away the sheets to get out of bed. He inhales again. The smoke circles up in the cone of light created by the lampshade, vanishes in the shadows. Fifth floor, Loiacono said. An apartment building near the Palazzo dello Sport. The cigarette has a disgusting taste.

*

The girl with no shoes has already made one and a half trips and is still sitting in the same place. The first time he got to the end of the line in Via Battindarno, Francesco was a little behind schedule and went on almost without stopping. She, motionless in her seat, seemed to be asleep. They went back across the city, arrived at the other end of the line, and she was still there, in the same seat she had sat in when she got on.

Francesco continues to examine her, in the mirror, wondering again if she might be a little crazy. She crosses and re-crosses her legs, stretches them out, shifts her position. Earlier, when they passed Via San Felice again, he noticed that she turned suddenly to look out the window.

When they reach the end of the line in Via Battindarno the second time it's 5:45. Francesco looks at his watch. He engages the hand brake. He straightens his back. He gets out to stretch his legs.

He breathes deeply and looks up. The night is clear. He lights a cigarette, bends his neck one way, then the other, to release the muscles.

For the first time, the girl gets up from her seat. She gets off the bus. She raises the collar of her jacket. She

144

takes a few steps, silent. Francesco takes another drag on his cigarette and tries not to look at her. She comes over.

"Excuse me, aren't you going to offer me one?"

Francesco takes out the pack of MS, holds it out to her. He watches as she takes a cigarette, her bare feet moving restlessly on the asphalt. She thanks him with a tired smile. Francesco searches his pocket for the lighter. The flame illuminates her face. Crazy or not, she really is pretty.

"Do you like riding the bus at night?" he asks, as she inhales deeply.

The girl looks him in the eyes. Then she makes a half smile and shrugs her shoulders.

"When I have nothing better to do."

"Ah. And tonight there was nothing good on at the cinema?"

She smiles again, blowing the smoke out the side of her mouth.

"Tonight some people were looking for me who I preferred not to see, so I thought I'd take a little ride."

Francesco decides she's not crazy, or an addict, or anything of the kind. But she is agitated, she takes quick, deep drags, she taps her finger on the cigarette continuously, even when there's no ash to knock off.

"And how was the trip? Did it bore you?"

"So-so. But I didn't expect anything special."

"Too bad you didn't get on earlier. It was quite a busy night."

"For that matter, so was mine. What happened to you?"

"The usual. A drunk told me his misfortunes in love, a group of Nazi skinheads repainted the bus, a transvestite offered me a blowjob."

Leila laughs, throwing her head back.

"No, really, you made that one up. I don't believe it."

"Really, I swear. You want to know his name? Susanna, Susy to his friends."

"Are you serious?"

"I swear on the thing I love most. This bus."

"Come on, you're kidding me."

"All right, I admit it. I don't give a shit about the bus. But the story about the transvestite is true. Word of honour."

The cigarettes are finished. They throw them on the ground. Francesco crushes his with his shoe. He looks at the girl's bare feet, stamps on the other one.

"By the way, if I'm not being intrusive, why are you going around barefoot? Aren't you afraid of hurting yourself?"

Leila looks at her feet, then at Francesco. What if she were to ask him for help? Why not? Ultimately, what has she got to lose? She has no keys to her house, no money, no documents, no nothing. Except a suitcase full of money locked in the boot of her car, which is impossible to retrieve.

"It's kind of a complicated story," she tells him.

Then she decides to go for it.

"Listen, I may seem a little bold. But I don't have anywhere to sleep and I don't have money for a hotel. Is there any way that I could stay with you? Just for tonight."

Francesco inclines his head slightly, with an expression of curiosity. The proposal has taken him by surprise. He smiles, shrugging his shoulders.

"Well, I don't know . . ."

"I'm sorry, I don't mean to embarrass you. Are you married? With someone?"

"No, it's not that. I live alone. And it's been four, no, wait, five months since I've been with someone."

"But?"

"Listen, if you need money, you've made an unlucky landing. I'm broke, and I owe money to half Bologna."

"Sorry, but did I ask you for money? I don't think so."

Francesco puts his hands in his pocket, embarrassed. She's offended, and he can't say she's wrong.

"The fact is that I've never thought I was so irresistible to women, so I started to suspect that . . ."

"That I was a prostitute."

"Well, yes," he admits, shrugging his shoulders.

Leila smiles. He has a way of acting that arouses tenderness in her. He stands there, his hands sunk in his pockets, searching for words to apologize for having thought she was a prostitute.

"No money," she says to him. "And no ulterior motives. Really, all I need is a place to rest a little. As I was telling you, my evening was also rather a mess. I lost my handbag with my documents, my house keys and everything else. And I'm exhausted."

"If you want, I could call the police. There's an emergency radio on the bus."

"No," she interrupts him too quickly. "I just need a bed for a few hours, nothing else. But I don't want to make trouble for you. If you don't feel like it, it's OK."

Francesco is confused. She got nervous hearing talk of the police. In the darkness he looks for her face. He meets two dark-circled eyes, frightened and tired.

"OK, OK, it's not a problem. No need to get excited. I don't get on that well with the police myself."

He lifts his wrist and glances at his watch.

"I still have half the route to do. I get to the station, then go back to the bus garage and I'm finished. If you don't mind staying on the bus for another half hour, afterward we can go to my house."

Leila smiles, nods in agreement.

"Thank you. You're doing me a real favour."

Francesco shrugs. Then he holds out his right hand.

"Since we're going to sleep under the same roof, we ought to introduce ourselves. My name is Francesco, but almost everyone calls me Franz."

Leila hesitates a second. Then the old survival instinct takes over.

"Alessandra," she says, shaking his hand.

His palm is warm, just a little damp. Leila wonders if before closing her eyes she'll have to fuck him too.

*

As soon as he enters his room, Matera locks the door, places the two suitcases on the bed, and, with his thumbs, unlocks the clasps. He runs his fingertips over the compact surface of hundred-dollar bills. Three rows by four. Twelve bundles in each suitcase, perfectly aligned. Twenty-four portraits of Benjamin Franklin, which stare into the space above his right temple.

He takes off his jacket, hangs it on the back of a chair. He stretches his arms, loosens the knot of his tie. He opens the door of the closet. He takes out another suitcase, deeper, longer and more worn than the others, with steel-reinforced edges and corners. Carefully, he places this too on the bed.

A tenor saxophone is lying in the moulded case, which is lined with burgundy fabric. He takes the instrument out of the case. He sits down, sticks the neckpiece in the saxophone, holds it in place by tightening the screw on the metal band. Then he pushes the ebonite mouthpiece into the neckpiece until it stops, in line with the shallow furrow that over time has been impressed into the cork. He opens the box of

148

reeds. He takes one between two fingers, delicately, a Rico Royal No. 2. He brings it to his mouth. He licks it over and over, moving it back and forth between his lips. When it's wet, he sticks it in the mouthpiece with the clip. He places the saxophone on the bed and goes into the bathroom. He comes back with a towel, which he sticks in the bell. Then he puts on the collar and hooks the sax to it.

His tongue slides once again along the reed, his fingers rest on the instrument, finding the proper keys by instinct. His lips tighten. The breath gently penetrates the sax.

So, la, ti, re, mi, so, and a held *la*, on which, in his mind, he hears the piano starting off in D minor, the *la* of the bass and the rustle of the brushes as they start caressing the cymbals.

As the notes of "In a Sentimental Mood" flow from the sax, his gaze rests on the open suitcases. As if in a transparency, beyond the rows of bills packed inside, Matera sees the dark-haired girl walking quickly, with one of those very two suitcases in hand, under the powerful neon of the airport lobby. With every step, the black fabric of her miniskirt emits little flashes.

*

Francesco parks the bus in the place indicated by the garage man.

"Done," he says, pressing the button to turn off the engine. "Now let's go home."

Leila smiles with a tired look.

As they pass in front of the glass booth, he notes the curious and envious looks of a couple of colleagues, who are chatting with the dispatcher. They walk along the road that leads to the car park without speaking.

Francesco doesn't know what to say. The girl walks beside him in silence, huddled in her leather jacket. She walks almost on tiptoe, cold. She must be incredibly sleepy.

The Peugeot is a dark shadow crouching near a row of trees. As Francesco approaches the car, one hand searching in his pocket for the keys, he feels himself grabbed by the shoulders. He tries to react, but his attacker shoves him against the side of the car and with his own weight keeps him from moving. Leila looks around, ready to flee. She wonders how the hell those men can have found her, and where the second man is. But in the whole car park there are only the three of them. Her, Francesco and that man who came out of nowhere.

"What the fuck..." Francesco gasps, almost breathless.

"Shut up, asshole. If you don't, I'll break your collarbone."

"Oh, it's you! Shit, Bear, you practically gave me a heart attack."

"So I scared you? I'm sorry."

The Bear grabs Francesco by the lapels. He picks him up and begins heaving him around, slamming his back against the car, with a series of dull thuds. *Sbam. Sbam. Sbam.*

"Hey, that's enough, Bear," Francesco begs, with the little breath left in his lungs. "Let me go."

"Like hell." *Sbam.* "You think you can keep on doing your own damn thing forever?" *Sbam.* "And cheat everybody else?" *Sbam.* "Right?"

Sbam. Sbam. Sbam.

Francesco is gasping. Every blow is like an axe cracking his spine.

Sbam. Sbam.

"Stop it!" Leila cries. "Hey, I'm talking to you. You want to kill him?"

The scene freezes. Francesco is suspended some three feet off the ground, a sack of rags in the hands of the Bear, who turns his head in the direction of the voice. He narrows his eyes. Standing out against the faint light of the street lamps behind him, he sees a straight, thin profile.

"What the fuck do you have to do with it?"

"Let him go, then we'll discuss it."

Francesco takes advantage of the truce to look for some means of escape. But it doesn't seem to him that there are many possibilities. Not as long as the Bear has him lifted off the ground by the lapels. Out of the corner of his eye he looks for something with which to defend himself. A few feet away, between the hedge and a mound of excavated dirt, he can discern an iron stake, left by the workers who replaced the fence last week.

"Listen to me, you little bitch, if you don't get out of my way I'll smack you one you'll remember for a while."

Francesco, with his neck wedged between his shoulders, rotates his head laboriously in the direction of Leila. He would like to make her understand that it's better to forget it, but before he can utter a sound he sees her take a step forward and point one arm at the Bear's face, as he lets out a cry and jumps back, bringing his hands to his eyes.

Francesco winds up with his rear end on the ground. When he tries to stand up, he can't keep his eyes open, and a sharp pain in his back forces him to stay bent over. He struggles along on all fours, blinking his eyes in order to see.

The Bear meanwhile is staggering around with his hands over his face.

"Goddamn whore!" he cries. "What the fuck did you do to me?"

Francesco's fingers find the metal stake, grab it. Now he has to make an effort. He contracts his jaw, struggles to his feet. He sees Leila with her arm lowered at a forty-five-degree angle, while the Bear moves like a drunk, waving one hand in an attempt to catch her. Francesco takes a short run-up, hits him on the neck with the stake. The Bear staggers forward as if he had stumbled. Then he falls to his knees.

"Oh shit," Francesco says. "Sorry, Bear, I didn't mean to hit so hard."

"Son of a bitch. This time you've really done something stupid, Franz. I swear I'm going to break your balls."

"What do you expect?" says Leila. "Come on, give him another!"

Francesco looks up at her, then lowers his gaze to the Bear, who is trying to stand up.

"I'll murder both of you. You and that whore."

Francesco knows there's nothing else to do.

"I swear I'm sorry, Bear. I would never want to hurt you, but I have to."

He raises the iron stake and cracks him hard on the head.

*

Loiacono said *butchered*. What the hell does he mean, *butchered*?

Luckily at this hour there's no traffic. There aren't many cars on Via Andrea Costa. Commissioner Roccaforte passes a truck from the sanitation department, speeds towards the centre.

This city frightens him more and more.

It used to be different. In the late sixties, when he joined the police, Bologna was like a big village. A few delinquents, an isolated robbery, some strikes. Then came the seventies, and the tension increased. Sometimes they had to get rough. OK, he did it. A punch or two never killed anyone. It's true that a few hotheads went around with pistols stuck in their jeans, and at a demonstration it might happen that three or four of them waved guns in the air just to create a little scene. He recalls them, those kids with the balaclavas or kaffiyehs over their faces, who acted like gunslingers, with their legs wide, knees bent, guns held in two hands. Sometimes a few shots went off, and at headquarters they began to get nervous. He recalls the tense faces of the cops before they got in the tanks. Apprehensively, they made sure that everything was in place, clubs, helmets, shields. It happened that in '77 that boy, what was his name, Lorusso, Francesco Lorusso, had lost his life. But he himself had never worried much. He did his job and advanced. Then politics had gone down the tubes and there seemed to be nothing left of that whole big mess. But Bologna grew and the criminals changed, became tougher. With the nineties had come shootings, torture, carabinieri murdered. Now a day didn't pass without some disaster, and he feels in his bones that things are going to hell. He doesn't know how many dangerous individuals are at large or who they are. He doesn't know precisely how many businesses pay bribes, nor where those who collect them are based. Drug dealers, criminals, prostitutes, everything comes through. The gangs resemble businesses; they manage their affairs from other cities. And he doesn't have a single thing under control.

The Commissioner lets a bus arriving from Via di Sant'Isaia pass, then turns left into Viale Vicini.

At one time he had more guts, that's the truth. But maybe he was merely younger; he had a head full of nonsense, the gun in its holster made him feel invincible. Sheriff John Wayne enters the saloon and they all go quiet, out of fear. In the end he was made of the same clay as those kids at the demonstrations, but on the other side. He was on the side of reason. Or, at least, when he was thirty he thought he could put order into a piece of the world, felt in his veins the courage to risk his life. Now that he's old, a terrible fear of dying has grown in him.

The signal at the intersection with Via San Felice turns green as he approaches. He shifts gears and accelerates. A fat black woman standing on the edge of the pavement watches him go by.

Loiacono seemed agitated. What awaits him this time? Blood, certainly. And wounds, staring eyes, smell of dead flesh. What a shitty job. It's not surprising if at night he's tortured by these revolting dreams.

He needs a cigarette.

Commissioner Roccaforte lowers the window, lights a Nazionale. He no longer has any desire to look at corpses. He no longer has any wish to risk his life, or to interrogate people who look at him with distrust, fear, hatred. He no longer has the desire to arrest anyone. He no longer has any desire for anything.

He would like to open up his skull, take out the brain, give it a good washing. Wash away the filth encrusted inside it. Stop everything, give up smoking, go on holiday somewhere near the sea, sit in the shade and watch the waves and the people swimming. The tanned girls walking on the beach, in those microscopic outfits they wear these days, with their tits bouncing in the wind. Perfume of suntan oil, a few clouds in the sky, cries of children playing, a nice glass of icy orange juice. Paradise.

He turns into Via Calori and immediately right into Via Battistelli. In front of number 8 police cars are stopped with their lights on. He parks on the pavement, gets out, throws the butt on the ground. A sad-looking pigeon approaches it, lowers its beak onto the butt, then goes off, its thin featherless neck swaying. Commissioner Roccaforte looks up and puts another cigarette between his lips. The fifth floor, Loiacono said. Now all he has to do is go up.

*

As the Peugeot moves along Via Della Pietra, a hint of greyish light begins to dirty the air. Francesco, driving, holds his back rigid because of the pain.

"Shit, this time I really thought the end had come. If you hadn't been there I'd've been done for. What was that stuff?"

"The stuff I sprayed in his eyes? Teargas."

"Wow. Not bad, you go around prepared."

"Well, yes, I manage. But what did he want?"

Francesco inclines his head, a grimace on his lips.

"I'm afraid he wanted money."

"He seemed pretty mad. Do you owe him a lot?"

"I don't even know how much. A ton of money I lost at poker. But not all to him. Except that lunatic got it into his head to start collecting on behalf of the others, and for me that's trouble."

"In other words, you're a champion at cards."

"If I think back at the whack I gave him, I feel bad."

"Why, what would you have wanted to do? After all, he was practically murdering you."

"It would have been better if I'd tried to reason

with him. Next time he gets his hands on me, he'll massacre me."

"But what in the world are you saying! You want to know what that monster is going to do now? Have a nice sleep. That's all."

*

Garofano, leaning forward, works the lock, while Diolaiti checks the landing and stairs, the handkerchief pressed to his eye.

"So is it going to be much longer?"

"Don't hurry me. If you breathe down my neck, I get nervous."

"The important thing is that we get in before noon."

"There we are. Happy?" Garofano says, straightening up.

He places one hand on the door and pushes. He lifts up his arm to make way for his colleague.

"You just have to have a little patience!"

The two men enter. Diolaiti turns on the light.

"So this is the whore's den," Garofano says, looking around.

"Hmm . . . it doesn't look like an apartment rented by the month."

"It remains to be seen, if we can get her. You think she's stupid enough to come home?"

Diolaiti opens a closet.

"Who knows? Anyway, there's no harm in taking a look."

"No doubt about that," Garofano says, opening the refrigerator. "In fact, you know what? I've got half a mind to cook some spaghetti."

Diolaiti stares at him, incredulous. The other smiles

and circles his fingers in the air, to simulate the movement of a fork.

"You're not really going to?"

"You bet I am!"

"Can't you think about anything but eating?"

"What do you mean? If that little slut makes the mistake of coming back, I'll show you."

Diolaiti shrugs his shoulders, opens a drawer at random.

"Well, well. There's a choice. Tell me, Diolaiti, do you prefer aubergine, *amatriciana* or tuna?"

"I couldn't care less."

"Just for a change you have no appetite. I should have guessed. Well, in that case I'll make *amatriciana*. And to be safe I'll throw in three handfuls of pasta, because I bet that as soon as you smell it you'll think again."

"You can't be serious. What if she comes back?"

"So what? What's wrong with that?" Garofano says, winking. "It means we'll offer her a plate too."

*

The door opens onto a narrow entrance hall crowded with coats and jackets hanging on a hook that doesn't look very secure. An old bicycle leans against the right-hand wall. Francesco sees with a fresh eye the chaos of his apartment. And notices the dust balls gathered along the edges of the floor.

"What can I say? Don't pay any attention to the mess."

"Don't worry, I'm not easily shocked."

"Just as well. Come on, I'll lead. Keep an eye on that shelf. If you touch it, it'll fall."

Francesco opens a door, shows Leila into a room full of shelves, books, old records. Shirts and socks thrown everywhere. Francesco sniffs the air, to make sure the smell is above the safety level.

"Here, this is what I can offer you."

In a corner is a big armchair covered with dark green material. Leila takes the teargas canister out of her jacket pocket, places it on the night table.

"Satisfy my curiosity on one thing," says Francesco, pointing with his chin at the spray. "Where did you get that stuff?"

Leila shrugs.

"I bought it in Holland. But, if you want, you can find it here too."

"Isn't it illegal?"

"Gambling is illegal too."

"True."

The bed is a simple double-width mattress on an unpainted metal base that's resting on eight large leather-bound volumes. Two for each corner. Leila approaches, curious, tilts her head to read the gilt lettering on the books' spines.

"Grand Encyclopedia of Arts and Crafts."

Francesco smiles, his hands sunk in his pockets.

"Nice, isn't it?"

"Is it interesting?"

"I haven't even opened it."

Leila looks at him, raising her eyebrows.

"I'll explain. One morning, a couple of salesmen pounced on me here and started an endless boring harangue on the advantages of having an encyclopedia like this.

"According to them, it was practically impossible to live without one. A real bargain, eight volumes for only 580,000 lire! All I cared about was getting them out of here. So, since the previous night the cards had gone my way, and I had a generous million in my pocket . . ."

158

"You bought it!"

Francesco spreads his arms.

"Yes, I bought it. And, as you see, the eight volumes have been useful. The week before, one leg of the bed had broken off, so I had had to take off the other three and put the mattress on the floor."

"Are you kidding? You spent 600,000 lire for some books that you use as a support for the bed?"

"And also to get rid of those pains in the ass. They were worse than the Jehovah's Witnesses."

Leila bursts out laughing.

"It's incredible!"

"The only trouble, you see, is that the eighth volume has fewer pages than the others. I had to add some magazines to make up for the height."

Leila drops onto the bed.

"In my view you're out of your mind. With that amount you could have bought a new bed."

"Maybe, but they were only selling encyclopedias."

*

"It's an old question. There are those who say that the true *amatriciana*, the original, was white, that is, without tomatoes. Pork cheek cut in strips and browned, to which you add only hot pepper and a generous amount of grated pecorino. Others don't agree. Who said that one must go back to historical research? I, for my part, don't give a damn about history. The best known *amatriciana* is the one with tomato. Except that usually it's made with pancetta, but this is another subject. The fact is that almost no one uses pork cheek anymore. Like lard, fat and all the other stuff that has gone out of fashion. As if the crap people eat today were good for your health. For example, I feel sick to my stomach at the idea of soy beefsteak. What the fuck is a soy beefsteak? Does it seem logical that, with all the meat we have available, we should start concocting fake beefsteak, using shit like soy? Anyway, to return to our *amatriciana*, there are some who sauté the pork by itself, with a drop of oil, or even with a chopped onion. Then, of course, you add the hot pepper, the crushed tomatoes and the pecorino. This is definitely the most common recipe. But I've worked out a couple of small variations. Pay attention. First of all, I heat a spoonful of oil in a pan with a couple of crushed slivers of garlic. As soon as the garlic colours, I take it out and throw in the pork cheek, cut in strips. I sauté it for a bit, then pour a couple of spoonfuls of dry white wine over it. As soon as the wine hits the hot pork, it creates a steam that fills your nostrils with perfume and opens up the stomach nicely. In this way the pork cheek loses its fat and becomes crusty and has a delicious taste. When it browns, I add the pepper and some tomato purée. I cook it down until I get a thick sauce, then I sprinkle it with a spoonful of chopped basil. When the spaghetti is cooked, I drain it and put it in the pan along with the sauce and a generous amount of cheese. Half pecorino and half Parmigiano. What a perfume. Come on, don't tell me you don't want to taste it."

Diolaiti looks with disgust at the giant plate that Garofano has filled. He glances at his watch.

"It's got to be heavy. And at this hour."

Garofano sinks a fork into the steaming mountain of pasta before him, twirls the spaghetti carefully around the fork and brings the red forkful to his mouth. He chews slowly, his eyes half closed.

"Every moment is good for a good dish of spaghetti," he says, as soon as he's swallowed the mouthful. "Tell me something, is it maybe that it bothers you to eat after what you did? I mean, all that cutting."

"Don't talk crap," Diolaiti says, touching his shirt over his stomach. "It's gastritis."

"Oh, yes, of course. Burning?"

Diolaiti nods, takes the handkerchief out of his pocket.

"In my opinion, it's because you have trouble relaxing," Garofano says, twirling spaghetti around his fork. "A man with no appetite isn't a serene person. My grandfather often said so. You really don't want any?"

"Maybe I'll have a Coke," Diolaiti answers, drying his eye with the folded handkerchief.

"A Coke! That stuff burns a hole in your guts!" Garofano exclaims, with the fork suspended in front of his mouth. "Didn't you know that if you put a ten-lire piece in and leave it all night, it corrodes almost to nothing?"

"I've always heard that story, but I don't know if it's true. Have you tried it?"

"What a conversation," Garofano answers with his mouth full. "No, I haven't tried it. But I haven't tried to down trichloroethylene, either. The label shows a skull and crossbones with 'poison' written on it, and I believe it. Tell me, Diolaiti, why are you always suspicious of everything? Earlier, when the moron on the autostrada told us what we wanted to know, you kept insisting that it might be lies. But what sort of lies? It was perfectly clear that he was telling the truth. The way we squeezed him, that poor fellow couldn't have invented a story even if we had suggested it to him."

"Better to be certain."

"You know what I say? I'd say it was an excuse to go on amusing yourself," Garofano throws out, sticking another forkful of spaghetti in his mouth. "It's obvious that you have a taste for it, with that razor of yours. You can't deny it."

"Are you finished playing the psychologist?"

"And why not?" Garofano says, chewing. "I've finished, I've finished. Not that I care. I eat my sandwiches, my spaghetti and anything else I feel like, while you suffer from acid stomach, you're always in a shitty mood, and your only relief comes from carving people up."

Diolaiti stares at Garofano's lips, which are red with sauce, and move to the rhythm of his chewing. In the corner of Diolaiti's eye a tear is forming again.

"You know what you should do? Pay a little more attention to your own affairs And above all to your health. It's not good for you to stuff yourself like that."

Garofano washes down the mouthful with a glass of wine. Then he leans against the chair seat, balances the chair on its back legs, burps with his mouth wide open.

"That's all?"

"That's all. That should be enough."

The two men look at each other in silence.

"Listen to me, Diolaiti, maybe we've misunderstood each other. When it's a question of physical force, I don't hold back. On the contrary – why not admit it? – I like to go heavy. But I feel that you do this job just so you can have a free hand. I don't know how to explain it. You seem to have a kind of obsession."

Diolaiti is silent. He stares into Garofano's eyes without saying a word. He pulls the handkerchief out of his pocket. He dries his eye. Then he reaches his hand out across the table, and with his fingers just grazes the cold bottle of mineral water. The tips of his index and middle fingers leave a double trail on the steamy glass. Garofano lowers his gaze to follow the movement of that white hand. He feels uneasy. Diolaiti doesn't shine when it comes to a sense of humour and there's nothing to be gained by quarrelling in the middle of the mission.

He twirls another forkful of spaghetti, sticks it in his mouth.

"OK, do what you like. But this *amatriciana* is delicious. You don't know what you're missing."

*

"I don't have any clean pyjamas. If you want I can lend you a T-shirt and a pair of boxers," Francesco says, throwing some clean sheets on the mattress.

Leila puts out her cigarette in the ashtray.

"Thanks, the T-shirt will be great. So is there a bathroom?"

"Yes, but I warn you, it's not the toilet at the Hilton."

"I think I'll be able to pee just the same, what do you think?"

"Probably yes, if you really have to go. In any case, it's certainly more comfortable than going down to the street."

As he rummages in a drawer in search of a clean T-shirt, Francesco hears the jet that streams into the toilet bowl. The flush of the water surprises him in the middle of an erotic fantasy. He balls up the dirty sheets and throws them in a corner, trying to think of other things.

Leila, in the bathroom, takes off the body stocking, squeezes some toothpaste onto her fingertip and rubs it on her teeth. Then she washes her neck and her armpits. She looks up, sees her own face reflected in the mirror. She can't help thinking of all that money, left sitting in the boot of her Y10. At all costs she has to try to retrieve that suitcase. But for now the best thing is to try to relax, sleep, recover her strength.

*

"Excuse me, did you already have the X-rays?"

The Bear tries to stay calm.

"For that matter, they've given me the results."

"Then come," the nurse says to him, gesturing with her hand.

The Bear gets up from the bench, passes a boy lying on a gurney, enters the clinic.

"What did the technician tell you?" the nurse asks, taking the sheets out of the light-brown envelope.

The Bear gives a snort of impatience.

"I don't know. Wound with lacerations and bruising, I think. And possible cranial trauma."

"You certainly had a good knock. But how did you do it? Did you bump into something?"

The Bear gives her a homicidal glance and the nurse lets it go. She shrugs her shoulders, slips the X-rays back into the envelope.

"All right, sit down and wait here. The doctor will be here in five minutes."

*

When Leila comes back into the room, Francesco is sitting in the chair smoking a cigarette.

"There were no mice, anyway," she says. "That's something."

"There used to be some, but they complained about the hygiene and ended up moving to the sewers."

"They're certainly fussy. I can assure you I've seen worse."

164

"Are you sleepy?"

"Exhausted."

"Listen, this is a sofa-bed. If you give me a hand, we can move it into the hallway and I'll manage there."

Leila inclines her head, smiles.

"If you're doing it for me, it doesn't matter. You can sleep here too. I trust you."

Francesco scratches his neck.

"Well, if it doesn't bother you," he says, putting out the butt in the ashtray. "OK, then. We avoid a hell of a job. Do you snore very loudly?"

Leila bursts out laughing, tossing her hair back.

"No, I don't think so. Do you?"

Saturday, 3 April 1993, 9 A.M.–4 P.M.

The murderers calmly measure their numbered days
perched like nocturnal birds on their guns
whose triggers they are about to pull
as one plays a card knowing one is going to lose
in the morning the shots fly around like handcuffs.

Léo Ferré, *The Death of Wolves*

From the crowd in the apartment you'd think it was an end-of-the-season sale. Cops, stretcher-bearers, photographers, medical examiner, even a couple of reporters whom no one has bothered to get rid of. Commissioner Roccaforte, hands in his pockets, is looking out the window. He stares at the broad path that cuts through the park across the street. A man in a green raincoat walks a cocker spaniel on a long retractable leash. The Commissioner puts another Nazionale in his mouth.

"Excuse me, sir, can we take the dead man away?"

"What, Loiacono? Oh, the body. Yes. I think so. What did the doctor say?"

"He said he's finished and he's going to have breakfast."

"Then yes, take it away."

Roccaforte clicks his lighter. Already the tenth cigarette of the day and it's barely nine o'clock. Not a bad start.

Loiacono turns to the stretcher men, claps his hands.

"OK, now let's clear him out. Let's go, boys, zip it up."

Farina, the medical examiner, approaches the Commissioner.

"Poor guy, they really did a job on him. Want to go down and get a coffee?"

"No, not yet. I'll have another look around, then maybe I'll join you."

"As you like. I'll be at the bar just around the corner."

Roccaforte nods, and inhales. He feels the smoke scrape his lungs.

Loiacono is getting rid of the reporters.

"Please, boys. *Pul-ease.* You can't stay there, what language do I have to speak?"

Roccaforte feels his headache getting worse. He taps the ash into the palm of his hand. What the hell happened here last night? Why did the murderer persist so savagely? Farina said that almost certainly the victim was alive the whole time he was being tortured. A maniac? Could be. Or a spectacular settling of accounts, to serve as an example. Meanwhile he has finished his cigarette. Using his handkerchief he opens the window, careful not to touch it with his fingers. He leans out and looks down. He lets the butt and the ashes that have gathered fall. He closes the window, puts the handkerchief in his pocket, wipes his hand on his pants. When he turns, he is facing Loiacono, standing stiffly in his uniform.

"I told you. Quite a butchery, eh, sir? Shall I go ahead and question the residents of the building?"

"Yes, go on, Loiacono, go on. See if you can find out anything about the victim. How long he'd been living here, job, habits, et cetera, et cetera."

Loiacono clicks his heels and goes off.

"Oh, Loiacono!"

"Yes, sir?"

"Call headquarters and light a fire under the boys. In half an hour I want to know everything there is to know about this Andrea Fabbri. Am I clear?"

"I'll take care of it, sir! Don't worry."

The Commissioner nods, yawns inside his closed fist. The signs of torture on the body might indicate an attempt to get information. It could turn out that this Fabbri was involved in some shady operation. Roccaforte turns towards the window again. The man with the dog is no longer in sight.

*

He feels something hard pressing against his ribs, half opens his eyes with a grunt. The light from the window is faint, but he can make out clearly the square outline of the closet. His neck hurts and his left arm is numb. He moves his hand down along his side. His fingers meet the metal of the sax. He lifts his body just enough to extricate the instrument from the covers. He places it on the floor. The reed has splintered.

He must have played for a while before falling asleep. But the music didn't help him get anywhere. The girl, her random journeys with the suitcase, Garofano and Diolaiti, the police sirens. Sooner or later he'll have to telephone the Secretary, to report that the exchange came to nothing. He has a terrible taste in his mouth. His left arm is still tingling. He rotates his wrist to look at his watch. Seven-ten. He sneezes four times, one after the other. Then he lets his head fall back on the pillow.

After half an hour he gets up to go to the bathroom

to pee. He turns on the tap, throws cold water on his face. To gain a little more time, he decides to shave. He shakes the shaving-cream can hard, sprays some cream onto the palm of his hand. He distributes it on his chin, his cheeks, his neck. He goes back to his room to turn on the radio, then plants himself in front of the mirror. He brings the razor towards his right cheek, draws it down from the hairline on the side, following the line of the jaw.

When the news comes on, he puts the razor down on the edge of the sink, hurriedly turns off the tap and goes in to turn up the volume. One of the first news items has to do with a crime the previous night. But the announcer reports that the victim is a man. Of the girl not a word. Matera sits on the bed, half his face covered with shaving cream, and listens to the rest of the news story. The police, called by building residents, arrived and discovered the body of a young man, completely naked, tied to a chair. The body was disfigured by numerous wounds, made by a weapon with a very sharp blade. Probably a scalpel or a razor. Of the culprit, or culprits, for the moment no trace. The victim has been identified. Andrea Fabbri, twenty-eight, born in Bologna, had been living in Rome for some time on account of work.

The name hits Matera like a hammer. Andrea Fabbri! It's not possible. Is it the Andrea Fabbri he knows? Of course! He disappeared a couple of weeks ago, and no one seemed to know where he had gone. And every time he tried to ask about him, the Secretary found a way of not answering!

Struck by a kind of illumination, for an instant he seems to see the whole picture. That ass-licking Fabbri must somehow have come into possession of some compromising document and decided to blackmail the Minister. Somehow, the intelligence services must have found out about the exchange and stuck their noses into it, causing the screw-up. It's not impossible that Fabbri himself let them know. Maybe that jerk put the document up for auction, to try and get as much as possible. If the Minister didn't pay up, he could have handed it over to whoever made the best offer.

After a moment, though, the picture that seemed so clear clouds again, and while he finishes shaving the uncertainties increase. What the hell could have happened in that apartment while he was waiting down in the street? Was it Garofano and Diolaiti who killed Fabbri? And where in the world did the girl come from? Does she also work for intelligence? And, above all, what has become of her?

A few minutes later, as he knots his tie before the mirror, Matera decides that, before taking any other initiative, he must absolutely call the Secretary. The moment has arrived to seek counsel.

*

Garofano shakes himself abruptly, alarmed by a noise that has interrupted his sleep. He remains motionless, trying to figure out where the hell he is. The noise is repeated and he raises his head. In front of him is the screen of a television that is on with the sound turned down. A man and woman smile in his direction. The man is wearing a jacket and tie, but on his head is a ridiculous silver, sequin-covered pointed hat. The woman adjusts the angle of the hat and the man's response is to look like a moron, imitating Stan Laurel when he laughs while he's scratching his head. Garofano looks around. He is lying on a couch. And it's the apartment of that little whore!

From the bedroom comes another sound. Garofano looks for his gun. He sees the holster hanging on an arm of the sofa. He reaches out and grabs the .45. He takes off the safety. He places his feet softly on the floor. Without putting on his shoes, he walks cautiously towards the other room. He leans carefully around the doorway.

Diolaiti is looking in the wardrobe. Garofano sticks the gun in the waistband of his trousers, enters scratching one ear.

"Tell me, do you have insomnia on top of everything else?"

Diolaiti turns suddenly.

"Oh, you finally woke up! I thought you might go on snoring till noon."

Garofano yawns, stretches his back, pats the comb-over into place.

"What are you doing? Looking for porn magazines?"

Diolaiti pulls out a drawer. He overturns the contents onto the floor. With the tip of his shoe he kicks a pile of knickers.

"I'm looking around, just to resolve some doubts."

"Good idea," Garofano says, massaging his neck. "And have you found anything?"

Diolaiti lets the empty drawer fall on the pile of underwear. He pulls out another one.

"Nothing interesting. But I'm sure that this apartment isn't any kind of cover. There are clothes for every season, lipsticks, perfumes, creams. And also supplies. Toilet paper, soap, cans of food."

Garofano nods, while with one finger he picks something out of his eye.

"Full-size bed with one pillow," he says, looking at the mattress. "And in the bathroom only one toothbrush. She lives alone."

"And she doesn't see many people, to judge from her address book."

"Doesn't mean anything. She may have another one somewhere with more important numbers. Have you found anything to do with our business?"

"So far not even a hint."

"Any idea about what she does?"

Diolaiti shakes his head, pulls out another drawer.

"No pay slips, no client lists, nothing of that sort. If she works, she may have an office where she keeps all that. But I doubt it."

Garofano sneers, looking at the mountain of stuff piled on the floor. He picks up a pair of black knickers and buries his nose in them, inhaling deeply.

"Mmm . . . You mean she gets by on giving it away?"

"Or she has some money put aside."

"All right," Garofano says, throwing the knickers on the pile again. "What do you say I make us a little breakfast? I've got a really vile taste in my mouth."

"How surprising. Maybe it's that mountain of spaghetti you finished off last night?"

"Or maybe it's that I slept on the couch."

"Oh, of course. And now what do you think we should do?"

"Besides breakfast?"

"Besides breakfast, obviously."

"In my opinion, for the moment the best thing is to station ourselves here and wait for the bitch to show up."

"She's not going to come back. She knows we have her handbag and her documents."

"True. But what's our alternative? The two main players in this game are both dead, we haven't managed to find the documents, and we've let the only person who could tell us something get away."

172

"A nice picture. The chief will certainly be satisfied."

"Listen to me, Diolaiti. Good or bad, that is the situation. And now we're starting again from zero. Where do you think the whore slept?"

"A hotel?"

"I don't think she's that stupid. But no harm in calling Alvisi and getting him to check."

"We might as well inform the chief. We'll have to report something."

"Breakfast first, Diolaiti. One doesn't reason well on an empty stomach."

*

Even through the Secretary's usual enigmatic circumlocutions Matera has had his suspicions confirmed. Behind this whole business is a blackmail scheme devised by that boy with the designer jackets who, during the past two years, has been performing confidential duties for the Minister. Fabbri must have thought it was better to take a shortcut rather than waste time and energy and risk waiting in a lot of waiting rooms forever.

The long silence that comes from the other end of the telephone is a clear sign that the Secretary isn't satisfied with how things are going. How can you say he's wrong? But Matera has no intention of taking the blame. He has nothing to do with the fact that the intelligence services and that girl out of nowhere have got mixed up in it.

"Did you at least retrieve the money?"

"Yes, I still have both suitcases."

"That's something. But what worries me is the document. I can't understand what this girl you've mentioned has to do with it. What do you think? Is she an accomplice of Fabbri or of intelligence?"

"The truth is," Matera says, scratching one cheek, "I was hoping you could tell me."

"Did you say you have her name?"

"Not exactly. But I've written down her licence plate number."

"Bravo, you've done well. Let's hope it really is hers. I'll look into it, and let you know."

Matera reads out the licence plate number of the Y10.

"Now listen to me. I'll make a couple of phone calls, to try to slow down the investigation and prepare the ground for it. I don't want the exchange Fabbri was involved in to become public, and I think I can count on a certain amount of cooperation. Naturally, you'll have to take care of things in person. I'll call you back."

*

To wash the coffeepot, Francesco had to shift to one side the mass of dirty dishes that have accumulated in the sink. Leila, still wearing the T-shirt and boxers he lent her, observes his manoeuvres as she smokes a cigarette, standing with her back against the credenza.

He barely managed to close his eyes. He kept touching his back, in the darkness, as he listened to the breathing of the girl who was sleeping in his bed. At a certain point it seemed to him that she was talking in her sleep. Some incomprehensible bits of sentences as he moved his fingers along his lower spine, trying to figure out if the Bear had cracked any vertebrae. He kept changing positions, unable to find one in which his back didn't hurt. Around eleven he couldn't stand it any longer. He got up, trying not to make any noise. He went to sit in the kitchen and to pass the time had begun to leaf through a magazine from a couple of months ago. After a quarter of an hour she appeared in the doorway, with her hair dishevelled and the T-shirt rumpled. She smiled at him as she rubbed her eyes, wished him good morning. He smiled back, pretending to be in a good mood.

"Can I take a cigarette?" she asked, pointing to the pack lying on the table.

He nodded affirmatively, then closed the magazine and got up to make coffee. While he emptied the filter, he tried to recall when he last had breakfast with a girl in that kitchen. Maybe with Monica, at the beginning of October, before things went definitively to the dogs.

While he waits for the coffee, Francesco too lights an MS. Then he sits down, reaches an arm across the table to move the ashtray closer. He has to make an effort to take his eyes off Leila's slender thighs. He sits there, smoking, trying to think of something to say.

"So did you sleep well?"

"I did, yes. But you, on that chair, I don't think so. I heard you moving around all night."

"My back was hurting."

"I can believe it. With the beating you got. I can't understand why you feel guilty for giving that monster a crack in the head."

"Guilt doesn't have anything to do with it. I'm thinking of the next time I run into him."

The coffeepot starts gurgling. Francesco gets up, a little stiffly, to turn off the gas. He rummages in the cabinet in search of a couple of cups, but finds only an old aluminium pot, a stem glass and a big red cup with a broken handle. He takes out the cup and the glass. He pours the coffee, offering the chalice to Leila.

"How chic! I've never had coffee in a champagne glass!"

"Sorry, but as you see my kitchen is a bit of a mess."

Francesco lets a spoonful of sugar fall into his own cup.

"Forget it," Leila says. "It was really nice of you to have me."

He makes a gesture with his hand, as if to say *don't even mention it.*

"Not counting the fact that you didn't try to take advantage of the situation. I wanted to tell you that that really was a pleasure."

"You know how it is, we gentlemen of the old school are made like that. Our house may be swarming with ants, but we don't let go of our code of honour."

Leila smiles.

"Ants? On the third floor?"

"Climber ants, obviously. They love heights and they must have got attached to the apartment."

"Where are they?"

Francesco lifts a finger in the direction of the window.

"Down there, between the sink and the wall. I've tried everything, but can't seem to get rid of them."

"Did you try salt?"

"No, but I've used all kinds of commercial insecticides. No good. In fact, I think that, all in all, they like insecticide."

"Listen to me, sprinkle salt along the corner where they come in, and you'll see, they'll go away."

"Salt?" Francesco asks, not entirely convinced.

"It's the most effective thing," Leila says, taking another MS from the pack. "Try it and you'll see."

*

Garofano hangs up the receiver. Diolaiti looks questioningly at him.

"What does he say? Is he nervous?"

"No, what makes you think that?" Garofano answers, putting out his cigarette on a dirty plate. "He's in excellent humour. He swore that if we don't find that girl, he'll break our balls with his own hands."

Diolaiti shakes his head then pulls the handkerchief out of his pocket and dries his right eye.

"The chief," Garofano continues, "says that he'll have Alvisi look for the girl's record and that he'll get busy to make sure the police don't arrest her. But we have to find her. That document seems to be of great concern to him."

He gets up and with the palm of his hand smooths the comb-over on his bald head.

"You want to know what I think? I think that the bitch had nothing at all to do with it. She must have ended up there by mistake."

"That would mean she's not a professional."

"I don't like dealing with amateurs. It's true that you can hope for a false move, but at the same time you never know what to expect from them."

"I see you're optimistic today."

Garofano looks at his watch.

"Tell me, how's your ulcer?"

Diolaiti twists his mouth.

"Who ever said I had an ulcer? I hope it's only gastritis."

"If you have nothing against it, I'm going to start cooking something to eat. I found a bag of aubergines in the refrigerator. I thought of making a nice *parmigiana*."

Diolaiti seeks in the eyes of his comrade a sign to confirm that he's joking, but Garofano widens his mouth in a broad smile.

"What do you say? Is your mouth watering?"

Francesco, lying on the bed, is enjoying the back massage that Leila is giving him.

"Ah! There, right there it hurts like hell."

"I can believe it. You've got a frightful bruise."

"You know what? I have half a mind not to go to work tonight."

"Good idea. Is it better?"

"Yes, thanks."

Leila's hands go back up towards the shoulders, loosen the stiff neck muscles. Francesco closes his eyes and relaxes, while the fingers slide over his skin with deep, decisive movements.

"Mmm . . . how lovely . . ."

After a few minutes, Leila gets up.

"There you go," she says, cracking her knuckles.

"Just what I needed," Francesco murmurs, with a blissful expression, his eyes still closed.

Leila sits on the edge of the bed. She lights two cigarettes and hands one to him. Her gaze is drawn to a small poster on the opposite wall. The photograph shows a beach with blue water, palm trees, and sand as white as powder. Leila has the impression she's seen that image somewhere.

"Where is that? Cuba? Costa Rica? Jamaica?"

Francesco half opens his eyes, barely raises his head.

"I don't know. It was an advertisement for a travel agency on the bus. I liked it. I took it down and brought it home. I cut off the writing."

Last night, on the bus. That's where she saw it.

"Anyway, I think it's the Caribbean. I've been around there."

"In the Caribbean?"

Leila blows smoke out of her nose and nods.

"I travelled around half South America. A long time ago."

Francesco turns onto his back, puts an arm under his neck.

"My dream is to go and live in a place like that. The hell with all this, the city, the buses, the traffic, the rent, everything, go and live in a hut on the beach. An ordinary one. Until I feel like changing huts. Or beaches. Or seas. People who've been there tell me there's an embarrassment of choices."

Leila turns towards him.

"If you're so eager to do it, why don't you?"

Francesco stretches his arm towards the night table, taps his cigarette in the ashtray, then picks it up and places it on his stomach.

"Who knows? Look, you see that other photo on the wall?"

"The photo of Naomi naked?" she asks, smiling.

"Farther to the right. The one with all those marks."

Leila squints and observes the rectangle of paper he's pointing to, tacked to the wall with four drawing pins.

"What does it look like to you?" Francesco asks.

"I don't know. A big spider web."

"It's a map of Bologna."

"A map of Bologna?"

"The plan of the streets, traced from a topographical map. But you're not far wrong. The way I see it, that's just what it is. A big spider web, in which I am trapped. I know those streets by heart, but I can't get out of them. For years I've had a kind of obsession to leave this city, and I haven't done it."

"But why not?"

Francesco shrugs.

"For one reason or another. For example, I have no money."

"I don't buy that. If you seriously want something, you always find the money for it."

"You're right. Basically, rather than losing a ton of money at cards, I could have bought myself a one-way ticket and goodbye. I don't know, maybe I lack the courage."

"Courage?"

Francesco takes a drag on his cigarette, blows the smoke out towards the blue sea of the photograph.

"Yes. It isn't easy to throw over everything and change your life from one day to the next. Habits, friends, the places you go."

"But you've got a lot of troubles here. Or am I wrong?"

"You even get used to that."

Leila smiles, puts out her cigarette in the ashtray on the night table. She's silent for a few moments. Then she gets up, stretching her arms.

"Can I take a shower?"

"Go ahead. I could take advantage of that to wash that mountain of dishes in the sink. Otherwise the next time I'll have to drink the coffee right out of the pot."

Leila stops on the threshold.

"Sorry, but do you have anything I could wear?"

Francesco swings his legs down from the bed and scratches his head, with the cigarette butt in the corner of his mouth.

"Wait, I'll have a look. Whatever it is, you'll have to adjust it."

He manages to dig up a pair of cotton socks, a blue sweater, a leather belt, some old jeans that are tight on him and even a pair of sneakers that Monica left, who knows when.

"I'm afraid this is all I have to offer."

180

"It will do very well," Leila says, heading for the bathroom. "I'll be five minutes. Then the bathroom's all yours."

*

The Secretary's voice sounds preoccupied. And its cadence is more rapid than usual.

"I have the information about the owner of the car. Do you have a pen?"

"Yes."

"Then take this down. The car belongs to a certain Leila Ronchi, born in Venice 3/5/1960, living in Bologna, in Via Borgo di San Pietro, number 16. It turns out that she has never had any contact with the intelligence services. From what I was told, it doesn't seem likely that she was directly involved in our exchange. This Ronchi has had some brushes with the law in the past. But a matter of ordinary crimes, unremarkable. Do you think this could be the person you followed?"

Matera thinks back to the girl in black, but what he recalls above all is her legs, her beautiful legs, and her way of walking. And the dark helmet of hair.

"I don't know. Yes, it could be her. The age more or less coincides."

"Good. Now let's go to the second point. I've learned that the commissioner charged with the investigation is a man called Roccaforte."

"Roccaforte?"

"Does the name mean something to you?"

"I knew him personally several years ago. When I worked in Bologna."

"All to the good. The first thing you have to do is get in touch with him. I've already spoken with the appropriate authority, and I'm sure that Roccaforte will do his best to meet our requirements. Try to find out what they've discovered up to now. Then get busy tracing the girl. The Minister and I are counting on you. Keep us informed."

Matera immediately tried headquarters, but Commissioner Roccaforte wasn't there. When he asked where he could find him, they said he had gone back to Via Battistelli, for a last inspection before sealing the apartment.

*

The Commissioner takes out the creased pack of Nazionali.

"May I smoke?"

"But of course," Sacchetti answers. "Please, go ahead."

The Commissioner lights the cigarette, blows the smoke out towards the ceiling. Sacchetti's wife gets up and goes to open a window.

"So, you heard a noise on the stairs."

"To be precise, my wife was the first to be aware of it. Isn't that right, Luisa?"

The woman nods in agreement and places a crystal ashtray, perfectly clean, on the little table in front of the Commissioner. Then she sits down again.

"And what did you do?"

"We got up and looked through the peephole."

"Who looked?" asks the Commissioner, addressing the wife.

"Him," she says dryly.

"Good," Roccaforte says, tapping the cigarette in the polished ashtray. "And what did you see?"

"At a certain point a stranger went by."

The Commissioner checks the notes on his pad.

182

"You said the man was armed."

"Oh yes, indeed! He had a gun!"

"Can you describe him?"

Sacchetti shakes his head, with an expression of regret.

"Well, I don't know . . . He didn't have much hair, and it seemed to me that he was quite large . . ."

"Do you mean fat? Or muscular?"

"Commissioner, try to understand, I saw him only for a moment. And when I realized that he was armed . . ."

The *ding-dong* of the doorbell interrupts Sacchetti's sentence. His wife gets up, goes towards the entrance.

"You see, yes. He had a very big gun. I was struck by the length of the barrel."

"It probably had a silencer," Roccaforte concludes, blowing out the smoke.

The ballistics expert from forensics appears on the threshold.

"Excuse me, Commissioner, could you come here a moment?"

"Yes, here I am," Roccaforte says, putting out his cigarette in the ashtray. "You'll excuse me a moment? I'll be right back."

The expert leads the Commissioner to the main floor, has him enter the lift, points the beam of the flashlight at the holes made by the bullets. They have ripped right through the metal.

"Good lord, what holes! What calibre is it?"

"A .45, I'd say."

The Commissioner pinches the lobe of one ear.

"If he had hit his target, we would have found another body."

*

If there's one thing in his life that functions regularly, it's his intestines. In general, in the morning, after coffee and a couple of cigarettes, something in his guts begins to move. And this morning is no exception. So for the moment he forgets about washing the dishes. He opens the kitchen window and, while he waits for the girl to finish her shower, lights another cigarette. From outside come the notes of a song by U2 and a smell of fried onions. Francesco leans on the sill, looks down. In the doorway of a garage two boys are messing with the engine of a Vespa. A woman with bleached hair and a flowered apron is hanging laundry on a clothesline stretched from one balcony to another.

Leila reappears rubbing her hair with a towel. She is beautiful even in that assortment of ill-fitting clothes. Francesco tosses the butt down into the courtyard.

"If you're finished," he says, trying to appear casual, "I'm going into the bathroom for a moment."

As he's about to go into the toilet, he suddenly feels embarrassed at the idea that she might hear him. He goes rapidly to the bedroom and turns on the stereo. He chooses the first record he happens on, an old David Bowie album, and sets the volume on high.

He sits on the toilet, protected by Mick Ronson's piano and the Thin White Duke's voice, as, outside the bathroom door, he sings: "The boy in the bright blue jeans jumped up on the stage." He wonders where that girl came from and what in the world could have happened to her last night, before she got on the bus. He tries to imagine what she intends to do now. As far as he understands, she hasn't a penny and maybe no place to go. And yet her clothes appear rather expensive. He looks up and examines them, hanging on a hook next to the shower. They are not the clothes of someone who spends the night in a sleeping bag on the floor of a squat, or on a bench in the train station. What's keeping her from going home? And if she really lost her keys, why the hell doesn't she simply call a locksmith and have him open the door? There must be something behind this that she hasn't told him.

Francesco tears some paper from the roll. The girl said she appreciated his behaviour, and he wonders what would have happened if he had tried to get in the bed. When all is said and done, maybe it was better that way. He is not at all sure that he would have managed to get up to much, with his back hurting like this.

*

Loiacono halts suddenly and raises the palm of his hand to chest height, to signal Matera to stop and wait. Then he executes a stiff about-face and crosses the room diagonally, heading towards Commissioner Roccaforte, who, talking on the phone, merely gives him an interrogative nod. Loiacono bends his left arm, signalling with his thumb towards a point behind him. The Commissioner follows the trajectory indicated and sees a fairly tall, grey-haired man, muscular but heavy, standing a little beyond the threshold and looking in their direction.

"I'm going to be here a little longer," the Commissioner says, continuing his telephone conversation. "If you find out anything, call me at the same number."

"Sir," Loiacono informs him, as soon as he hangs up, "this gentleman says he wants to talk to you."

"Yes, certainly. Come in."

He lights another cigarette, makes a sign to Matera to approach. He observes him as he walks and it seems to him that there is something unsteady in his gait, as if

185

he were limping slightly. Matera hints at a smile, gives him a broad hand, the back covered with grey hairs.

"Commissioner Roccaforte, do you remember me?"

"Of course," the Commissioner says, shaking his hand. "But I have to admit that I was surprised when I was told that a certain Signor Matera was coming to speak to me. I wondered if it would be the one I knew, or someone with the same name."

The other smiles.

"My job has changed a bit since the last time we saw each other."

"Yes, I imagine it has."

Matera tries to remember what sort of policeman Roccaforte was. Someone you could reason with? In any case he has surely accepted some compromises. Who knows how far he will be disposed to cooperate?

"You see, as the person who informed you of my arrival must already have explained to you, the situation is very . . ."

The telephone begins to ring. The Commissioner gestures with his hand.

"Excuse me a moment," he says before lifting the receiver. "Hello? Yes, it's me. Ah, excellent, I didn't expect such a quick response. Yes, I agree. Until later then."

He hangs up, then fixes his gaze again on Matera.

"What were you saying?"

"Therefore, I imagine you understand that the situation is very delicate. I think it would be in the interest of everyone if you and I can cooperate."

The Commissioner makes a sign of agreement, exhales the smoke downward.

"You mention cooperation. Do you think you might have some information for me?"

Matera widens his arms in a shrug, but Commissioner

Roccaforte, even before he begins to speak, interrupts him.

"Excuse me, I've finished here for now. And it's almost time for lunch. What do you say we continue the conversation over some pasta? There's a trattoria nearby where the food isn't bad."

Matera smiles, caught off guard.

"Certainly. Why not? That sounds excellent to me."

*

Leila finishes rubbing her hair, hangs the towel on the back of a chair. She combs her hair as well as she can with the tips of her fingers. She can't get that suitcase full of money out of her mind, sitting in the boot of her Y10. It's her only hope, she absolutely has to retrieve it as soon as possible.

On the kitchen table is a pack of cigarettes. She shakes it, realizes it's empty. She opens a couple of drawers in the cabinet in search of another, but she finds only a deck of cards, two non-matching napkins, some rubber bands, a stapler, a pair of dishtowels, some old postcards.

She goes into the bedroom, deafened by the voice of Bowie, who from the speaker is shouting, "and Lady Stardust sang his songs of darkness and disgrace". She glances into the drawer of the night table. She finds a ball-point pen, an old Zenith wristwatch with a splintered face, a couple of buttons and a wallet. The holes in the leather watchband are torn, and the watch's hands are stopped at nine twenty-five. She looks up at the door. She takes the wallet, opens it. Inside are two 10,000-lire bills, one fifty and a few thousands. She bites her lower lip. That money would be useful. If she wants to get her car, she has to get something to force the lock with and strip the wires. It's true, she could ask Francesco, but he would have questions, and she would have to invent a plausible story to palm him off with. Meanwhile the money is there, within reach. Since when has she hesitated in the face of a good opportunity? David Bowie is singing, "Femmes fatales emerged from shadows", and the door of the bathroom, for the moment, is still closed. If she wants to take it, she has to decide in a hurry.

Rapidly she tries to calculate risks and advantages. The teargas spray is right there in front of her, on the shelf of the night table. She shakes the can. It's almost empty, but what remains could be useful. She puts it in the back pocket of the jeans, takes the 50,000 out of the wallet. Then she puts everything back and closes the drawer.

From the hook in the hallway she grabs a blue canvas jacket, careful not to bump the dangerous shelf and the bicycle leaning against the wall. Gently she closes the door, just as the last notes of Bowie's song sound.

As she goes down the stairs, she realizes that her shoes are untied.

*

Commissioner Roccaforte picks up the carafe, fills their glasses with white wine.

"Do you have any idea how much he was spending on rent, the man who was killed last night?"

Matera looks at him without responding.

"A million two hundred thousand a month," the Commissioner says, putting the carafe down on the table. "Not bad, eh? What do you think about that?"

"I don't see . . ."

"I've tried to reconstruct the victim's movements.

188

Let me summarize for you. Fabbri arrives in Bologna about three weeks ago and goes to a rental agency to find an apartment. He puts down four months' rent as a deposit, for a place with cooking facilities. Bologna is expensive; if you want to find a house in a hurry, you have to be willing not to be fussy and to pay. For Fabbri, money doesn't seem to be a problem. He pays, he settles in the new place. Unfortunately, he didn't get to enjoy his stay for long. After less than a month he's murdered."

The Commissioner interrupts himself to take a swallow of wine. Then he plants his eyes on Matera's face again.

"Second instalment. We arrive at the place and try to get some idea of what happened. While I'm starting the routine procedures, I get a couple of phone calls. It seems that this investigation is of concern to some bigwig. I'm given to understand that it isn't worth going too far. Someone informs me that a certain Signor Matera is coming to see me, and that I am to do whatever I can to be useful. Well, here we are. But don't think that in the meantime I've been sitting here twiddling my thumbs. It didn't take much to get a little information about Fabbri. I know who he worked for. I imagine it's the same person who sent you here. Am I mistaken?"

"No, you're not mistaken."

Commissioner Roccaforte seems satisfied. He smiles, takes a Nazionale out of the pack. He taps it on the table.

"As soon as I knew whose lackey Fabbri was, I realized that I was in a minefield. As you see, there was no need for you to come and tell me that."

Matera can't figure out what's going on in the policeman's mind.

"May I ask what else you've found out?"

The Commissioner lights the cigarette, stares at it for a few seconds, before he answers.

"Between the sheets, for instance, we found something interesting. A couple of dark hairs, some pubic hair and a bunch of keys that didn't open any doors in the house. Neither the apartment nor the entrance to the building."

The waiter arrives with two steaming plates.

"The *tagliatelle al ragù*?"

"For me, thanks," the Commissioner says. He stubs out the burning end of the cigarette he just lit and rests it on an indentation in the rim of the ashtray.

"And the *maccheroni alla boscaiola* for you," the waiter says, leaning over to set the plate in front of Matera. "*Buon appetito.*"

The Commissioner sprinkles cheese on his tagliatelle.

"On those keys we found the prints of a person who has had some trouble with the law in the past. A woman."

Matera jumps in with a guess.

"Is her name by any chance Leila Ronchi?"

Commissioner Roccaforte is twirling tagliatelle onto his fork. He interrupts himself, looks at Matera.

"I see you are very well informed. Do you also know if she's the one who murdered Fabbri?"

"That I can't tell you. But, if you want my opinion, I'm pretty certain that someone else is behind the homicide."

"In fact, Ronchi's record shows crimes of a completely different type. Several years ago, she was mixed up with a group of small-time criminals involved in smuggling, receiving stolen goods and auto theft. I would be amazed if she were responsible for a murder."

"Have you arrested her?"

The Commissioner shakes his head, as he continues to chew.

For a few minutes the two men are busy eating their pasta, sunk in their own thoughts.

"If you don't mind, Commissioner, I'd like to ask you a couple of favours."

Roccaforte nods. He wipes his mouth with the napkin, takes a swallow of wine.

"Sooner or later we would have got to that. Go ahead."

"First of all, I'd like to ask the maximum discretion concerning this case and what I am about to tell you." Matera clears his throat and tries to imagine the diplomatic formulas the Secretary would use to explain to the Commissioner what is expected of him. "You realize that if anyone knew about the collaboration of Fabbri and the Minister . . ."

"I understand, don't worry. Go on."

"I would be grateful if you would keep me informed of developments in the investigation, and . . ."

"And?"

"If it's not asking too much, I think it would be better, at least for the moment, not to continue the official investigations of Ronchi."

"You won't believe it, but someone else just asked me the same favour."

"Ah! May I ask who?"

"You have no idea?"

"The intelligence services?"

"Bravo. You've hit the bull's-eye on the first shot."

Matera's pupils are clouded. The Commissioner puts another forkful of tagliatelle in his mouth and looks at him, chewing in silence for a few seconds.

"This girl," Roccaforte says, "seems to know a lot of influential people who are concerned about her."

Matera shakes his head.

"Yes. It does seem that way."

"In any case, even if you're sure she's not the killer, it seems to me clear that, one way or another, she must be involved. You understand that I can't pretend not to notice. For how long am I to suspend my investigations?"

"Twenty-four hours."

"You know it's like asking me to let her escape." The Commissioner slowly sips his wine. "On the other hand, with the type of pressure I've had, I am more or less obliged to agree. Let's talk about us. Can I really count on your cooperation, in exchange for these favours?"

"I give you my word. But I warn you that, if things are as I think they are, you won't be very happy to know who is responsible for the crime."

"Excuse me, Matera, with all due respect, I'm the one who's stuck with these crimes. If you don't mind, I would prefer to know something about them."

"Crimes?"

"Maybe you're not up to date yet. So let me inform you. Tonight, along the A14, in a field next to a rest stop, another body was found."

"On the A14? And what makes you think that the two homicides are connected?"

"The body left beside the autostrada has a series of wounds very similar to Fabbri's. But there's something else. The victim is a man named Roberto Magagnoli. From the early investigations we learn that this Magagnoli lived in Bologna and got by doing occasional jobs. Bouncer in a discotheque, messenger, security guard at the stadium. His record wasn't immaculate. Nothing big, let's be clear. A couple of arrests for threatening behaviour, fights, a little drug dealing, you follow? Good, now listen closely. Magagnoli was the same age as Fabbri, and it turns out that the two victims knew each other. Until he was twenty, Fabbri, too, lived in Bologna, and the two went to the same school. Classmates and, it seems, close friends. Over time, they took very different roads. But it's not impossible that they kept in contact. At this point, what would your hypothesis be?"

"I don't know. Fabbri could have asked Magagnoli for help, involving him in an affair that cost both of them their lives."

The Commissioner retrieves the extinguished cigarette from the edge of the ashtray, relights it.

"That also seems to me among the most likely hypotheses. And I asked myself what the affair could be."

"And what conclusions did you reach?"

"It wasn't all that difficult. When I found out who Fabbri worked for, I smelled a rat. If the aide to a politician that powerful is tortured and murdered, a lot of suspicions begin to buzz around in my head. When, afterwards, the big shots take the trouble to try to keep my investigation under control, these suspicions are transformed into certainties. Another drop of wine?"

Matera signals yes, the Commissioner again refills the glasses.

"If you want to know what I think, I think that Fabbri, with the help and complicity of his old schoolmate Magagnoli, has attempted blackmail. It doesn't matter if I tell you who, in my view, is the person being blackmailed."

The waiter approaches the table.

"May I?" he asks, indicating the empty plates.

The Commissioner pulls on his Nazionale, nods. Then he asks Matera: "Will you have something else?"

He opens the menu, while the waiter goes off with the dirty plates balanced on his forearm. Commissioner Roccaforte shifts his weight and leans back in his chair, looking at Matera, who is scanning the list.

"All right," the Commissioner says. "I'll do what you ask. But don't you make a mess for me too because, between you and me, I don't enjoy washing other people's dirty laundry. I'll give you twenty-four hours. And I'll trust you at your word. For the moment, I won't continue the investigation into Ronchi. But if you find out anything regarding either of the two murders, you'll call and let me know. Are we agreed?"

*

Francesco comes out of the bathroom.

"You know what I was thinking?" he says, then realizes that she can't hear him because the music is too loud.

He goes into the bedroom, lowers the volume.

"Alessandra," he repeats, in a loud voice. "You know what I was thinking?"

No answer. He goes into the kitchen. The girl isn't there, either. Francesco remains standing, hands in his pockets, staring at the towel hanging on the chair. After a few seconds, he leans over the table to grab the pack of cigarettes. It's empty. He crumples it and throws it back on the table.

He looks disconsolately at the stack of dirty dishes. Come on, sooner or later they have to get done. He looks for the rubber gloves. He finds only the left, stuck under a dirty saucepan. As he puts it on, he realizes it's torn. He throws it in the waste basket and rolls up his sleeves. He reaches one hand down to stick the plug in the drain. He pours a generous amount of detergent on the heap of dishes, runs hot water until the basin is filled. He begins to wash a cup, a couple of glasses, some silverware. Suddenly he stops, with a plate in midair. He puts it back on the pile, washes the soap off his hands and goes into the bedroom.

He opens the drawer of the night table. His wallet is still in its place. He can't be mistaken about the amount because it was the last of his cash. Of the 74,000 lire, however, only 24,000 remain. He looks in the change compartment. A 500-lire piece and two fifties fall onto his palm.

He goes back into the kitchen, tapping the wallet against the tip of his nose. His gaze falls on the sink. To hell with the dishes. His back hurts, and he doesn't feel like washing them. He drags himself back to the bedroom, falls onto the bed. He places the wallet on his stomach and lies there, on his back, staring at the ceiling, which has needed painting for a long time.

Fifty thousand, more or less, with all the debts he has, is a drop in the ocean. But the situation depresses him anyway. If she needed money, she could have asked him, couldn't she? He wonders why she didn't take it all. Maybe she went to buy a carton of cigarettes. He turns this hypothesis over in his head for a while, without convincing himself.

*

On the table are two glasses, one half filled with a red liquid and the other almost empty. The Rabbit aims his gaze between the two glasses and a pack of Camels. He doesn't have the courage to look at the Bear, except with brief, almost furtive glances, between one swallow of Campari and the next. He can't recall ever having seen him so furious and he wants to make sure at all costs that not even a tiny fraction of that rage is directed at him. The Bear really took a beating. His eyes are bloodshot, one grazed cheek is stained purple with antiseptic, he's got a bandage on his head. And the Rabbit is afraid that if he stares too hard at the bruises the Bear might get even more irritated, so he limits himself to looking at him when he speaks and avoids letting his eyes rest on the bandages.

"No, I mean, do you know what that son of a bitch did?"

The Rabbit makes a sign yes, of course, he understands, even if he really can't imagine how the hell it occurred to Franz to bang the Bear on the head with a metal bar. Doing a thing like that means you dig your grave with your own hands, no more, no less. The Rabbit listens to the Bear cursing and swearing on everything he holds most dear in the world that he is going to squeeze the living daylights out of that fucking son of a bitch, and as he listens, with an expression of extreme attention pasted on his face, he searches for something intelligent to say. Anything, really, that would let the Bear understand that he is sincerely sorry about what happened but that might also diminish his rage and provide justification, at least in part, for Franz's behaviour. Then he concludes that it's impossible and gives up. He takes his glass and empties it in one swallow.

"I'm having another. You want one? It's on me."

The Bear fixes him in the eyes, as if he were trying to evaluate his level of idiocy.

"Forget it, Rabbit, I don't feel like it. Want to do me a favour, though? If you see that dickhead, tell him that this time there's no way out. His days are numbered."

196

*

With the 50,000 she stole from Francesco she can't be extravagant. There's already 18,000 gone, just for the taxi. And while she calculates what she can buy with the amount remaining, she wonders for what absurd reason, since it was there, she didn't take it all. What difference would it have made?

She takes a small screwdriver from a shelf and revolves it in her hands, trying to recall when was the last time she felt something like a sense of guilt. The screwdriver doesn't cost much and seems strong enough. Leila drops it into the basket she has on her arm, along with the paper cutter, the tempered-steel chisel, a pair of pliers. She can't help thinking of Francesco's expression when, coming out of the bathroom, he realizes that she's gone. She wonders if he's really as broke as he said. She squeezes her lower lip between her teeth. At least she could have fucked him. There, she thinks, that is really a whore's type of reasoning. There are some ideas that only a bitch who hasn't the stomach to endure regrets could come up with. She chooses a hole-punch with a black plastic handle and throws it in the metal basket.

*

Even with his eyes closed, there's no way he's going to fall asleep. This is what you get for being hospitable! You find yourself down 50,000 and your morale under the soles of your shoes. He turns onto his left side. But the more he turns, the more agitated he gets. And the slight sleepiness he seemed to feel has now completely vanished.

The problem is that that thief has left her smell in

the sheets. And what makes Francesco even angrier is that the smell appeals to him. He sniffs the pillow and the damn perfume descends to his stomach, mixing with a kind of desire that's almost painful.

The only certainty is that at this moment he would prefer to be closed up in a coffin rather than driving a bus. Come to think of it, what's to keep him from staying in bed for a couple of days? There's also the possibility that the Bear will try to intercept him again during work. Ultimately, a phone call is enough, he just has to tell the shift supervisor that he doesn't feel well. Tomorrow or the day after he'll go to the doctor and get the certificate. He looks for the number in his address book. The chief answers on the fifth ring, takes down the information without comment. Surname, name, registration number, garage he works out of.

As soon as he hangs up, Francesco goes into the toilet to pee. His gaze falls on Leila's clothes. He takes them off the hook. He sees her sitting on the bus, barefoot, with that jacket and miniskirt on. He remembers her face, tired yet attractive, while he helped her make the bed last night. He sees her thighs beneath the edge of the T-shirt, barely an hour ago, when they were having breakfast. The image of her legs provokes a spasm in the pit of his stomach.

Francesco feels his mood descending in a free fall. He is on the verge of crying. An idiot, that's what he is. An idiot who takes home a thief and is robbed. He should have known. He feels stupid. Betrayed and made a fool of. Suddenly, a painful rancour rises in him. He crumples up the clothes into a ball, returns to the kitchen, hurls them angrily into the waste bin.

The ring of the telephone makes him jump. He grabs the receiver with his sweaty palm.

"Yes? Who is it?"

"Franz, it's Rabbit. I saw the Bear."

"So?"

"Well, I wanted to warn you that things are looking really bad."

"Hey, Rabbit, did you suddenly get stupid? You already told me yesterday that he's furious at me."

"Yes, but yesterday you hadn't split his head open."

"I had no choice. If I hadn't stopped him he would have killed me."

"I take your word for it, Franz. But it's not me you have to convince. Anyway, you beat him up pretty badly. He spent the night in the emergency room and now he's going around with his head bandaged, swearing to God that if he sees you he'll kill you."

*

The Commissioner insisted on paying his share. Then, when they left the restaurant, he accompanied Matera to Via San Felice, to show him the shortest way back to Via Battistelli.

Matera follows the Commissioner's directions. He crosses through a series of buildings and emerges into a piazza full of parked cars. He recognizes the place where he left the Alfa. On the other side of the street he sees the burgundy Y10, still in the same place it was the night before. He wonders if he should have talked about it with the Commissioner. Then he decides it's not that important, since the investigation into Leila Ronchi has been suspended. But it might not be a bad idea to take a peek inside the car. He is heading in that direction when he sees a girl with a plastic bag in her hand approach the car. He stops. Ten to one it's the brunette he followed last night. He hides behind a column of the portico. He watches as she approaches the car and takes a pointed gadget out of the bag. Matera realizes that she's trying to force the lock with a screwdriver or something like that.

That lunatic will never cease to amaze him.

He sees her open the door, get in, bend over under the dashboard. Unbelievable. Not only does she return, at the risk of being arrested, but she steals her own car, practically under the eyes of the police. On the other hand, with three-quarters of a million dollars at stake, he too would get busy.

Matera quickly goes back along the portico. He gets in his Alfa 90.

He's just in time to start the engine, because the Y10 is taking off. She's a smart girl. She connected the wires as quickly as a professional.

Matera lets four or five cars get between them. He's in a good mood. He had been resigned to wasting a lot of time and energy in finding her; instead here she is, showing up out of nowhere to throw herself into his arms. Holding the wheel with his left hand, he reaches out the right to open the glove compartment. He rummages around for a cassette. He takes one at random, sticks it in the tape deck.

It starts out with a piano phrase, and after a few minutes a sax enters, embroidering a sly, melancholy melody. Amazing what he came up with! A live version of "My Romance". The old Ben Webster on tenor and Kenny Drew at the piano. If memory serves, it was recorded one night in the Montmartre of Copenhagen, somewhere in the mid-sixties.

Some maintain that Webster is too sentimental. It may be true, but he's also elegant and velvety, like the walk of a cat. Matera's always had a weakness for Ben's style. His sax doesn't want to scorch you, doesn't want to astonish you or even hit hard. He prefers to caress you, with melodies that are a little sweet. As you listen, you have the impression of rolling a soft sip of bourbon around in your mouth.

Matera takes a Marlboro out of the pack. He presses the button for the lighter, tries to release the tension in the muscles of his neck and shoulders. Now that he's got her, he just has to stay with her. The lighter pops out. He brings the glowing disk to the cigarette. The smoke rises between his face and the windscreen, slow and sinuous as Webster's solo.

He smiles, thinking of the expression on Leila's face when she finds out that the suitcase is no longer in the boot.

*

The grains of coarse salt that he sprinkled on the pieces of aubergine have been transformed into little bubbles swollen with water.

Diolaiti, with his elbows resting on the edge of the table, observes his colleague stirring the sauce with a wooden spoon. For more than a quarter of an hour Garofano has been talking about cooking, and he has been forced to listen.

"There are a lot of ways to prepare aubergine *parmigiana*. My mother, who was from Caserta, used this recipe, which remains my favourite. First, you cut the aubergine, spread the pieces out on a flat surface, and cover them with coarse salt. While the salt absorbs the liquid from the aubergine, you prepare the tomato sauce. Here I've had to manage with what I can find, but the way my mother did it was to melt lard and minced bacon fat in a pan. Then you sauté some crushed garlic, a *battuto* of parsley and marjoram, sliced onion, celery and carrot. After it browns, you add a couple of cloves and some hot pepper, a little white wine, and when the wine has evaporated you throw in the tomato pulp. At this point you have to add salt, stir, and cover the pan. You lower the flame and let it simmer slowly for an hour. While the sauce cooks, you pour a good amount of oil into a big pan and put it on the stove. You dry the aubergine and, when the oil is hot, you brown it. Then you drain it well, salt it, grease the bottom of a baking dish and put in a layer of aubergine slices, alternating them with the strained tomato sauce, grated Parmesan, a few torn-up basil leaves and thick slices of mozzarella. Then you put the pan in the oven to brown the top.

He brings the wooden spoon to his mouth, tastes the sauce.

"Ah, delicious! Today, my friend, you will be able to taste a perfectly cooked *parmigiana.*"

Diolaiti twists his mouth.

"I don't know if it's good for me to eat this stuff. It looks heavy."

"Heavy?" Garofano asks, turning to him with his eyes wide and the wooden spoon in his hand. "Are you joking? A dish prepared with such care can't be heavy! You know what makes food indigestible? The wrong temperature. The flame has to be lively to fry properly, and reduced as low as it will go for the cooking of the sauce. Listen to me, Diolaiti. If you don't taste this *parmigiana*, you don't even deserve to have a mouth under your nose."

*

Leila drives around the traffic circle at Porta Lame, turns onto Via Zanardi, heads for the outskirts. She doesn't have a precise plan, but, first of all, she wants to check the contents of the suitcase. And she prefers to do it without running risks, in a quiet place, far from indiscreet eyes.

She goes through an underpass and continues, driving slowly. The important thing is not to draw attention. She passes one grade crossing, then a second. The houses begin to thin out. She takes a couple of wide curves, then the road narrows, bordered by trees that throw dark shadows on the asphalt. She seems to feel the blood fizzing in her veins with excitement. Now that she has the suitcase again, she can at least count on a big pile of cash to help her out of trouble.

As she comes around a bend, she notices on the right an unpaved road that leads deeper into the countryside. She slows down, shifts into second, turns. The sun is reflected on the white gravel that covers the road surface, dazzling her. She rolls up the window to keep out the dust. On her right is a fence, on the other side of which a couple of horses watch her pass, swishing their tails. The smaller of the two, a male with a light brown coat, beats one hoof on the ground, shakes his mane, raises his nose in her direction.

The car jolts on the uneven terrain, which is marked by the imprints of tractor tyres. Leila turns right onto a side road. After about half a mile she comes to a small open space, protected by a grove of spindly, dusty trees. She stops the car, turns off the engine, takes a deep breath. Now all she has to do is open the boot. She rummages in the plastic bag on the seat next to her, chooses a couple of tools.

She gets out of the Y10, looks around. The countryside is still and silent, submerged in a clear light that forces her to half close her eyes. The only sounds are the sharp cry of cicadas and the muffled, distant sound of the cars passing on the main road. She walks around the car. She leans over the boot, kneels with one knee on the bare ground. She inserts the chisel into the gap between the boot lid and the body, levers it downward with the palm of her left hand and, meanwhile, sticks the point of the little screwdriver in the lock. She tries to force the cylinder, revolving it in one direction and the other, until finally the lock gives, allowing the chisel to lift the latch. Her eyes dart to the inside of the boot as it opens, and her head begins to spin. She leans on the edge of the car, stares disoriented into the empty boot.

"Surprise!" says a voice behind her.

The blood turns to ice in her veins. She turns suddenly. She finds herself facing the outline of a man, so close she can't understand how she didn't hear him arrive. Instinctively her hand rushes to her pocket to grab the spray.

*

The bar as always is very crowded. Politicians, businessmen, aides, journalists, ministerial functionaries, jackals in search of recommendations. An aroma of coffee and sandwiches hangs in the air, which is saturated with a persistent, chaotic shouting.

The Minister and the Secretary, sitting at a small table for two, have just finished lunch. The Secretary stirs his coffee, observes, preoccupied, the face of the Minister, who smiles in all directions and meanwhile torments the sugar wrapper. His colour has noticeably worsened in recent days. It must be his liver.

"The doctor told me I should avoid caffeine. If we don't resolve this affair in a hurry, I'll end up with another ulcer. You know how many nights it's been since I closed an eye? I'm a step away from nervous exhaustion. And everyone is worried, like me, what do you think? Look around. You see what the atmosphere's like. We look each other in the face, we greet each other as if everything were normal, but no one can say with certainty who of us will still be here tomorrow. Difficult times, my friend. Times like the Inquisition. For years these fanatical judges have been expecting to dig our graves. And meanwhile the world is going to rack and ruin. The Americans have tied the purse strings, and the whole country is turning against us. I know that I shouldn't say it, but our problems began because of this Pope. Who knows, maybe the break-up was inevitable, but the fact remains that this Pope, with his *idée fixe* of tearing down that damn wall, marked the beginning of our misfortunes. On top of that, Gorbachev got it into his head to be democratic, and if you add it all up you can understand the reason for the general breakdown. The truth is that we were doing fine in the shadow of that wall, no point in being hypocritical. As long as the divisions were clear, there was something to eat for everyone. The Russians stood in line for bread, but they were used to it, and the governments on both sides spent billions on nuclear tests. But meanwhile the money circulated and no one could complain. We were in the middle and had everything to gain. And now?"

The Secretary wears a regretful expression on his face. But the Minister doesn't even look at him. He removes a handkerchief from his pocket, blows his nose, shakes his head, lost in the catastrophic visions in which his party, which once seemed an impregnable force, appears to him a grain of sand in a desert roiled by a storm of global proportions.

"But let's get to our problems," the Minister says,

putting the handkerchief back in his pocket. "When did you say that Matera would get in touch?"

*

Without even realizing what's happening, Leila finds herself lifted up bodily. The man grabs her wrist and tears the spray can out of her hand. Then he twists her arm behind her back. The pain forces her up onto tiptoe, her face pressed against the stranger's jacket. Maybe, if she had enough breath, she could scream. Instead all she can do is gasp, breathing in that odour of aftershave and tobacco, while the man, holding the can in his free hand, reads the tiny print on the label.

"Bravo. So you wanted to spray this stuff in my face?"

Leila is tempted to try shoving a knee into his testicles, but the man seems to read her thoughts, because suddenly he pushes her backwards. As soon as she regains her balance, she realizes that he is pointing the barrel of a gun between her stomach and her breast.

"Listen to me," he says. "I've been following you since last night. If I had wanted to kill you, I could have done it at least fifty times."

It doesn't seem to be a question, but Leila nods. And she'd like him to calm down, if only to gain time.

"Good. The important thing is that we understand each other. I don't want to hurt you, but if you force me to, I assure you, I won't think twice. So, what do you want me to call you?"

Odd question. He asked not "What is your name?" but "What do you want me to call you?"

"Leila."

A second later she is sorry. What in the world got into her to reveal her real name to this guy?

He smiles, though, as if the answer satisfied him.

"Good, Leila. You're an intelligent girl. It's much better if you tell me the truth. Now we need to have a few words in order to clear this matter up."

He closes the lid of the boot. Then he indicates the car with the barrel of his gun.

"What do you say we sit there? No, you on the other side. If you don't mind, I'll take the driver's seat."

*

He has to put something in his stomach. Francesco opens the refrigerator door, bends over to gaze at the empty shelves. In the vegetable drawer he finds a mummified lemon and an onion from which a long white leg has sprouted. From the cupboard he retrieves a package of spaghetti and a carton of tomato purée that expired only two months ago. In a jar he finds a couple of garlic cloves and three dried peppers.

He fills a pot with water, puts it on the cooker. While the water comes to the boil, he minces the garlic and onion, brooding grimly about his future.

A tunnel, that's what he has before him. A dark tunnel, with no exit. The Bear is chasing him and all he has in the world is 24,600 lire. You can't get far with an amount like that. He might as well just open the window and throw himself out.

At least the onion gives him a good excuse to cry.

At the bottom of a bottle smudged with fingerprints are the muddy remains of some oil. Francesco drips it into the pan, down to the last drop. He waits for it to heat up, then adds the garlic and onion. A rancid odour is released. As soon as the onion becomes transparent, he adds the tomato, the pepper and a pinch of salt.

The sound of the doorbell catches him with the ladle in the sauce. Who the hell can that be?

He balances the wooden spoon on the edge of the pan, goes towards the door. The second ring surprises him halfway down the hall. Maybe it's something in the angry protraction of the sound that makes him slow down. What if it's the Bear? The third ring, though shorter, seems to him even more threatening than the first two. Suddenly, he has a clear view of the Bear, standing in front of the door of his building, as he takes a step backwards on the pavement and looks up, trying to make out which are Francesco's windows. Francesco takes the last steps as if he were walking in a minefield.

The silence that follows worries him.

He seems to hear someone coming up the stairs. He brings his eye to the peephole just in time to see the Bear emerge on the landing. A shudder of fear keeps him at the door, like a cat surprised crossing the street, hypnotized by the headlights of the car that's about to hit it.

He sees the enormous shape, rendered even more frightening by the distortion of the fisheye lens, moving decisively towards him. This time the Bear doesn't waste any time ringing the bell, he pounds on the door a couple of times with his fist. Francesco jumps back suddenly.

"Franz, open up. I know you're in there!"

Not a chance, he thinks, motionless, a couple of feet from the door.

"Open up, I'm telling you!" the Bear shouts, banging on the door as if it were made of cardboard.

Francesco knows that he could tear that door off its hinges with a push of his shoulder if he wanted to. He could try to slide the bolt in, but that doesn't seem like a very intelligent move. It would be like admitting he's home, and the bolt isn't strong enough to guarantee safety. It's more prudent to wait for the Bear to decide to leave. Meanwhile, however, that beast has begun kicking the door, making the whole building rumble.

Francesco wonders if it wouldn't be better to flee through the bathroom window, when he hears the voice of a neighbour coming from the stairwell.

"Stop that! What's all the noise about, anyway?"

He recognizes that irritating voice. It's the retired army officer on the floor below, a first-class pain in the neck. For once, however, the intervention of the ex-soldier might turn out to be useful. He holds his breath, listening to the voices shouting at each other. The Bear is telling the army officer to go to hell. But Francesco knows the man's stubbornness. He wouldn't stop even if he were facing a tribe of head-hunters.

"Look here, there's no point in being so arrogant. I warn you that if you don't stop disturbing this entire building, I am going to call the police *immediately.*"

"Fuck you and fuck the police!" cries the Bear.

He punches the door a couple more times and finally decides to give up.

Francesco stands listening to the sound of the foot-steps going down the stairs. He goes back to the peep-hole, carefully, and observes the deserted landing. Then he turns, leans his back against the door, takes a deep breath. At that moment he realizes there's a smell of burning in the air.

*

The barrel of the Berretta along her right thigh, his left hand on the backpack she's holding in her lap, Matera lets his gaze float beyond the windscreen. It seems that the girl didn't know about the exchange. She claims she's never met Diolaiti and Garofano before and that she picked up Andrea in a bar. Of course, she also tried to tell him some lies, but that's normal – he expected it, and it wasn't difficult to make her understand that lying to him was a wasted effort. If she had a hope of saving herself, it was by owning up and telling him everything she knew. That is to say, practically nothing. She's just a petty thief, caught up in this business by accident.

Matera made her repeat her story three times. He made her reconstruct every move. Then he searched her and examined the car. But the only thing he found is that backpack, from which emerged a lighter, a paper cutter, a ballpoint pen, a tie clip. Of the document that interests him not a sign.

"Now," Matera says to her. "Think hard. You're sure that everything you took from that apartment is in here."

Leila is exhausted.

"Yes. No, maybe not. I don't remember. Maybe I also put something in my handbag."

"And where is it?"

"I've told you ten times! Those two men took it."

Matera seems to feel something deflate inside. If the girl put the document in that damn handbag, it means that the men from intelligence have it now. But still something doesn't fit. Why would they worry about stopping the police investigation if they already had what they wanted? Maybe they mean to silence her before the police get their hands on her, in order to cover up the whole thing for good.

There's another possibility. The document could still be in Fabbri's house, carefully hidden somewhere. Yet this hypothesis seems to him the least plausible. The police searched the apartment from top to bottom. And before them Diolaiti and Garofano went through it, and they tortured Fabbri to make him spit out the truth. Matera can't imagine that gutless youth resisting the methods of those two thugs.

No, the most probable thing is that Leila took the document along with the rest of her booty and lost it. And the worst thing is that, if it really is lost somewhere, sooner or later it could turn up in the hands of someone else. Let's suppose that it ends up with Commissioner Roccaforte. Would the Secretary manage to keep it quiet? The Minister's power isn't what it once was. Just a few years ago it wouldn't have been a problem, but today?

And if Commissioner Roccaforte should be seized by a mania for justice? If behind him there was an aggressive prosecutor? Matera tries to imagine the Secretary's reaction, when he finds out how things stand. The document, which the Minister is waiting for with bated breath, lost, who can say where.

There is, of course, another possibility. The girl might have realized the value of what she found and hidden it. He can't be a hundred per cent sure that she hasn't made up a nice little story to stall him. She doesn't work for the intelligence services, but she's still a thief. She finds herself in possession of a suitcase full of money, she realizes she's stumbled onto something big, she has the idea of getting more out of it. All right, suppose things are like that. What would be the best thing to do? Kidnap her? Try to scare her a little, using some more persuasive method? Eliminate her?

Matera can't decide. Maybe it would be wiser to call Rome, pass this hot potato along to the Secretary.

He taps the gun barrel against the steering wheel. Even admitting that the girl has lied, what would he gain by getting rid of her? One of the already faint possibilities of recovering the document would disappear.

Matera notes the worried expression with which she is observing him. She's not stupid and certainly is aware that her life is in the balance. He wonders if, in fact, all these reflections are nothing but an excuse not to have to shoot her. But yes, why not admit it? Killing her does not appeal to him.

"In essence," he says to her, breaking the silence, "you have no idea where that money came from . . ."

"No, I told you. I thought I'd got lucky, that's all."

"Well, there's no use in wasting more time. At this point you realize that you're in big trouble. There are already two corpses and you could be the third. No, don't worry, I'm not going to kill you. But you've seen with your own eyes that there are a lot of unscrupulous people chasing after the same thing I'm looking for."

"Those two men."

"Yes, for example, them. But others might show up as well. And then there's the police. They found your keys in Fabbri's apartment and identified the fingerprints."

Leila stares at him, concentrating her attention.

"I hoped that you could be useful to me and for the moment I've managed to delay the investigation. But the police won't stand still for long. Starting tomorrow they'll be on your trail, and sooner or later someone will catch you. Do you understand?"

Leila nods. She understands. She understands that she is in shit up to her neck and hasn't the slightest idea how to get herself out. She runs her tongue over her lips.

"But what can I do?"

At the very moment she formulates the question, she sees the absurdity of the situation. This man she doesn't know, who's got a gun on her, is the only person she can ask for advice.

"What can I tell you?" Matera says. "If you were to find that . . ." He interrupts himself. He shakes his head. "No, it's hopeless. You see? I can't even tell you what it is. And on the other hand there would be no point. If you don't have what I'm looking for, it's useless for me to tell you what it is. If you do have it, however, you would already have realized that the best thing is to hand it over. I could cover you, and even give you the money."

Leila furrows her brows.

"The money in the suitcase?"

"The money was intended to buy something and the offer is still good. But unfortunately you don't have the slightest idea what I want in exchange . . ."

She shakes her head wearily.

"I swear to you. If I knew, why wouldn't I tell you?"

"Then I'm sorry. I can't help you."

Leila remains silent. He observes her. It's too bad, such a good-looking girl.

"In other words, either the police or those two murderers."

Matera shrugs his shoulders.

"What can I tell you? If they've found what they were looking for, maybe they'll forget about you."

"But it's not certain."

"No, it's not certain. Nothing is certain."

The girl now has a desperate look. She seems on the point of collapse.

"It's blackmail, right?" she asks. "This whole business . . . Andrea was blackmailing somebody . . ."

Matera doesn't move a single muscle of his face. Now he's sure that she is sincere. She would never have thrown out a comment like that if she had known the situation. She has made a guess and hit the mark. But, if she really is involved in this affair by chance, the wisest thing would be to eliminate her here, immediately, get rid of the thought once and for all. She knows almost nothing, but what she knows is still too much. He looks her in the eyes.

"You want some advice? The less you talk about this, the better. You should disappear from circulation. And the farther you get, the more hope you have of surviving."

Then he puts the gun in the holster, takes out the pack of Marlboros and lights a cigarette. She senses that the gesture represents a form of leave-taking. She'd better take advantage of the opportunity right away.

"Can I . . . can I go?" she asks.

Matera lowers his eyelids in a nod. He puts the lighter back in his pocket.

They open the doors of the Y10. They get out. Leila walks around the car. Even to place one foot in front of the other costs her an effort of concentration.

"Excuse me, may I ask you a favour?"

Matera scowls.

"Let's hear it."

"The fact is that at this point I'm totally broke. You know that better than I do. I don't have a penny or a place to go."

He hesitates. He makes a circular motion with the hand holding the cigarette.

"And so?"

"Well, I wanted to ask you . . . could you give me a little money?"

This is good, now she's asking for a loan! He shakes his head, puts the cigarette in his mouth. He takes out his wallet. He fingers a 100,000-lire bill and two fifties.

"Will two hundred do?"

Leila nods, stretching her colourless lips into a semblance of a smile. She reaches out her hand to take the money he offers.

"If I were you," he says to her, putting his wallet back in his pocket, "I wouldn't go around in that car. By now even the rocks must know your licence plate number."

Leila nods yes, while she sticks the bills in a pocket of her jacket. She gets in the driver's seat. Matera closes the door carefully. She leans over to connect the wires and starts the engine. As she is fumbling under the dashboard, with trembling fingers, she imagines him pulling out the gun and taking aim through the window. Maybe he preferred to do it from a greater distance, to avoid getting spattered with blood.

Matera taps his knuckles against the window.

She is paralysed, her muscles tense. She has to make an effort of will not to start screaming. She recovers slowly, holding her breath. She looks up. She sees him scribbling something on a notepad, his eyelid half closed so that the smoke doesn't get in his eye. Leila lowers the window, he tears off the sheet and hands it to her. His fingers are covered with grey hairs. It's a piece of graph paper.

"Here. If for some reason something should come to mind, you can find me at this number."

She takes the piece of paper, looks at it without focusing on the numbers. She tries to swallow and realizes her throat is dry.

"Can I go now?"

"Go on," Matera answers, putting his notepad in his pocket. "And good luck."

*

Garofano leans over, puts the pan in the oven and

215

adjusts the dial. Then he stands up, massaging his kidneys.

"There we go. Less than ten minutes and it'll be ready. I'm going to take advantage of it to call home."

Diolaiti, sitting at the table, is leafing through a magazine. He nods without even looking up.

Garofano rinses his hands under the tap, dries them, throws the towel on the sink, takes the phone from his jacket pocket.

Diolaiti hears him greeting his wife in a low voice.

"Giovanna, this business is dragging on. I'm not sure if I'll be home for the weekend. How's Betta?"

Diolaiti turns the page of the weekly. Ad for a cologne for men. Black-and-white photograph. Face of a young man in profile, hair falling over his forehead. The cologne bottle is the only object in colour. On the next page, an interview with a judge from the Milan judiciary. The journalist plays with the details, trying to give the article a sensationalist tone, but in substance it says nothing new. Corruption at every level. Politicians who have been pocketing money for years. Mountains of public money vanished into thin air. Diolaiti stretches his lips in a sneer. What nerve! As if they had only now discovered it! Next to the article, a photograph of the judge. He looks like someone who just showed up there by chance, with tousled hair and thick glasses. Probably he doesn't know yet how far he can push. Diolaiti closes the magazine and leaves it on the table. He looks at the cooker. The workspace in the kitchen has been reduced to a battlefield. Garofano may be a good cook but he certainly doesn't worry about cleaning up.

"I told you not to get involved!" he hears him shouting. "All right, I spoke to him. Violent? What do you mean violent? Let's not get all worked up. Nothing, what do you think I did to him? I only explained that I didn't like him and Betta going out together. What should I have done? Given him my blessing?"

Diolaiti stands up, walks around the table. He joins his hands behind his back. He examines the splatters of tomato and oil, the dirty knives, the salt and pepper sprinkled everywhere, the crumbled pepper flakes.

"You'll see, sooner or later she'll get over it," Garofano says, lowering his voice a little. "Just let her cool down."

Diolaiti leans over towards the oven. He pushes the button to turn on the light. This aubergine *parmigiana* looks good, he can't deny it. He brings his face to the window, sniffs. It also smells good. But surely it would sit like a brick in his stomach. He takes his finger off the button, and the inside light goes out.

"Listen, Giovanna, I've got to go now. And about this? If she wants to stay locked in her room, let her. I told you, right now I can't come home. Yes, I'll get in touch."

Diolaiti takes the TV remote. He raises the volume, changes the channel a couple of times.

"Goddamn," Garofano says. "That shit called up Elisabetta and, it seems, told her about our little chat."

Diolaiti looks at him questioningly.

"You know," Garofano explains, stretching out his arms. "That pig who does it with my daughter. Well, as soon as we've settled this, I'll show him! And next time he won't go complaining about my manners!"

*

Leila pushes the supermarket trolley in front of her and tries to figure out if what she feels is fever or only the effect of the tension.

She was sure that she had her hands on a suitcase

full of money, instead she finds herself empty-handed and obliged to run. First, however, she would like to go by her apartment, to pick up just a few things. The indispensable minimum. The money she put aside, passport, credit card. Today is Saturday, the banks are closed. And Monday will be too late. That man was clear. The police know she's involved; starting tomorrow they'll be after her. The first thing they'll do is block her bank account. The fact is, though, that those two criminals could be stationed on the pavement in front of her house, waiting for her to return. On the other hand, if she doesn't try today, she'll never be able to go there again.

Into the cart she throws a couple of pairs of dark tights, some knickers, two T-shirts, a black undershirt, a charcoal-grey cotton pullover with a wide neck. A pair of black jeans in her size.

She left the Y10 in a car park opposite the station, then took a bus out of the neighbourhood. When they find her car, they'll think she got on a train and ran off. Who knows? Maybe it would have been better to do that. Use the 200,000 the man loaned her to buy a ticket and leave town. Only she hasn't the least idea of where to go. To ask for help from her family is impossible. Apart from the fact that her father would slam the door in her face, it's the first place the police would go to look for her.

Then she thought of Francesco. With his help she could go to her apartment to get the stuff she needs. As far as she can understand, he's got money troubles. Who knows? Maybe promising him a small reward for the favour . . . the problem is to justify her disappearance and, above all, the theft of the 50,000.

So now she's in this supermarket. His cupboard and refrigerator were empty. She'll tell him she took the money to do some shopping. Ultimately, it might even seem a nice gesture. And even if he takes it badly, at the most he'll make a scene. The important thing is to save face. In any case, she has no alternative. At worst he'll throw her out and she'll be where she started. It's worth a try.

Leila pushes the cart down the aisles. In the shoe department she finds some short black suede boots. Into the cart she throws two packages of pasta, a can of tomato puree, a couple of tins of tuna. Salad greens, some bananas and oranges. A box of biscuits, crackers, potato crisps, bread. A couple of ounces of Parma ham. A container of milk, six eggs, cheese. A bottle of Cabernet-Sauvignon. Some cans of beer.

What else does she need? Kleenex, deodorant, toothbrush, moisturizing cream and sanitary pads, in case all the risks she's run don't keep her from getting her period. Powder, lipstick, hair gel, mascara, cleansing milk, a packet of hair dye. She chooses a very light blond, to change her appearance as much as possible. Then, in the hardware department, she looks for a pair of scissors and a knife with a folding blade.

*

The trill of the intercom makes him jump. The Secretary leans forward to press the button.

"Yes?"

The voice of the assistant answers him: "The Minister would like to see you."

"Tell him I'll be there right away," the Secretary says. Then he closes the file in front of him and gets up.

The Minister receives him standing in front of the window, his back to the door, hands clasped behind him.

As soon as the Secretary closes the heavy inlaid door behind him, the Minister turns and stares at him, frowning.

"Have you heard from Matera?"

The Secretary stretches his arms in a shrug.

"Unfortunately no, Minister."

The Minister takes a handkerchief out of his trouser pocket and blows his nose. Then he refolds it carefully and uses it to mop his forehead.

"Dear God. I'm beginning to fear the worst."

"Don't worry, Minister. You'll see, Matera will solve our problem."

The Minister is too agitated to listen to what he's saying.

"Don't you read the papers?" he bursts out, raising his voice. "Don't you understand what the atmosphere's like? We are in the middle of a witch-hunt! At this moment everyone thinks only about saving himself and doesn't give a damn about his friends. There are traitors in the party who would denounce their own mothers to get themselves out of trouble. And you come and tell me not to worry!"

"Minister, we are doing everything we possibly can. I'm ready to answer personally for the capability of . . ."

"Do you want to know what I'll do with your capability?" the Minister interrupts him, waving the hand holding the handkerchief in the air.

The Secretary lowers his eyes. It's of no use to persist on this track.

"Minister, what can I tell you? I am on pins and needles as much as you, believe me."

The Minister puts the handkerchief back in his pocket.

"You're right, I'm sorry. The fact is that we have little

time and any false move means the possibility of disaster. As soon as you have any news, let me know."

The Secretary inclines his head.

"I won't fail, Minister."

*

Too late. While the Bear was pounding on the door, the sauce stuck to the bottom of the pan. Not that the sauce is, at this moment, of much interest to him. Francesco turns off the flame under the water too, goes into the bedroom. The Rabbit was right. If he wants to escape, he has to move on. From on top of the wardrobe he pulls down a suitcase wrapped in a plastic bag. He throws it on the bed, opens it, then opens the doors of the wardrobe to decide what to take. Not that there's much choice. A pair of dark-green trousers, three shirts still in need of ironing, some blue jeans, some sweaters. Almost all his T-shirts and socks are in the laundry basket. Francesco goes to the bathroom, picks up the basket. The movement causes a sharp pain in his back. He returns slowly to the bedroom. He overturns the basket's contents onto the floor. He kicks aside the knot of dirty sheets. He kneels down, rummages among underpants and dirty handkerchiefs in search of any salvageable items. He chooses four T-shirts and five pairs of socks. He sniffs them one by one, evaluating whether he should put them in the suitcase. While he is crouching down, the doorbell rings again. He stops, then raises his head, like an animal scenting its prey.

If it's the Bear again, he must have returned with the intention of getting in at any cost. Maybe this time he's brought a crowbar to pry the door open. He tries to calm himself, thinking that in that case he wouldn't have rung the bell. And yet suddenly he feels in a big hurry to do something. Anything. Escape. Call the police to ask for help. Look for a weapon to defend himself with. Go to the door to see who's ringing.

Moving on all fours, he reaches the wardrobe and from under it pulls out a toolbox. He opens it. He grabs a hammer. He stands up, his back stiffened by pain. He heads for the door with legs that feel like lead. He approaches the peephole cautiously. Before looking out, he takes a deep breath and grips the handle of the hammer. The palm of his hand is clammy with sweat. Now all he has to do is look.

*

Garofano sweeps the table with a broad movement of his arm, knocking onto the floor the remains of dinner and breakfast. Then on the tabletop he arranges silverware, two plates, two glasses, the already uncorked bottle of wine. Finally, the steaming pan.

"Here we are. Now all we have to do is eat."

Diolaiti lowers the volume on the television and gets up from the couch. He approaches the table hesitantly. Garofano, using a broad knife, is cutting the *parmigiana*. Diolaiti leans over to observe the sauce-covered surface of the pan.

"I'm not at all sure that I feel like it," he says distrustfully.

Garofano, with an enormous portion balanced on the knife, raises his eyes. Then he shrugs, deposits the portion on his own plate. He sits down, grabs the knife and fork, starts cutting. He sinks his fork into the mixture, spears a steaming, streaming piece, puts it in his mouth. With his tongue he catches the threads of mozzarella hanging down his chin. He rests the fork on the edge of the plate and, chewing, refills his glass with wine.

"You should taste it," he says with his mouth full. "I ask you as a personal favour."

Diolaiti looks at him, not totally convinced.

"I admit it's tempting. But are you sure it won't cause problems with my digestion?"

"You want to know the secret of a good digestion? First of all, concentrate on what you're eating. Enjoy the taste. And then chew well. Don't forget that digestion begins in the mouth."

"I'll take a little."

"Make me happy!"

"It's too much," Diolaiti protests, seeing the gigantic piece his colleague is cutting.

"Big? You must be kidding!" Garofano says, scooping up the rectangle and setting it down on the plate. "Whatever you don't feel like eating, just leave it – where's the harm?"

*

The lens of the peephole frames a girl, with two big plastic bags in hand, who is reaching forward to press the doorbell yet again. He was so sure of seeing the Bear that it takes him a few seconds to recognize her. Then he opens the door.

"Finally," Leila says with a smile. "I thought you had gone out!"

Francesco looks at her with a dazed expression, cranes his neck to take a look behind her.

"Are you alone?" he asks.

Leila frowns.

"Well, of course. Who would I be with? What are you doing with that?" she asks, indicating the hammer.

Francesco follows the trajectory of her gaze, observes the tool that is hanging at the end of his arm.

"Come on, come on in."

He leads the way along the hall. Leila puts the bags down on the floor in the kitchen.

"This morning I noticed that your cupboard was pretty bare. So I allowed myself to take some money from your wallet to buy a few things. I hope you don't mind."

In Francesco, now that the fright has vanished, anger suddenly rises again.

"Mind, shit, yes," he cries, throwing the hammer on the counter next to the sink. "That 50,000 was practically all I had left."

Leila looks at him with an expression of regret, says nothing for a few seconds.

"I'm sorry. I didn't think you'd take it like that."

"How did you think I would take it? And where the hell did you go? You were out a long time! I was sure by now you weren't coming back."

"Were you making something to eat?"

"Yes, but the sauce burned."

"I see," Leila says, leaning over the pan to smell it. "Well, anyway, as I told you, I bought some stuff. We'll manage with that."

"I told you I had a pile of debts, and you, without even asking me, spend the last money I had."

"Listen, about the money, I have a proposal to make."

"What sort of proposal?"

"We'll discuss it at the table, while we're eating. I'm going to the bathroom and I'll be right back."

Francesco shakes his head without answering. Leila's gaze falls on the waste basket, from which the sleeve of a jacket is sticking out.

"Hey, what's in there?" She lifts the lid. Hands sunk

in his pockets, he watches her take from the waste basket the jacket, the miniskirt, the body stocking.

"But these are my clothes!" she says. "What are they doing in the rubbish?"

Francesco shrugs.

"I thought you weren't coming back."

"All right. If you feel like a cigarette, I bought some. They're in one of the bags."

Francesco watches her head for the bathroom, then leans over the bags. A sharp pain in his back makes him grimace. Among the various purchases, three red packs of Gauloises stick out. He takes one. He tears the cellophane, removes the foil. He inhales the first drag with pleasure.

Three packs?

He bends over the bag again, to look through the contents. The cigarettes alone cost more than 9,000 lire. The Parma ham and the cheese have labels showing the price on them. So that's more than 20,000. Then there's wine, eggs, milk and an assortment of cosmetics. Damn, this is expensive stuff! In the other bag, he finds clothes. On the bottom he digs out the receipt. He stares, scowling, at the total, marked at the bottom: 132,870 lire.

From the bathroom comes the sound of flushing.

When Leila comes back to the kitchen, Francesco is sitting with on elbow on the table and the cigarette between his fingers.

"Tell me," she asks, "why in the world is the suitcase open on the bed and all that mess on the floor? Were you going to take a trip?"

"First I'm going to ask you a question, Alessandra, if you don't mind."

For an instant, she's taken by surprise. Alessandra? She remembers at once, nods.

Francesco plants the receipt in front of her eyes.

"This is the bill from the supermarket. A hundred and thirty thousand and change. Plus there are three packs of cigarettes. That's at least a hundred and forty. From my wallet you took 50,000, and you said you were broke. I'd like to know where the rest came from."

"I met someone in the supermarket," Leila improvises. Immediately she realizes she's said something stupid. Francesco stares at her without moving a muscle If she wants help, she has to have his trust. She can't continue lying to him.

"I'm sorry, I think at this point I should explain a few things to you."

"I think so too," he says, putting out the cigarette in the ashtray.

"It will take a little time. It's a rather complicated story."

"That's OK. There's nothing I like better than to sit and listen to complicated stories in which I play the part of the moron."

Leila bites her lip, takes a deep breath.

"OK. But I'm warning you, what I'm about to tell you you certainly won't like. In the last two days some things happened to me that are so absurd I have trouble believing them myself."

He folds one arm over the another.

"It sounds interesting. Do secret agents enter into it?"

Leila lets a smile escape.

"Maybe."

*

Garofano tears off a big piece of bread and wipes it carefully across the plate.

Diolaiti watches him with a sneer of disgust.

"I can't believe it. You also mop up after all that good food you've devoured?"

The other sticks the bread saturated with sauce in his mouth and replies, chewing, "Luckily I don't have problems with my digestion. In fact," he adds, standing up, "from the moment I saw some pecorino in the refrigerator . . ."

Diolaiti watches as he brings a big chunk of cheese on a wooden breadboard to the table.

"Do you want some?" Garofano asks, knife in hand.

He shrugs.

"At this point . . . All right, give me a little piece."

"Ah, today, I see, you're in shape!"

"I hope I don't regret it," Diolaiti says, while a tear slides slowly down his cheek.

Garofano watches him take the handkerchief out of his pocket.

"I've been wanting to ask you for a while." He points to his colleague's eye with the tip of the knife. "Why is it always tearing?"

"Because of a cut," Diolaiti says, putting away the handkerchief.

"A splinter during a shoot-out?"

"No. I had to have an operation to take out a chalazion. And while the surgeon was removing it he touched the tear duct with the tip of the scalpel. The skin there doesn't grow back together."

"A chalazion? What kind of thing is that?"

"A sort of cyst. There are glands on the edge of the eyelid, which can swell. And if . . ."

The ring of the mobile phone interrupts him. Garofano grabs the phone.

"Yes? Ah, it's you? I'm listening. How about that. You're sure? All right, all right. OK, thanks. If I need anything else, I'll call you. Of course, soothe the boss, we're working here! Talk to you later."

Diolaiti nibbles his cheese.

"That was Alvisi."

"What did he say?"

"It seems the girl is some kind of a lowlife. First she gave up university to go around the world with a guy who later was arrested for drug trafficking. Then she was with a Genovese crook, a guy named Baccigalupo."

"Big stuff?"

"What do you think? Stolen cars, prostitution, smuggling, supplying drugs to small-time pushers."

"And her?"

"Since they split up, it seems that she's moved several times, going from one city to another. It's not clear how she lives. Probably prostitution. Maybe she cleans out her clients."

"Would you say that someone could have hired her to rob Fabbri?"

Garofano shrugs without responding. Then he pours a glass of wine, takes a long swallow.

"Not bad, this Nobile di Montepulciano! The whore has good taste."

Having emptied his glass, Garofano takes a pack of cigars out of his shirt pocket. He cuts one in half, then chooses the half that draws better. He runs the flame of the lighter back and forth over the point where the cigar was cut, until the tobacco is glowing. He puts it in his mouth, inhales for a few seconds and, immediately afterwards, exhales. Thick puffs of smoke disperse slowly in the air. Diolaiti fans his hand in front of his face.

"Do you have to smoke that? I wonder how you can possibly like it."

Garofano looks at him from through the cloud of smoke.

"And I, my friend, wonder what it is you like, besides cutting people up."

*

The bottle of Cabernet-Sauvignon is sitting on the edge of the bathroom sink, almost empty. Near the tap, beyond a bar of soap and an orange comb, are two glasses. Leila is sitting on a chair in front of the mirror. Francesco, standing behind her, has a pair of scissors in one hand and a lock of hair in the other. Leila's hair has changed in appearance. It's like a crew-cut on the sides, while on top of her head some irregular tufts are sticking up. Francesco takes a step back and, looking dubious, studies the result of his work.

"I warned you. I'm not a barber."

"Don't worry, it's just fine. In fact, make it a little shorter on the sides."

He starts cutting at the temples.

"But I can't say I understand much of the story."

Leila raises her eyes, looks at Francesco's face reflected in the mirror.

"Nor do I, for that matter, but I swear that it's completely true! What reason would I have to invent an adventure like that? Besides, I don't exactly come out looking good, do I?"

"You can say that again! As far as I understand, you make ends meet by picking up guys, taking them to bed and then robbing them."

She shrugs.

"More or less."

"A system like any other. And does it pay?"

"So-so."

"But you get by. Better than nothing, right? In practice, a middle road between thief and whore. Correct me if I'm wrong."

"Come on, you're not going to get moralistic on me, are you?"

"Who's getting moralistic? Not at all! And not that I care. But the fact remains that you stole 50,000 from me, I don't know if you remember. So I don't think you should be offended."

Leila twists her lips without responding.

"And so your name isn't even Alessandra."

"No, I told you. My real name is Leila."

Francesco shakes his head.

"Even your name seems false."

"You don't like it?"

"Maybe I should get used to it. Anyway, that guy who dropped the 200,000 on you stole the suitcase."

"From what I understand, he was the one who put it in the locker. Except that the person who took it was supposed to leave something in exchange."

"What?"

"That's what I don't know. Anyway, when he realized that the exchange was screwed up, he must have decided it was better to retrieve it himself."

"How much was there, in the suitcase?"

"I didn't have time to count it. A pile of dollars. What do I know? More or less, it could have been half a million."

Francesco whistles.

"Half a million dollars? Not bad! Anyway, it's gone now, there's no point in crying over it. So let's hear it. What's your idea?"

"Those two men took my handbag last night, with all

my documents in it. I don't know what happened afterwards. It could be that they've already got what they wanted and couldn't care less about me. But it wouldn't be very smart to go to my house alone, to check. If they're hiding out somewhere waiting for me, they would recognize me, even in this state. The fact remains that I don't have a thing. Money, clothes, documents, nothing. And, starting tomorrow, as if that weren't enough, the police are going to be looking for me."

"You do seem to be in deep shit."

"Thanks. If I want to survive, I have to disappear. But to have a chance, I have to get to my apartment and get some things. That's where you could help me."

"What could I do?"

"I thought you might come with me and look around to see if anyone is watching the place."

"You must be nuts! Why the hell should I run the risk of being murdered instead of you?"

"That's not what I asked you."

"No? What happens if I find myself face to face with those thugs?"

"They don't know you."

"Don't talk nonsense! If they're stationed somewhere and they see me going into your apartment, it won't take much for them to put two and two together!"

"But how are they going to know you're going into my apartment? Even if they're watching the building, they're expecting me, not you."

"It's pointless to go on talking about it. I wouldn't even consider it."

"I was hoping you'd be a little grateful. Basically last night I saved you from that monster who wanted to smash you to pieces."

"Forget it. Thanks to you, now the Bear is angrier than before."

"I could pay you for the favour."

"Nothing doing. I've already got enough troubles of my own. And then how do you think you'd manage to open the door? With a magic formula?"

"I never said that you had to go alone. I'll take care of the lock."

"Oh yes, I forgot that it's your speciality."

Leila clenches her teeth, her nostrils dilate with anger. She grabs the pack of cigarettes lying on the sink. She lights one. She inhales nervously a couple of times, crosses her legs, stares at Francesco furiously.

He, with an indifferent air, puts the scissors in his pocket.

"If your hair's OK like that, I'll have one of those too."

"All right," she says. "Maybe I deserved it. But let me at least explain what I had in mind. You put on a workman's outfit and pretend to be, I don't know, someone who's cleaning the radiators or an electrician. While you ring the bell, I'm hiding. Who would be suspicious of an electrician? Even if someone asks who you're looking for, you say that I called a couple of days ago because of some problem or other. Then you pretend to get mad that there's no one home and you leave. If, on the other hand, the situation seems peaceful, you let me know and I'll go up too. Then I'll manage by myself. I open the door, get what I need and we take off. And you earn the reward."

Francesco taps the ashes into the sink, sits on the edge of the tub.

"How much would it be, just out of curiosity?"

"I haven't thought about it yet. Would two million do?"

He laughs.

"You would give me two million to ring a doorbell? Why not three, then?"

Leila inhales her cigarette. She holds the smoke in her lungs for a few seconds, then blows it out towards the ceiling.

"Let's make it five."

Francesco raises his eyebrows.

"And where are you going to get it from, this five million?"

"I have thirty, if that interests you. The problem is to get it."

He stares at her, lowering his eyelids halfway.

"You keep thirty million at home?"

"At home I have six and change, in cash. The rest is in the bank."

"Why don't you simply withdraw it?"

"What day is today?"

"Saturday?"

"Right. The only hope is to at least get my credit card. But that's in the house too."

"Listen, if you're thinking of rolling me again . . ."

"Francesco," Leila interrupts him, holding his gaze, "I swear to you that I have no intention of robbing you."

They continue to stare at each other in silence. Then he puts the cigarette in his mouth and Leila sees his gaze clouding. She inhales again, stands up, throws the butt in the toilet. She runs a hand through her hair.

"So?" she asks. "Will you tell me what you're thinking about now?"

Francesco looks up at her.

"About my brother."

"Why's that?"

"Because he's a plumber."

*

Garofano revolves the stub of the cigar between his teeth.

"Are you feeling any better?"

Diolaiti, sitting on the couch, is drinking big swallows of a cloudy liquid, holding the hot glass with the tips of his fingers.

"Not even a little," he complains, his face pale and shiny with sweat. "I knew I shouldn't pay any attention to you! You and your *parmigiana*!"

"Now, don't get mad at me! I didn't force you to eat it! And besides I'm not at all sure it's the fault of the *parmigiana*. Shit, you ate hardly a mouthful! You're not by chance allergic to dairy products, are you?"

Diolaiti glares at him with pure hatred. Garofano puts his hands in his pockets.

"Anyway, that should help."

The other massages his stomach.

"I hope so," he says.

"What do you feel, exactly?"

"I told you, I'm nauseous. And then my stomach is in turmoil. I've got cold sweats, shivers, in other words, I feel terrible."

"Diarrhoea?"

"Damn, I should never have let myself be convinced . . ."

"You certainly don't have a good colour!"

Without a word, Diolaiti sets the glass on the arm of the couch, jumps to his feet and runs towards the bathroom.

Garofano heads in the same direction. Then, hearing the noises coming from behind the door of the bathroom, he stops in the middle of the room. He takes the cigar out of his mouth.

"Grit your teeth," he shouts. "You'll see, you'll feel better afterwards!"

"Hello, Leo. It's Franz."

"Oh, so you're still alive!"

"Why?"

"I wouldn't have put money on it. Word's going around that the Bear is looking for you so he can bash you to pieces."

"It's a relief to know that you're all thinking of me. Listen, Leo. I have a favour to ask."

"Oh no, Franz. I'm sorry, but you've chosen the wrong person. This time I'm not falling for it."

"It's not money. I need to borrow your Renault."

Leo is silent for a few seconds.

"The Renault? Will you tell me what the fuck you're going to do with the Renault?"

"I promised a friend that I would help her get some stuff out of her house. It'll only take a couple of hours."

"A move? You know, you can't load an awful lot in my van."

"Yes, I know. But for what I have to carry it will do just fine."

"I don't know, Franz. When do you need it?"

"Now. I'll come by and get it and bring it back in an hour and half at most. It's a promise."

Another silence.

"You're not afraid I'll ruin it?"

"All right. But only because today is Saturday and I just have a few small jobs in the neighbourhood. I'll leave the keys with Stefania, who's doing the bills here in the shop. But I'm warning you, Franz. Remember I have to work in that van!"

Francesco hangs up, raises his eyes and finds Leila in front of him, wearing a pair of black jeans and a dark grey sweater. The wide neckline reveals the pale skin of her chest, against which the edge of a black T-shirt stands out. But the most astonishing thing is her hair. Very short and dyed almost white blond, with tufts sticking straight up, fixed in place with hair gel.

"Hey, what's that face?" she says, smiling.

Francesco studies her. He purses his lips and tilts his head.

"You look like a punk. But you know what? It's not bad at all!"

"What did your brother say?"

"Unfortunately he agreed. So it seems it's up to me to help you."

"Tell me the truth, you're already thinking of the five million you're about to put in your pocket."

"No. I'm thinking that I'm about to do the dumbest thing in the world and that I'll certainly regret it."

*

"I hope you're happy. Your cure has certainly been effective!"

"What do you mean? Everybody knows that hot water and lemon is beneficial!"

"Then I'm the stupid one for still listening to you."

"Excuse me, Diolaiti, now you're starting to bug me!"

"Oh, shit!" says Diolaiti, bringing one hand to his stomach. He crosses the room in a hurry. Garofano decides it's better not to persist. He sits in front of the television, turns up the volume so that he can't hear his colleague's curses coming from the bathroom.

When he reappears, Diolaiti has the face of a corpse;

his lips are an opaque colour between purple and blue.

"Holy God, I've never been so bad. The next time I hear you talk about one of your recipes, I'll shoot you."

"Forget about it. Do you want me to run out to the pharmacy and get you something?"

"Maybe that would be a good idea. I don't want to spend the whole weekend in the toilet."

*

"So we're all set?" says Leila, through the little window that connects the cab to the rear of the van.

"Yes, I've got it. Now I get out, take a look around, and if everything seems quiet, I signal to you."

"But first ring my bell. You never know. If no one answers, I'll get out of the van and come with you. We'll try ringing Signora Ruffini. She's almost always home."

Francesco parks the van. He turns off the engine.

"Don't worry," Leila whispers to him from inside. "You'll see. It'll all be fine."

He nods, then gets out, clutching a toolbox. He's wearing the work clothes that Leo lent him, which are too short. The trousers barely reach his calves. He feels ridiculous and out of place. Before crossing the street, he looks right and left. He doesn't seem to see anyone suspicious in the vicinity.

On one of the nameplates he finds Ronchi L. He presses the button and waits, toolbox in hand. Nothing. He tries again, this time pressing for a longer time. No answer. Up to here, everything all right. He glances at the other nameplates. On one of the two bells for the third floor he sees the name Ruffini, Aldo. That

237

must be the husband. He turns towards the van and signals with his arm.

*

Diolaiti is sitting on the toilet seat, hunched forward as if he hasn't an ounce of energy left in his body. Right now he's trying to decide if it's worth the trouble of getting up or if it's better to stay there, waiting for the next wave. He just hopes that Garofano gets back soon with something that works.

He feels another attack about to arrive. The ringing of the doorbell surprises him in the middle of a cramp. He looks towards the bathroom door. It can't be true. That moron Garofano must have forgotten the keys! The contraction required to get up provokes another sharp pain. He stiffens and sinks back again, pressing his stomach with his hands. He curses his colleague through his teeth. Him, his obsession and that god-damn whore of a mother, the origin of the lethal recipe that has reduced him to this state.

When the bell rings again, much longer and more insistent than the first time, Diolaiti is bent forward. His face, livid and covered with an icy sweat, is touching the dark blue tiles of the floor. There's a desperate-sounding gurgle in his throat. If curses had an effect, Garofano would die on the spot, struck down with his finger on the bell.

And if by some chance it isn't him? With an extreme effort of will, Diolaiti tears off a piece of toilet paper and wipes himself. Then with a further effort he pulls up his trousers, drags his feet towards the door.

A glance is enough to see that the bunch of spare keys is no longer hanging in its place. He hobbles to the shelf where he placed his .9 calibre. He grabs the automatic with trembling fingers.

As he takes off the safety, he hears a metallic sound from the landing.

*

Leila jumps out of the van and hurries across the street.

"Everything OK?"

"Seems like it. I rang twice, but no one answered."

"Good," says Leila, pressing the Ruffinis' bell.

After a short wait a voice asks who it is.

"It's Leila Ronchi, signora. The tenant on the floor below. I forgot my front-door key. Could you let me in?"

The electric buzz of the lock sounds almost immediately.

"Thanks," Leila says.

Francesco follows her through the doorway.

"You're sure you can open the door with that stuff?"

"I hope so."

They go up the stairs two at a time. On each landing there are three doors. Arriving on the third floor, Leila indicates the middle one.

"Come on, take out the tools."

Francesco sets the metal box down on the mat. He is about to raise the lid when he hears a sound and sees the door in front of him open. He looks up with a start. A man with a pale angular face is staring at him.

Saturday, 3 April, 1993, 4 P.M.– 12 A.M.

Leila jumps aside, flattening herself against the wall a fraction of a second before Diolaiti looks out, holding the doorknob in his left hand. The right, hidden behind the doorjamb, holds the gun.

"Hello," says Francesco, still bent over the toolbox.

Diolaiti inclines his head sideways. Where did this guy come from? And what the hell is he doing?

"Are you the one who rang the bell?" he says.

Leila, with a shiver of fear, recognizes the voice of the man with the razor.

"I was about to leave. I was sure no one was home."

Slow down, Franz. Slow down. Don't speak too fast.

"Who are you looking for?"

Francesco stands up without managing to contain a grimace. Every movement causes a sharp pain in his back. Leila, flattened against the wall, stares at him. He tries not to look even for a second in her direction. He keeps his gaze fixed on the angular face of the man in front of him. He has the impression that he is staring into the eyes of a gigantic ant, suspicious and ready to strike.

"I had an appointment to fix a broken tap."

Diolaiti lowers his eyes to the toolbox. His gaze moves slowly upwards along the work clothes and stops on Francesco's face. He smiles, trying to look casual.

"The lady isn't home?" Francesco asks. He immediately regrets it. He has to be careful not to say too much. But the man's eyes make him uneasy and that silent stare is unnerving.

"She's not home. When did you speak to her?"

Francesco shrugs.

"I don't remember exactly. She called me Monday, maybe. Or Tuesday."

"And why are you coming only today?"

"I've been busy. And she said it wasn't urgent."

Leila breathes with her mouth open, very slowly, careful not to produce the slightest sound. Francesco manages to get a view into the apartment, behind the man. It's a huge mess. Doors open, drawers emptied, a lot of stuff piled on the floor. His house, in comparison, is a paradise.

"Well, whatever," Diolaiti says, breaking the silence, "I've got things to do now."

The pain in his intestines has started up again. Sudden, terrible cramps, which feel as though they are tearing his guts. He has to clench his teeth in order not to fold forward.

"OK, I understand," Francesco says. "I'll come back another time."

Diolaiti has an attack of vertigo. There is something that isn't convincing about this plumber. But the spasms are rapidly increasing and becoming more painful every second. He's afraid of going in his pants at any moment.

Francesco, meanwhile, has closed his toolbox.

"Well, then, I'm going. Goodbye."

Diolaiti closes the door and hurries towards the bathroom. He puts the .9 calibre on the edge of the sink, fumbles with his belt buckle.

As soon as the door is closed, Leila nods towards the stairs and moves off on tiptoe. Francesco, with the toolbox in his hand, hurries after her.

They go down three steps at a time, reaching the street at the same moment as a violent burst of diarrhoea strikes Diolaiti with his trousers at his knees. As he sinks onto the toilet seat, exhausted, he suddenly realizes what it was that didn't make sense. In the whole house he hasn't noticed a single leaky tap. He grabs the gun, but he's too weak to go in pursuit. He drops the barrel of the automatic on the white skin of his thighs and lets his back fall against the top of the toilet.

*

Garofano is returning up the street with the cigar in his mouth. His hand, in his pocket, plays with the packet of Imodium he's just bought. When he's just about at the entrance to the building he sees two people coming out in a hurry. He jumps forward to grab the door before it closes. Then, instead of entering, he stops on the threshold, turns to observe the couple who have just left. He sees them run into the street and get in a van parked on the other side.

One detail has struck him, but he can't focus on what it is. Maybe it's the way they're dressed. The man is wearing work clothes and carrying a toolbox, and the girl's hair is cut in an absurd manner. Garofano shakes his head. She really looks ridiculous! He shrugs his shoulders, turning. But the bell in his head starts ringing louder. Just a second. Where has he seen that face? But of course, shit, it's the whore from last night!

He runs into the street, sticking his hand under his jacket. The two have just got into a white van. Garofano, with his palm on the butt of the .45, sees a traffic cop approaching the van. He slows down, without taking his hand off the gun. He sees the plumber lower the window, the cop leans over towards him. Garofano hesitates. He could follow them in the car and stop them somewhere else. He takes his finger off the trigger, rummages in the pockets of his jacket. Nothing to be done. Diolaiti must have the keys of the Audi. Meanwhile the man at the wheel has started the engine. Garofano sees the cop take a step back, smack the roof of the van, wave his arm, signalling it to move on. As he watches it leave, he memorizes the writing on the rear door.

LEONARDO LAMBERTINI

PLUMBING REPAIRS

BOILER INSTALLATION AND MAINTENANCE

TEL. 700377

*

"What do you mean the girl doesn't know anything? So where is the document?"

Matera scratches his ear.

"I don't know. I don't think she ever had it . . . or maybe she lost it."

"Lost? You're telling me that that document has been lost?"

"I'm not at all certain about it. But that's what might have happened."

"I pray to God that you're wrong. And what do you think about the two men from intelligence? Couldn't they have it?"

"Not impossible. But in that case I imagine that sooner or later you'll be informed."

At the other end of the telephone is a long silence.

"I would say so. Now what do you propose doing?"

"I'm asking you. With the girl a dead end, I don't think there's much else for me to do here in Bologna."

Another silence.

"Listen, Matera. These last developments have caught me by surprise. Let me speak to the Minister. I'll call you back as soon as I can."

*

Leila and Francesco leave the building, hurry across the street and jump into the Renault. As he is about to start the engine, Francesco sees a cop approaching the van. He lowers the window. He tries to smile.

"Excuse me, you know there's no parking here?"

"Yes, I know," says Francesco, looking disconsolate. "But I stopped just for five minutes, for an emergency. There was a leaking pipe; it was flooding an apartment. I'm leaving right away."

"Hurry up, then."

Francesco turns the ignition key. He goes into first.

"Move it," says the traffic cop, slapping the roof with one hand. "Get out of here!"

As soon as they leave, Leila drops her head back against the seat.

"Shit, I was afraid that asshole wouldn't let us go!"

"All we needed was a fine . . . But what the hell was that guy doing in your house?"

"What do you think he was doing? Waiting for me! Luckily you pulled it off really well."

"I almost didn't make it! That man gave me the creeps."

"He had a face like an insect, right? With cheekbones sticking out and thin lips."

"And pale as a corpse."

"It was him. I recognized his voice."

Francesco turns into Via Irnerio, glances at Leila.

"You mean one of the men who killed that guy?"

"Yes."

"Well, then it seems to me that you are in big trouble."

Leila stares at the street beyond the windscreen, without focusing.

*

"You should have shot them!"

"I told you there was a traffic cop! You think I should have shot him too?"

"Meanwhile you let them get away!"

"No, to be precise it's you who let them get away! You had them within reach and you didn't lift a finger to stop them."

"It's all the fault of that damn *parmigiana*!"

"All right, there's no point in getting all worked up. I managed to read the name of the plumber and I remember the phone number. If we find him, we'll trace the girl too."

"Then let's move. There's no time to lose."

*

After returning the van to Leo, they decide to go back to Francesco's.

"Now what are you going to do?"

Leila shrugs.

"I don't know. I'll have to think about it."

"If you want, you can stay with me for a few more days."

"But didn't you say you wanted to get away?"

"True. I ought to cut out, and so should you. We could take a holiday together. Too bad we don't even have enough money to fill the petrol tank."

"I'm sorry about the reward I promised you."

Francesco shakes his head.

"Forget it. With my luck, I would be amazed if I had found it in my pocket."

He pulls up to the curb and turns off the engine of the old Peugeot. Before getting out, he checks to see if the Bear is around. They go up the stairs in silence. In the house, the usual mess.

"Shall we have some coffee?" Francesco proposes, with his hands in his pockets.

Leila smiles without joy. While he pokes around in the sink, she sits down, rests one elbow on the table, lets her chin fall on the back of her hand.

"To cheer ourselves up, we need a hit of coke, not coffee."

"You said it," Francesco answers, managing to get a cup out from under the pile of dishes. "But for the moment, apart from caffeine, the only available drugs are a couple of beers and some teabags."

"Wait a second. Not so fast!"

Francesco sees her jump to her feet, go to the other side of the table, bend down and dig through the pockets of her jacket, which is hanging on a chair.

"Here we go!"

Triumphantly she shows him an envelope folded in four.

246

"What is it?"

Leila doesn't answer. She tears the upper side of the envelope and empties it on the table. Francesco approaches, observes in astonishment the snowfall that pours out, forming a small mound. Leila looks up and smiles, radiant, while she shakes the envelope to empty it completely. Along with the last particles of powder, a piece of paper slides out, falling onto the mound of cocaine.

*

Stefania, the girl who helps Leo with appointments and the accounts, looks up from the ledger, sees two men wearing jackets and ties come in. The bigger one runs the palm of his hand over his head, smoothing down his comb-over. The other seems about to cry.

"Good evening. How may I help you?"

"We're looking for Signor Lambertini," the bigger one answers, while the thin one takes out a handkerchief and runs it over one eye.

"Leo left about ten minutes ago. He said he was running out for a coffee. He should be back soon."

"Yes, but we're in a hurry. Do you know where we can find him?"

"He's at Bar 28, on the next cross street. Just a few steps away."

The two men turn their backs without saying another word.

*

The Bear is playing cards at one of the tables under the portico. And he's losing. Gandini, who's his partner, takes responsibility for their losses and avoids at all cost looking at the bandage around his head.

"Sorry, Bear. As you can see, it's not my day today."

The Bear gives him a harsh glance.

"It doesn't matter, Gandini, but let's try to win at least one game."

"I'm trying, but when the cards aren't right, there's not much you can do."

Balduzzi and Rangoni, who are playing against them, exchange a glance. In order not to irritate the Bear, they are doing as much as they can to favour the other two, but fate continues to provide them with trumps – aces and threes. Even when they try, they can't lose a hand.

In the bar, Leo is drinking a glass of white wine. Meanwhile he's talking to Bobo.

"Was it really Franz who put the Bear in that state?"

"Even I couldn't believe it. It's madness. Your brother is digging his grave with his own hands."

"Well, we're only half-brothers. Still, I'm wondering how before my mother died she had the bad idea of marrying that good-for-nothing and even having a child."

Leo sips his wine thoughtfully.

"Imagine, today he asked to borrow my van."

"The van? To do what?"

"How should I know? He said he had to help a friend move some stuff. I was sure he wouldn't return it until Monday. Instead he brought it back in less than half an hour."

Bobo shakes his head.

"It would take a real genius to figure him out," he says, continuing to stick cups and glasses in the basket of the dishwasher.

*

The van is parked on a diagonal across the street.

"There it is," says Garofano, elbowing Diolaiti. "It's that one."

"Let's go, then. Let's not let him get away."

Four men are sitting at a table under the portico, playing cards. Diolaiti and Garofano walk by the players, checking their faces carefully.

"He's not here."

"Let's try inside."

They enter the bar and look around. Then they head for the counter, where a red-haired man is chatting with the bartender.

"Good evening," Bobo greets them. "What can I get you?"

"We're looking for a plumber. One called Lambertini."

Bobo shifts his gaze to Leo, who wipes his lips and says: "That's me."

Garofano and Diolaiti look at him, then exchange a glance.

"Then the person we're looking for is someone who works with you."

"I don't have employees or partners. Only a girl in the office. What's the problem?"

"Excuse me, would you mind if we went outside and had a few words in private?"

Leo looks at Bobo, who shrugs and returns his questioning glance. He drains his glass, then goes outside and stops next to a column, a few steps from the table where the four men are playing. Diolaiti and Garofano follow him.

"So?"

Garofano points to the Renault parked on the other side of the street.

"Is that your van?"

"Of course it's mine. Why?"

"Do you know if it might have been in Via del Borgo San Pietro about three-quarters of an hour ago?"

This is beginning to look fishy.

"Maybe."

"I'm asking you if you did or did not use that van this afternoon. It doesn't seem like a difficult question."

Leo looks at one and then the other. The way the thin one continues to stare at him makes him uneasy.

"If you would explain exactly what you want from me, maybe . . ."

"Lambertini, if you really have nothing to hide, why are you making such a fuss?"

"Excuse me, but I don't see why I should give an account of who drives or doesn't drive my van to two people I don't know! Is it because of an accident? If that's it, there's no problem. The insurance is in order."

"No, not an accident," Diolaiti intervenes. "Don't worry. It's just that we urgently need to trace the people who used your Renault. That's all."

"But can't you tell me who you are?"

Garofano snorts. He hooks his thumbs on his belt, shifting the edge of his jacket to one side.

"No, I can't tell you. But, if you're interested, I can tell you that I'm about to lose patience."

Leo sees the butt of a gun sticking out from under his jacket.

"All right, all right," he says. "No need to get excited. I don't know what the heck Franz is up to, but I have no intention of getting involved in it."

"Franz?"

"Francesco Lenzi. The one I lent the van to."

*

Francesco looks up from the piece of paper, scratches his forehead.

"Can you understand anything from this?"

"I don't know," Leila answers. "It seems that these two million marks were moved from one account to another."

"And you think all those people are looking for this?"

"Let's say it seems possible to me."

"If that's the case, this piece of paper is worth a shitload of money. What should we do?"

"That man left me his mobile phone number. He said to call him if by some chance something useful should occur to me."

"You think he really is willing to hand over the money?"

"Why not? He was the one who said he was willing to pay to get what he was looking for."

"OK. But you're not sure that this piece of paper has anything to do with it. I see here only numbers. There's not even a name. It's impossible to tell who paid the money and who received it."

"Yes, but I can always . . ."

The ringing of the telephone interrupts her sentence in the middle. They both stare at the instrument as if it might have overheard their conversation.

*

The Bear is losing his eighth game when he seems to hear Franz's name mentioned. He glances behind him and, under the portico, a few feet away, sees Leo talking to two men. He concentrates, trying to grasp what they're saying, but only manages to pick up a few

251

shreds of the conversation. But he catches Franz's name immediately.

He waits until the conversation is over. As soon as he sees the two men going off, he abandons his cards on the table and gets up and hurries after them.

"Wait a second. I heard you're looking for Franz."

"You know him?" Garofano asks.

"Very well, unfortunately," the Bear answers, pulling out the notebook in which he's marked down all Francesco's debts. "And when it comes to collecting, I would strongly advise you to put yourself in my hands. I pay fifty per cent of what you're owed and your credit becomes my business. Half immediately is always better than nothing, right?"

Diolaiti and Garofano look at one another questioningly. With his teeth the Bear pulls off the top of his pen.

"So, how much has he lost to you?"

"Just a moment, I don't think we've understood each other. Can you tell us where we might find this Francesco Lenzi?"

The Bear gives an evil smile, clenching the cap of the pen between his teeth.

"Don't worry. I'll take care of rousting him out!"

Garofano pinches one earlobe, studying the beast in front of him.

"You don't trust me? You can ask around. I've already made the same proposal to a lot of people, and they all thought it was a good deal."

Diolaiti takes out the handkerchief and dries his right eye.

"If I were you," the Bear insists, "I wouldn't let the opportunity escape. You just tell me the figure and the names of the people who can testify."

"Just a minute," Garofano interrupts, indicating the

bandage. "You took a pretty bad knock in the head, didn't you?"

The Bear stops, with the point of his Bic resting on the notebook.

"What?"

Garofano glances at Diolaiti, who puts the handkerchief in his pocket and nods, to suggest to him that they should go.

"You're right, let's forget it. Since this fellow here seems to me a little soft in the head."

The Bear stares at them in astonishment.

"What? Are you talking about me?"

Diolaiti stretches his lips into a cold smile, his eyes narrow to cracks.

"No, my friend," says Garofano, slapping him on the back. "Why would you think that? You go on taking down your notes. We, however, are in a hurry, and if you don't mind we'll stop bothering you."

The two turn on their heels, leaving the Bear openmouthed in astonishment, as he watches them moving off, the pen and notebook still in his hands.

*

Standing in front of the metal shelves, Stefania arranges the invoices in a file. Out of the corner of her eye, she sees Leo hunched over the desk, while he grips the receiver hard, trying not to shout.

"What I just told you, Franz! Yes, you've got it, two men who were looking for you. Can you tell me what the hell you did with my van? Remember, if you get me in trouble I'll be seriously angry! If I were you . . . of course I gave them your address! You think I want to be shot covering for you? I'm not raving! I saw with my own eyes the gun one of them had under his armpit. Franz? Franz?"

*

Francesco hangs up the phone.

"Who was it?"

"My brother, mad as a wild beast. He says that two men he didn't know cornered him at the bar, looking for information about the van and the person he'd lent it to."

"And?"

"He realized that one of the two was armed and he caved. He blurted out who I am, where I live, everything."

"Shit! When did that happen?"

Francesco scratches his neck.

"I don't know. A little while ago, I imagine."

They look at each other in silence for a few seconds.

"I don't understand," Francesco says. "If they traced Leo, it means that they had already figured it out when we left your house and followed us."

"Maybe they looked out the window and recognized me, who knows? Anyway we'd better get out in a hurry."

"Damn!" Francesco cries, rushing towards the bedroom.

He climbs over the pile of dirty laundry and starts throwing stuff haphazardly into the suitcase. Leila joins him, throwing in the things she bought for herself. They both move rapidly, without exchanging a word. When the suitcase is full, Francesco closes it quickly.

As they're about to head into the hallway, Leila stops him.

"Wait a second."

He stands in the kitchen doorway, watches her as she takes a knife from the sink and with the blade separates from the mound of coke a small quantity, which she then divides into four parallel lines.

"Do you have a pen?"

"In the drawer," Francesco answers, moving towards the cabinet.

Leila grabs the Bic, takes out the ink rod and uses the empty case to inhale two of the four lines. Then she hands the pen to Francesco, who takes the two remaining ones.

"We needed that," Leila says, running her index finger under her nose.

Before going out to the landing, Francesco checks through the peephole.

"All clear?" Leila asks behind him.

"Looks like it."

Along the stairs they meet the army officer from the second floor, who is going up.

"Ah, excuse me, just you —"

"Bye." Francesco cuts him off, without even a glance.

The lobby is deserted. Francesco grasps the door handle and, with his thumb, pushes the button that opens it. He finds himself face to face with Diolaiti and Garofano, who are studying the nameplates. He is paralysed, and Leila practically falls on top of him. Garofano takes the .45 out of its holster and points it at Francesco, forcing him to retreat.

"Get inside," he says. "And don't even dream of opening your mouth."

Francesco backs up slowly, carrying the suitcase, while the two men enter, letting the door slam shut behind them. Now Diolaiti is holding his automatic and keeping Leila in its sight. Garofano approaches the stairwell, leans over to look up.

"What floor do you live on?"

Francesco swallows.

"Fourth."

"Then let's take the lift, what do you say?" Garofano says, winking at Leila. "I had enough stairs the other night."

*

The Bear returns to the table and sits down, but without resuming the game.

"I don't feel like it anymore," he declares.

"Just as well," Balduzzi says, rubbing his hands together. "It's starting to get cold out here."

"True," Rangoni says, standing up. "Besides, I have to go. I'm sure my wife is already expecting me."

"You're right," adds Gandini, following Rangoni with his gaze as he enters the bar, taking out his wallet. "And I'm tired of losing!"

The Bear glares at him.

"I'm not stopping because we're losing," he explains. "It's that I'm pissed off!"

He feels an acid rage foaming inside him. Those two shits treated him like an idiot. However you look at it, whenever Franz is involved, one way or another you always get screwed! He stands up without saying goodbye to anyone. He crosses the street, gets in his Volvo and takes off, tyres squealing. Gandini raises his glass in the direction of the car and drains what's left of the Fernet.

"I wouldn't say it to his face," he says, turning to Balduzzi. "But when he's in a shitty mood like this, he's a real pain in the ass!"

*

Francesco's fingers tremble as he tries to insert the key in the lock.

"Let's see if we can do this in less than a week," the big man snarls, pressing the gun into his back.

He has forgotten to warn them about the shelf. They're passing through the hall, and one of the two must have bumped it, because it crashes to the floor. Diolaiti, alarmed by the noise, shoves his elbow into the bicycle leaning against the wall, knocking that over too. The guns get jerked around in all the confusion, and it's a miracle that neither one fires a shot.

"OK," Garofano says, when silence has returned. "Now everybody try to stay calm. Come on, let's go. And no joking."

They make Francesco put the suitcase down. Then, with Diolaiti keeping the gun on him, Garofano pushes the table against the sink and arranges two pairs of chairs, facing each other. They all sit down.

Diolaiti dries his eye with his handkerchief. Garofano settles his buttocks on the chair, takes from his jacket a narrow metal cylinder.

"Now," he says, screwing the tube onto the barrel of the gun, "let's have a few words in peace and quiet."

Francesco feels the sweat dripping between his shirt and his skin. He glances sideways at Leila, sitting next to him, and realizes that she too is pale and rigid. Garofano indicates the girl's head with his arm.

"Why did you change your hairdo?"

She remains silent.

"If you want my opinion, you looked better before."

Diolaiti has the gun pointed at Leila, his lips tightened in a kind of painful grimace. The skin looks as if it had been stretched over the sharp bones of his face.

*

The Bear gets out of the Volvo and kicks the door closed. He looks up at the façade of the building. At that moment, the snout of a Dalmatian pokes out of the doorway, followed by a girl attached to a leash, who is trying to keep control of the dog. The Dalmatian drags the girl across the pavement. It stops beside the Volvo, sniffs it, then lifts one leg and pees on the front tyre.

*

The Secretary, in a funereal tone, has told him to return to base.

"I'm doing what I can, but the Minister is beside himself. There's no point in trying to hide our concern from you."

Matera has asked what he should do with the money. The Secretary told him to bring it back to Rome.

"That money is the least of our problems," he said. "We're pleased, of course, that at least it wasn't spent for nothing."

Matera folds his shirt carefully, lays it on the pile of socks and undershirts. Next to it he arranges the bag with the toothbrush, toothpaste, razor. Then, between the bag and the side of the suitcase, he sticks the bottle of aftershave and the can of shaving cream.

Before he leaves, he ought to make a phone call to the Commissioner to update him on what he knows. He can decide if it's worth the trouble to accuse the two intelligence agents of murder, or if it's more prudent to let the investigation follow its natural course and end up shelved. Maybe, he thinks, dialling the number of police headquarters, they'll manage to get their hands on the girl and try to pin the crime on her. Unless someone shuts her up first.

While the signal echoes in the receiver, he thinks that he hasn't accomplished much. But at least he got to hear Petrucciani, and the concert was worth the journey.

*

Francesco's hands are like ice. End of the line. End of everything. But why, why, why did he let himself get dragged into this mess? He listens to Leila stalling, improvising lies and admissions in a desperate attempt to delay handing over the piece of paper. But it's all too clear that sooner or later the two men are going to run out of patience. All they want to know is if Leila can help them find the document they're looking for. Francesco feels his brain fogging up. Their lives are bound to the piece of paper that Leila has stuck in the pocket of her jacket. All those men have to do is search her and for them it will be all over. His stomach is as tight as a fist.

"Listen, you little shit," Garofano says to her. "I'm sick of listening to your crap. If you don't tell me immediately what you know, I'll shoot your friend. And if you still don't want to talk, then it's your turn."

The man's enormous steel-coloured gun revolves towards Francesco's chest. He holds his breath and turns to Leila in terror. He sees her run her tongue over her lips.

"And remember, I don't want any more of your

nonsense. This time, don't tell me there's a guy down in the street waiting for you."

Leila opens her mouth to say something. At that instant the doorbell rings. For a second the scene seems to freeze.

"Now, who the fuck is that?" Garofano growls. "Diolaiti, keep the gun on them. I'll have a look."

He goes into the corridor. He climbs carefully over the bicycle and the stuff that fell off the shelf. He brings his eye to the peephole. On the landing he sees the man from before, that giant moron with the bandaged head. Then the moron raises his arm, presses the bell again.

"Franz," says the Bear, with his finger still pressing the bell. "There's no point in being clever. I know you're home!"

Garofano bites his lip. Is that jerk involved? It doesn't seem possible. But, given that he's up here, it would be better not to let him get away. He seems pretty agitated, there's always the risk that he could give an alarm. He turns the handle.

The Bear has just raised his hand to pound his fist against the door when it opens and he finds himself face to face with one of the two men who made fun of him in front of the bar. He doesn't have time to notice that the man has a gun. He continues the movement and lands a punch right in his face, with the full weight of the arm.

Garofano, thrown backwards, falls onto the bicycle. The moment the punch hits him the .45 goes off. The bullet hits the floor a couple of feet from the Bear's left foot. The shot is muffled by the silencer and covered by the crash of the body landing on the bike. The Bear is aware of nothing. He leaps forward and charges inside, moving like a bulldozer over

260

Garofano, the bike, the various objects scattered on the floor.

Diolaiti turns suddenly, in time to see him appear in the doorway. He aims the SIG-Sauer, but Leila lunges at him, knocking him off his chair. The bullet goes high and hits the doorframe. The .9 calibre doesn't have a silencer and the sound of the shot echoes deafeningly in the little kitchen. The Bear, startled by the detonation, stands paralysed in the doorway as a cascade of plaster descends on him. Meanwhile Leila is on the floor, struggling with Diolaiti. She punches him, again and again. The man, pivoting on his hip, manages to shake her off. Francesco looks around. He sees the hammer on the sink. He grabs it. The first blow hits Diolaiti in the right shoulder, eliciting a cry of pain. From the SIG-Sauer another shot fires, this one ricochets off the floor and lands in the door of the refrigerator. The Bear, hearing the shot, ducks his head between his shoulders. Francesco again raises the hammer, brings it down between Diolaiti's shoulder blades, while the Bear, exasperated now, advances towards the knot of bodies. Francesco, seeing him approach, hurls the hammer at him, and it strikes him in the chest. Diolaiti drags himself away on his elbows. The Bear, finding him at his feet, kicks him. Diolaiti rolls over on his side, faints. When the Bear looks up, he sees Leila, kneeling on the floor, aiming the .9 calibre at him.

"Stop right there," she says, panting. "Stop right there or I swear I'll shoot you!"

The Bear hesitates, confused, his arms hanging down at his sides.

Francesco, sitting on the floor, shouts at him, "Bear, please, stay calm. This is already a big mess. Don't make things worse."

The Bear's eyes are flashing with rage under thick eyebrows sprinkled with plaster.

*

The first drops struck the windscreen at Barberino, and after a few minutes it began to rain hard. Matera turns on the windscreen wipers and raises the volume of the stereo a couple of notches. "Sweet Georgia Brown", played by Dizzy, Pres and Bird. Three giants. Pity the recording's rather bad.

The trailer truck in front of him, in spite of the wet road and the poor visibility, is doing eighty. The fat tyres send up dense masses of water. Matera decides to pass it anyway. He increases his speed, puts on his indicator, shifts into fourth. He feels a sharp pain in his knee. He moves into the left lane and accelerates to the floor, just as "I Can't Get Started With You" begins. The Alfa takes off, gaining ground rapidly.

When he has just about got past, he seems to hear, under Lester Young's solo, the ring of his mobile phone. He lowers the volume on the stereo. It really is the phone. He presses the accelerator to the floor again, quickly gets back into the right lane, digs around with his hand among the folds of his jacket. Extracting the telephone, he presses the button to answer.

"Yes?"

"Hello? Hello, can you hear me?"

A woman's voice, muffled by the static on the line.

"Yes, who is it?" Matera answers, loudly.

"It's Leila. The girl you talked to today. Remember?"

Matera glances in the rear-view mirror and takes his foot off the accelerator. The Alfa Romeo slows down.

"Perfectly," he says. "Do you have any news for me?"

From the phone comes a dense crackle.

"Hello?" Matera shouts. "Hello? Hello?"

They're cut off. A deafening roar startles him, as the headlights of the truck he just passed flash in the rectangle of the mirror. Matera pushes the accelerator to the floor again, and the Alfa 90 leaps forward, leaving the Scania far behind. The broad headlights grow distant in the darkness.

*

Francesco, with his back pressed against the oscillating door of the telephone booth, looks at Leila hang up the receiver.

"Did you speak to him?"

"I could hardly hear him, then the line went dead."

"Great. Now what do we do?"

"I don't know. I think he was in the car. Let's wait a little, then try again."

"You really think he'll help us get out of this mess?"

"No, but I'm sure he's ready to hand over the suitcase to get this piece of paper."

"And then? There's still a risk of not getting very far, even with all that money."

"We have to figure out a plan of escape, then grab the money and disappear."

"No sooner said than done."

"Well, actually . . . I might know someone who can give us a hand."

"And who might that be? The genie with the lamp?"

"An old acquaintance. Anyhow, there's no way to accomplish all this now. We have to find a place to spend the night and make some phone calls in peace. What do you say we look for a hotel?"

"Maybe the fact that we don't have a shred of identification has escaped you."

"We'll find a clerk who's willing to turn a blind eye! A good tip is always useful."

"And where are we going to get the money?"

"Surprise," says Leila with a big smile. "See what I took from that guy's jacket before we cleared out."

"Shit! Don't tell me you stole his wallet!"

"The wallet and, while I was at it, the gun too."

*

"Alvisi, it's Diolaiti. We have a job for you. Yes, I know it's late, but it's an emergency. Do you have paper and pen? Good, then take down this name. Lenzi, Francesco. We need all possible information on him. He's with the girl. We'll wait for news."

He ends the conversation, looks at Garofano, who is touching his lip with the tips of his fingers.

"What I would like to know," he says, "is how you managed to get yourself laid out."

"I'd like to have seen you! I'd barely opened the door when that beast punched me in the face! You, though, how could you have been taken by surprise?"

"They were all on me at the same moment!" Diolaiti says, massaging the place where the Bear kicked him. "I think I have some broken ribs. And my shoulder took a beating!"

"Don't tell me," Garofano answers, continuing to touch in a gingerly fashion his upper lip, on which the blood, coagulating, has formed a dense wine-coloured clot. "That pig smashed my mouth. Two incisors and a canine. What a bill I'm going to get from the dentist!"

"And my wallet and gun were stolen!"

*

They managed to find a category four pension in an alley in the Bolognina neighbourhood. The reception-ist, a man around forty, with two big bags under his eyes, and the bluish cheeks of a badly shaved beard, proves to be reasonable. To soften him up they hand him a couple of fifties, plus payment in advance for the night.

They go up a dimly lighted stairway, covered by a purple carpet, which is perhaps the only new object in the entire place.

The room is at the same level as everything else. The floor has a brown carpet, pockmarked by an infinity of cigarette burns. On the walls is wallpaper of an indefinable colour, somewhere between indigo and pink, with an ornamental ship design. A threadbare camel-coloured bedspread is thrown over sheets that look as though they have already been used. A night table, a wardrobe, a squat armchair, with four narrow legs that end in a point, complete the furnishings. In the bathroom, a toilet with a swaying black plastic seat, a tiny sink with separate taps for hot and cold water, an eight-by-twelve-inch mirror, a tub whose yellowed por-celain is dotted with black encrustations, like cockroaches.

Leila sits on the bed. The mattress creaks under her weight.

"Well, at least we have a place to sleep."

Francesco, standing opposite her, takes out a pack of Gauloises. He lights one.

"So," Leila says to him. "Are we partners?"

"If that's OK with you."

"Anyway, at this point we don't have many alterna-tives. Neither of us can stay here."

Francesco nods, inhaling again. Then he lets the smoke out of his mouth slowly. A dense grey tongue rises in front of his face.

"And then, correct me if I'm wrong, wasn't it your dream to throw it all in and go to South America?"

The tufts of her hair, shooting straight up, emit orange reflections under the forty-watt bulb trapped behind the wavy glass of the ceiling lamp. Francesco answers her smile with a scowl, undecided whether to kiss her or slap her.

*

At the exit for Prato, Matera leaves the highway to find a place where the mobile phone reception is better. He parks the Alfa and lights a cigarette, waiting for the girl to call back.

After twenty minutes or so the rain stops, and the temperature drops suddenly. Every so often he has to bend his leg, so that the knee doesn't get completely immobilized. The minutes pass, and the girl doesn't call. He wonders if when she telephoned before she was being tailed by someone. By now they could have killed her. Still, he might as well wait.

The music stops, Matera replaces the tape that has just ended with Coltrane. *Dear Old Stockholm* on side A, *Blue Train* on B. Every so often he lights a Marlboro and from time to time turns his head to glance at the two suitcases, embedded between the seatback and the rear seat. Coltrane's sax fills the car with daredevil acrobatics.

Finally, after more than an hour, the phone rings again.

It seems that the girl has found the document. She is

willing to hand it over to him. In exchange for the suitcase, obviously.

"How do I know you're not inventing the whole thing?"

"Let's see . . . what you're looking for should be a certificate of credit at the Banque Commerce de Genève. The account number is —"

"That's enough," Matera interrupts her. "The less we talk about it on the phone the better."

"So we'll make the exchange?"

"When were you thinking of doing it?"

"Tomorrow," Leila comes to the point. "I'll call to let you know how and where."

She hangs up. Only the obsessive lament of Coltrane's tenor remains and the marks of the rain that is drying on the windscreen.

He lights another cigarette and thinks for a couple of minutes. When "One Down, One Up" ends, he turns off the stereo and punches in a number on his phone. The Secretary's voice has the same timbre it has at nine in the morning.

"Hello? It's Matera. I'm sorry to disturb you at this hour."

"Don't worry. Have you got some news for me?"

"The girl got in touch again."

"Ah, very good."

"She found what we're looking for. She's willing to hand it over in exchange for the money."

"Are you sure she's means it?"

"I can't swear to it. But it doesn't sound like a bluff."

"Then proceed. Do you want me to send someone to help you?"

Matera scratches his cheek.

"No, thank you. I think I can handle it on my own."

*

The bartender sticks the tip of his index finger in his
right ear while he presses the receiver into his left and
shouts: "What did you say? Paolo? Paolo Baccigalupo?
Yes, he's here! You want me to get him?"

Leila, at the other end of the line, breathes a sigh of
relief.

"Yes, please. Tell him that Leila is looking for him."

"Lella?"

"No. *Leila*, with an 'i'!"

"Just a minute."

The bartender lets the receiver dangle on its metallic wire and goes into the mauve-coloured lounge.

Leila hears music thundering in the telephone. She
gives an affirmative nod to Francesco, who, sitting in
the armchair, looks at her without changing expression and crushes the cigarette in the ashtray.

In the mauve lounge the music is muffled. Paolo
is having a discussion with a man from Mantua, who
claims he can resell him a consignment of Bulovas.

"Stolen?" Paolo asks, taking a swig of Chivas.

"I don't want to know where they're from. And, by
the way, I don't see that it matters to you. I'm offering
them at cut price."

"All right. But I'd like to have a more precise idea."

"It's my brother-in-law who's involved in the business. I know practically nothing. But if you say you're
interested, I can put you in contact."

The bartender appears in the doorway.

"Paolo, there's a woman on the phone who wants to
talk to you."

"*Woman*?" Paolo asks, scowling. "Who? She didn't say
her name?"

"She said her name is Leila."

"Leila? Are you sure?"

The bartender sticks out his chin, shrugging his shoulders.

"I made her repeat it."

Paolo puts his glass down on the table.

"Can you wait a moment?" he says to the man from Mantua. "I'll be right back."

He follows the bartender, goes behind the bar and takes the receiver.

"Hello?"

"Paolo, is that you?"

"Leila! What's happening?"

"I thought I'd never find you. I've been looking all evening."

"Goddamn, it's been a century since I've heard from you! Are you well?"

"I'm calling from Bologna, but I'm not going to be here long. The fact is I'm in trouble, Paolo, and I need some help."

"In trouble? What kind of trouble?"

"It's a long story. Listen, Paolo, you once said to me that if by some chance I needed something, I could count on you."

"I remember. Tell me."

"I need two passports."

"Two passports?"

"One for a man about thirty, thirty-five, brown eyes, around five-ten. The other is for me. Do I have to give you the details or do you still remember?"

"A little over thirty. Five-six. And stupendous green eyes."

"Well, yes, more or less. I'm a little under five-six, but it doesn't matter. I'll add the photographs."

"When do you need them?"

"As soon as possible. Tomorrow, actually."

"That's a real hurry. The trouble is that big?"

"I'm afraid so."

"Anything else?"

Leila is silent for a moment, she bites her lower lip.

"Can you also get me a bag with a false bottom? You know, a travel bag, not too big, the kind you can take on a plane? It should have room for something like . . . wait, let me think . . . let's say forty comic books."

"*Diabolik* or *Tex*?"

Leila lets a laugh escape.

"What's there to laugh about? They're not at all the same size!"

"Let's say forty *Diabolik*s. Maybe even more."

"For a false bottom that's not small. You're going to make money pushing comic books?"

"I have to organize the cartel, but it looks promising."

"I can imagine. In any case, about the bag there's no problem. You want it hermetic?"

"Hermetic?"

"For the drug-sniffing dogs."

"Oh no. That doesn't matter."

"And you need it all by tomorrow?"

"Do you think you can do it?"

"I'll do everything in my power. Are you going far?"

"I would say yes. Assuming I manage to leave."

"How am I going to get you the stuff?"

"I haven't figured it out yet. I'll call you tomorrow morning and we'll decide."

"You can reach me on my mobile. Wait, I'll give you the number."

Leila writes the number on the cigarette pack.

"You don't know what a favour you're doing."

"Forget it. I'll wait for your call."

"OK. Till tomorrow."

"Leila."

"Yes?"

"Be careful that you don't do something stupid."

"Of course," Leila says, smiling. "Don't worry."

Francesco puts another Gauloise in his mouth and gestures with his chin.

"So, what did your friend say?"

*

The Filipino maid answers the phone. The Secretary, pronouncing the words clearly, asks her if the Minister is still up.

He's up, and hurries to answer.

"Yes?"

"Minister, excuse me if I allow myself to disturb you at this hour, but you advised . . ."

"Make it brief. Do you have news?"

"I spoke to Matera, Minister. The girl got in touch. She has what interests us and is willing to negotiate. They're supposed to talk tomorrow to make the arrangements."

"You were right to call me. This news gives me a breath of oxygen. By the way, do you have any engagements tomorrow?"

"No, Minister. I would say no."

"Then I'll expect you at lunch. With your wife, of course. Let's hope we'll be able to celebrate together the successful outcome of this painful operation."

"Thank you for the invitation, Minister. We'll be there with pleasure."

*

The receptionist at the hotel widens his eyes, seeing him return with all his suitcases.

"A hitch," Matera explains. "I should be here until tomorrow. May I have the same room?"

"Unfortunately 326 is occupied," the clerk says. "But we have others available. I don't think it will be a problem."

After he eats, he goes to his room, hangs his jacket on the back of a chair. He lays a piece of material on the desk. On it he places the Beretta. He disassembles it. While he carefully oils the barrel and the mechanisms, he reflects on the details of the exchange. The Secretary has entrusted it to him, so it's up to him to decide what is the safest route. Maybe, after retrieving the document, it would be better to shut the girl up for good. It wouldn't be difficult. But is it really advisable?

What he has in hand is one and a half million dollars, in two suitcases. And the girl doesn't know anything about the second. It's worth considering.

The most important thing – the Secretary has repeated this to him ad nauseam – is to retrieve that damn piece of paper. So why not give the girl the suitcase with the first half of the blackmail, get the document and keep the other three-quarters of a million dollars for himself?

What the Minister cares about is the document. Once Leila has put her hands on the money, she'll be busy getting herself out of circulation. Even if, in a second act, the men from the intelligence services succeeded in tracing her and something should happen to her, why would anyone be suspicious of him? There is any number of ways in which the missing amount could have disappeared.

Matera reassembles the last pieces of the 92SB attentively. He slides in the high-capacity magazine, fixing it in place with a shove of his palm. A ray of light sparkles on the burnished steel of the gun. Matera screws the Hush Puppy silencer onto the end of the barrel. Then he places the gun on the desk, folds up the cloth, goes to wash his hands.

His face, reflected in the bathroom mirror, shows all his fifty-four years. Maybe even a few more. How long will he still be able to do this kind of work?

Three-quarters of a million dollars would be a good advance for his retirement.

*

Leila got up and stretched her back, extending her arms towards the ceiling.

"I'm really hungry. What do you say we go and get something to eat?"

Francesco put out his cigarette.

On the first cross street they saw a sign for a trattoria. They ordered grilled chicken and green beans, steak and baked potatoes. While they ate, Leila explained her plan. After sharing an order of apple cake, they went back to the hotel.

They agreed that he would take the first shower. He washed in discomfort, under a thin stream of cool water, with sudden spurts of boiling hot, while the plastic curtain kept sticking to him.

When he came out of the bathroom, Leila was already asleep. He stood looking at her, with the towel around his neck. Then he put on a T-shirt and a pair of clean underpants, turned off the light and slid under the covers. The mattress creaked under his weight, but Leila didn't change the rhythm of her breath and went on breathing out through her nose. Before Francesco fell asleep, their feet just touched.

*

He could try the Austrian in Lagaccio. Paolo looks at his watch. It might be too late tonight to get the passports, but it doesn't cost anything to try. He looks around. On the other side of the room he sees the Fez, gestures at him to get his attention.

"I need a travel bag, more or less this size." With his hands he draws an approximate size in the air. "But it has to have a false bottom where you can hide some stuff."

"And where do I find a bag with a false bottom at this hour?"

"Remember the Chinese I rented that old warehouse to in Le Vigne? Try them. If they don't have one ready, have them make it now."

"But there won't be anyone in the workshop. Those slant-eyes will have been in lullaby land for hours by now!"

"So? They sleep in the basement. Drag them off their bunks and make them understand that I need the bag for tomorrow. If they make a fuss, say I'll kick them out on their asses. Got it?"

Paolo watches the Fez hurry to the door and, before he leaves, steps into the mauve lounge to say goodbye to the man from Mantua.

"Excuse me," he says, draining the last of his Chivas. "But I have to run. About those watches, it would be better if your brother-in-law and I have a few words in peace."

"Trouble?"

"No, only a matter I have to take care of in a hurry."

"Don't worry," the Mantuan says, shaking his hand. "Give me a call when you feel like it and I'll arrange a meeting. Meanwhile, think about it. You could make a lot of cash out of this."

Paolo gets in his Saab. As he heads for the Principe

station, he keeps wondering what goddamn mess Leila's got herself in. After all these years, suddenly she calls him with a fire under her and asks him to get two passports and a bag with a false bottom. It seems interesting. The question is: what the hell does she intend to transport in the bag? It's not drugs. What else could it be? Contraband goods? No, he's cold. Leila told him she didn't have an exact idea of the volume, but gave him an approximate size in terms of comic books. Why the example of comic books? He would bet that in that false bottom she has some papers to transport. Warmer, warmer. Money? Yes, ten to one Leila has it in mind to clear off with a wad of cash!

Paolo takes out his Lucky Strikes and, grabbing one between his teeth, pulls it out of the package. Then he pushes in the lighter. Leila mentioned forty comic books. That would certainly represent, more or less, a serious pile of money. Even if, obviously, it depends on the cut. The lighter pops out. Paolo lights his cigarette, inhales deeply, then puts a hand in his jacket pocket and takes out his mobile phone. Keeping an eye on the street, he presses the numbers, with the cigarette dangling from a corner of his mouth.

"Hello, Fez? Listen to me. You remember that bag we were talking about? Good. I want two. But I'm telling you, it's important that they be identical. Same size, same colour. They should be indistinguishable. I want twin bags, with the false bottom and all, get it? Call Parodi and Ghiglione. Tomorrow morning I want all three of you at the Gabbiano, at seven. Are we clear? And another thing. Bring with you what you need to disguise yourselves as customs officers. I've got a job for you."

*

Leila sleeps with one arm folded under the pillow. Her right leg, from the knee down, sticks out from under the sheet. Francesco, sitting on the chair opposite the bed, observes the perfect line of her calf, ending in the slender ankle.

He woke a quarter of an hour ago with a start, in the middle of an upsetting dream in which he was fighting with a man whom he was trying in whatever way he could to push over the edge of a very high balcony. In the dream it was night, and the man's hands, like tentacles, were gripping his arms, while he struggled to get free. His energies were completely concentrated on that body, which managed to keep itself in equilibrium. Then, suddenly, the man yielded. As he watched the man falling backwards into the void, Francesco realized that, until then, he had seen only the chest and arms of the stranger. At that moment, however, he looked up: the man he was hurling down was himself. He leaned forward, but the man with his face had already been swallowed up by the darkness. He found himself sitting up in the bed, his heart in his throat, his mouth opened in a scream that wouldn't come out. He looked around in the dark, without recognizing where he was. Then he heard the breathing of the girl asleep beside him and remembered everything.

Running a hand through his hair, he felt it still damp. He bent his head one way, then the other, to release his back, then got out of bed and took a few steps, slowly, until one knee bumped into the chair. Then he bent over, following the shape of the arms with his hands. He sat down. Slowly, his eyes became accustomed to the darkness. First he saw her head lying on the pillow, then the folded arm, the outline of the face, part of the back. He followed the edge of the leg and remained staring at the ankle until the foot assumed a precise form.

Francesco continues to observe Leila, without being able to figure out what the dream means. He would like to smoke a cigarette, but he prefers to sit there, in the dark, watching her sleep.

It's the second night he's spent with her without even kissing her.

The second night? To digest the evidence that all this began only yesterday, Francesco is forced to replay the sequence of events. Leila hurtled into his existence like a meteor, barely twenty-four hours ago, and here they are, holed up in a hotel room, about to attempt blackmail and flee together somewhere on the other side of the ocean.

He can't help wondering who she is, where she came from, where the hell she is leading him. He knows nothing about her, except what she's told him.

How can a person organize her existence on the basis of occasional pickups and thefts? Do the shopping, pay the insurance, take pills for a headache and at the same time go to bed with strangers, rob them, change the colour of her hair, way of dressing, bars, cities. All this seems absurd to him. On the other hand, he doesn't have much to boast of. A bus driver who spends his evenings throwing away money on cards.

Two nights. How many things have happened, in this short span of time? Francesco thinks of his habits, his job, his debts. Is he really about to leave all this? Leila seems willing to offer him a way out on a silver platter. He wonders how far he can really trust her. She is used to lying, stealing, hiding. Why should it be different with him? What guarantee is there that, as soon as she has that suitcase in hand, she won't abandon him? And, even admitting that it's worth the risk, who can assure him that they'll come out of this mess alive? He massages his neck with the palm of his hand. Tomorrow at this time will they be rich or will they be dead?

Leila moves, turns her chest in the other direction. Now he sees her shoulders. He can see the hair on her nape, cut short, dyed that too pale blond.

But then why deny it? This girl fascinates him. She has the look of someone who has navigated a lot of seas. She is pretty, smart and seems able to handle any situation. He feels slow in comparison, with dull reflexes and little experience, little wit, little energy.

But above all, maybe, it's her odour. The odour of her skin.

He would like to tiptoe close to the bed, lean over and sniff her. He wonders if she likes his odour, at least a little. He wonders if odours have the power to attract people like magnetic poles, making them wander randomly through streets and cities, until finally they meet.

Now he can see the sheet rise and fall with the rhythm of her breath. He would give anything for a cigarette. He could grope around for the pack and go in the bathroom to smoke one. But he can't tear himself out of the chair. He can't stop sitting there, in the dark, watching her sleep and asking himself a million idiotic questions.

Sunday, 4 April 1993, 7 A.M.– 12:30 P.M.

Faithful to that postulate of adolescence
according to which if one jumps into the void
one ends up falling somewhere,
and this will always turn out to be better than the place
    of origin.

Paco Ignacio Taibo II, *Leonardo's Bicycle*

There aren't many people out and about in the neighbourhood at seven o'clock on a Sunday morning. The Gabbiano is one of the few open bars. The smell of last night's smoke persists in the air, the neon ceiling lights are on, an aid to the faint light from the street. The Fez and Parodi have already arrived, they are talking, leaning on the bar, with cappuccinos in front of them. Smoke rises from a cigarette between Parodi's fingers. Paolo comes in, followed by Ghiglione, who greets the others, rubbing his hands.

"A little chilly this morning, eh?"

Besides them there is only the barman, who is leafing through the paper, and a fat woman, somewhere in her sixties, with a sweater thrown over her shoulders and her hair in curlers. She is sitting on a stool smoking a cigarette and stares at Paolo with a glazed look.

"What's today?" says the barman, raising his head from *Secolo XIX*. "What are you two doing up at this hour?"

"The early bird catches the worm, Aldo. Can you make us a *macchiato* and a coffee?"

"Why not? Coming up right away."

Ghiglione, with the puffy eyes of someone who has just got out of bed, stretches a hand towards the pastry tray.

"OK, Fez," says Paolo. "Let me have a look."

The Fez opens the suitcase, takes out one of two blue travel bags. The woman in the curlers elongates her neck to see what's going on. Her wrinkled lips are covered with a bright lipstick.

"Lucky you!" she says, in a hoarse voice. "You going on holiday?"

The Fez ignores her. He holds out the bag to Paolo, who turns it over in his hands, feels the weight, unzips the zipper, studies the inside.

"How does the false bottom open?"

"With this hidden flap."

Ghiglione, a croissant in hand, leans forward to see the mechanism that the Fez is showing Paolo.

"Seems like the Chinese have done a good job."

"Here you go, a coffee and a *macchiato*," says Aldo, placing the cups on the bar.

Ghiglione adds sugar and stirs his coffee. Parodi takes a sip of his cappuccino, the old woman in the curlers tries again to start a conversation.

"If I went on a trip," she says, "I'd really like to go to Vienna. My daughter went at Christmas, with my son-in-law and the children. They told me it's beautiful."

Paolo drinks his coffee and lights a Lucky Strike.

"Now listen to me. I've got something going, in Bologna. I don't yet have a precise idea of what's in the pot, but I think it has to do with a lot of cash. Ghiglione, did you bring the uniforms?"

Ghiglione, chewing, widens his eyes. He makes an affirmative gesture.

"Of course, boss," he says, swallowing.

"Tell me, young man," the old woman behind him interrupts. "Have you ever been to Vienna?"

"Naturally, signora," says Paolo. He turns towards her and blows smoke out over her shoulder. "And once I threw a woman off the Prater wheel."

*

Leila half opens her eyes, finds herself looking at Francesco's face, a couple of feet away. She remains in that position for a few more seconds, then props herself up on her elbow, turns towards the window. Not much light comes in through the shades, but it looks like a beautiful day. When she turns around, Francesco is looking at her.

"Hi," she says to him. "Did you sleep well?"

"Not a wink," he says.

"You're anxious?"

"You could put it like that. Anxious and with a screaming pain in my back. If I go on like this, I'll end up in a wheelchair."

"We're practically at the finish line. All we have to do is get the money and clear out."

Francesco gets up and goes to sit on the bed, testing his sore vertebrae with his fingers.

*

Every time the Saab comes out of a tunnel the sun is blinding. It heralds a beautiful day. Parodi is napping with his head against the window. As the windscreen explodes with light, Paolo lowers his sunglasses. From time to time he checks in the rear-view mirror to see that Ghiglione's red Rover is following. At the Valle Scrivia service area they stop. Paolo gets out and tells the others to wait. Inside, he rakes up all the comic books he can find on the metal shelves. He'd like to get just *Diabolik*, but he can only find twenty or so and has to buy some old *Alan Ford*, at half price, as well. When he comes out, the Fez and Ghiglione are chatting, leaning on the hood of the Rover, while Parodi is smoking a cigarette and wandering around the back of a tractor-trailer, craning his neck to see the cargo. Ghiglione is telling a story about smuggled hi-fis, the Fez is listening with a smirk that reveals his yellow teeth.

Paolo packs the comic books in the false bottom of one bag, trying to picture Leila's face when she realizes the scam. He carefully closes the compartment, zips up the bag, calls his men. Parodi drops his cigarette and stamps on it, while Fez and Ghiglione get back in the Rover.

They've been on the A21 for about ten minutes when the mobile phone rings.

"Paolo? It's Leila."

"Hi. How are you?"

"Good. So what's the news?"

"Everything's ready. In fact, since I would have had to make a run to Bologna one of these days anyway, I thought I'd take the opportunity to bring you the bag and the passports in person. So I can say goodbye before you go."

"You're too nice."

"What do you expect? In an hour, hour and a half, I'll be in Bologna. Where do you want me to meet you?"

"Right now I'm in a hotel, but I'll be leaving soon, so for me one place is as good as another."

"OK, then let me think. Listen, from the exit on the autostrada, if I remember correctly, you take a street that leads to Via Emilia. A friend of mine has a bar just in that neighbourhood, towards the centre. Maybe you remember it, I Tre Randagi. It's a pretty big place, at the first intersection after the big supermarket."

"You mean the Ipercoop?"

"Yes, that's the one. I'll see you at ten-thirty?"

"That's good. Meanwhile, tell me the names on the passports."

"Wait, I'll check. Maurizio Soldati and Sonia Vecchi. Need anything else?"

"For the moment no. See you later."

*

Garofano, in front of the closet mirror, shifts his head to the right and the left, carefully examining his swollen lip. Then he gently lifts it with two fingers, to check on the gap in his teeth. The telephone on the night table begins to ring, and he grabs it like a cat that has to capture a bird with one paw.

"Hello."

"It's Alvisi. But who's that?"

"Garofano."

"Garofano? I'd never have recognized you."

"My mouth is banged up and it's hard to speak. What's up?"

"Boys, I have a nice present for you. Tonight your man slept in a hotel and registered with name and surname. He must be a real idiot."

"Good work! Wait, let me write down the address."

Garofano digs in his pockets. He takes out the pack of cigars, scribbles on it the information that Alvisi gives him. Then he hangs up and heads for the toilet, where his colleague shut himself up right after breakfast.

"Diolaiti!" he shouts, pounding his fist on the door. "Try to hurry. Alvisi has tracked down that shithead and I'd like to get him before he vanishes into thin air."

*

"Hello, Alitalia. This is Anna. How may I help you?"

"Good morning. I'd like to know if you have two seats free on a flight to South America."

"When do you want to go?"

"Today, if possible."

"Just a moment while I check. Do you have a preference? Rio? Caracas? Bogotà?"

"Anywhere is all right."

"I have two seats on the flight for Caracas. Leaving Bologna at 12.15, stops at Milan, arrives at Caracas at 8.40 in the evening, local time. One million one hundred and sixty thousand round trip."

"I'm interested only in one-way."

"You don't save much. It's 890,000 lire."

"What's that in dollars?"

"I'm sorry, what did you say?"

*

While he's driving at full speed towards Porta San Vitale, with Diolaiti gripping the handle over the door, the phone rings again. Garofano almost tears his pocket as he gets it out.

"Who is it?"

"Beppe, it's Giovanna. You sound odd. Are you ill?"

"A problem with my teeth. Listen, right now I'm busy. Can't you call me back later?"

284

Diolaiti, white as a sheet, nods questioningly. Garofano moves his lips to mouth "My wife."

"I'm worried, Giuseppe. Betta didn't come home last night."

"What?" Garofano cries. "Where did she sleep?"

"I don't know. Yesterday evening she said she was going out with Silvia Raggi. But I didn't hear her come home, and this morning when I went to her room I realized that the bed hadn't been touched."

"Shit! Did you try calling the Raggis?"

"It's the first thing I did. Silvia had already gone out, but her mother assured me that last night she was home with her cousin, watching a video."

"Listen, Giovanna. I have to take care of something now. As soon as I'm free I'll call you. Meanwhile try phoning the families of her other friends to see if by any chance she spent the night with one of them. We'll talk soon."

He hangs up and accelerates hard to get through an intersection before the light turns red.

"Goddamn, my daughter will end up giving me a heart attack!"

"Why?" asks Diolaiti. "What happened?"

"That idiot didn't come home last night. And I'm afraid I know where she was."

*

Matera woke early, shaved, went down to breakfast with his phone. Then he returned to his room, brushed his teeth and lay down on the bed, his arms behind his neck, to wait for Leila to call.

When the telephone rings, he has been napping for a few minutes.

"Hello?"

"It's Leila."

"Good morning. Everything OK?"

"If it's all right with you, I thought we might get this done as soon as possible."

"That seems best to me."

"I trust you, but I hope you won't mind if I take some small precautions."

"Meaning?"

"I thought of having a friend give me a hand."

Matera scowls.

"Listen to me carefully, Leila. The fewer people you involve in this affair the better. Am I clear?"

"Yes, of course. But you know my situation, so you realize I can't do everything by myself. This is a person I trust. In any case, I'm hoping to leave the country in a few hours. In fact, I was thinking of making the exchange at the airport."

Matera smiles.

"That's where I was supposed to do it in the beginning. Where do we meet?"

"In Terminal A, just under the escalator that goes to the first floor, there's a bar and some tables. We could meet there. You sit and wait for me. I'll come and pick up the bag, check that everything is in order, and my friend will hand over the document."

"What guarantee do I have that you won't try to cheat me?"

"None. But where I intend to go, I don't see what use your piece of paper would be to me."

"I warn you, Leila. I wouldn't like to have to change plans."

"I told you, you don't have to worry."

"All right. What time?"

"Eleven."

286

Sacchetti has chosen the squad for the kick-off, revising the plans. Simoni is on the bench, and his nose is out of joint. But he's the coach and his decisions can't be discussed.

The players from Calderara are among the best in the league, but his boys seem full of energy this morning, motivated to win. The outcome can't at all be taken for granted. The coach for Calderara is a fat bald man, with a rumpled shirt collar and a tie that looks like a rag for wiping windows. Sacchetti studies him from the opposite side of the stadium. He's never liked that fatso. He's known him for a long time and once, a few years ago, they had a real argument.

Apart from the Calderara fans, at the game are two classmates of Gerry's, Pisani's brother, and three girls Sacchetti has never seen before. While he gives the boys their final instructions, he finds a way of glancing at the girls. One is called Federica, she must be Boxer's new girl. A blonde with shapely legs and freckled cheeks. Very pretty. While the team piles onto the court, Sacchetti wonders if the story Gerry was telling about the blowjobs the other night after practice is true. The referee's whistle tears him out of his thoughts. The ball is theirs, Pisani kicks. The game begins.

*

This part of the city is a labyrinth of one-way streets. Garofano curses the signs that force him to go in a circle, wasting time. Diolaiti sweats as he follows the route with his finger on the map. He's nauseous and his intestines are cramping.

287

"I've had enough!" Garofano shouts. "I'm sick of this! We're not getting there. Shit, Diolaiti, do I go right or left at this fucking intersection?"

"Straight would be best."

"I can't go straight, for God's sake!"

The driver of the car behind them sounds his horn a couple of times. Garofano takes off in exasperation, so that the tyres skid. Diolaiti looks up from the map and tilts his head, trying to read the names of the cross streets.

"There," he says. "It should be the next one."

Garofano turns. He proceeds slowly, hunched over the steering wheel as he tries to check the house numbers. Arriving opposite the hotel, he pulls up with the front of the Audi on the pavement and turns off the engine. He is about to get out when Diolaiti grabs him by the sleeve.

"Wait! Isn't that them over there?"

Garofano looks up. He sees, from the back, a girl with blond hair and a man with a suitcase opening the door of a car.

While he restarts the engine, Diolaiti rolls up the map and sticks it in the glove compartment. Then he grabs the Colt revolver.

Francesco throws the suitcase on the back seat of the Peugeot, gets in, leans over to open the right-hand door. With her fingers on the handle, Leila hears the sound of a car nearby. A glance is enough for her to recognize the faces of the two men and realize that the thin one is holding a gun. She hurls herself onto the seat crying, "Go, go! It's them!"

Francesco starts the car with an acceleration to the floor. He goes into first, revving the engine, and turns the wheel as fast as he can. The Peugeot takes off, tyres squealing, with the Audi just a dozen yards away.

Francesco launches into the first left turn. The bumpers of the two cars hit. The back end of the Peugeot skids as Francesco takes the corner, while Garofano, unable to make the turn, jams on the brakes. The right side of the Audi scrapes a parked Renault 5. Garofano goes into reverse, the car jerks back, tyres screeching. Diolaiti puts on his seatbelt.

Leila sees the Audi manoeuvre and turn onto the street.

"Shit, they're right behind us!"

"How the fuck did they find us?" Francesco asks, going into third.

"How should I know? Let's just try to shake them."

"Easier said than done."

Francesco goes into fourth. Then he brakes, drops quickly into second and turns onto a cross street.

"That's good. If we zigzag maybe we can manage it."

Again in third, then fourth, engine racing. Francesco glances in the rear-view mirror, sees the Audi appear. On their left, a screech of brakes and a honking horn that angrily pursues them. Francesco tries to think what the best route is in that network of narrow streets and one-way signs. Leila, looking back, monitors the situation.

"They're gaining on us."

Garofano, jerking the gearshift, forces the car into third.

"Those shits aren't going to get away from me," he says.

Diolaiti swallows a mouthful of saliva.

"I'm going to be sick."

"What?"

"I said I'm not feeling well!"

"Fuck!"

Francesco brakes, drops into third, turns left. As he

skids sideways, the bumper hits a garbage can, which rolls over and ends up in the middle of the street. The Audi hits it straight on and sweeps it away, sending it flying against the lowered shutters of a fruit and vegetable shop. The garbage scatters on the pavement.

Francesco swerves again, turning into another side street. He notices too late the circular red and white sign.

"Shit!" he cries. "It's the wrong way!"

Leila looks ahead, sees a van emerge at the end of the street. It moves forward, flashing its headlights.

"Now what's that idiot doing?" asks Diolaiti, nervously.

Garofano, without responding, presses the accelerator to the floor.

The driver of the van sees the two cars heading towards him. In order to avoid an accident, he stops in the middle of the street. Francesco misses him at the last instant, going up on the pavement on the left. Leila holds her breath and squeezes her eyelids. The car door grazes a low wall on top of which is a railing. The left-hand mirror hits a bar of the enclosure and snaps off with a sharp crack, ricocheting with a bang against the window. Garofano grips the wheel so hard that his knuckles turn white as he steers into the narrow space. The truck driver looks with dismay at the two cars passing within a few inches of his truck. The side of the Audi brushes the wall and a blaze of sparks bursts from the chassis. Diolaiti holds the gun pointed straight up.

As Francesco guides the car back onto the street, the exhaust scrapes the edge of the pavement. The Audi is still on his tail. Diolaiti's back is bathed in cold sweat, he has to contract his abdominal muscles with all his strength to endure the painful spasms. Waves of nausea, vertigo and attacks of diarrhoea assail him, and with each one it seems to him that he can't hold out a moment longer. He clenches his teeth, while his insides shake.

"I can't make it," he laments.

"What the fuck is wrong with you?" Garofano asks.

"I'm shitting myself, that's what's wrong."

"Then shoot," Garofano says. "Try to get a tyre."

Diolaiti lowers the window.

At the end of the street Francesco sees the intersection with Via Corticella, where the traffic is heavier.

"Hold tight," he shouts. "Now I'll try to get them off our backs."

Leila grips the door handle, while Francesco brakes abruptly, swerves and suddenly veers to the right. Garofano curses. The two cars turn onto the street one after the other. A couple of vehicles coming from the left are forced to brake hard. Francesco goes into the opposite lane and the front of the Peugeot misses a motorcycle by a hairsbreadth. The car skids sideways, Francesco straightens it with an effort, bringing it back in line with a series of turns and counter-turns of the wheel that nearly put them into a spin.

On this street, which is wider than the preceding ones, Francesco is forced to swerve continuously to the right and to the left, to keep the Audi from catching them. Garofano, with rapid turns of the wheel, tries to insert the Audi in the gaps between cars.

The drivers of the other cars dodge them shouting and honking. Diolaiti leans out the window and takes aim. The detonation echoes above the noise of the engine. Francesco looks up at the mirror.

"What the fuck are they doing? Are they shooting at us?"

He speeds through an underpass, runs a red light

without slowing down. Leila looks back. She sees the thin one aiming a gun at them.

"Shit, now what do we do?"

Diolaiti fires two more shots. The first bullet ricochets off the asphalt, barely a foot from the right tyre. A jolt throws his arm off. The second bullet goes too high, pierces the rear window of the Peugeot, and ends in the metal of the roof.

"They want to kill us!" Francesco cries, seized by panic.

Leila looks with widened eyes at the hole in the back window.

"I'll try to stop them," she says.

"What?"

She doesn't answer. Out of the corner of his eye, Francesco sees her kneel on the seat, climb over it and jump into the back seat. Then, through the rear-view mirror, he sees her digging around in the suitcase.

Leila retrieves the gun she stole from Diolaiti, lies down on the back seat, kicks the window. The glass cracks and a couple of pieces fall into the street, disappearing under the wheels of the Audi, which is on their tail, only a few yards away.

"What the fuck is she doing?" Garofano says.

Diolaiti, with his eyes tearing, fires two more shots at the tyres of the Peugeot.

Leila, sheltered by the seatback, aims the SIG-Sauer and pulls the trigger. The recoil whips her wrist back.

"Shit," Garofano cries. "That whore is shooting at us!"

Diolaiti pulls back inside the car and wipes his eyes with the sleeve of his jacket.

Leila clutches the gun in both hands and, with all her strength, extends her arms forward and empties the barrel. She looks up, panting, her nostrils filled with the odour of gunpowder, and sees that the Audi is still there, a few yards away. She can clearly distinguish the faces of the two men staring at her. Then, suffocated by fear and rage, she hurls the empty gun at them. The .9 calibre spins through the air, strikes the windscreen with a crash. A sunburst of cracks opens up. Garofano curses and brakes. The left wheel scrapes against the traffic divider that separates the two lanes in that stretch, he loses his grip on the steering wheel. The car jumps the divider, crosses the opposite lane on a diagonal, and ends up crashing into a reinforced concrete pillar.

Leila follows the accident with a look of astonishment. When she sees the Audi hit the pylon, she exults, with all the voice she has left. The Peugeot gets away at full speed.

After the crash of the crumpling car body, the silence seems almost absolute. Only a few seconds later does Diolaiti begin to distinguish a creaking of metal, an escape of steam, the liquid dripping on the asphalt. In the impact, he got a jerk from the seatbelt that's left him dazed. He reopens his eyes, runs his fingers over his forehead. Some tiny splinters of glass have stuck in his skin but he's hardly bleeding. He has the impression that at any moment his head might burst. He turns towards Garofano, but in his place he sees only the empty seat. Through the open window he sees a poster advertising the Togni Circus, stuck to the yellow plaster of a wall. A clown, his face covered by white greasepaint and an enormous red ball of a nose, stares at him, laughing.

*

Paolo flicks on the indicator and pulls up on the right.

Ghiglione stops the Rover behind him. They get out. Parodi takes a comb out of his pocket and smooths back his gelled hair. The Fez does a couple of knee bends to stretch his legs.

"Wait for me here, I don't want the girl to see you. I'll take the empty bag with me. Keep the phone on. As soon as I get away I'll call you and we'll make our plan."

He gets in the Saab, heads towards Via Emilia.

He parks right in front of the bar. I Tre Randagi is a little more desolate-looking than he remembered. But it must be different at night, with the right illumination and the rooms full of music and people. Entering now, he has the impression of a big dark room, too big, in which sounds echo as in an empty hangar. Paolo takes off his sunglasses and looks around, searching for Leila. Then he sees Gigi, his friend, the manager. He gives him a nod of greeting as he approaches the bar.

"Paolo! What are you doing here?"

"I have to meet a girl. About thirty, slender, green eyes. You haven't seen her?"

"All morning only one woman has been in here. But she was over fifty. Not the type for appointments."

Paolo glances at his watch, then shrugs.

"It looks like she's late too. So, how's business?"

"I can't complain. What can I offer you?"

"A Martini, straight up. I'm going to sit back there. That way when my friend arrives I'll see her."

Gigi lowers his eyelids with a smile of complicity.

Paolo heads towards a series of small tables of thick wood, with the short side at the wall. The seats are two facing benches, and the padded backs are high enough to form a kind of screen. Paolo sits so that he can keep an eye on the entrance. He places his sunglasses on the table and settles the bag on the seat beside him.

294

While Leila is in the booth getting her picture taken, Francesco is trying with a screwdriver to get the last bits of glass out of the rear window.

"Done." Leila takes the strip with the four instant photos out of the slot. "How do I look?"

Francesco holds the strip between two fingers. In the last picture, at the bottom, Leila is making a face, widening her eyes, puffing her cheeks and sticking out her tongue.

Francesco looks up at her. Then he bursts out laughing, shaking his head.

"You must be out of your mind! We've just risked getting blown away and you seem as carefree as if you'd won the lottery."

"What can I do? I'm in a good mood. Come on, now it's your turn to immortalize yourself. Give me the screwdriver, I'll finish this."

*

The Bear's tongue is coated with a pasty, bitter saliva. He didn't sleep a wink, then he spent a good part of the morning wandering aimlessly, hoping to catch Franz somewhere. He even tried the bus depot, but the supervisor said he was sick. And of all the people he met, not a single one could tell him where the hell he was hiding.

The taste in his mouth is disgusting. It's a mixture of old cucumber and mud. He'd like a drink to clean out his mouth, but more than anything he'd like to strangle someone.

He stops at Bar 28 just long enough for a glass. First of all, he has no desire to look at the usual assholes.

Second, the news of what happened yesterday has already spread and everyone's eager to hear the details. Third, he hasn't the slightest intention of explaining anything to anybody. It's true that he knocked out two men and stopped only when he found a gun in his face, but the fact remains that Franz and that whore he's got with him made a fool of him yet again, and the mere thought of it makes his head spin.

"Bear, how's it going?"

"Terrible! Give me a double grappa."

Bobo understands immediately that something's wrong. He fills the glass in silence.

The Bear gulps down the grappa as if it were fruit juice, throws two 1,000-lire notes on the bar and leaves, filing past the curious, timid glances of the other customers. But as soon as he's in the driver's seat, he's seized by the desire for another drink. He turns left on Via Emilia and after a quarter of a mile sees a sign for a pub.

He drives the Volvo halfway up on the pavement, enters the place and orders a grappa. He drains it, then immediately asks for another.

"Triple," he clarifies, as the bartender is about to pour.

"What do you mean, triple?" asks the other, with bottle in midair.

The Bear stares threateningly at him, and the man fills the glass to the top. The Bear empties it in one gulp, pounds on the bar.

"Where's the toilet?" he asks.

The bartender indicates a stairway with his eyes.

"Down one flight. First door on the left, at the bottom of the stairs."

Commissioner Roccaforte lights a Nazionale. Loiacono, at his side, takes a few steps inside the apartment. The closet doors are wide open, objects and
clothes are scattered all over the floor.

"Nice mess, eh, sir?"

Roccaforte nods. He advances, moving a drawer with
his shoe.

"Would you say that the thieves stopped here?"

"What do you think?"

"Me?" Loiacono shrugs his shoulders. "If the girl
who lives here has to do with the butchery of the other
night, I think there's some complicated business
behind it. There's a stink here of somebody looking
for something. Am I wrong?"

The Commissioner shakes his head, blowing out
smoke.

"Not at all, Loiacono."

"But, sir . . ."

"What?"

Loiacono raises his head and widens his nostrils,
sniffing.

"You don't smell something?"

Roccaforte lifts his chin and sniffs.

"An odour of food?"

"Aubergine *parmigiana*, sir. Come and have a look,
the sauce is still liquid."

The Commissioner leans forward to look inside the
aluminium pan.

"So?"

"So, it would seem that someone cooked a short
time ago." Loiacono touches with one finger the
remains of the *parmigiana*. "Roughly, no later than yesterday. You see all the rubbish on the floor?"

"I see it, Loiacono. Go on."

"Well, it seems obvious that they ate and then ate again, not giving a damn about cleaning up. But who can it be? The girl? Do you see her stopping to cook herself a nice *parmigiana*, knowing that someone is after her? And then it's her house. And, sir, in her own house does she clear the table by throwing the plates on the floor?"

"You don't think so, right?"

"Me? No, not in the least."

"Who do you think could have been here?"

"Sir, what do I know about it? But pigs certainly!"

*

"Are you coming in?" Leila asks him.

"No," Francesco answers. "I'll wait for you in the car."

"Whatever you like. I'll try to be quick."

As he takes a Gauloise out of the pack he watches her hurry across the street and disappear into the pub. He lights the cigarette, then gets out of the Peugeot. He walks around the car, stops at the rear window that has no glass in it. He looks around. A car in this condition doesn't go unnoticed. Above all, Bar 28 isn't far from here. It wouldn't be that surprising for someone he knows to pass by. He inhales deeply, hoping that everything happens quickly, because the tension has transformed his stomach into a wrung-out sponge. At this rate he'll end up with an ulcer.

He gets back in the Peugeot. He lowers the window, rests his neck against the seat, tries to relax.

*

As he's being loaded into the ambulance, Garofano makes a sign to Diolaiti to approach. Two cotton swabs stick out of his nostrils, inserted to stop the bleeding.

"How are you?" Diolaiti asks.

"A mess," he answers, holding out his mobile phone. "Take it. It's better if you have it, so we can keep in touch."

The ambulance people push the gurney inside, then close the doors. Diolaiti watches the ambulance drive off and wonders what's left for him to do. The Audi is a wreck. And who knows where those two are hiding. Can't be helped – when a job begins badly, everything goes wrong.

Now he's alone, on foot and, furthermore, with no papers, since that bitch must have stolen his wallet. He touches his hurting side and looks around, in search of a solution. Just at that moment, Garofano's phone begins to ring.

*

Gigi arrives and puts the Martini on the table, along with bowls of salted peanuts, olives, and potato crisps. Paolo lights a Lucky Strike, takes a swallow. With the point of a toothpick he captures an olive. As he's sucking on the pit, he sees a large, tall man, with a bandage on his head, going towards the bar. The giant gulps down two glasses, one after the other, asks Gigi something, heads towards a corner of the pub.

Paolo puts a handful of nuts in his mouth. He's still chewing when he sees a thin girl come in, wearing tight black jeans, and with blond hair cut very short, who stops just beyond the threshold and looks around. Only then does he recognize her. He crushes the cigarette in the ashtray and waves his arm. Leila sees him, smiles. She arrives at his table. She leans over and just touches his lips with a quick cool kiss, which gives him a little tug of nostalgia.

"Hey, what's this? I've never seen you go punk before!"

Leila tilts her head, smiling.

"A little change, that's all. Have I aged?"

"On the contrary. With that haircut you seem even younger. And cuter than ever."

"When we were together I was a mess. Thanks to your lifestyle."

"Forget it, you stood up to it very well. Really!"

They look at each other in silence for a few seconds. Paolo offers her the pack of Lucky Strikes.

"Want one?"

"Yes, thanks."

He brings the flame of his Zippo to Leila's cigarette, then lights one for himself.

"It was nice of you to help me. And to come here."

Paolo blows the smoke out, above the yellow tufts of Leila's hair.

"Don't worry. I was happy to do it. So, you're not going to tell me what kind of trouble you're in?"

Leila shakes her head.

"There's not time now, Paolo. I'm in a hurry, and it's a complicated story. I don't exactly understand it myself."

"And have you decided where to go?"

"For the moment Venezuela. Then we'll see."

Paolo nods, tapping the ash. Then he pushes aside the bowls and the sunglasses. He picks up the blue bag from the seat, places it on the table.

"This is the bag," he says. "And here are the passports."

Leila puts the documents in a pocket of her jacket.

"I've also brought the validation stamps. Here, I put them in this envelope, along with some adhesive plastic to apply after you've put in the photos."

"Perfect," Leila says, then unzips the bag.

Paolo watches her as she examines the inside.

"There's a hidden flap, to open the false bottom. That's it, good for you, right there."

At that moment, the voice of someone who is quarrelling with the bartender echoes through the room.

"If I tell you I want the bottle, you sell it to me! What the fuck do I care if it's Sunday and it's the last one you have?"

Leila turns to see what's happening, sees the Bear pounding his fist on the bar and yelling. She turns abruptly back to Paolo.

"Oh, shit!" she says, staring at him, her eyes wide. "This we didn't need."

*

"Garofano, is that you?"

"No, Alvisi, it's Diolaiti."

"Did you get them?"

"They got away again. And this time Garofano ended up in the hospital."

"Was he shot?"

"Are you kidding? We went off the road and he broke his leg."

"That's a real bit of bad luck! Anyway, I've done some checking that may help you. As soon as I found the hotel that guy was in, I got a list of phone calls and checked the ones coming from his room."

"And what did you discover?"

"Three calls. The first to a mobile phone that belongs to a criminal. The second to the reservations office of Alitalia. The third to another mobile phone, property of the Minister. I thought this might be useful to you."

"Yes. I'm sure the two of them are going to make the exchange and then take a flight right afterwards."

"Yes. That's what I thought too."

"Thanks, Alvisi."

"For what? Try to nail them. And good luck."

"Thanks!" Diolaiti says, wiping away a tear that is about to slide down from his eye.

He ends the call and puts the phone in his pocket. The only problem now is to find a means of transport.

*

From the broken rear window comes a breeze that hits him on the back of the neck. Francesco opens his eyes and looks at the time. If Leila doesn't hurry, they'll be late at the airport. He rotates his gaze towards the door of the bar, sees the Bear appear on the threshold with a bottle in his hand. Their eyes meet. The Bear stands immobilized on the pavement for a second or two, staring at him in dismay. Then he rushes towards him. In a flash Francesco climbs into the passenger seat, leaps out of the right-hand door. He doesn't try to flee, because he knows that the Bear would get him in less than no time. He takes shelter behind the car, touching the car body with his fingertips, ready to jump one way or the other.

The Bear slows down, approaches the Peugeot.

"This time you're finished, Franz!"

"Bear, please, calm down."

"I'm extremely calm," says the other, throwing the bottle at him.

Francesco ducks just in time. The bottle goes over

his head, crashing on the pavement behind him. The Bear tries to circle the Peugeot on the bonnet side, but Francesco isn't unprepared and darts towards the boot. The Bear stops, tries a fake, goes in the other direction. Francesco manages to keep the car between them.

"I'm going to kick your teeth out, Franz! Wait till I get my hands on you, you'll see, the desire to fuck with me will vanish!"

"Jesus! When did I ever fuck with you?"

The Bear feels his stomach churning with rage. He and Franz barely a yard apart, between them the Peugeot. He'll never stop him like this, he has no intention of continuing to play ring around the roses with this shit car in the middle. He puts his hands on the roof and gets set to jump. But just as he's about to take off, he feels something cold and hard on his neck.

"What's happening here?" asks Paolo, pressing a Walther against his neck.

The Bear is immobilized, with his palms on the car. The pressure of the gun forces him to bend his neck to one side. Out of the corner of his eye he sees Leila, a couple of feet away.

"You ugly bitch," he growls. "I should have figured you were around here somewhere!"

"Hey, pay attention," says Paolo, pressing the gun barrel harder. "It's true that you hit your head and you're a little out of it, but there's not much room between you and a bullet right here."

"And who are you?"

"I'm the one with a gun in his hand. And that should be sufficient."

Leila looks around nervously. It would be really unfortunate if a police car were to show up at this moment.

"And now what do we do?" Francesco asks from the other side of the car.

"I'll tell you what." Paolo gets to the point. "Get in your car and leave. I'll take care of this asshole."

The Bear is furious, but the man behind those black glasses seems calm and decisive, and he doesn't want to get a bullet in the head.

"Back up," he orders. "Slowly."

The Bear obeys. He backs up slowly. When Francesco walks in front of him to get to the driver's seat he glares at him with bloodshot eyes.

"I'm not done with you yet, Franz. Sooner or later I'll get you and make you shit blood!"

Paolo increases the pressure of the gun barrel.

"Will you stop being a pain in the ass?"

Francesco closes the window and starts the car. Leila, before getting in, looks at Paolo over the car roof.

"Thanks for everything."

"For what? Stay well, Leila. And good luck."

As the Peugeot drives off, Paolo says, "It's just the two of us now. Do you have a car?"

"Yes," says the Bear, sullenly. "It's that Volvo over there."

"Then let's go. I'm coming with you."

Paolo pushes him with the butt of the Walther. When they reach the car, he puts a hand in the Bear's pocket and roots around. He finds the keys, puts them in the lock of the boot, lifts the lid.

"What are you doing?"

"Me, nothing. You're the one who has to get in there."

The Bear looks at the boot.

"Are you joking?"

"Not at all. Come on. Try not to make me lose patience."

"But I can't fit in there!"

"You try it," Paolo says, pointing the gun at him. "You'll see. If you squeeze a little, you'll make it."

The Bear looks around. But on the street only a few cars are going by, speeding, and no one pays attention to them. He lifts up one leg and places the foot on the floor of the boot. Then he gets the rest of his body in, and curls up slowly.

"See?" says Paolo, looking down at him. "I was right."

The Bear, huddled on the floor of the boot, stares at him with hatred. He looks at his big shot smile, his dark glasses, his 50,000-lire haircut waving sinuously in the breeze.

"You aren't really going to close me in here."

"That's exactly what I intend to do. Watch your head!"

"You shit! You'd better hope that you and I don't meet again," the Bear growls, as the door closes.

The click of the lock seals him definitively in darkness.

*

He has eyed a red Renault 5 with a faded body. Stealing cars is not his speciality. At least old low-cylinder cars don't have alarms. In any case, he has no recourse, he just has to get to the airport in time to catch them.

As he leans under the dashboard to strip the wires, he has a foretaste of the pleasure of killing them. Maybe it won't be that simple, but it's not the first time that he's eliminated someone in front of dozens of witnesses.

He puts together the bare ends of the two wires. Nothing happens. He stifles a curse, his ribs, compressed in that uncomfortable position, hurt like hell.

All he needs now is to be caught stealing a fourth-hand car.

*

The maid greets the Secretary and his wife, leading them into the living room. The Minister emerges from a side door, with his arms stretched out towards them.

"Signora Letizia," he says. He grasps her hand and brings it to his lips. "It's been so long since we've met! How are you?"

"Very well," the woman says. "And you, Minister?"

"I? How do you think I am? It's fashionable these days to take shots at us and we submit like Christians, dear lady. What else can we do? Let's hope that the truth will triumph in the end. And let us trust that in time liars and slanderers will be unmasked. Those who have made mistakes should pay, I'm the first to say so, but this tenacity is extreme. You will admit that I'm right."

"Of course, Minister. Of course!"

"And you," says the Minister, turning to the Secretary and questioning him with a nervous smile. "Everything all right?"

The Secretary extends the muscles at the sides of his lips, trying to respond to the smile.

"Of course, Minister. But unfortunately not yet . . ."

"Make yourselves comfortable, my friends," the Minister, almost shouting, interrupts. "This way, please. If you will allow me, I will offer you an aperitif, while we wait for my wife to finish making herself beautiful. Ah, the vanity of women, how we love it!"

*

As soon as he's locked the Bear in the boot Paolo takes his mobile phone out of his pocket. He punches in the number quickly. While the telephone rings, he checks his watch.

"Hello, Fez? I've made the delivery. Just one little hitch, but I've taken care of it. The girl is with a guy, but that shouldn't create any problems for us. We have to hurry, because they've already left. I think they're headed for the airport. No, it's better if you come and get me. I'm at the third light on Via Emilia. You know the street? Good, then move it. I'll wait for you on the pavement."

*

"You think we'll get there in time?" Francesco asks, while Leila pastes the photos in the passports.

"That man will wait for us, don't worry. He's too attached to his piece of paper."

"Let's hope that at least he won't rip us off."

Leila presses the star-shaped stamp, careful to make it match up with the original outline. Then she sticks the rectangle of sticky plastic to the page.

"Done," she says. She looks up and checks the result. "I think it came out well. What do you say?"

"What's my name?"

"Maurizio Soldati. Do you like it?"

"Not much."

"Well, you'll get used to it. And in South America you can call yourself whatever you like."

"What makes me nervous is driving with the car in this condition. It's too noticeable. If some cop stops us, we're screwed."

Leila reaches out a hand towards his face, caresses it.

"Try to stay calm. You'll see. It will all be OK."

*

Matera pulls out the magnetic card. He waits for the bar to go up, enters Section One. He parks the Alfa 90, turns off the engine, checks the time. Ten-forty. The appointment is for eleven. There's enough time to get to the end of the piece he's listening to. "The Girl from Ipanema". Stan Getz on tenor, João Gilberto voice and guitar, and his wife, Astrud, who sings, taking turns with him. Just as Getz's sinuous solo begins, he sees a red Renault pass in front of his car. The man driving is the Crocodile. Matera looks around. Of Garofano and the Audi in which he saw them the other night there is no sign. He turns off the stereo, waits until Diolaiti has started on the descent to the underground car park, then turns the key in the ignition.

At the bottom of the ramp, the Renault turns to the right, drives around an area occupied by parked cars, heads into a space between a van and a concrete column. Diolaiti detaches the wires. As soon as the engine is off he opens the door, looks up and finds himself facing the dark tube of a silencer.

Matera shoots twice, in rapid sequence. The first bullet hits Diolaiti in the middle of his forehead and knocks him backwards. The second grazes him as he's already falling and shears a shred of skin and a tuft of hair off his forehead. The bullet is deflected off the frontal bone through the right window, and ends up in the body of the van next to it.

Matera puts the Beretta in the holster and looks around. One less. He places the suitcase on the ground, leans forward to arrange the body inside the car. When he supports himself with his knee on the edge of the seat, the joint sends out a sharp stab of pain. He clenches his teeth and tries to pivot on his other leg. He grabs Diolaiti's jacket with two hands, pushes the body down into the front seat. Then he lowers what remains of the right window, so that the bloodstains and the bullet holes can't be seen from the outside.

Finally he slides out of the Renault and stands up. He closes the car door. He adjusts his jacket, picks up the suitcase from the ground and goes off with an elastic step, in spite of his bad knee, because the velvet, sensuous voice of Astrud Gilberto has given him a soft samba rhythm.

*

The Bear's cheek is resting on the floor mat. Inside there is an odour of petrol, rubber and grease. A point in the middle of his back itches terribly. He would pay anything to be face to face with that big shot and have a few words without the gun getting in the way. Is it possible that for the past several days everyone around here has been treating him like a halfwit?

Suddenly he hears the voice of the shit, outside, speaking to someone. The Bear concentrates, but, stuck in that lousy boot, he can't pick up more than one out of about five words. Among the many that escape him, however, there is one that does not, and that stamps itself in his brain. Airport.

*

"That's it, Signor Garofano," says a male nurse with buckteeth, pushing the gurney into the lift. "You've got quite a fracture, you know? In any case, with this cast and the bone in traction, you'll see, your leg will recover and be like new."

"Will I have it for long?"

"You have to be patient. But I think that it will take about six weeks. Plus a period of rehabilitation, of course."

"Excuse me, but I really can't move?"

"In a week, perhaps. With crutches. Better still a wheelchair. But you'll have to ask the doctor."

"I meant now."

"With the plaster still fresh? You must be joking!"

Another male nurse, this one with oily hair, helps the other unload him onto the bed. They stick a couple of pillows behind his back and attach the leg in its cast to a harness hanging from a support bar in the ceiling. When the nurse with the buckteeth takes his things from the gurney to settle them in the little chest of drawers, he stops a moment, weighing in his hands the holster with the gun. He is about to ask something, then lets it go.

"Rest. And just remember, it could have been worse!"

As soon as the nurses are gone, Garofano raises himself on his elbows to take a look at the room. The effort causes a sharp pain in his leg.

"Oww! Shit!"

A boy lying on the bed next to his and reading a basketball magazine looks at him.

"Excuse me, but it's best to take it easy. The first two days it really hurts like hell."

"Yes, but I have to make a phone call."

"Didn't you hear what the nurse said? You can't walk on the new plaster."

"I can't stay stuck in here."

The boy thinks about it. Then he closes his magazine.

"Excuse me, are you a cop?"

310

Garofano looks at him. The boy has a potato nose, fan ears and alert eyes that shine with curiosity.

"Yes," he says. "Something like that."

"Well, if it's really so important, you can use my crutches. But I'm telling you, if the nurses see you, they'll kick your ass big time."

Garofano, clenching his teeth, tries to free his leg from the harness it's hanging from. The boy gets down from his bed.

"Wait, I'll give you a hand."

Sweating with the effort, Garofano hobbles to the doorway. Before going out, he sticks his head into the corridor, to make sure no nurses are around. Going back along the hall to the telephone costs a lot of time and effort. Reaching his objective, he leans one crutch against the wall and props himself up with his shoulder against the wall. He puts all the money he has in the machine, dials the number of his mobile phone.

The phone rings and rings in Diolaiti's pocket, as he's lying on the front seat of a Renault, in the underground car park at the airport.

Garofano hangs up cursing and a cascade of coins falls noisily into the coin-return compartment. He retrieves the change. He puts it back in the slot. This time he calls headquarters.

"Hello, Alvisi? It's Garofano."

"Look who it is! How's the leg?"

He scowls.

"How do you know about my fracture?"

"Diolaiti told me, what do you think?"

"And when did you talk to him?"

"It must have been half an hour ago more or less," Alvisi says. "He said you'd had an accident and he was calling on your mobile phone."

"Yes. But I just tried to call him and he doesn't answer. Do you know what he was up to?"

"Sure. He told me he was going to the airport."

*

Sitting at one of the tables of the bar, Matera keeps an eye on the escalator coming up from the floor below. Behind him, a broad window looks out on the area where the buses arrive. He finishes his coffee, lights a cigarette. The table has one leg, in the centre, that descends to a round steel platform, next to which he has placed the suitcase. He checks his watch. By now waiting at the airport has become a habit. Provided this too doesn't turn out to be a cheat.

*

The Bear has no wish to find himself facing a gun empty-handed again. So he waits patiently until that swine has cleared off. Eventually, hearing nothing, he suspects that the man has left and that he is waiting there pointlessly, trapped like a mouse in the boot of his Volvo. A few seconds later, though, he hears a sound of tyres braking on the asphalt and the voice of the bastard talking to someone.

He hears a door slam, the sound of a car growing distant, disappearing. He waits another long, suffocating minute, then, with a big effort, turns his body, so that he can press his right shoulder against the boot lid. Propping his elbows on the floor, he pushes up with all his strength. The metal creaks as it bows. The Bear fills his lungs and increases his effort. The lock gives suddenly.

An old man passing by on the pavement stops,

frightened by the crash of the door opening, and stands staring, eyes wide, at the enormous individual who emerges from the boot. Tall, broad and with a dirty bandage around his head.

"Excuse me, but what were you doing in there? Taking a nap?"

The Bear wipes his hands on his trousers and lowers his gaze to the old man.

"Mind your own business, Grandpa," he says, landing with a jump on the pavement.

*

"What did you say your name is?"

"Stefano," says the boy, chewing his gum.

"Giuseppe. Put it there. Listen, Stefano, you seem like a reasonable fellow. If I have to wait to go through the whole bureaucratic procedure, I'll be out in a month. But I'm in a hell of a hurry. I'm afraid my friend is in trouble and needs help."

"In your condition you won't be able to do much for your friend."

"That's my affair. Now listen to me. I have a proposition. I would like to buy your crutches. How much do you think they're worth?"

"I don't know. My father rented them."

"OK, I'll pay you for them and you can say you lost them or someone stole them. Invent whatever you like. You think that 200,000 might be a reasonable figure?"

The bubble that Stefano is blowing bursts. With his fingers, he detaches the gum from his lips and sticks it back in his mouth.

"Excuse me, mister, for two hundred I'll throw in a packet of anti-inflammatory capsules I have left. I'm not taking them anymore anyway."

313

"It's a deal," says Garofano, opening his wallet.

*

Francesco goes up first, carrying the suitcase. Arriving on the upper level, he heads for a bank of telephones along the wall, between the bar kiosk and the shop selling newspapers and cigarettes. He stops in front of a phone, places the suitcase on the floor. As he pretends to make a phone call, he turns to get a view of the group of tables in front of the window.

At that moment, Leila steps off the escalator. Francesco, with the receiver pressed to his ear, watches her walk around the railing and head for a table where a robust, grey-haired man in a herringbone jacket is sitting.

*

Ghiglione parks the Rover in front of Terminal A, far away from the entrance. The four men get out of the car. Paolo puts on his sunglasses. The Fez, Parodi and Ghiglione are wearing the uniforms of customs officers. The Fez's uniform displays an officer's stripes. Parodi holds the suitcase in which they have hidden the second blue carry-on bag, its secret compartment stuffed with comic books. As they hurry towards the main hall, Paolo quickly reviews his plan.

"So, is everything clear? I point out the girl, and from that moment on you have to take it by yourselves. I'm certain that in the secret compartment of the bag I brought her she's hiding a lot of money. She told me she's going to Venezuela, so I think the best thing is to stop her just before she boards. She'll be tense and in a big hurry to get on the plane. You have to play on this. Try to keep her calm, tell her it's a routine check, but insist on inspecting her baggage. At this point Ghiglione finds a pretext to distract her. There's no need for me to tell you how to do it. The girl and her friend are extremely anxious to leave, they'll do whatever they can to keep things moving. While the Fez and Ghiglione are talking, you, Parodi, take advantage of it to exchange the two bags. The important thing is that the operation has to be quick. I trust you, you've spent twenty years playing this game and you should have it in hand. If everything goes smoothly, they won't be aware of a thing. Any questions?"

The three men in uniform shake their heads.

"Good," Paolo says, while the automatic doors open in front of them. "Then all we have to do is go into action."

*

Matera watches her approach. Black jeans, jacket, short hair, cut roughly and dyed very pale yellow. A blue bag in hand. The same elastic walk. In that getup, she looks even thinner. Maybe it's the tight trousers. Leila stops in front of him, with a half smile on her lips. She grasps the back of a chair and sits down on the other side of the table.

"What did you do to your hair?" he asks, indicating her head with his chin.

Leila pats a blond tuft.

"A little retouching."

Matera arches his eyebrows and nods silently, without appearing to believe her.

Leila narrows her eyes to better see the face of the man who is opposite her, dark against the window

315

illuminated by the sun. Then she looks down at the overnight bag placed on the floor, next to the table base.

"Is the money in there?"

Matera lowers his eyelids in a sign of assent.

"And have you brought the paper?" he asks.

"Of course. As we agreed."

He looks up over Leila's shoulders and glances at the crowd of people passing through the lobby. Probably her friend is around here somewhere to make sure that everything goes smoothly.

"Good," says Matera, leaning over and grabbing the handle of the bag. "Then all we have to do is conclude the exchange."

He places the overnight bag on the table, rotates it 180 degrees, until the lock is facing Leila.

"Do you want to have a look?"

"If you don't mind."

"Not at all. From now on it's yours."

With her thumbs Leila clicks the two metal clasps, raises the lid a few inches. The beating of her heart accelerates.

"I'm not going to see if it's all there. I trust you."

"At least you know how much it's supposed to be?" Matera asks.

"To tell you the truth, no."

"Three-quarters of a million dollars. All in hundred-dollar bills."

Leila tries to contain a cry of joy.

"And it's clean?"

Matera smiles.

"You can relax. It's straight from the bank."

"Good. Because I have to pay for the plane tickets."

"So you can go away with your friend?"

"Yes."

"You must be very fond of him, if you've decided to share this windfall with him."

Leila inclines her head to one side, smiles.

"You want to know the truth? I just met him the other night!"

"Who is he? The driver?"

"Yes, him."

"He's a lucky man. I wouldn't mind being in his place. And not only for the money."

"Thanks," Leila says.

The light that comes in through the window strikes her face, lighting up her intense, bright green eyes, which are sparkling.

*

The boy chews his gum. He looks at Garofano in fascination as he buckles the holster and laboriously puts on his jacket. The tie partly covers the bloodstains on his shirt.

"So you've decided?"

"I'll say. Thanks again for the crutches. Stay well."

Stefano raises one hand to wave, watches him hopping towards the door.

In the corridor the greasy-haired nurse pounces on him.

"Excuse me," he says, touching one shoulder. "What do you think you're doing?"

"What does it look like?" Garofano answers, without stopping. "I'm bowing out."

"But you can't just leave like that! The plaster is still fresh!"

Garofano clenches his teeth and continues to hop.

"Do you know what you're saying? You are my

317

responsibility. I am not authorized to let you leave the hospital!"

Panting, Garofano advances towards the metal door at the end of the corridor. He leans against the handle and emerges onto the landing.

"You have to at least sign the discharge papers!" the nurse insists.

The doors of the lift open in front of them. Inside is a parchment-faced old woman who is covered with necklaces and bracelets, and has a big red hat on her head. Garofano plants his crutches on the floor and enters with a jump. The greasy-haired nurse reaches his hand in front of the photoelectric cell.

"Get out of there immediately! I repeat. I have no intention of letting you leave like this!"

Garofano sticks the crutches under his armpits, takes the Smith & Wesson out from under his jacket and aims it at the man's shirtfront, where the buttons are stretched over his broad stomach.

"At least you're in the right place to get fixed up. Do you want me to pull the trigger?"

The nurse takes away his hand and the doors slide closed over his stunned face. The old woman stares at Garofano in amazement, while the lift descends.

"Why are you in such a hurry?" she asks.

Garofano looks at her, putting the .45 back in its holster.

"I have to get to the airport. And I have no time to lose."

"If you like," says the bejewelled old woman, "I can give you a ride."

*

Commissioner Roccaforte exhales smoke towards the

extinguished neon light, crushes the butt in the ash-tray. Then he closes the folder in front of him, places his palms on the desk and gets up with a sigh.

"Good, boys," he says, taking his jacket from the hook. "That's enough for today. It's time to go and eat. In case . . ."

The ring of the telephone interrupts him halfway through the sentence. The Commissioner, with one arm in the sleeve of his jacket, looks at Loiacono and nods at the phone with his chin.

"No. Oh! Yes. Yes. Yes. All right, I understand. We're coming now."

Loiacono hangs up and finds himself facing the questioning looks of his colleagues.

"Sir, it seems they've found a man murdered at the airport. Shot and shut up in a car. I guess we'd better go."

*

He waits until Leila walks away. Then he hangs up the phone, picks up the suitcase, heads towards the table where the grey-haired man is sitting.

"Hello," he says, with an expression of embarrassment.

Matera responds to his greeting with a nod. Francesco bends over, a little stiffly, to place the suit-case on the floor.

"Here," he says, taking out of a pocket the piece of paper. "I'm supposed to give you this."

Matera takes the rectangle of paper, glances at it, then looks up at Francesco. He has the impression of having seen that face somewhere. Francesco holds his breath. A terrifying suspicion crosses his mind, like a flash, that that paper has nothing to do with anything and the man was looking for something else entirely.

"Good," Matera whispers instead, making the document vanish into a pocket. "With this, our business is over. I have only to wish you a good trip and good luck."

"Thank you," Francesco says. He can't believe that his role is over already.

Matera notes a grimace of pain on his face as he bends over to grab the suitcase.

"Bad back?"

"What do you mean?"

"Your back seems to be hurting you."

"Oh yes, in fact. A couple of days ago I got banged around and since then it's just got worse."

Matera searches for something in his jacket pockets.

"Here," he says, offering him a blue-and-white box. "These capsules may be useful."

Francesco looks at the box in puzzlement.

"Go ahead, take them. I have plenty more. I know something about pain in the joints. I've been going around for years with a piece of iron in my knee. This stuff kills the stomach but at least it helps ease the pain."

*

Reaching the cemetery, the Lancia Delta turns left onto the state road leading towards Bologna. Sacchetti smiles to himself. The boys made such a racket in the locker room at the end of the game that his ears are still ringing. The victory exhilarated them and a little of that happiness has stayed with him.

During the last phases of the match the shouts of the other coach, on the opposite side of the gym, echoed like the hopeless curses of a man condemned to death. Sacchetti watched the fat man waving and was beside himself with joy. Incredible but true, his boys were thrashing those fatheads of the Calderara sports league. There's not much you can do, when Gerardo is in shape, he becomes practically unstoppable. And today was a big day for Gerry! He had them over-powered from the start. And he ended the match with an unbeatable smash that crossed the other team's field with the power of a missile. The enthusiasm of his team-mates exploded. Sacchetti leaped up from the bench as if he had a firecracker under his butt, and the boys' euphoria was transmitted to him like a virus, while they jumped up and down, embraced, high-fived each other excitedly, threw themselves on him, and he laughed and at that moment didn't give a damn about his tweed jacket and their sweaty T-shirts.

So now, as he heads for home in the Lancia Delta, Sacchetti is no longer thinking of the homicide in his building two nights ago. In the sky a beautiful clear sun shines, it's almost time for lunch. He feels on top of the world. Hunger and the team's victory make him happy.

Along the road that joins Calderara and Bologna, a few miles before the industrial zone of Ca' di Zoppo, there's a complex of buildings that rises suddenly in the middle of the countryside. A couple of playing fields, a shopping centre, a hotel, a huge apartment building, its walls blackened by the smoke of the factories and the diesel fuel of the tractor-trailers that pass along the highway that crosses the plain, a few hundred yards away. The desolate apartments of Bologna 2, as it's called, are inhabited by workers in the nearby industries, most of them immigrants. A dozen prostitutes stand, night and day, on the big dusty plaza in front of the buildings, walking between the bus stop and the parked trucks of the drivers who have stopped to sleep or to fuck.

Sacchetti decreases his speed and takes a moment to glance at the girls, who, made-up and dressed provocatively, look at him with boredom. Three-quarters of a mile on, he catches sight of another one, in green miniskirt, net stockings and high heels, walking alone along the edge of the road. Sacchetti slows down, looking at her legs. She, hearing the sound of the car, turns and sticks out her thumb for a ride.

Sacchetti passes her, then thinks why not, what's the harm in offering a ride? He presses the brake pedal and in the rear-view mirror sees her running towards the car. When she reaches it, she opens the door and leans in. Bright-red lips, heavy make-up and a face that has seen many seasons.

"Hello, handsome," she greets him, in a low voice, panting a little. "Will you give me a lift to Bologna?"

"Of course," he says, staring at her décolletage. "Go on, get in."

As the girl settles herself, the miniskirt goes up, revealing the red edge of her knickers. Sacchetti goes into first and starts off.

"God, what a workout," she says, with one hand on her chest. "I went to pee, and I missed the noon bus. Luckily, you came by."

Sacchetti smiles, embarrassed, while his gaze continues to ricochet from the street to the woman's thighs, even if those legs are no longer much of anything. But the fishnet stockings and that line of red fabric sticking out from under the emerald-green miniskirt are like flypaper for his eyes.

"My name is Susanna. But my friends call me Susy."

Sacchetti, holding the wheel with his left hand,

shakes with the right the hand that she is holding out to him.

"A pleasure," he says. "My name is Walter."

Only then, noticing the thickness and size of that hand, is Sacchetti seized by doubt.

*

Francesco follows the signs for the restrooms. He enters and finds himself in a deserted vestibule, with walls and floor of red tile. In front of him are three doors, with the signs for men, women and handicapped. On the right wall is an automatic condom dispenser. He pushes the door that displays the symbol of the wheelchair. A line of sinks on the left. Two doors closed and one open. He places the suitcase on the floor and takes out the box that the man gave him. He removes a pill, swallows it with water from the tap. Then he puts the box back in his pocket and approaches the doors of the toilets.

"Leila," he whispers. "Are you there?"

He hears the sound of a lock clicking. The door on the right opens a crack and the girl appears, nods at him to enter. The suitcase is sitting on the lid of the toilet. Francesco looks at it while she quickly picks up the last bundles of bills and leans down to pack them into the blue bag, open on the floor.

"Perfect," Leila says, closing the false bottom. "Now open the suitcase and hand me some stuff to put in here."

Francesco offers her a couple of pairs of knickers, the beauty case, some T-shirts, the cosmetics, handkerchiefs. Leila arranges everything inside the bag.

"I'd say it can go like that. Wait, as long as we're

323

here, I'll take along the package of sanitary pads. It's a long trip and you never know."

Francesco nods, without comment. He feels stunned. He tries not to think what the consequences would be if they should be discovered now, while they are about to leave with fake passports and a bag with a false bottom full of cash. In the air is an odour of disinfectant that makes his head spin.

In the suitcase open on the toilet three bundles remain.

"I kept these aside," Leila says. "Here, it will be useful to have a little cash on hand."

Silently, Francesco takes the two packets of bills that she's holding out to him. While he puts them in his pocket, he tries to calculate their value. It must certainly be the largest amount he has ever touched at once.

*

Ever since she took his hand, Susy hasn't let it go. After holding it for a long time, she revolved the wrist and began to study the palm.

"What a lovely hand!" she told him, with that masculine voice of hers. "Look at the life line. It's long and straight. And the work line, that isn't bad at all."

Sacchetti continues to look at her in perplexity. Is she really a man? He never knew that transvestites worked in the area of Bologna 2. Susy, with the tip of her index finger, follows the lines on the palm of his hand.

"You're married, right?"

"Yes," he says, looking at the ring on his left hand. "But that wasn't hard."

"OK, then I'll tell you something else. I see that you

are very attracted by sex. And also well endowed. But one would say that in this area you don't have a lot of satisfaction. If it were up to you, you would prefer something more intense, more frequent and maybe even a little naughty. Am I wrong?"

Sacchetti has never believed all this nonsense you get from people who read palms, interpret cards or prepare horoscopes, but he doesn't see any harm in listening to her.

Meanwhile Susy continues to caress him gently. Her fingers go up along the wrist, tickle the skin of his forearm. Even though he doesn't want to, Sacchetti begins to feel excited.

"You know something, Walter?" she whispers. "Your wife is very fortunate. I'm serious. You really are a handsome man."

He smiles in embarrassment, while Susy lifts up his arm, brings his fingers to her lips, and starts sucking them, one at a time.

"Very often, Walter, we're not happy simply because we're unable to seize the opportunities that come our way. Don't you think so?"

Sacchetti raises his eyebrows. He is about to answer when Susy puts a hand on his thigh.

"And yet life is beautiful, Walter. And it is our right to enjoy the good things that are offered to us."

Her hand moves up towards his crotch.

"In fact, I say it's more than a right. It's a duty."

She pulls down the zipper. He keeps his gaze fixed on the road and clears his throat.

"Listen, Susy, I don't want to offend you, but . . ."

"There's nothing impure about physical pleasure, Walter," she interrupts him, slipping her fingers, with a delicate, graceful movement, under the elastic of his underpants. "Our body asks nothing but happiness.

325

And what it demands is right and natural. There's no sense in denying it."

Sacchetti opens his mouth to make an objection, but just at that moment Susy takes out her dentures and lowers her head.

*

The Bear gets out of the Volvo and hurries across the car park towards Terminal B. His head is hurting more and more, but rage gives him energy and determination. He's going to catch those sons of bitches and make them pay.

The sliding doors open before his enormous mass. As soon as he emerges into the hall, he stops and looks around. A group of nuns. A girl pushing a baggage cart, holding the hand of a blond child with a checked skirt and red sandals. Three black men, with short hair and flashy ties. One of them, with a big belly, wears an orange baseball cap. An old man and woman go by, dragging enormous suitcases. The old man stops, takes off his hat and wipes the sweat, while the old woman fans herself with the palm of her hand, breathing hard. And now?

The Bear heads for the check-in counters. From his six-foot-four-inch height, he scans the people in line handing over their bags. He seems to feel the blood fizzing in his veins. He doesn't see anyone he's looking for. Neither Franz, nor that whore his friend, nor that other pig who locked him in the boot of his car. And yet they can't have escaped him. He heard that bastard mention the airport clearly. Maybe they're in the other terminal. The Bear does an about-face, hurries towards the exit.

*

"You're lucky," says the ticket agent, checking the electronic list. "Your tickets are still there. But you're late. If you want to get the flight, you'll have to hurry. The plane has already begun boarding."

The girl pushes a couple of keys on her computer, stares at the screen attentively. Long lines of amber-coloured data on the monitor's black background are reflected in her eyes.

"The total for two seats is 1,780,000."

Leila takes out twelve bills and slides them over the counter, while Francesco nervously checks his watch.

*

Paolo, staying hidden behind one of the big red metal columns, points out Leila and Francesco to the three men in grey uniforms.

"There they are. Those two at the Alitalia counter, did you see them? The girl in black, with short blond hair, and the guy next to her, who's looking at his watch."

Fez scratches his chin.

"OK, boss. Now where are we going to station ourselves?"

Paolo looks around.

"You'll have to grab them before they go through the other controls. I would say you could stop them while they're heading for the check-in. The important thing is to find a good place, secluded enough, where you can work undisturbed. The rest is child's play. I'm going to wait for you in the car park."

*

As he swallows his non-alcoholic aperitif, the Secretary

hears the sound of his mobile phone ringing. He places the glass on the crystal table.

"Excuse me," he says, getting up from the leather armchair. "I was expecting an urgent call and I allowed myself to keep the phone on."

The Minister follows him with his eyes as he glides with little steps towards the hall.

"Hello?"

"It's Matera. I wanted to let you know that it's all resolved."

The Secretary sighs.

"You can't imagine what a weight you've taken off us. I'm sure the Minister will know how to demonstrate how grateful he is."

Matera smiles. Ah yes, my old friend, you can bet on it.

"Of course," he says. "But I still need to clarify a couple of things."

"I'm listening."

"On the way to the place of exchange, I intercepted one of the persons we spoke of. I didn't have much time. To make sure that no problem arose, I thought it was best to resolve the matter in a radical way. Do you follow me?"

"Perfectly. Continue."

"That's it. I only wanted to let you know, in case there should be some complications of a diplomatic type."

"Don't worry. If someone complains, I'll arrange things."

"And one last question. What should I do with the document?"

"Hmm. The situation is calm now?"

"I would say yes, but I can't guarantee it a hundred per cent."

328

"Then destroy it, Matera. I'm sure that the Minister desires nothing other than to end this ugly business once and for all."

*

Finally he's run them down! The Bear sees that pig with the sunglasses conferring with three individuals in grey uniforms. You can bet your life it's a farce! Those men are from the customs just like he's an altar boy.

Now the bastard gives a slap on the back to each of his three cohorts, turns around. The Bear retreats quickly. He just has time to slip around a corner, before the son of a bitch passes by a few feet away from him, with that gigolo's hair that sways at every step.

*

While they walk quickly towards the check-in counter, Leila stops to wait for Francesco.

"Come on," she urges him, grabbing the suitcase from him. "Try to hurry!"

"Sorry," Francesco says. "But I can't run. I feel like my back could break at any moment."

"Once we're on board, you'll have at least twelve hours to rest. But now try to go faster."

Francesco hopes the medicine that that man gave him will take effect soon. He tries to accelerate. Then he looks up and sees three customs agents approaching Leila.

"Excuse me," says Ghiglione, raising an arm to bar their journey. "Only a moment. May we inspect your suitcases?"

Francesco feels his blood freeze and drop to his feet.

Leila stops, confronts the three guards with the bags grasped tight in her hands.

"I'm sorry," she protests. "We're really late."

The Fez advances, smiling reassuringly with his yellow teeth.

"Please, ma'am. I assure you that there's no reason to be alarmed. It's only a routine check. If everything is in order, you'll lose only a couple of minutes."

"Yes, but we really are in a hurry. We're in danger of missing the plane!"

"Yet another reason," the Fez insists, strutting in his fake uniform, "to let us do our job."

*

The Bear knows that those sons of bitches are armed, but he is filled with a bloody rage that makes him feel invincible. He's like a war machine, loaded with fury and destructive energy, he's sure he could tear them to pieces alone, guns or no guns. The important thing is to take them by surprise, without an instant's hesitation.

He opens the glove compartment, rummages around until he finds some brass knuckles with studs on them. He puts them on his fingers, fitting his own knuckles tightly to the indentations inside. Then he gets out, circles the car, unties the piece of rope with which he closed the lid of the boot, and opens it. From under the spare tyre he takes out a leather sack that contains his equipment. He turns it upside down, digs among the tools scattered on the floor of the boot. He takes a large wrench, tests the heft against the palm of his hand, and sticks it in the belt of his trousers. Then he unhooks the jack from the elastic that fastens it to the car. He inserts the crank into the slot, turns it until the jack is at its greatest expansion. He holds it with two hands, gripping it so hard that his knuckles turn white.

The grand army is ready for battle.

*

Leila ties the identification tag to the handle, places Francesco's suitcase on the moving walkway. Then she turns to look at him.

"You're pale."

"I believe it," he says. "Shit, I thought I was dead."

"Would you like to check that bag too, miss?"

The check-in clerk points to the blue bag.

"No," she says. "I'll take this with me."

"I was about to pee in my pants," Francesco whispers to her. "I was sure they were going to throw us in jail."

"Luckily, we put the money in the false bottom."

"When they asked for our passports, I practically threw myself on my knees to beg them to be merciful."

"A real poker player!"

"Have you forgotten that I always lose?"

"Excuse me," says the check-in clerk. "You may proceed to boarding."

*

Lowering his gaze, Sacchetti can see Susy's head rising and falling. Her too-sweet perfume fills his nostrils. He takes one hand off the wheel to caress her neck. Her hair is rough and dry. It seems fake. Sacchetti puts his hand back on the wheel.

"Are you uncomfortable?"

The tone of his voice is much sharper than usual. He clears his throat.

"Do you, do you want me to stop the car?"

"It doesn't matter to me," Susy says, almost without interrupting herself. "Don't you like it like this?"

Like it? He could faint, it's so wonderful! The important thing is not to think about who is performing the act. Even though, after all, who gives a damn if it's a woman or a transvestite? Staring at the road in front of him, Sacchetti swallows hard. To the left the flat, sun-struck countryside goes by. On the right, behind the fences, are the tall grey outlines of the factories, with extended geometries of pipes that wind along the external walls and then plunge into big tanks.

He breathes with his mouth half open. As long as he doesn't run into someone from the team returning home on his motorbike.

A hundred yards farther on, an orange cat slips from under a fence and hurries across the road.

*

Where the hell has that imbecile Diolaiti got to? Garofano hops through the lobby, sweating and panting. He reached the entrance a moment ago and, an instant before the smoky glass doors slid open to let him enter, he saw the reflection of a man with a bruised and swollen face, hobbling on a pair of crutches. He had difficulty recognizing himself in that poor jerk who looked so beat up.

Beppe, he says to himself, try to be objective. Do you really believe that you can stop the two of them in this condition?

The broken bone makes him wince in pain. He stops. He looks at the people sitting on the benches of the waiting area. No trace of those shits. And even if he should find them, how could he stop them? Take out the gun and threaten them? In the middle of all those people?

At the end of the lobby, beside the luggage lockers, there are three telephones on the wall. Garofano heads slowly towards them.

He props his back against the Plexiglas divider. He mops his forehead, arranges the comb-over on his scalp, takes his wallet from an inside pocket. He dumps all his change into the palm of his hand, puts the coins one by one into the slot. He presses on the keypad the number of his own mobile phone. What else to do? It rings and rings, but no one answers.

Who knows? Maybe the battery is dead. Or that asshole Diolaiti has left it somewhere. He hangs up the phone. He retrieves the money and puts it in again.

"Hello?"

His wife's voice sounds worried.

"Hello, Giovanna? It's me."

"Good God, Beppe, what happened? I was expecting you to call me back!"

"Yes, I know, but I had an accident."

"An accident? What happened to you? Are you hurt?"

"A broken leg. Nothing serious, don't worry. Tell me about Betta instead. Did she come home?"

At the other end, silence.

"Giovanna, are you there?"

"Yes, Beppe, I'm here. No, Elisabetta hasn't come home."

"Shit! You haven't even heard from her?"

"She called a couple of hours ago."

"Ah, thank goodness! What did she say? Where is she? What in the world got into her to spend the night somewhere without even letting us know?"

"She said she was leaving, Beppe. A trip, a period

away from home, I don't know. She hadn't decided. She said she was sick of feeling suffocated and couldn't go on this way."

"This way? What way? What do you mean? And where the hell would she go? Let's hear it."

"She's gone, Beppe. She wouldn't even tell me where she was. All I know is she went with that man, you know, her drawing teacher."

"It's not possible, Giovanna! He's a joke!"

Just then, looking around, he sees an old acquaintance pass by behind him. He turns back quickly to the telephone, following out of the corner of his eye Matera's profile, which is heading for the toilets. His wife, at the other end of the line, is trying to explain something to him.

"Listen, Giovanna," Garofano says, cutting her off. "I have to hang up now. I'll call you later."

*

Francesco makes an effort to breathe slowly as they approach security. Leila places the bag on the roller and walks through the metal detector. Francesco follows with his gaze on the bag, which is swallowed up by the X-ray machine. He tries to look casual. Passing through the archway of the metal detector, she grabs the bag, and the policeman on duty, with a bored wave of the hand, indicates that they can proceed.

"We've done it!" she says to him, in a low voice, as they approach the boarding ramps.

Francesco looks straight ahead.

"Wait," he says. "We haven't taken off yet."

*

Parodi, the Fez and Ghiglione come out of the airport, walk under the metal awning and quickly cross the plaza. Parodi is carrying the suitcase in which he has hidden Leila's bag. The Fez takes off his cap, Ghiglione loosens the knot of his tie. Paolo, beside the Rover, is smoking a Lucky Strike. As soon as he sees them, he throws the cigarette on the ground.

"So?" he asks.

The Fez gives a thumbs-up and smiles broadly.

"Parodi should get an Oscar," Ghiglione explains. "In less than no time he transferred their stuff into the second bag. They weren't aware of a thing."

Parodi, without saying a word, places the suitcase on the hood of the Rover. He clicks the lock and lifts the lid.

"Good work, boys," says Paolo. "I was sure you would manage."

He throws the suitcase on the asphalt. He opens the zipper of the bag, tugs on the flap that opens the false bottom.

"Holy shit! It's full of dollars!"

The others lean forward to look over his shoulders, but Paolo quickly zips up the bag and slaps Fez on the shoulder.

"Later, later. Now let's clear out."

They get in the car. Ghiglione in the driver's seat, the Fez beside him, Paolo and Parodi on the rear seat.

Ghiglione turns to Paolo.

"Have you got the keys, boss?"

"Oh, yes. Here," he says, holding them out to him.

Ghiglione is about the start the engine, when the windscreen explodes, causing a rain of glass fragments to spatter in his face.

The Bear plants his foot against the bumper, pulls the jack out of the shattered windscreen. From inside come the cries of Ghiglione and the Fez. The Bear opens the door, seizes Ghiglione by the jacket and drags him bodily out of the car. As the customs officer's hat rolls over the asphalt, Ghiglione, blinded, reaches out his hands. The Bear lets him fall to his knees, raises the jack and hits him with all his strength on one shoulder, breaking the clavicle. Ghiglione crashes to the ground, while the Bear rotates the jack and hits the rear window, shattering that too. The Fez meanwhile is rubbing his eyelids, removing the fragments of glass from his eyes as well as he can. His nails scratch on the holster as he tries to get out his gun. Paolo, in the back seat, still doesn't understand what is happening. He is clutching the bag in one hand, while with the other he goes for his jacket pocket. Just as he manages to get his hand on the Walther, Parodi shoves him and it falls to the floor of the back seat. The Bear sticks an arm through the broken window, seizes Parodi by the jacket, tugs him through the shattered glass. The splinters dig into the fabric of his uniform and tear his flesh, making him scream like a pig at the slaughterhouse. Paolo's fingers grope for the door, as he tries to escape on the other side. The jack strikes Parodi on the neck. Silence. His chest is hanging over the side of the Rover. A door opens. The Bear looks up, sees the Fez aiming a gun at him over the roof of the car. Instinctively he hurls the jack, which spins heavily through the air and hits the Fez in the forehead, knocking him backwards. The Bear hurtles around the Rover. The first kick sinks into Fez's ribs, the second is full in the face.

Paolo is hurrying away. The Bear rushes after him. When he is close enough, he strikes with the brass knuckle, hits him in the middle of the back. The blow cuts off Paolo's breath, makes him stagger forward as if he had stumbled. He falls to his knees and before he can recover and get to his feet, the Bear is on him. His arm draws an arc in the air, the iron fist comes down with all the force of the windup on one of Paolo's cheeks. His head spins, the rest of the body follows. Paolo pirouettes on himself and lands on his back, with his arms spread in a cross, on the asphalt of the parking lot. In his hand he is still holding the handle of the bag.

The Bear looks down at him, panting triumphantly, while behind him the Fez, writhing on the asphalt spitting blood and splinters of teeth, groans weakly.

*

The police car speeds under an overpass. Loiacono accelerates and passes in fifth, while the Commissioner inhales the last drag on his Nazionale.

"Another homicide," Roccaforte says. He lowers the window and throws out the butt. "I can't take any more homicides. I can't take any more blood and people murdered and bodies in pieces."

"May I give you my opinion, sir?" Loiacono says, looking at him out of the corner of his eye. "My opinion is that you are exhausted. You've seemed odd for a while."

"I wonder how people can go to the cinema to watch people shoot each other and screw. They should come and do our job for a while. I'm sure the desire would go away."

"I'm serious, sir. You seem tired to me. And then you smoke too much. You know, all those cigarettes are bad for you. Why don't you take a nice holiday?"

"You're right, Loiacono. I need a holiday. But I'm almost more afraid of free time than of work. If one could at least do this goddamn job in a serious way! If you could investigate, arrest the guilty people and put them in jail!"

"Why, sir, isn't that what they pay you to do?"

*

Matera passes the row of sinks and enters one of the stalls. He locks the door. These toilets give him claustrophobia. Red floors, red tiles, red metal toilet-paper holder. He takes out the document that Leila gave him. Sheer madness. Who would ever imagine that a piece of paper like this could be worth so much money? He's satisfied with the way he's conducted things. Letting the two kids go was a really good idea. The Minister got what he wanted, the two of them are heading off somewhere to enjoy their three-quarters of a million dollars, and he has the second suitcase for himself. And they all lived happily ever after.

With his left hand he searches his pocket for the lighter. He brings the flame to a corner of the piece of paper and watches it burn. When the flame gets close to his fingers he lets the small, blackened film fall into the toilet, following with his eyes its downward spiral, until it's extinguished in the water. Then he unzips his pants and pees on it, making it disintegrate under the jet of urine. When he opens the door he finds himself face to face with Garofano, supported on a pair of crutches, and aiming at him a silencer screwed to a .45.

*

The Bear steps on Paolo's wrist. He bends over, wrenches the bag out of his hand.

"So, you piece of shit, see what a nice surprise I had

338

for you? You don't feel like being funny now, do you?"

Paolo, stunned, gazes at the enormous shadow standing over him.

The Bear lowers his face to his and says in an undertone, "Good night, dickhead!"

He raises his arm and punches him in the face, breaking his nose with the brass knuckle. He stands up and hurries back to his own car. He opens the door, throws the bag on the passenger seat, gets in. He starts the car and accelerates quickly, because the first curious bystanders have gained courage and are already heading over to the wounded. The Bear follows the prescribed route for getting out of Section 3, emerges at the barricade, sticks the magnetic card in the slot. He drives around the rotary with screeching tyres, turns flat out onto the exit road. Along the straightaway he shifts into fourth and glances at the blue canvas bag.

"All right," he says out loud, extending one hand towards the bag. "Let's see what the fuck is in there."

With a decisive gesture he unzips the zipper, overturns the contents. As the Volvo takes the last fifty yards before the intersection at full speed, the Bear stares, wide-eyed in astonishment, at the cascade of hundred-dollar bills scattered on the seat.

*

A hundred yards from the traffic light, Loiacono puts on the indicator and moves to the left lane, for the airport entrance. As the squad car approaches the central traffic divider, a sound of squealing brakes makes the policeman and the Commissioner turn around suddenly. Loiacono half closes his eyes, hearing the dull thud of two cars colliding. A brown Lancia Delta, which is coming from the opposite direction, hits the front of a Volvo that is emerging at full speed from the airport access road. The impact makes the Volvo spin in a quarter-turn and throws it up on the shoulder, smashing it against the guardrail. The Lancia absorbs the blow, crumpling the metal of the bonnet and the right wing, executes a complete about-turn, stops sideways on the road.

"Bingo!" says Loiacono.

"Great," the Commissioner fumes. "That's all we needed!"

"What shall I do, shall I stop?"

"What do you think, Loiacono? At least we'd better see if anyone's hurt."

"And the dead man, sir?"

"The dead man isn't going anywhere, Loiacono. Just the time to take a look and radio the traffic police."

*

With the call over, the Secretary returns to the living room. He clears his throat with his fist in front of his mouth.

"Minister, if I may, I'll steal you away just for a second."

"But of course, my friend," says the Minister, getting up. "Dear ladies, with your permission ... Unfortunately, our work pursues us even on the day the Lord dedicated to repose."

He approaches the Secretary.

"So?"

"All taken care of, Minister. Matera just confirmed that he has retrieved the document."

"My friend, that is good news."

"Minister, as soon as the situation became less than calm, I permitted myself to tell him to destroy it."

"You know I have complete faith in you. If you decided that it's more prudent to act this way, you have my approval. Now, my friend, let's not keep the ladies waiting any longer."

The Minister takes the Secretary under the arm and pilots him towards the two women.

"My dear ladies, we assure you that for today there will be no more interruptions! Now all we have to do is to enjoy in holy peace the good lunch that awaits us. Thomas!"

The Filipino butler appears in the doorway of the dining room.

"Yes, Minister?"

"Where are we?"

"Ready to serve the antipasti, Minister."

"Good. So, dear friends, if you will follow me, an excellent *carpaccio* of marinated sturgeon and a tray of fresh oysters are waiting for us!"

*

"Don't fuck with me," Garofano says to him. "If you try to close the door in my face I'll shoot you. Come on, Franco, step back and keep your hands in plain view."

Matera backs up a couple of steps, slowly, with his arms away from his sides. Garofano advances, hopping on the floor of the bathroom, with the Smith & Wesson pointed and the crutches stuck as solidly as possible into his armpits. With a shove of his elbow he closes the door. Then, keeping Matera covered, he reaches his left hand back to lock the door.

"So, here we are," he says smiling. "A lot of time has gone by!"

"Yes," says Matera, staring at Garofano's toothless mouth. "A lot of time indeed. What happened to you?"

"Forget it. There's nothing worse than getting involved with amateurs. If you don't get rid of them immediately, you never know what to expect."

"Amateurs? You mean it was the two kids who got you into this mess?"

"Precisely. And while we're on the subject, we might as well get to the point right away. I don't have to tell you why I'm here."

"I can imagine. But I'm sorry. I don't have what you're looking for."

"Don't give me that crap. Who else would have it?"

"Don't you smell something?"

Garofano half closes his eyes, studying Matera's face distrustfully. Then he lifts his chin, and breathes in a couple of times, sniffing.

"Stink of pee."

"Nothing else?"

"Burned paper?"

"Bravo. Now try to guess what I just burned."

"And you think I'm going to believe you? You were supposed to retrieve the document, not destroy it!"

"I just received instructions by telephone," Matera says, shrugging. "You can search me, if you want."

"So that you can take advantage and grab my gun? Like shit. I have no intention of getting beaten up in these conditions."

"Just as well. In any case you should resign yourself. This time you've arrived too late."

"And the money?"

Matera raises his eyebrows.

"The money? I handed it over in exchange for the thing I burned."

"Don't bullshit me! Do you take me for a moron? You gave a shitload of cash to those two kids? You could eliminate them, swipe the document and go back to Rome, having your cake and eating it too."

"The two kids aren't so clueless, they took their precautions. And anyway I don't see why I should have murdered them. They kept their word and gave me what I wanted. I thought it was right to respect the agreement."

"You certainly have a lot of nerve. If I hadn't known you a lifetime, maybe you'd even manage to make me swallow that."

"Listen, I don't give a damn what you believe or don't believe. The two kids, by now, must be in the air, on their way to some tropical island. And I'm happy about it."

"So you want me to understand that you gave them the money and let them get away?"

"Exactly. I gave them the money and let them get away. Even if it may seem incredible to you that there is anyone in the world who respects an agreement."

Garofano shakes his head with an air of regret and fires a shot that hits Matera in the chest, throwing him against the wall. His neck hits the tiles, he falls to a sitting position on the toilet. A dark stain spreads rapidly over his blue shirt, around the big hole where the bullet entered.

"Shit, Franco," says Garofano, continuing to shake his head. "And to think you were a smart guy! Who would have said that you could be so stupid?"

Matera's shoulders hunch over. His legs kick a couple of times, the heels of his shoes slide along the red tiles. From his mouth comes a gurgle of blood that trickles over his chin and chest. His arms hang limply and his gaze clouds, staring at a point on the floor.

Garofano puts the .45 in the holster and turns,

struggling to manoeuvre the crutches in the narrow space of the stall.

*

Susy is squashed under the dashboard, her face crushed against the pedals, Sacchetti's knees pressed against her back. As she tries to extricate herself from that knot, she realizes that her right shoulder is hurting terribly. And meanwhile Sacchetti begins complaining.

"God, what a shock. God, God, God, God. Oh, holy God, what a shock."

Susy is panting, trying to extricate herself. Her dentures have gone who knows where. And her wig too is down there, stuck somewhere. Sacchetti's hands are still gripping the steering wheel. His dick hangs limply between his legs.

"Damn! The car is ruined, ruined, ruined. My car is ruined."

"Are you hurt?" Susy asks.

"No, I don't think so," Sacchetti answers, on the verge of tears. "But I'm in trouble. Real trouble. God-damn what trouble."

"It might be better if you put your dick back in your pants," Susy says, trying to pull the door handle.

The door yields, she gets out of the car. She's lost a shoe. She takes off the other one and, limping, crosses the street, holding her right arm, which is hurting more and more. She approaches the other car, looks through the window. Thrown forward against the dashboard is a mastodon of a man, with huge shoulders and a bandaged head. The bandage, probably in the collision, has come unrolled a little. Blood is trickling down one cheek.

Susy leans over, raps with her knuckles on the glass.

"Hey, how are you? Everything OK?"

The man lifts his head and stares straight ahead. Just then Susy notices the sea of bills scattered in the car.

Loiacono, followed by the Commissioner, approaches the Lancia Delta. One beside the other, the two cops squat down to look inside. Clutching the wheel is a man who turns terrified eyes to them.

"I've seen this man before," says Loiacono.

"Yes, of course," Roccaforte says. "He's one of the tenants that we questioned yesterday."

"Oh, right. Anyway, he doesn't seem hurt. You want to check, sir? Meanwhile I will go and have a look at the other car."

Loiacono heads towards the Volvo. The person he saw get out of the Lancia Delta is knocking with one hand on the window, and shouting in an agitated voice.

She hit her head, thinks Loiacono. Or she's arguing with that guy, who cut across in front of her.

"Why are you shouting, ma'am? Are you hurt?"

The woman turns. But it's not a woman, it's a man, his face smeared with make-up, a head covered by a thin, mouse-grey down, a mouth of smooth pink gums, completely toothless.

"It's full of money, officer!" mumbles the transvestite, jumping up and down on her bare feet. "This car is full to the brim with money!"

Loiacono takes off his cap and with his index finger scratches his head, while Susy, in front of him, continues to wave her left arm, pointing agitatedly at the inside of the Volvo.

*

The whistle of the engines becomes more acute, the vibrations increase in intensity. The runway is sliding. Under the wing, the asphalt becomes an out-of-focus stripe, whose details can be distinguished only if you narrow your gaze. Suddenly the head of the airplane climbs upward, the bodies are pressed against the seatbacks. The jet detaches itself from the earth and the runway grows distant beneath them. The little buses that carry the passengers from the terminal look like blue-and-white models abandoned in a courtyard.

The plane turns, on its way to altitude. Francesco bends his head to look down, at the dense agglomerations of roofs and the small green squares of parks and gardens, cut by the pale lines of the streets. There it is down there, the old spider web. Francesco feels like a fly who by a miracle has managed to escape the trap. Quickly the green areas become broader, the few structures grow tiny in the irregular chessboard of tilled fields, and in a moment, before he has time to realize it, Bologna has disappeared, hidden by the other side of the fuselage, or too far away to be visible.

A voice informs the passengers that they can take off their seat belts.

"Shit," Francesco sighs. "We made it!"

"Why, didn't you think we would?"

"I think it's going to take me a little time to digest it all."

Leila smiles. Her eyes are shining, full of iridescent specks. Francesco arches his upper back, stretches his legs forward, extends his back against the padding of the seat. The pain is slowly diminishing. Maybe the pill is having an effect. He runs a hand through his hair. He seems to feel a slight tingling all over his body.

"And now?" he says.

"Now what?"

"I mean, what will we do when we get there?"

"What we feel like. We'll go around, go swimming, sunbathe. We'll enjoy our money."

"Ours?"

"Were you afraid I'd abandon you?"

Francesco looks at her without answering.

"Why should I do that? There's enough for both of us." She lays a hand on his arm. "Relax, I have no intention of pulling a fast one."

Leila leans over and kisses him.

"Can't you trust me?" she asks, with her lips on his.

Francesco is about to say something, but Leila pulls back suddenly.

"Oh damn!"

"Now what is it?"

"My period. Right now . . . Maybe it's the effect of the takeoff. Or the release of tension, who knows, after all we've been through. Wait a moment," she says, leaning down to get the bag.

She unzips it, rummages around inside.

"Where the hell did the sanitary pads go? I was sure I put them in. Oh, here they are! I'll make a trip to the bathroom. Back in five minutes."

Francesco nods. He watches her with as she goes off down the aisle. The blue canvas bag is still on the seat. He stares at the open zipper, from which the white material of a T-shirt sticks out. He looks around. No one is paying any attention. He takes the bag, settles it on his thighs. With his left hand he shifts the stuff around, while with the right he searches on the bottom for the flap. He grips it between two fingers, lifting the bottom just enough to glance into the hidden compartment.

Francesco feels his pulse accelerate. He forces up the divider, compressing underwear and cosmetics on one side of the bag. Stunned, he sits staring at the dozens of comic books lined up in the false bottom. He closes the compartment, moves the contents around, places the bag on the other seat.

When could it have happened? He breathes deeply, his gaze pointed at the headrest in front of him. Those customs agents. It must have been them. *Excuse me, it's only a routine check.* A sleight-of-hand, executed professionally. Yes, but how the hell did they know about the money? Leila's friend, he was the only one who knew about the bag.

Slowly, Francesco's heart returns to its normal rhythm. His hand goes to his pocket, to touch the two packets Leila gave him in the airport bathroom. About 50,000,000 lire. Maybe a little more.

When Leila returns from the toilet, Francesco is again looking out. The plane is flying over a vast flat area, through which winds a long grey-blue river. The sun's rays, reflected on the metal sheets of the wing, send out pink and orange flashes. Leila picks up the bag. She puts the package of pads inside, closes the zipper, places it on the floor. She drops onto the seat, exhausted. He looks away from the window.

"So," Leila asks, with a tired, relaxed smile. "How are things? Everything OK?"

Francesco looks at her. Her grey-green eyes, half closed to filter the light. The blond tufts of hair shooting straight up.

"Yes," he says. "I would say everything's fine."

THE MANNEQUIN MAN

Luca Di Fulvio

Shortlisted for the European Crime Writing Prize

"Di Fulvio exposes souls with the skills of a surgeon, It's like turning the pages of something forbidden – seduction, elegant and dangerous." *Alan Rickman*

"Know why she's smiling?" he asked, pointing a small torch at the corpse. "Fish hooks. Two fish hooks at the corners of her mouth, a bit of nylon, pull it round the back of the head and tie a knot. Pretty straightforward, right?" Amaldi noticed the metallic glint at the corners of the taut mouth.

Inspector Amaldi has enough problems. A city choked by a pestilent rubbish strike, a beautiful student harassed by a telephone stalker, a colleague dying of cancer and the mysterious disappearance of arson files concerning the city's orphanage. Then the bodies begin to appear.

This novel of violence and decay, with its vividly portrayed characters, takes place over a few oppressive weeks in an unnamed Italian city that strongly evokes Genoa . . .

The Italian press refers to Di Fulvio as a grittier, Italian Thomas Harris, and *Eyes of Crystal*, the film of the novel was launched at the 2004 Venice Film Festival.

" A novel that caresses and kisses in order to violate the reader with greater ease." *Rolling Stone*

"A wonderful first novel that will seduce the fans of deranged murderers in the style of Hannibal Lecter. And beautifully written to boot." *RTL*

£9.99/$14.95
Crime paperback original, ISBN: 1–904738–13–3
www.bitterlemonpress.com

THE SNOWMAN

Jörg Fauser

"A gritty and slyly funny story. About the life of the underdog, the petty criminal, the fixer, the prostitute and the junkie. With a healthy dose of wit." *Cath Staincliffe, author of the* Sal Kilkenny *series*

"German author Jörg Fauser was the Kafka of crime writing." *Independent*

Blum's found five pounds of top-quality Peruvian cocaine in a suitcase. His adventure started in Malta, where he was trying to sell porn magazines, the latest in a string of dodgy deals that never seem to come off. A left-luggage ticket from the Munich train station leads him to the cocaine. Now his problems begin in earnest. Pursued by the police and drug traffickers, the luckless Blum falls prey to the frenzied paranoia of the cocaine addict and dealer. His desperate and clumsy search for a buyer takes him from Munich to Frankfurt, and finally to Ostend. This is a fast-paced thriller written with acerbic humour, a hardboiled evocation of drug-fuelled existence and a penetrating observation of those at the edge of German society.

"Jörg Fauser was a fascinating train wreck: a fiercely intelligent literary critic who also wrote the occasional nudie-magazine filler; a junkie who got clean in his thirties only to become an alcoholic; a tragic figure who died mysteriously at 43 in a 1987 Autobahn accident. Oh, and along the way he managed to crank out one of the most indelible crime novels in Greman history. Fauser writes with a gimlet eye and a black, acerbic (so, German) wit, creating an unflinchingly brilliant tale of a perspective – the outsider among outsiders – he knew all too well." *Ruminator*

£8.99/$13.95
Crime paperback original, ISBN 1–904738–05–2
www.bitterlemonpress.com

HAVANA RED

Leonardo Padura

**Winner of the celebrated Café de Gijon Prize,
the Novela Negra Prize and the Hammett Prize.**

**"A scorching novel from a star of Cuban fiction. Lt Conde's
quest follows the basic rhythm of the whodunit, but Padura
syncopates it with brilliant literary riffs on Cuban sex,
society, religion, even food."** *Independent*

On August 6th, the day on which the Catholic Church cele-
brates the Feast of Transfiguration, the body of a strangled
transvestite is discovered in the undergrowth of the Havana
Woods. He is wearing a beautiful red evening dress and the
red ribbon with which he was asphyxiated is still round his
neck. To the consternation of Mario Conde, in charge of
the investigation, the victim turns out to be Alexis Arayán,
the son of a highly respected diplomat. His investigation
begins with a visit to the home of the "disgraced" dramatist
Alberto Marqués, with whom the murdered youth was living.
Marqués, a man of letters and a former giant of the Cuban
theatre, helps Conde solve the crime. In the baking heat of
the Havana summer, Conde also unveils a dark, turbulent
world of Cubans who live without dreaming of exile, grap-
pling with food shortages and wounds from the Angolan war.

Leonardo Padura was born in 1955 in Havana and lives in
Cuba. He is a novelist, essayist, journalist and scriptwriter.
Havana Red has been published in Cuba, Mexico, Spain,
Portugal, Italy, Germany and France, and is the first of
the Havana quartet featuring Lieutenant Mario Conde, a
tropical Marlowe, to be published in English.

**"So many enchanting memories, sultry Cuban nights and
music in this novel that you let the author take you by the
hand, impatient to find out what comes next."** *Lire*

**"Nothing is what it seems in this case, which has less to do
with crime than with the struggle for identity in a corrupt
society where outsiders are exiled in their own country.**
Daily Mail

£8.99/$13.95
Crime paperback original, ISBN 1–904738–09–5
www.bitterlemonpress.com

INVOLUNTARY WITNESS

Gianrico Carofiglio

"Involuntary Witness raises the standard for crime fiction. Carofiglio's deft touch has given us a story that is both literary and gritty – and one that speeds along like the best legal thrillers. His insights into human nature – good and bad – are breathtaking." *Jeffery Deaver*

A nine-year-old boy is found murdered at the bottom of a well near a popular beach resort in southern Italy. In what looks like a hopeless case for Guido Guerrieri, counsel for the defence, a Senegalese peddler is accused of the crime. Faced with small-town racism fuelled by the recent immigration from Africa, Guido attempts to exploit the esoteric workings of the Italian courts.

More than a perfectly paced legal thriller, this relentless suspense novel transcends the genre. A powerful attack on racism, and a fascinating insight into the Italian judicial process, it is also an affectionate portrait of a deeply humane hero.

Gianrico Carofiglio is an anti-Mafia judge in Bari, a port on the coast of Puglia. He has been involved with trials concerning corruption, organized crime and the traffic in human beings.

"A powerfully redemptive novel beautifully translated from the Italian." *Daily Mail*

"I enjoyed every moment of the book. Bitter Lemon Press have yet another winner on their hands." *Eurocrime*

"A new template for our literature, the mechanics and suspense of the American court procedural made profoundly Italian by its characters, its atmosphere, emotions and concerns." *La Stampa*

A best-seller and a major TV series in Italy, *Involuntary Witness* has won a number of prizes, including the Marisa Rusconi, Rhegium Julii and Fortunato Seminara awards.

£8.99/$13.95
Crime paperback original, ISBN 1–904738–07–9
www.bitterlemonpress.com